Wolf Moon

Lycanthropic Book 2

Steve Morris

This novel is a work of fiction and any resemblance to actual persons living or dead, places, names or events is purely coincidental.

Steve Morris asserts the right under the Copyright, Designs and Patents Act 1988 to be identified as the author of this work.

Published by Landmark Media, a division of Landmark Internet Ltd.

Copyright © 2018 by Steve Morris.
All rights reserved.

stevemorrisbooks.com

ISBN-10: 1985896397
ISBN-13: 978-1985896390

The Lycanthropic Series

Acknowledgements

Huge thanks are due to Margarita Morris, James Pailly and Josie Morris for their valuable comments and help in proof-reading this book.

Chapter One

King's College Hospital, Lambeth, South London, New Year's Day

Police Constable Liz Bailey slowly blinked her eyelids open. Blinding yellow light burned her eyes and she screwed them quickly shut again. Darkness was better. She was somewhere warm and soft, and her head felt fuzzy like she was inside a cocoon.

A cocoon. That's what she needed now. A warm, dark, safe corner that she could curl into and hide. Too much had happened, and she just wanted it to stop. The world began to fade as she drifted back into the tender arms of sleep.

'Are you awake?' asked a soothing voice, rich and smooth as honey.

The voice might have been real, or just a dream. Liz ignored it, sinking back into the softness that enfolded her.

'How do you feel?'

She didn't know whether hours had passed since she'd

first heard the voice, or just the beat of a heart. The voice was gentle but insistent and impossible to ignore. She forced her eyelids open a crack. The bright light still burned, but not as painfully as before.

A nurse was leaning over her, a concerned look on her face, a well-worn caring look. 'You've been in a deep sleep since you arrived in the Emergency Department,' said the nurse. 'We administered stimulants, but you didn't respond. We were wondering if you were ever going to wake up.' Her mouth turned up at the corners in a faint smile, deep dimples hollowing her caramel-coloured cheeks.

'I know you,' murmured Liz. 'I've seen you somewhere before.' Was it in a dream? She couldn't remember. She remembered nothing.

The nurse smiled again. 'It was here,' she said. 'In the hospital. My name is Chanita. I treated your colleague, PC David Morgan.'

Chanita. Liz's lips moved soundlessly. *David Morgan.* Strange names. Names from long ago, a lifetime ago. 'He's dead,' said Liz. 'Dave Morgan is dead. The wolf bit him. I saw it myself.' Had that really happened, or was it part of the dream? She hoped it was a dream, but a coldness in her heart told her that it was true. 'So tired,' she muttered. 'Light hurts.'

The nurse frowned at that. 'Let me take a look at your eyes.'

'Need to sleep,' said Liz. She felt her eyes closing again, lead weights pulling them shut, the warm darkness dragging her back into wonderful oblivion.

A hand shook her arm gently. 'Open your eyes for me,' said the nurse.

It took a colossal effort to force them open. A light shone into them and she snapped them shut again. 'Too bright.'

'You have acute photo sensitivity,' announced Chanita. 'And your eyes are dilated with a pronounced yellow tint.

Do you have any idea what that means?'

Liz shook her head. She had no idea what anything meant.

'Have you been bitten?' asked the nurse. 'By a wolf? Did it bite you?'

A wolf. An image presented itself to her, a huge black beast, its yellow eyes glowing in the dark like searchlights, its teeth bared, tongue dripping with drool. A memory, not a dream. A memory from last night. Had the wolf bitten her? No. She had thought it would, but it had sniffed at her and walked on by. Then it had run. Run at the others.

She snapped her eyes wide open, ignoring the painful stab of the lights. 'The others! My colleague, Dean, the children he was protecting? What happened to them?'

'They're all okay,' said Chanita calmly. 'They were brought in at the same time as you. Your colleague is being treated for a head wound. The teenagers have minor injuries.'

Liz allowed her eyes to drift closed again. They were safe. She was safe.

'We're going to keep you in for observation for a few days,' continued Chanita. 'One of the doctors will be round to see you later, but at the moment we're very short of staff. A lot of casualties were brought in during the night after the riots and the wolf attacks.'

Liz curled up in the bed. Riots. That's right. She had been in the middle of the rioting. She remembered the looters, the petrol bomb, the injured people. She had done her best to help them. She had done something terrible too. But what? The answer was just out of reach, and for now she wanted to keep it that way. It would come to her, in its own time, when she was strong enough to deal with it. Now was the time for sleep.

Chanita said something else to her, but it was too quiet to hear, coming from too far away. The nurse spoke again, but Liz let the distant voice wash over her. The darkness was calling her, and couldn't be refused.

She continued to drift in and out of sleep. How many times, and for how long, she had no way of knowing. Other nurses came to her bedside, and a doctor too. They questioned her, but she couldn't remember what they asked, or how she answered. All that mattered was sleep.

At first the sleep was sweet and healing. Her battered body craved the relief it brought her aching bones. Her exhausted mind uncurled into its soothing embrace. Then the dreams began.

Fire, darkness, screams – a vision of Hell. Yellow eyes, bright in the night. The stuff of nightmare. Yet this was no nightmare, this was memory. A giant wolf, panting hot breath in the frigid air. An explosion. Police officers wreathed in flames. The fighting in the alleyway. It was coming back to her, the memories unfolding one by one like blood red roses.

What had she done? The horror of the memory flooded over her in a wave. The moon shining on her skin, its silver rays filling her with superhuman energy. And then the violence. She had attacked those vigilantes with her bare hands. Drawn dark red lines in their flesh with her fingers. Smacked them to the ground like flies. Left them for dead.

The moon had changed her. It had made her a monster, yellow-eyed like the wolves. And Chanita knew.

Liz sat up in bed, suddenly alert. The bright hospital lights half blinded her, but she narrowed her eyes, gritted her teeth and hauled her legs over the edge of the bed. It was like dragging huge weights up a hill. An IV drip tethered her, feeding liquid into the back of her hand, but she pulled the tube out and dropped onto the floor. Her legs sagged and she had to grip the metal frame of the bed to stop herself falling. She held it for a moment, regaining her balance, and used it to drag herself forward. She had to get out of the hospital before Chanita returned.

A privacy curtain hung around her bed. She drew it aside and peeked out at the hospital ward. It was bedlam.

Every bed was full, and nurses and doctors hurried around tending to patients. No one took any notice of her. She looked around for Chanita and saw the nurse attending to a patient down the far end of the ward. Liz lurched off in the opposite direction.

She reached the ward exit and stumbled down the staircase. A woman at the bottom of the stairs frowned at her, staring at her eyes, but Liz pushed past, following the signs to the main exit. Everywhere people hurried. Patients, doctors, visitors, nurses and support staff. The bright lights overhead burned down relentlessly and every limb felt dead with exhaustion. She sat down on a plastic bench in the corridor to rest for a moment, before coming to her senses.

Chanita knows.

As soon as Liz was discovered missing, they would come for her. They would catch her. And what would they do when they caught a monster? An image of villagers wielding pitchforks and flaming torches sprang into her mind. She lurched back to her feet, forcing the exhaustion aside, ignoring the pain in her eyes. The corridor twisted and turned, intersecting with other corridors like a maze, until eventually she pushed out and found herself in the open air. To her surprise, it was still dark, still the early hours of the morning. She must have been in the hospital for only a few hours, unless days had somehow passed.

She looked around and stumbled over to a black taxi. The driver had the window wound down and she placed her hands firmly on the metal door to steady herself.

'Where to, love?' asked the driver.

'What day is it?'

'Eh? You what?'

'What day is it?' she asked again.

'New Year's Day,' said the man cheerfully. 'Blimey, you must have had a big night.'

New Year's Day. Only a few hours had passed since the rioting. Since she had become a monster.

'So where to, then?'

'Brixton Hill,' she told him, climbing into the back of the cab. Her home wasn't far from the hospital. Just a short journey and she would be safe again.

'Bloody hell,' said the driver, peering at her in his rear-view mirror as he pulled into the early morning traffic. 'You look like you've been in a battle.'

Chapter Two

Department of Genetics, Imperial College, Kensington, London, New Year's Day

Leanna Lloyd watched from her rooftop vantage as the last pale glimmer of moon dipped behind the London skyline. Dawn was slowly breaking across the city, the sun turning the eastern sky from grey to pink. She roared one last time before the change took her in its cold embrace. From wolf back to human this time.

She winced as the fur that clothed her vanished, leaving her pale naked skin exposed to the chill night air. Her sharp teeth retracted into her gums and her claws turned back to manicured nails as the rising sun began to cast a glow over the rooftop where she crouched. She felt the weakening in her limbs as her muscles wasted away and the wolf blood that flowed through her veins turned back to ordinary human blood.

Not quite ordinary. She would never be truly ordinary again. But in human guise she was only half the woman she knew she could be. The dawn had robbed her of her power. Wolf form was her true nature now, and one night a month would never be enough to satisfy her.

She cast one last glance at the cold dawn before turning away. Black smoke from the overnight fires still rose into the sky, filling the air with the sharp smell of burning. Leanna smiled grimly to herself. Those fires would burn higher yet. She would turn this city into a funeral pyre before she was done.

But now she had other needs. She left the open rooftop of the university building and climbed down the stairs to the genetics lab where she had left her clothes before going out to hunt the previous night.

Her phone was already ringing when she reached the deserted lab and she answered it before dressing. Warg Daddy. She was glad to hear his deep booming voice again.

'Leanna,' he said. 'Good. Are you safe?'

'I'm safe. What about the others?'

'All the Brothers are with me. None were harmed.'

Last night had been the first time for Warg Daddy and the Wolf Brothers to change. The first time was always a risk, but she had been confident that the biker gang could take care of themselves.

'I've seen Adam,' continued Warg Daddy. 'He's safe too. But Samuel is dead. He was shot by a police marksman. And James has gone missing. We won't see him again, the traitor.'

She winced at the reminder of how James had betrayed her last night. He had sided with humans over his own kind. She had never trusted James, and Samuel had been a fool to bring him home. Samuel had paid a dear price for his folly, but Leanna would shed no tears for him. 'Tell me again about James,' she said. 'Tell me exactly how it happened.'

The Leader of the Pack began to speak in his deep, rumbling voice. 'It was after midnight. The Wolf Brothers had gathered to wait for the moon. I was there with

Snakebite and the others. We waited together. When the moon came, I felt the change begin.' A kind of awe crept into his voice as he recounted the experience. 'At first the moon burned my eyes. It seemed to set my skin on fire. Then the change went deeper, right to my bones. The moon fed me power, it gave me new life. Strength poured into every pore and muscle of my body. Then, when the change was complete, I killed.'

Leanna nodded eagerly. The intensity of that first change was without compare. Warg Daddy's words brought it back sharply. That feeling of unimaginable power, the knowledge that anything was now possible, the undeniable lust for blood.

'And James?' she asked. 'Where did you see him?'

'It was down a blind alley. After the police started shooting, the Brothers split up and ran. I found some kids sheltering with a police woman in the alleyway. The woman was strange. She smelled of wolf, but she hadn't changed under the moon. I didn't know what she was, so I left her, and went to the kids. I killed some of them. Then James came, with Samuel. I knew them immediately, even in wolf form. They were running from the police too.'

'What did they do?'

'James stood in my way. He challenged me for the kids. He told me to leave them. I gave him plenty of warning but he wouldn't back down. So I fought him. I would have killed him, but Samuel joined him. Then the police came, and the bullets. I ran.'

'Did you see what happened to James and Samuel?'

'No. I just heard shots. Gunfire. But Snakebite saw them. He watched Samuel dying while James looked on. He would have killed James then if he had known. But he didn't know.'

'No,' agreed Leanna. 'It wasn't Snakebite's fault.' She knew where the blame lay. With James, and James alone.

In savage fury, Leanna had killed when she had first heard the news of James' betrayal. She had roamed the streets, killing, and killing again. But slaughtering innocents would never purge the black hate that boiled her blood. Only James's death would quiet that rage. Until then it would burn inside her, a reminder of the betrayal.

Leanna had learned a hard lesson about trust. She had been too weak with James and Samuel. From now on she would trust no one and tolerate no dissent. Anyone who stood in her way would be crushed. Anyone.

'Leanna?' Warg Daddy's voice growled from the phone. 'Leanna? Are you still there?'

She stilled her fury and bottled it up inside. It would keep for later. She would not permit a rogue werewolf to derail her plans. She would have her revenge one day. One day soon. 'I'm still here,' she said.

'So what next?' asked Warg Daddy. 'The Brothers are ready to search for James. We'll hunt him down and kill him like a rat.'

'No,' said Leanna. 'I want to kill him myself. Besides, we have other things to do. It's time to gather a War Council. Meet me at the house in one hour. Make sure Adam is there, and bring Snakebite with you too.'

Warg Daddy hesitated before responding. 'Adam, yes. But Snakebite? Are you sure? He's not such a good one for meetings.'

'Are you questioning my decision?' she demanded.

'No, it's just that …'

'Bring him,' she snapped. The sooner Warg Daddy learned to obey her commands and not question them, the better. She would have to teach him that lesson soon. She ended the call and pulled her clothes back on. After a night cloaked in nothing but her own fur, the clothing seemed like an unnecessary constraint, a reminder that she must still hide. But her plans were already in motion. Soon it would be the humans who would need to hide. And there would be nowhere for them to go.

Chapter Three

*Upper Terrace, Richmond upon Thames,
West London, New Year's Day*

The news networks were calling it the New Year's Massacre. Hundreds had been killed in the overnight riots, either in the street battles started by vigilantes, or else by the mysterious and sinister creatures that had suddenly appeared just after midnight, bringing London's New Year's Eve celebrations to a sudden and violent close. Sarah Margolis sat glued to the TV, at Grandpa's bedside.

The old man's mind was wandering erratically, the brief moment of clarity that had come upon him during the night now replaced by brain fog. 'I don't understand it,' he kept saying. 'I just don't understand. Who are these people dressed as wolves?'

'They're not dressed as wolves, Grandpa. They really are wolves. Now be quiet and listen.'

'Wolves in London? Impossible! It's an April fool.'

Part of Sarah wished it was just an April fool. The violence of the overnight rioting had been dreadful to watch, and the sight of armed police opening fire in crowded streets barely two miles from her own house was terrifying. But most frightening and terrible of all were the wolves, or Beasts, or whatever they were. Even though she had already watched dozens of replays of them prowling and attacking, the initial shock of seeing them hadn't faded in the least. In fact, as more and more amateur footage and CCTV images were shown, the picture that was emerging was increasingly strange and unbelievable. One of the most startling images was of an enormous red-haired wolf stalking down the middle of St John's Road in Battersea, its yellow eyes glowing in the dark like doorways to another dimension. The shot had been captured by a news photographer with a high magnification lens, and the pin-sharp quality of the photograph made the creature seem terrifyingly real, despite its fantastical nature.

Nobody could say with certainty where the wolves had come from, or, perhaps more worryingly, where they had gone. Some witnesses reported hearing the creatures speak. They were obviously suffering from some kind of hysteria or collective delusion.

'The wolves spoke English,' insisted one man. 'They talked with London accents.'

'London accents,' repeated the news reporter raising a single eyebrow. 'What did they say?'

But the man didn't know. Blood ran down his face from a head wound, and his hollow eyes gazed out of Sarah's television screen in shock. He was clearly in a state of disarray, but was adamant about what he had heard. Paramedics came to treat his head injury then, and he was taken away in an ambulance. The whole scene was one of absolute chaos.

'Madness,' muttered Grandpa. 'The whole world's gone mad.'

Sarah gripped his age-mottled hand tightly. The

thought that her sister might be out there and caught up in the mayhem was too awful to contemplate. Melanie had been missing for two whole weeks now, and Sarah had still heard nothing from her. She could only hope that Melanie was still alive and out of danger, perhaps not even in London at all. She might be living it up in some luxury resort halfway across the world. Sarah clung ever more desperately to that slender hope as the night wore on. If she let it go, she was lost.

And yet despite her worries, the shaky and grainy videos of dangerous beasts on the streets of London had awakened something unexpected and visceral within her. She had discovered an unexpected delight in watching real-life horror unfold before her. Although she tried to deny it even to herself, a small but growing part of her was cheering on the strange creatures as they prowled through the city, chasing their victims, spreading fear and chaos before them. More and more, Sarah was living her life anew, this time through the eyes of monsters. For the wolves could do something that she no longer could. They could go out.

It was months since she had stepped foot outside the house. Her social life had long ago dwindled to nothing as she cared for the old man beside her. But she couldn't blame Grandpa for her social isolation. No, it was her sister that she blamed. She had always secretly resented the glamorous and charmed existence that Melanie enjoyed. Envy, you might call it, though that seemed a petty word to describe what Sarah felt. It was more than that. As twins, it seemed that whatever Melanie possessed, Sarah lacked. They were mirrors of each other, and the brighter Melanie's candle burned, the darker Sarah's own world had become. The more Melanie went out, the more Sarah stayed indoors, until the fear of leaving the house had become a paralysis. She couldn't resent her sister for that. One of them had to live, and if Sarah couldn't or wouldn't, then Melanie must, for both their sakes.

She hurried into the kitchen to make some tea for herself and Grandpa. When she returned, carrying the two mugs on a tray, the scene on the television had switched to a new location that was instantly recognizable to anyone.

'Shh now, Grandpa, something important's happening.' A nervous presenter stood immediately in front of Number Ten, Downing Street, fiddling with her earpiece and microphone. A group of other reporters clustered around her, jostling for position, quickly adjusting dress or hair, more TV crews and microphones jutting into shot in the general chaos. They were clearly waiting for something to happen. Behind them all stood a uniformed policeman outside the familiar black door of Number Ten, a single calm figure amongst the excitement.

The voice of the anchorman cut across the buzz and noise. 'We're going live now to Downing Street, where we understand that the Prime Minister will shortly be making an announcement.'

'That's right, John,' said the reporter, a thirtyish woman wearing a jade suit and a string of red beads around her neck. Her daily wardrobe had become familiar to Sarah over the days and weeks of the growing crisis. 'The Prime Minister and her most senior ministers and advisers have been meeting this morning to discuss the overnight rioting and attacks by the unidentified creatures known popularly as the Beasts of London. The so-called COBRA meeting was chaired by the Prime Minister at Cabinet Office Briefing Room A, a secure location within the heart of Whitehall used by the government to discuss urgent responses to major security events and other crises with national or regional implications. It's not known exactly who was present at this meeting, but typically we would expect key government ministers, the Mayor of London, the Police Commissioner and other senior security advisers to attend in order to brief the Prime Minister and enable her to make any necessary decisions.'

'And we understand that the Prime Minister herself will

be speaking to the press to explain what actions are to be taken?'

The reporter touched her earpiece. 'That's right, John. In fact, I believe that the Prime Minister is about to come out of Number Ten right now to speak to us.' She stood to one side, turning to where the black door with its lion head knocker and polished brass letterbox was already opening. The modest Georgian house always seemed to Sarah to be a strangely low-key location for such important briefings to be made. It seemed more likely that the Prime Minister would share her secret for preparing souffles than make a national security announcement. Curiously, the familiar domestic setting made the situation somehow less believable than if the Prime Minister had descended some grand spiralling staircase, amidst marble and gold pillars.

The camera zoomed in to reveal a number of burly men wearing black suits and sober ties emerging from the building onto the pavement outside. Behind them stepped a small woman dressed in a grey suit, her high heels failing to make her reach even as high as the men's shoulders.

'Who's that, Barbara?' asked Grandpa.

'It's the Prime Minister.'

'How can it be?' moaned the old man. 'She's a woman.'

'It's normal these days, Grandpa. Now be quiet, she's about to speak.'

Chapter Four

King's College Hospital, Lambeth, South London, New Year's Day

Vijay Singh sat upright in the hospital bed, waiting for the nurse to return. His right arm was bandaged and in a sling. A burning pain shot from the tips of his fingers up to his elbow whenever he tried to move it.

Rose Hallibury had accompanied him and Drake to the hospital last night, and she was still sitting at his bedside now as the faint light of the early morning sun began to push the darkness away from the windows. But even the rising sun couldn't compete with the glow of her curly copper hair. Her beauty was hardly diminished by the dirt and blood that stained her face and clothes.

Vijay tried not to stare at her too much. He turned away, and winced as another jolt of pain shot along his arm.

'What is it?' she asked, leaning forward and resting a

pale, freckled hand on his good arm. 'Is it the pain?'

'No,' he said Vijay, feeling his neck flush as she touched him. 'Well, yes, it still hurts when I move it.'

'Just keep still then,' said Rose.

The nurse returned from wherever she had been. 'Good news,' she said. 'Your arm isn't fractured after all. It's just a sprained elbow.'

'Are you sure?' asked Vijay. 'It feels like every bone in my arm must be broken.'

'The X-ray was clear,' said the nurse. 'The bones are undamaged. But the ligaments around the elbow joint are torn. You'll need to rest your arm until it's healed. Holding an ice pack against it for twenty minutes every few hours will help to ease the pain.'

'How long will it take to heal?' asked Vijay.

'It should be fully healed in a few weeks,' said the nurse.

'Really?' he said doubtfully. 'I can hardly move it.'

'That should improve in a day or so. But you should wear the sling for a few days and try not to move your arm.'

'So how long will I have to stay in the hospital?' he asked.

'You don't have to stay at all,' said the nurse. 'You can leave right away. I'll give you a leaflet explaining how to self-treat at home.'

'That's great news,' said Rose, smiling.

'I suppose so,' said Vijay. He had really expected to be staying in the hospital bed for weeks after being struck by the thug with the baseball bat. He ought to have been glad, but somehow being told there was nothing much wrong with him made him feel like a failure. The fact that he'd needed Rose's help made things even worse. If he'd been hoping to impress her with some heroic act, he'd failed utterly.

Rose didn't seem to notice his discomfort. 'As soon as they've finished with Drake, we can all go home,' she said.

'Yeah,' said Vijay glumly.

'What's wrong?'

'It's just that … if it was nothing more than a sprained elbow, I ought to have done more last night to protect everyone.'

'You did your best,' said Rose. 'You fought those men, even though they had weapons. I thought you were very brave.'

'Really?'

'Yeah.' She rested her fingers on his hand, squeezing it gently.

Suddenly the burning pain in his arm didn't matter. He would suffer gladly if Rose thought he was brave. 'I'm not as brave as you, though,' he said. 'You were amazing. You're always amazing.'

She smiled at him, a pink flush coming to her freckled face.

Vijay swallowed nervously. This was the moment he'd been waiting for. Ever since the day Rose had first spoken to him at school he'd been unable to get her out of his mind. Before meeting her he'd always imagined that one day he would marry a girl his parents chose for him. An arranged marriage, with a girl from a good Sikh family. But now he'd met Rose, he didn't think he could ever love a girl who didn't have her pale freckled skin and copper hair. He hoped that his parents wouldn't object to the match. How could they, when Rose was so amazing?

He just needed the courage to tell her how he truly felt. He'd always been too scared of what she might say. But if Rose thought he was brave, then perhaps he did have the courage after all.

'There's something I want to say to you,' he said. It was almost as if fate had brought them together in this way, so he could speak to her now. Perhaps his sprained elbow had a purpose.

'Is it about Drake?' asked Rose.

'Drake?' Vijay screwed up his face in puzzlement.

Drake Cooper was the last person he wanted to talk about right now. If it hadn't been for Drake they would never have got into so much trouble last night. Why on earth did Rose think he wanted to talk to her about Drake?

'About what Drake did last night to that man,' she prompted.

An unwelcome memory intruded into Vijay's thoughts. His friend, Drake, beating the injured thug who had attacked them with a baseball bat. Kicking him half to death as the man lay helpless on the ground. Vijay's sister Aasha watching, her dress torn, her face hard, full of vengeance and without pity.

'I know you tried to stop him,' continued Rose, 'but Drake just gave that man what he deserved. That thug was going to rape your sister.'

'No,' cried Vijay, dismayed. He knew it was true. But that didn't make it right. No one deserved the cold-blooded beating Drake had given that man. That kind of violence could never be justified, whatever the man had done, or intended to do.

'Anyway the man's dead now,' said Rose dismissively. 'The wolf killed him.'

'That doesn't make it any different,' said Vijay defensively.

'Yes it does. The dead don't matter. Only the living.' She withdrew her hand from his.

Vijay stared back at the red-haired girl sitting at his bedside. He wondered if he really knew the first thing about her. One thing he did know for sure – he loved her, and love was all that mattered. He was losing control of the conversation though. If he didn't say what he wanted to say now, he might never have the chance. 'I wanted to talk to you about something else. I wanted to –'

A shout cut his words off before he even knew what he really meant to say. 'Vijay!' It was Drake. His friend swaggered confidently toward him in his ripped jeans and T-shirt, his cropped hair sticking up and even messier than usual. His arm was in a sling too, and his lip was badly swollen where the baseball bat had caught him in the mouth, but he was up and about, unfazed by his injuries. But what truly astonished Vijay was that Aasha was with him, holding his free hand in hers. They walked close together, too close, much too close for Vijay's liking. They came over to his bed, looking elated, despite Drake's damaged arm, despite what had happened to Aasha last night.

'Look at us!' said Drake, showing his injured arm to Vijay. 'We both got slings. Wicked. You and me, we're like brothers now, yeah?' He turned to Aasha and gave her a wink.

'How's your arm?' Vijay asked, trying not to notice the way Aasha gazed admiringly into Drake's eyes.

'It's not really my arm that hurts,' said Drake. 'That bastard with the iron bar hit me in the shoulder. The doctor said I damaged a tendon. But it's no big deal. I reckon I can handle it.'

'Yeah?' teased Aasha. 'Think you're a tough guy, do you?'

'Reckon so,' said Drake. 'How about you, Vijay?'

'It's just a sprained elbow,' said Vijay miserably. 'Nothing to fret about.'

He heard his name being shouted again then, and Aasha's too. He looked up to see his parents bustling onto the hospital ward.

'Vijay!' His mother sobbed when she saw him, and rushed to him with open arms.

'Don't touch my arm,' said Vijay, before she tried to give him a hug. 'It hurts when it moves.'

'Is it broken?'

'No. I thought it was, but it's just a sprained ligament. The nurse said it will heal in a few days.'

His mother looked aghast. 'A sprained ligament,' she repeated. She turned then to face Aasha, her earlier look of concern replaced with anger. 'And you?' she demanded.

'Are you hurt?'

Aasha shook her head.

His mother's expression didn't change. 'And Drake is here too, I see.' She glared at the couple holding hands. 'Are you hurt, Drake? Is your arm broken?'

'I'm okay, thank you, Mrs Singh,' he said. 'My arm will be fine in a couple of days too.'

'That is something at least,' said Vijay's mum. 'No thanks to Aasha.'

Vijay knew what was coming next. So did his father, who stepped forward to take his wife's arm.

She shrugged it off angrily. 'Aasha, this is all your fault. If you hadn't gone out last night, the boys wouldn't have followed you.'

'I didn't ask them to follow me,' said Aasha petulantly. She turned her gaze to Drake. 'But I'm glad they did. You should have seen what Drake did to the guy who tore my dress.'

His mother threw a startled hand to her mouth. When she withdrew it, her face had hardened further. 'I don't care whose fault it was. And I don't want to hear any more about what happened. You could all have been killed last night.' She swept her gaze back to Vijay. 'You should have known better. You are not like your sister, you have always been a good boy.'

Vijay hung his head in shame. He knew he had let everyone down. His parents didn't even know how close they had come to being attacked by werewolves. He decided to keep that detail to himself.

His mother turned her attention to Rose then, sitting quietly by Vijay's bedside. 'Who is this?' she asked.

'It's my friend Rose,' said Vijay.

Rose stood up.

Vijay's mum looked her up and down, taking in the girl's bedraggled appearance. 'Were you there last night too? Did the boys drag you along?'

'I was there. But they didn't drag me along. I wanted to

go.'

'And what do your parents think of that?'

Rose said nothing.

'I see.' Vijay's mother was boiling with anger now. 'Vijay, you should think about other people first. You put yourself in danger, and this poor girl too.' She rounded on Aasha. 'And if you hadn't insisted on going out, none of this would have happened. You were lucky to escape with just a torn dress. From now on, you two are grounded,' she said to Aasha and Vijay.

Aasha protested loudly at this, but her mother was adamant. 'Your friends may come to visit you if they wish, but you will stay at home until further notice. And that is all I have to say on the matter.'

Chapter Five

South East London, New Year's Day

Chris Crohn was still trapped in London, despite all his carefully laid escape plans. Worse, the car that belonged to his best friend Seth had been smashed and wrecked during the overnight riots and was now useless. Worse still, all the survival gear he'd so carefully stockpiled in the preceding days and weeks had been stolen from the back of the car.

But there were positives too. He and Seth had come through the riot unharmed. Better still, Seth now finally believed in the werewolf apocalypse, having fought off a werewolf himself with nothing more than a pen knife. Chris still had his map of the British Isles, and Seth was clutching the Japanese origami book that Chris had given him for Christmas. It wasn't much, but it was a start. To survive the apocalypse you needed to look on the bright side.

Seth was having trouble seeing the bright side of

anything right now. 'My car,' he groaned. 'Look what they did to my car.'

They were standing in the road near where the car had finally ground to a halt the previous night, hemmed in by rioters and hooligans. A werewolf had attacked them while they sat huddled in the car, but together they had fought it off. For a brief moment they had been heroes, champions, apocalypse warriors valiantly charging into battle. But now their steed was just a burned-out husk. The car, or what was left of it, stood in the middle of the street. Only its steel frame remained. The tyres were gone, the windows were smashed, one of the doors had fallen off, and the interior was blackened and bare. A gang of rioters had stolen all their stuff from the rear of the car and then set the vehicle ablaze while Chris and Seth sat huddled in the front seats. They had barely escaped with their lives.

'It's gutted,' said Seth. 'Destroyed. Trashed. Finished. Useless. Broken.' He stopped, his lower lip quivering, but seeming to have run out of words to describe the ruined car. 'Dead,' he added finally.

'We were lucky to get out unharmed,' Chris told his friend. 'We can fix this.'

Seth raised his mournful face to look at him. 'How?' he wailed. He turned back to look at the remains of the car. 'How can we fix it?' His heavy mop of brown hair had fallen over his eyes and he seemed to lack the energy to flick it away like he normally did.

'We still have money.' In fact, Chris was carrying more money than he'd ever had in his entire life. Technically, none of it was his. It all belonged to the banks. In theory he would have to repay the loans very soon, but that didn't matter. Very soon the banks wouldn't exist, and neither would money. By Chris' reckoning, money was already worth a lot less than it had been the day before. People were freaking out, trying to withdraw cash from the banks, panic-buying food and other essentials. The financial markets would open in a day or two, and they were bound to crash. The money he carried would soon be almost worthless. The only problem then was how to spend it quickly.

In view of the fact that they had lost their car and most of their possessions during the riot, it seemed likely that one problem might solve the other.

'We'll just hire a new one,' he said. 'A black SUV. A big one with tinted windows and extra-wide wheels. It'll be incredible.' He could picture it already. The two of them driving the black beast through a post-apocalyptic wasteland, headlights blazing in the darkness. He could hardly wait to get going.

'I just want my old car,' said Seth, gazing miserably at the blackened wreck.

'Come on, Seth. This is going to be a huge adventure. Remember how good it felt when you fought off the werewolf last night? That was just the start. We're going on a journey and it's going to be packed with awesome.'

'My car,' repeated Seth mournfully. 'I want my car.'

Chris sighed. Seth was behaving like a baby. It was probably the shock of having his entire world tipped upside down. Yet hadn't Chris warned him enough times that the apocalypse was coming? It seemed that some people just weren't emotionally equipped to handle the end of the world. Someone needed to take charge, and that someone would have to be Chris.

He took hold of Seth's sleeve and led him gently away from the burned-out wreckage. 'Come on,' he said. 'Your car's dead, and we will be too if we stay here. We need to be out of London before nightfall so we don't get caught up in any more rioting.'

Seth said nothing as Chris dragged him across the street.

Chapter Six

*Upper Terrace, Richmond upon Thames,
West London, New Year's Day*

Sarah watched as the Prime Minister walked forward onto the pavement immediately outside Number Ten, Downing Street, a grim but determined look on her face, her security team fanning out to either side of her. Behind her, three more men appeared and took their places at her side. Sarah recognized the Mayor of London and the Police Commissioner, but the third man was a stranger to her. He wore a dark blue military uniform decorated with elaborate gold sashes and shoulder epaulettes. His silver hair was shorn short, although his eyebrows were untamed, meeting in the middle in a bushy monobrow. The peaked cap fixed rigidly to his head looked as much a part of him as the stony scowl he wore on his face, and the row of brightly striped medals pinned to his chest was almost too wide even for his broad girth to encompass.

'That's the head of the army,' commented Grandpa, and for once he was right.

'Standing with the Prime Minister are the Mayor of London, the Commissioner of the Metropolitan Police, and General Sir Roland Ney, Chief of the Defence Staff,' explained the reporter. 'General Sir Roland Ney is the head of the British Armed Forces and reports directly to the Secretary of State for Defence.'

The Prime Minister stepped up to a lectern that had been hastily positioned by the roadside in front of Number Ten. She gripped the edges of the lectern with thin, bony fingers and looked around at the cameras and journalists arrayed before her. In characteristic style, she wasted no time in getting to the point. 'Good morning to you all. I have come to you directly from an emergency meeting of the government's COBRA committee, called in response to the terrible overnight events that you will all no doubt have seen on your television screens.

'Present at that meeting were the Mayor of London, the Metropolitan Police Commissioner and the Chief of the Defence Staff.' She indicated the three men towering at her side. 'First, let me extend my sincere condolences to the families of those who were killed last night. Secondly, let me assure you all that this country will take whatever action is necessary to ensure the safety of its citizens. While the precise nature of the threat is still to some extent unclear, I have today authorized a number of actions that I believe necessary to restore order. All police leave is cancelled, with immediate effect. Since last month one thousand specially-trained police officers equipped with SIG 516 semi-automatic carbines, sniper rifles, and Glock nine-millimetre sidearms have been patrolling key public spaces. A further two thousand Authorised Firearms Officers will now join them. These officers will be authorized to use their firearms where necessary to restore order and ensure the safety of the public.'

The Mayor shuffled uncomfortably at her side and

glanced down at his feet as the Prime Minister made this announcement, but the Police Commissioner faced the cameras with grim resolve.

The Prime Minister continued. 'Make no mistake. Rioting, looting and violence on the scale we saw last night will not be tolerated. Furthermore, in recognition of the severity of this crisis, and to deal with the threat posed by the as-yet unidentified creatures that were witnessed in this city last night and in recent weeks, I have asked the Chief of the Defence Staff to deploy the army at strategic locations throughout the country, and in particular in London. The presence of the army on the nation's streets is intended to bring about the prompt capture or destruction of these dangerous animals, and to make the country safe for ordinary people to go about their everyday business. General Sir Roland Ney will now explain the details of this operation.'

A hubbub went up from the TV reporters, but the PM stood back to allow the General to take his position at the lectern. The tall, barrel-chested man waited patiently for quiet to return to the briefing. 'Thank you, Prime Minister,' he began, in the clipped voice of command. 'I have been asked by the Prime Minister to restore order to the streets, towns and cities of Great Britain, and I intend now to explain the operational details of how that will be brought about. First, let me state that while the primary role of the police and military in the days and nights to come will be to prevent any repeat of the looting, rioting and vandalism that occurred on New Year's Eve, our secondary purpose will be to capture and exterminate the creatures that now roam the streets of our capital, and which have become known in the popular press as *Beasts*. To that end, the army will be deploying soldiers in London and other cities, including Birmingham and Manchester, to root out and destroy this threat.'

The General paused briefly, and a few voices called out questions. He raised his hand to silence them. 'With immediate effect we will be deploying troops from the Air Assault Brigade, comprising the Air Assault Task Force and associated units, drawing from several battalions of the Parachute Regiment. These units have served recently in Afghanistan and Iraq, and are experienced in full spectrum rapid reaction combat missions. The Parachute Regiment is a light and agile force, able to deploy to any part of the world in five days. The Prime Minister has requested their immediate deployment in their home country, and so I can tell you that they will begin their duties later this day, and will be fully operational by midnight tonight.'

The General frowned, and his steely eyebrows knotted together with fierce determination. 'I am therefore able to announce the imposition of a curfew beginning at midnight and extending until six am tomorrow morning. The army will patrol the streets of the capital during these hours and will arrest anyone found breaking the curfew. This curfew will remain in place until the current situation has been resolved.'

The General stood down from the lectern amid a huge wave of shouts and questions from the waiting journalists.

Once again the Prime Minister returned to the microphone. She waited for the noise to die back before she spoke again. 'I realize that the curfew and the troop deployment that the General has announced are unprecedented in modern British history. But so, too, is the threat we face. I do not mean simply the criminal behaviour of the rioters, looters and arsonists who attacked our country last night. I refer to the dangerous creatures that also spread mayhem and destruction. Until these twin threats have been dealt with, I ask all of you to fully support and cooperate with the police and military operations I have outlined. I promise you that if we stand together as a nation, we can defeat this grave threat. And now, if you will excuse me, there are many urgent tasks that I must attend to.'

Sarah stared at the TV screen in disbelief. A curfew?

She had never heard of such a thing. And the army deployed on the streets of Britain to arrest curfew breakers? It was unthinkable.

The old man in the bed coughed loudly and gripped her arm weakly. 'That's all very well,' grumbled Grandpa, frowning in irritation, 'But now my tea's gone cold.'

Chapter Seven

Brixton Village, South London, New Year's Day

Ben Harvey woke early on New Year's morning, the first rays of the winter sun forcing their way through a crack in the bedroom curtains and triggering a headache he knew would stay with him for the rest of the day. He manoeuvred himself carefully out of bed, his head buzzing as furiously as a wasp's nest when he stood. He propped himself against the bedroom wall for a minute until his vision cleared. Headaches, blackouts and dizziness had been a part of his life ever since Mr Canning, the headmaster, had landed that kick on his head that fateful day at school. *Minor traumatic brain injury, more commonly known as concussion,* had been the doctor's glib assessment. *Keep taking ibuprofen and call back if the symptoms haven't cleared in a few weeks.* It had been two weeks so far, and he didn't need to swallow quite as many pills now. Another week and he ought to be okay.

The mirror in the bathroom seemed to tell another story. Bloodshot eyes, dark rings framing them, and the scar on his forehead gave him the appearance of a reanimated corpse. His headache was worse than any hangover he could remember, and he hadn't even been out for a New Year's drink. *Happy New Year, Ben.* Never mind. Things could only get better.

Unless they got worse. He'd slept fitfully after watching the violence unfold on his TV screen the previous night. Rioting, looting, arson. Dozens feared dead. And something even worse – bizarre images of dangerous beasts on the streets. Creatures like giant wolves, attacking and killing people. He shook his head and instantly regretted it. If he could just remember to keep his head still, the world wouldn't feel like it was constantly exploding.

He washed a couple of pills down his throat, showered quickly, dressed and hurried into the kitchen to switch on the radio. The news that greeted him was as bad as he'd feared. Not just dozens killed, but hundreds, and many more with serious injuries. People were blaming the mysterious beasts for the worst of the carnage. The *Beast of Clapham Common* had graduated from rumour to fact, and had brought its friends along for a New Year's Eve party, if the eyewitness reports were to be believed. Ben would have said it sounded impossible if he hadn't personally witnessed the headmaster devouring one of his own students at school. After seeing that, it was difficult to rule anything out.

He couldn't face breakfast, but made himself a cup of coffee and went to look out of the window. The sunny morning had banished the night horrors, welcoming in the new year with a brightness that was completely at odds with his own mood. People were already out in the street, and a group of neighbours had gathered outside his house. Watching their body language, it was quickly apparent that they weren't there to enjoy the sunshine. Their raised voices were audible even over the sound of the radio.

He switched the radio off and took his cup of coffee outside to see what was happening. About half a dozen people had gathered in the street. He recognized Mr Kowalski, the shopkeeper from the local Polish supermarket, his bushy walrus moustache completely covering his mouth. A couple of other faces were familiar, but most were strangers.

Mr Kowalski was gesticulating angrily with his heavy hands at a man Ben knew vaguely by sight but not by name. 'What use are police?' he demanded. 'They do nothing when people break into my shop. They do nothing.'

The other man shrugged. He was taller than Mr Kowalski, and heavily built, with beefy arms visible under his shirt. He wore no jacket or coat, even though it was only just above freezing. 'What do you expect? The police have bigger problems to deal with than your shop.'

'I expect protection,' shouted Mr Kowalski. 'Protection for honest working people. Is that too much? What are police for, anyway?'

Before the argument could get more heated, a woman stepped between the two men. Ben recognized her from his regular morning journeys to school. He had exchanged pleasantries with her and they'd sometimes shared their grumbles about the state of the buses or the weather. Her name was Salma Ali, and she was some kind of human rights lawyer, if he remembered correctly. Even though it was a holiday, she wore a smart black trouser suit, her long dark hair tied back neatly. Ben had never seen her in any other kind of outfit. 'Mr Kowalski, Mr Stewart, please, this is no time for us to be arguing amongst ourselves. We need to pull together as a community.' She spotted Ben standing on his doorstep and beckoned him over. 'Ah, Mr Harvey, perhaps you can help us here.'

Ben walked over to the group reluctantly. 'I don't know what I can do to help,' he said. 'What exactly is the problem?'

Mr Kowalski began speaking first. 'My shop is broken into last night. Looters from the rioting. They are common criminals.' He punctuated each statement with a jab of his blunt fingers.

'Did you call the police?' asked Ben.

'Of course. I dial 999. Police too busy to come.' He lifted his hands in frustration. 'What use are they?'

'They were dealing with the rioting and the wolves,' said the other man, Mr Stewart. 'Do you think your shop matters more than that?'

'If my customers have no food to buy, then it matters, yes.'

The raised voices were making Ben's head throb angrily. He threw up his hand to quieten the two men. 'Okay, okay, but what do you expect me to do about it?' he snapped. The question had come out all wrong. He hadn't meant to sound critical of the shopkeeper, but he was out of patience lately.

Salma Ali stepped in. 'An excellent question, Mr Harvey. What can each of us do to protect our community?' It seemed to be a rhetorical question. Everyone waited for her to elaborate. 'The police are clearly tied up dealing with the big picture, and rightly so. But that doesn't mean we are powerless to act locally. We can start by building on the existing Neighbourhood Watch scheme. If we organize groups to patrol the area we can keep everyone safe. All we need are some volunteers, and someone willing to coordinate.' She cast her gaze around the group. 'Do I see any volunteers here?'

Mr Kowalski was the first to pledge his support. 'Ms Ali is right. We must do this thing ourselves. I volunteer. My two sons as well.'

The others in the gathering looked sheepish, but the outcome was inevitable. Salma Ali turned first to Mr Stewart. 'Can we count you in, Mr Stewart?' She smiled at his nod of assent. 'Mr Harvey, I'm sure we can depend on you, especially after your recent act of heroism?'

There was no way out. If only he'd stayed inside to enjoy his coffee, none of this might have happened. Then again, from what he'd seen of Salma Ali, she wasn't the kind of woman to permit anything to stand in her way once she'd set her mind on it. 'I'm happy to help if I can,' he said.

'Excellent,' she said, smiling. 'And I'm happy to volunteer my services as coordinator. Give me a little time to get organized. I'll see you all back at my house in one hour's time.'

The little group broke up, leaving Ben standing alone on the pavement outside his home. The dull throbbing in his head had grown steadily throughout the conversation and now a sharp pain lanced through his skull, worse than ever. He tried a sip of his coffee, but it had gone completely cold. He'd been awake for less than an hour, and already he wished he could rewind the clock and start the new year over again.

Things can only get better, he reminded himself.
Unless they get worse.

Chapter Eight

Brookfield Road, Brixton Hill, South London, New Year's Day

When Liz arrived home from the hospital there was no sign of Kevin or Mihai in her apartment. Her father and the Romanian boy had disappeared without leaving a note of explanation.

She dropped into a chair and pulled out her phone. She needed to know that Mihai was safe and she just didn't have the energy to go looking for her father in her current state of near-exhaustion. It was funny. She'd never imagined that monsters could feel so tired, so sleepy. But that's how she felt. And there was no doubt in her mind that she had become a monster. Any bright light stung her eyes, reminding her that the yellow-eye sickness had claimed her, just as it had claimed PC David Morgan. Just as it had claimed the madman who'd attacked her on the Common. She was one of them now. There was no denying it.

'I am not a monster,' she whispered to the silent apartment, but it was a lie.

She stabbed at the phone with her finger, speed-dialling her father's number. She hoped he'd remembered to take his phone with him and not leave it in the apartment. She hoped the networks were still working after all the recent trouble.

A muffled ringtone answered her. Oh, no. He'd left it behind again. The ringtone continued, audible but from somewhere nearby. She couldn't be bothered to go and look for it. She was just about to cancel the call when her father answered it.

'Hello? Liz? Where are you?'

Her tired brain could barely make sense of the reply. 'Dad? Where are you? I heard your ringtone. Are you in the apartment?'

'Just outside. Hold on.'

A key slid into the lock and the front door opened. Her father entered, Mihai by his side. 'We was just getting in when you called,' he said into the phone. 'Oh, sorry.' He ended the call and spoke directly to her. 'Are you all right? You look terrible.'

Liz didn't need any reminding about how bad she looked. 'Where have you been?' she asked. 'There's been rioting all over London. Why did you go out?'

'We just went to the newsagent's around the corner to pick up a pint of milk. A kid like this can't get by with no breakfast, can he?' He ruffled Mihai's hair affectionately.

Mihai ran to her and threw his arms around her neck. 'You back, Liz, you back!' he shouted excitedly.

She was pleased by the boy's obvious delight. She'd never imagined herself as the maternal type, but she must be doing something right. She gave him a hug. 'Why did you take Mihai with you?' she asked her father.

'What am I supposed to do with him? He ain't made of glass. He's a tough kid. He's seen worse than this.'

'Sure,' said Mihai, 'Much worse.'

Lycanthropic

Her father took the milk into the kitchen and started preparing breakfast. 'What about you?' he called. 'Are you okay? I saw the rioting on TV. You didn't get caught up in all that, did you?'

There was nothing to be gained from telling them that she'd been right in the middle of the fighting, so she decided to keep it to herself. 'A bit of rest and I'll be fine.'

'I'll fry some sausages,' he said, and set to work.

She dragged herself out of the chair and followed him through to the kitchen. The smell of sausage, bacon and liver soon made her mouth water. She hadn't realized just how ravenous she was.

Mihai put plates, cutlery and tomato ketchup on the table while Kevin played at being chef. The man and the boy had forged a strong, if unlikely bond in the few days they had known each other. A chauvinist truck driver wanted in connection with a murder enquiry, living happily with an orphaned Romanian boy and a police officer turned part-time monster. Somehow Liz had gone from living alone to being in the middle of a three-generational extended family. They were almost like a functioning family unit. Almost.

She sighed. 'What am I going to do with you, Dad?'

'What do you mean?' he said, his back to her as he turned the sizzling sausages.

Liz glared at him. He knew well enough. Being wanted for a triple murder wasn't the kind of thing someone forgot – even someone as unreliable as her father. 'About what we discussed previously. About you going to the police station and handing yourself in for questioning. Don't pretend you've forgotten.'

'I ain't forgotten. I was just waiting for the right moment. Things have been a bit hectic, like. Just give me the word, and I'll go straight over.'

Mihai frowned at Liz. 'Grandpa Kevin go to police station? What for? He do something bad?'

'Don't ask,' she said lightly. 'Trust me, you don't want

to know.'

'Grandpa Kevin not bad man,' said Mihai defiantly. 'He stay here, look after me.'

'Here you go,' said her father, serving generous portions of fried bacon, liver and sausages for them all. 'Tuck in.'

Mihai half-drowned his plate in tomato ketchup and got straight to work. Liz was just about to eat too when her phone rang. Reluctantly she checked to see who was calling. She groaned when she saw. 'I have to take this call,' she said. 'It's Samantha, my partner Dean's wife. Dean got hurt in the riots and got taken to the hospital.'

She answered the call.

'Liz? Oh, thank heavens!' Samantha sounded like she was almost in tears.

'Samantha? Have you heard anything? Any news about Dean?' Liz had been so caught up in her own hospital escape that she hadn't given much thought to her injured colleague. She hadn't seen him since they'd been taken into the hospital in the same ambulance.

'He phoned me from the hospital. They gave him some stitches for a blow to his head, but he seems to be okay.'

'That's good news,' said Liz, relieved. She had been by his side when the iron bar had struck his forehead and knocked him unconscious. It sounded like he'd got off lightly.

'They want to keep him in for observation,' continued Samantha, 'but he's well enough to receive visitors. I was wondering if you could give me a lift to the hospital?'

'Sure,' said Liz. 'I'll be with you in fifteen minutes.'

'You not going out again, are you?' asked her father when she hung up. 'You only just got back.'

'I know,' she said, cramming hot food into her mouth. 'I'm sorry. But Samantha needs a lift to the hospital. I can't let her down.'

'No problem,' said Mihai. 'I stay here with Grandpa Kevin.'

'Okay,' agreed Liz. 'Just be sure to stay indoors. It's not safe out there. I'll be back as soon as I can.'

She drove over to Dean's house where Samantha and her two-year-old daughter, Lily, were waiting for her. 'Hop in,' said Liz. Samantha strapped Lily into the child's car seat that she'd brought and Liz drove them to the hospital. The sun shone brightly through the window of the car, making her eyes sting. She stopped at some traffic lights and pulled on her sunglasses. Samantha jabbered nervously to her the whole journey, telling her about the violent scenes she'd watched unfold on the news overnight, but Liz hardly heard a word she said. She must be mad returning to the hospital she'd only just escaped from. Was *escaped* too melodramatic? She didn't think so. If Chanita saw her, she might call security and have her apprehended.

When they arrived at the hospital, Samantha and Lily got out, but Liz remained in the car. 'I'll just stay here and wait for you,' she said.

Samantha gave her a curious look. 'Don't you want to come and see Dean?'

'No. I'll let you have some family time together. Just you, Dean and Lily. Take your time. There's no rush.'

'Thanks,' said Samantha. She walked slowly toward the main hospital building, the bump in her belly clearly showing. Liz couldn't remember how many weeks it was until the baby was due. The little girl at her side clutched her hand, a doll held tightly under her arm. A model family unit, so unlike the family Liz herself had known growing up.

She studied her reflection in the car's mirror. Dark glasses stared back at her, concealing an even darker secret: that she was infected by the yellow-eye sickness.

So here she was, hiding in her car. A fugitive, too afraid to show her face in the hospital in case someone screamed, 'Monster!' Yet there was no point denying it to herself. The full moon had done something to her, changed her in some unfathomable way. For a brief moment last night she'd gained superpowers – unimaginable speed and strength. And how had she used those powers? She'd attacked two members of the public and left them for dead. They'd been criminals for sure, but what she'd done to them had hardly been *reasonable force*. How was she going to explain that when she wrote her report of the night's events? She would be suspended if anyone found out. And if they discovered she was hiding a wanted murderer in her own home … it would be the end of her career as a police officer. She might even go to jail herself.

So this was how it happened. A little white lie here, a careful omission there. Saying whatever it took to make it through to the next day, and the day after that. Soon the lies would be flowing freely until she didn't even notice anymore. This must be the murky moral world her father inhabited. There was no way out. She could only go deeper.

One thing was crystal clear – she couldn't look after Mihai on her own. She had been stupid to try. She needed her father's help if she was going to give the boy a chance. And that meant that she would carry on telling lies, just as often and for just as long as she needed to.

At least she no longer had any flu symptoms, and the scratch marks on her arm had disappeared. The injuries she had sustained last night had also mysteriously healed under the light of the full moon. Now her only remaining symptom was her light-sensitive yellow eyes. That, and total exhaustion.

She closed her eyes for a while and tried to rest, but her brain kept spinning, turning the same thoughts over and over again. A sudden banging on the door of the car made her jump in her seat. She spun round to look. Samantha and Lily had returned, and Dean was with them.

She unlocked the car doors and Dean swung himself gingerly into the passenger seat next to her. The others got into the back, and Samantha began strapping Lily into her car seat.

Dean's face was red and black with bruising. A row of stitches in the middle of his forehead gave him the appearance of Frankenstein's monster.

'You look terrible,' Liz said to him. 'What the hell are you doing out of hospital?'

'I could ask you the same.'

'Yeah, well,' she said. 'They said I could leave.' Another lie, and this one so easy she hardly felt it.

Dean grinned. 'Well they told me to stay in the hospital, but I feel okay, and I'm not staying there while there's a job to do.'

Samantha touched Liz on the shoulder. 'Can you persuade him to at least stay home and rest for a few days?' she asked. 'I've tried, but I can't talk any sense into him.'

Liz looked at her partner and saw the look of resolve on his face beneath the grin. 'I'm sorry, Sam, but I don't think I can.'

Chapter Nine

Upper Terrace, Richmond upon Thames, West London, New Year's Day

Sarah sat rooted to her television screen. News had never been so astonishing, so unbelievable, so utterly compelling. What had begun as an interest had bloomed into an obsession, then a compulsion, and now an addiction. She couldn't bear to leave it, not even to fetch a drink, or use the bathroom.

Grandpa grumbled when she refused to let him watch his usual quiz show, but missing out on the constant stream of speculation and reports was unthinkable. 'You can watch it another time, Grandpa,' she told him, although she knew it was a lie as soon as she said it. As long as Sarah controlled the remote, the TV would be showing nothing but news channels until this crisis was over. If it ever was.

One TV reporter had managed to track down a woman who claimed to have witnessed one of last night's *Beast* attacks at close quarters. He was interviewing her in central London, on the north bank of the River Thames. The glass and steel triangular tower of the Shard thrust above the jumbled skyline behind her. Bright shafts of sun burst through the clouds that scudded overhead, turning the muddy water blue and silver wherever it struck.

'Tell me where you were standing when you saw the creature,' prompted the reporter.

The woman was young, with shoulder-length ash blonde hair and black-framed glasses, smartly dressed in a navy suit. 'I was watching the fireworks, on the south bank of the River Thames, with friends.' She paused and pointed at the bank opposite. The area was still sealed off, lines of police cars visible across the river, their yellow, blue and white checked patterns garish in the winter light. 'We had a good spot, right at the front of the crowd. From where we stood, we could see the laser show at the Houses of Parliament and the London Eye about a mile downriver.'

'What time was this?' the reporter asked.

'Just after midnight. We heard Big Ben chime the hour, and then the fireworks began. It was a minute or two later that I first noticed the man.'

The reporter pushed the microphone closer. 'Can you describe him?'

'He was a young man, not much more than a boy really. He looked like a student, with blonde hair, neatly parted. He was dressed well, with a kind of preppy look. No jacket, just a polo shirt and some chinos. Honestly, I wouldn't have paid him any attention except that he was fixated on this girl standing next to him.'

'Fixated?'

'Staring at her intensely. His eyes hardly left her. Everyone else was watching the fireworks, including the girl. But he just kept looking at her. I don't think she even noticed. So I watched.'

'What happened then?'

'The firework display was in full swing. Suddenly the moon came out from behind a cloud and the man looked up at the sky. He began to change. His skin started moving, rippling, like there was something underneath trying to get out. It was hideous. I grabbed my friend's arm and she saw it too. At first I couldn't understand what was happening, then I realized that hair was growing all over his body, even over his face. That's what was making his skin appear to move. In less than a minute he was entirely covered in sandy hair.'

'Covered in hair. What else?'

'His body was changing shape, becoming more muscular. His shoulders broadened, his chest expanded. His arms were bare, so I could see the muscles tightening, all the sinews stretching taut. And his face was changing too. That was the most awful part. His nose grew longer, like a dog's snout. He even started sniffing at the girl. That's when she noticed, I think.'

'What did she do?'

'Nothing. She just stood there, looking back at him. I think she was too terrified to move. It was too late anyway. The man lunged at her and bit her throat. It was horrible. He wasn't a man anymore.' She trailed off, dabbing at tears that ran down her cheeks. Behind her, a small gathering of onlookers stared at her, while others hurried past. A police siren blared out suddenly and blue lights flashed briefly across the street.

The reporter raised his voice above the noise. 'What happened to the girl?'

The woman gestured with her hands, her fingers curling and uncurling as she remembered the details. 'There was blood everywhere. She just fell to the ground. I think she was already dead. I've never seen so much blood before. Then a second creature appeared, with black fur. I don't know where it came from. The two of them ran away through the crowd, just seconds before the police came. Then there was gunfire, and people started running, and ... it was all just chaos.'

'Some people may find your description of events incredible,' the reporter said. 'Is it possible you may have been mistaken?'

The woman fixed the reporter with an icy stare. 'I know what I saw,' she said. 'I saw a man become a wolf.'

'Preposterous,' sneered Grandpa. 'What are we watching? Some kind of prank show?'

'It's the news, Grandpa.'

'How can it be?'

Sarah shrugged. 'I don't know. It just is.'

The weirdest thing of all was that none of this seemed unbelievable anymore. In fact it had taken on an air of inevitability, like a train that had been set in motion. Something had shifted, whether it was the world, or just Sarah's mind. It seemed obvious to her that this series of extraordinary events, whatever it was, was only just getting started. The old certainties had gone, as if her old life had simply been a dream, as if the world was one of those movie sets made of cardboard, nothing more than a surface illusion. Push at a seemingly-solid wall too hard and it fell away revealing an emptiness behind. Now, anything felt possible, anything at all. And Sarah, having lived her entire life in the shadows at the edge of a dream, could hardly wait for it to get started.

Chapter Ten

*Greenfield Road, Brixton, South London,
New Year's Day*

Leanna sat at the head of the big wooden table at the house in Greenfield Road, the house that she shared with Adam Knight. It had been home to Samuel Smalling and James Beaumont too, before their betrayal.

She studied the two men sitting either side of her. Adam sat to her left, leaning his long, slim body back in his chair, stretching out his well-toned arms, trying to affect a nonchalant attitude. But Adam fooled no one. Leanna could see the nervousness in his sharp eyes. She could sense the simmering resentment bubbling beneath the surface. Adam was a seething ball of nerves and discomfort, and that was how she intended to keep him.

Warg Daddy sat opposite him, clothed in the black leather jacket and dark shades he wore everywhere. The leader of the Wolf Brothers seemed to fill the space with his bulk, rippling his huge arm muscles and flexing his wide shoulder blades, as if the constraints of sitting at the table in this domestic setting caused him some kind of physical discomfort. He gazed suspiciously across the table at Adam, clearly making him even more nervous than ever.

Leanna permitted herself a small smile. Warg Daddy had many uses, and keeping Adam in his place was one of them. But the big man needed to be kept in his place too. Not only had he questioned her orders, he had explicitly disobeyed her. The chair where she had expected to see Warg Daddy's second-in-command was empty. 'Where is Snakebite?' she demanded, her voice like a whip. 'I specifically instructed you to bring him to this meeting.'

She noticed Adam smirk at the word *instructed*. Let him smirk. She had things to say to him too. Things that would wipe the smile from his face.

Warg Daddy looked stung by her words. He lifted one huge hand and began to rub his smooth bald head with his thumb. 'I don't understand why you want him here,' he said defensively. 'Snakebite isn't so good at talking. Or thinking. He gets bored too quickly. He's better with his hands, especially when he has a knife in one of them. Know what I mean?'

Leanna treated him to a cold stare, watching him shrink under her gaze. She remembered the night on the Common when she'd first encountered him and his sidekicks, the Wolf Brothers. They'd had a plan to catch a werewolf, but she had caught them instead. It had been tempting to kill them all, but Warg Daddy had convinced her to spare them. *We could be good together*, he'd suggested, and he'd been right. She had changed him into a werewolf, taken him as a lover, and he had already proved his worth as her henchman. But headstrong men like Warg Daddy responded well when she gave her affections sparingly. They responded best when she withdrew them entirely. Besides, she had particular reasons for wanting Snakebite at the War Council. The flame-haired giant had skills that even Warg Daddy didn't know about.

'I told you to bring Snakebite,' she said icily. 'There is no need for you to understand why. Next time, do what I tell you.'

Warg Daddy rubbed his head again and nodded unhappily.

Leanna had been studying Warg Daddy's DNA back at the lab. It had changed in many ways since he'd become lycanthropic and those changes were having physiological effects on his body. He had gained strength, and his athletic abilities were greatly enhanced even while in human form. His blood was able to carry significantly more oxygen, and his lungs had altered their structure to absorb oxygen and remove carbon dioxide more efficiently. His performance on the treadmill and exercise bike had improved dramatically.

His brain had altered too. The parts that processed his sense of smell and sight had grown larger. She had tested his night vision and found that he could see almost as well during the hours of darkness as during the day. His hearing had sharpened and his sense of smell was now as good as any dog. The increase in brain size had come at a cost however. The internal pressure on the skull gave him severe headaches and she had prescribed pills for him to take each day. Judging from the way he rubbed his head more and more often, the pills weren't having much effect.

She turned her attention to Adam. 'Where were you last night?' she barked. 'I ordered you to follow Samuel and James. I told you not to let them out of your sight for a second.'

That wiped the smirk off his face, just as she had intended. Suddenly he was like a sullen little boy, caught doing something naughty at school. 'I did follow them,' he protested. 'But they gave me the slip. They must have planned it in advance.'

Leanna lashed out at him with her tongue. 'That was why I gave you your instructions,' she snapped. 'I wanted to know what they were up to.'

Adam had changed too, in interesting ways. His cardiovascular capacity had increased enormously, stimulated by his intense training regime. His brain structure had also changed, but in a different way to Warg Daddy's. His senses had not developed to the same level. Instead his motor functions were evolving in tandem with his physical advances, giving him almost superhuman athletic and gymnastic performance. His intelligence level had increased too, making him useful but dangerous. She would need to keep him on a short leash, and eliminate him if he became too much of a threat.

'Warg Daddy should have killed James last night when he had the chance,' said Adam.

'I will kill him,' said Warg Daddy. 'Just as soon as we find him.' His nose still bore a red scratch where Samuel had clawed him during the fight with James.

'No!' shouted Leanna. 'I already told you. I will kill him myself.'

'Why don't you just forget about him?' said Adam sullenly, not looking at either her or Warg Daddy. 'James is a distraction. There are more important things for us to deal with now.'

'I will never forget about James,' hissed Leanna. 'Never. One day soon I will kill him. And I want you to find him for me.'

'Me?' said Adam in surprise. 'Why me? Why not the Wolf Brothers?'

'Because you know him better than any of us.'

'But where should I look?' asked Adam. 'He could be anywhere by now.'

'Use your wits, Adam,' said Leanna. 'Start with his family home. Check the school he used to go to, and the church where he killed that priest. Talk to the people he knew. Find out the places he might have gone. But stay out of his sight. I don't want to scare him off.'

Adam shrugged, but he didn't argue this time.

'I have a task for you too, Warg Daddy,' she said. 'I want you to find us somewhere new to live. Somewhere safe and secure.'

The Leader of the Pack looked puzzled. 'What's wrong with this place?'

'James knows about it. He might tell someone. We need to move out of here, and I want to move today.'

Warg Daddy still wore a frown. 'It's New Year's Day,' he said. 'How can I find us a house? All the rental agencies will be closed today.'

'I know,' said Leanna. 'But I'm not asking you to use a rental agency. You have a particular skill set. I was thinking that you and the Brothers might be able to acquire a vacant property without anyone knowing. Somewhere large. Somewhere discreet.'

Warg Daddy stroked his thick black beard. 'I catch your drift,' he said.

She treated him to a small smile. 'Good. That's excellent, Warg Daddy. I knew I could rely on you.' She watched his face and saw a faint glimmer of relief at her words.

Rewards and punishments. These were the tools she used to control her followers. Simple tools, but effective. It was how you trained a dog, and Warg Daddy and Adam were nothing more than dogs, even though they didn't know it.

Warg Daddy might believe that she was his lover, but the idea that she might actually love him was preposterous. Love was a stupid human emotion. Warg Daddy was useful to her, and he pleased her in bed, but there was nothing more to the relationship than that. One day he might no longer serve a useful purpose, and she would discard him just as easily as she had picked him up. She was free of the shackles of emotions.

Her own brain scans had shown that since becoming lycanthropic the parts of her brain that handled emotion and empathy had diminished in size. Her feelings had become muted and dulled. She remembered that as a girl she had been full of love. She had loved her parents and brother dearly. She had even loved her pet puppy. That kind of sentimentality disgusted her now. How could she have indulged in such weak and stupid behaviour? She was better off without it. When her puppy had died, she had cried for days, cried until her eyes and nose were red and raw. Yet all that grief had been for naught. It had not brought the dead pet back to life. Her father had bought her another puppy as a replacement, and the new one had been just as good as the one that had died. Why had she continued to cry, even after the new puppy arrived? It was senseless. She had cried when her mother had died too. A mother could not be replaced, but Leanna could no longer remember what had saddened her so. All mothers died eventually. It was the way of the world.

Last year, when she had murdered her father and brother, she had shed no tears. Her only feeling then had been the satisfaction of well-laid plans coming to fruition. But not all of Leanna's feelings had shut down. Love may have gone, but in its place burned anger and hate. And all that hate was now directed at James. Adam would find him for her, and then she would kill him. The pleasure would be all hers.

'That's everything for now,' she said.

'Is that it?' asked Warg Daddy in surprise. 'I thought you had big plans to discuss.'

'I do. We'll talk again when Snakebite is with us. In the meantime you both have jobs to do.'

'What about you?' asked Adam. 'What are you going to do?'

'I need to go back to the university one last time and clear everything away. I don't want any of my research falling into the wrong hands.' She thought of the DNA samples she had collected. Her own, Adam's, and one from each of the Wolf Brothers. Analyzing the genetic changes had been a fascinating research project. Each one of the Brothers had changed in a different way since she had passed the condition to them with her bite. All of them had grown in strength and athletic ability. Some had developed super senses, some enhanced memory skills, some had faster reaction times. All were more capable than they had been before.

Most interesting of all was Snakebite. The man had started out a brute, performing poorly in all the IQ tests Leanna had given him. Yet in just a few weeks, Snakebite's cognitive functions had sharpened dramatically. The *corpus callosum* that connected the left and right halves of his brain had grown by an order of magnitude. His IQ was approaching genius level, and his advances showed no signs of stopping. She was keen to run more tests to see if any further changes had taken place since last night's full moon. Snakebite was well worth watching.

Adam had one final question for her. 'What about that supervisor of yours at the university? Does she have any suspicions about what you've been doing? Perhaps you should eliminate her as a precaution.'

Leanna smiled her cold smile. The idea was tempting. Doctor Helen Eastgate had merely been a route to gain access to the laboratory equipment Leanna needed to carry out her tests. It would be a pleasure to dispose of her, just as she had taken care of Professor Wiseman back in Romania. But while losing one professor may be regarded as a misfortune, losing both would look like carelessness and would raise far too many suspicions. Besides, Leanna might still need access to the lab to carry out further tests. 'Don't worry about Doctor Helen Eastgate,' she said. 'I have her under control. She suspects nothing.'

Chapter Eleven

Brookfield Road, Brixton Hill, South London, New Year's Day

'Come on, kid,' said Kevin. 'Get your coat on. We're going out.'

Mihai peered at him from beneath his unruly mop of hair. 'But Liz say we stay indoors. Is not safe outside.'

'Yeah,' said Kevin. 'She's a good woman, Liz. But mothers always fuss too much. That's why you need your old grandpa, so you can have some fun now and again.'

Mihai grinned, his face seeming to light up. 'Okay, Grandpa Kevin. We do what you say.'

Kevin reached out and ruffled the boy's hair. 'Just keep it a secret, okay? This is just between you and me. Liz don't need to know what we get up to when she ain't around.'

Their first stop was the butcher's shop down the road.

'All right, Kevin?' said the butcher when he saw him.

He was a big man with a red face and straw hair. He wore a navy striped butcher's apron over a white coat, but his sleeves were rolled up, revealing a pair of beefy arms. An old-fashioned trilby hat perched jauntily on his head. 'How you doing there, mate?'

The butcher reminded Kevin of his own father. The traditional butcher's clothing, the cheery smile, the polished metal worktop, the smell of hung meat. Entering the shop was like walking back into his own childhood. The butcher was in his early forties by the looks of him, about the same age Kevin's old man had been when he passed away. Kevin could have taken over the family business then if he'd wanted to, following in his father's footsteps, just as his father had followed his own father before him. *Bailey & Son* could have become *Bailey & Grandson*. But Kevin had longed for adventure. He'd wanted to travel beyond South London, so he'd joined the army, hoping to see the world. To his dismay he'd spent the next five years posted to Northern Ireland, trying to stop the Catholics from killing the Protestants and the Protestants from killing the Catholics. Senseless. He'd never understood what their problem was. But he'd learned one thing from his time in the army – loyalty. You picked your side, and you stuck with it, through good times and bad. Mostly bad, in Kevin's case. If only he could have learned that lesson before he'd left his family home, he would never have gone in the first place, but that was life for you.

'I'm not so bad, Gary,' he said to the butcher. 'Not so bad. Have you met the kid? This is Mihai.'

'Hey, kid, nice to meet you,' said Gary. 'I'd shake your hand, but I got a bit of blood on me right now.' He raised his hands to show the stainless steel chainmail gloves he wore, spattered with gore.

Mihai peeped nervously over the counter at the big man, staring apprehensively at his metal gloves.

The butcher gave a hearty laugh. 'So what can I do for

you gentlemen this fine morning?'

Kevin looked up at the meat hooks that lined the wall behind the counter. Usually they were all hung with carcasses, but today half the hooks were empty. 'What you got in today, Gary? Any specials?'

The butcher gesticulated with his brawny arms. 'We're a bit short, to be honest, Kev, what with the market being closed for the holidays.' He lowered his voice and leaned over the counter conspiratorially. 'And I'm not too optimistic after all the trouble last night. The soldiers are closing roads, searching vehicles, generally getting in everyone's way. To tell the truth, I don't know when I'll get fresh supplies. If I were you, I'd stock up now.'

'Good advice,' agreed Kevin. 'We'll take as much as we can carry.'

They hauled the meat back to Liz's apartment and stowed it safely in the freezer. 'This'll keep us going for a while,' Kevin told Mihai. 'But we're gonna have to do some strategic thinking if we're gonna keep our bellies full. But you know what they say? Crisis breeds opportunity. Know what that means, kid?'

'Crisis, bad; opportunity, good?' suggested Mihai.

Kevin beamed at him. 'You're a bright spark, ain't you? You and me, we'll go far. Come on, there's something I want to show you.'

'What is it, Grandpa Kevin?'

'Come in here,' said Kevin, leading the way to the room where he slept. A sleeping bag was rolled up on an old mattress that Liz had given him. He reached inside the sleeping bag, pulled out a cardboard shoe box and placed it on the mattress.

'What's in the box, Grandpa Kevin?' asked Mihai excitedly.

'Open it and see.'

Mihai kneeled down cautiously and flipped the lid of the box open. He stared at the contents of the box in amazement. 'Is money,' he said in a hushed voice.

'Yeah, money,' said Kevin. 'That's my entire life savings in there, kid. Don't seem like a whole lot, when you look at it like that.'

'But Grandpa Kevin, I never saw so much money. You are rich man.'

Kevin chuckled. 'Not exactly rich, but I reckon it's enough for us to get started.'

'Started on what?' asked Mihai. 'What you going to spend it on?'

'Good question,' said Kevin. 'You put your finger right on it. It's a funny thing, money,' he mused. He picked up a wad of bank notes from the shoe box and flicked through it. 'It's just pieces of paper, ain't it? Paper's cheap. It grows on trees. Don't cost a lot to print money, I reckon. Money's only worth something if people think it is. In times like this people start to wonder, do they really believe in money? Can they trust pieces of paper? They start to put their trust in things they can hold in their hands. Things they can eat or drink, for instance.'

Mihai was listening to his words carefully. 'So we going to buy food?' he asked.

'Not food,' said Kevin. 'We already got enough food to keep us going for now. Buy too much and it just goes off. We're gonna buy something else. Something better than food. Something that will keep a long time and that will be worth more and more the less people believe in money.'

'What is it, Grandpa Kevin?' asked Mihai excitedly. 'What we going to buy?'

Kevin punched him playfully on the shoulder. 'Just you wait and see, kid. Just you wait and see.'

Chapter Twelve

Brixton Village, South London, New Year's Day

Salma Ali was true to her word. In less than an hour, she was back, hammering on Ben Harvey's front door, making his head pulsate with each quivering thump. 'Sorry, did I disturb you?' she asked, when he yanked the door open. Her hand was poised to knock again.

'I have a headache,' he explained. 'Is it time for the meeting already?'

'Everyone's gathering at my house now,' she said, smiling. 'Number sixty-eight. See you there?'

He swallowed some more painkillers and made his way across the road. Ms Ali's house was one of the largest in the street, a prime example of the kind of property that had powered the housing market in this part of Brixton to sky-high levels in the past few years. Ben had bought when house prices were still relatively cheap, although at the time it had felt like an extortionate amount to pay for a two-bedroomed terraced house.

A group of neighbours had already assembled in her elegant living room, and more were arriving as he entered. The chairs and sofas were fully taken, so he found a place to lean against the back wall. Bright sun shone through the French windows, making his head ache more than ever, and he found himself wishing darkly for more seasonal weather. A black thundercloud would have better matched his mood.

More people pressed into the room, and Ben was surprised at how many had turned up. Then again, Salma Ali wasn't a woman to take no for an answer. She had probably spent the last hour knocking on doors up and down the street and bullying her neighbours until they relented. Ben was slightly alarmed to realize just how few of his neighbours he recognized. Modern life didn't seem to leave much time for building local community relations. Perhaps this meeting was well overdue.

Salma Ali waited for everyone to arrive before she started speaking. She was dressed in her customary black jacket and white blouse, black trousers and shoes. Her black hair was tied back from her face, and she wore a concerned expression. Her delicate hands crossed and uncrossed impatiently as she waited for everyone to sit or stand.

'Thank you all for coming, and welcome to my home,' she began as the last person squeezed in next to Ben. 'I'm sure you all know why we are here. Last night, rioters and so-called vigilantes took to the streets of London, unleashing a wave of criminal activity. Our local supermarket was attacked and looted and the police were unable to do anything to protect us. Isn't that right, Mr Kowalski?'

The Polish shopkeeper nodded vigorously, his oversized moustache bristling with indignation. 'That's right. They steal cigarettes, they steal alcohol. I try to stop them, but they are too many. They steal from me, and the police do nothing.'

'If Mr Kowalski's shop can be attacked, then none of us is safe,' continued Salma Ali. 'We must hope that the police will be able to stop these rioters and looters before too long, but in the meantime we are not powerless to help each other. We must take action to protect our own community. Am I right?' There was a general murmur of agreement. 'I propose that we organize around the principle of the existing Neighbourhood Watch scheme. I will be the coordinator, and I will organize groups to patrol the local area at night. I will also organize a network of contacts, so that anyone who notices anything suspicious can report it to the Watch.'

'Who will be in these patrol groups?' asked a woman sitting on the sofa.

'I will ask for volunteers,' said Salma Ali. 'The task is not without some risk, so no one will be asked to join if they don't want to.'

'I will join,' said Mr Kowalski. 'And my two sons.' He indicated two strapping young men at his side. Both nodded enthusiastically. 'And we will fight!' declared the shopkeeper.

The woman who had asked the question frowned. 'Surely we aren't authorized to fight anyone? We aren't vigilantes.'

Ms Ali smiled widely. 'An excellent point. And speaking as a lawyer, I can give you a definitive response. The law states that a person may use reasonable force in the prevention of crime. They may also effect or assist in the lawful arrest of suspected offenders or persons unlawfully at large.'

'A citizen's arrest?' queried Ben.

'Thank you, Mr Harvey. Exactly. As long as the offenders are engaged in criminal conduct, reasonable force can be used to prevent the crime, or to detain them afterwards.'

'And what exactly is reasonable force?'

'Another excellent question. The law defines reasonable force as whatever a reasonable person regards it to be.'

'That sounds a bit circular to me,' said Ben, rubbing at his forehead. 'So what is a reasonable person?'

'Let's not get too hung up on this,' said Ms Ali. 'The law always sides with honest people acting to defend themselves against criminals, especially when protecting their own homes.' She smiled her practised smile. 'Trust me. I'm a lawyer.'

'I wonder if we shouldn't just leave this to the police?' wondered Ben aloud. 'I mean, they've drafted in a lot of additional armed officers, and now soldiers too.'

Ms Ali turned her smile up another degree. 'The police? Did you watch the news last night? Did it look to you as if the police had the situation under control?'

'Well, …'

'With every respect, Ben, when the law breaks down, it's not people like you that are most vulnerable. It's people like Mr Kowalski here. Many of those thugs on the news were racists and hard-line political extremists. They're using this opportunity to further their own hateful agenda. When the rioters come, anyone whose name doesn't fit, or whose skin is the wrong colour will be the one who gets hurt. We can't afford to stake our lives on police protection.'

There was a murmuring of agreement from some of the others present.

'So who will volunteer for night patrols?' asked Salma Ali.

The three Polish men were first to raise their hands, followed quickly by half a dozen others. Mr Stewart, the man who had argued with Mr Kowalski earlier, nodded and lifted a muscular arm. Reluctantly Ben raised his hand too.

Salma Ali went around the volunteers, taking names, addresses and phone numbers. 'That's excellent. I suggest dividing into three groups, each with three or four men. That will be enough to patrol the district between the hours of six and midnight, when the curfew begins. Mr Harvey, you can go with Mr Kowalski and Mr Stewart.' She reeled off a list of names for the other groups. 'I will drop leaflets through all the doors, letting people know what is happening, and explaining that you are authorized to patrol the area. If anyone sees anything suspicious they can report it to me, and I can pass the information on. Any questions? No? Then good luck!'

The meeting began to break up. Mr Kowalski came over to where Ben and Mr Stewart were standing and shook hands solemnly with them, closing his thick fingers tightly over Ben's hand and pumping it vigorously. He seemed to be assessing how well the two men might handle themselves in a tough situation, a thought that had occurred to Ben too.

'You have weapon?' enquired Mr Kowalski. 'Knife? If not, I give you one.'

'A knife?' said Ben. 'Hold on, you can't just wander around the streets with a knife.'

'Not in normal time,' agreed Mr Kowalski. 'This is not normal time.'

But even Ms Ali looked uncertain about the suggestion. She hesitated, then said, 'No knives, Mr Kowalski. We must stay within the boundaries of the law, if the law is to be on our side.'

The Polish man narrowed his eyes. 'Okay then. No knives for us. Then hope that looters don't bring knives.'

Chapter Thirteen

Upper Terrace, Richmond upon Thames, West London, New Year's Day

The sound of a key turning in the front door of the house could only mean one thing. Sarah dragged herself away from the TV screen and ran down the stairs. The door to the house was opening wide as she reached the entrance hallway. 'Oh my God, Melanie!'

It had been weeks since she'd seen her sister. In all that time she'd received not a single message. Not one of her voicemails had been answered. Neither the police nor the local hospitals had any record of Melanie, or anyone matching her description. Sarah had almost abandoned all hope of seeing her alive again.

She ran to her sister, expecting to be scooped up in an extravagant embrace, but Melanie stood still in the doorway, stooping forward pitifully. She looked dreadful, her hair dulled and dry, her skin pinched and pallid, her bloodshot eyes vacant and hollow. Worst of all, dark bruises covered one side of her face. Her arm trembled as she leaned against the doorframe for support.

'What's happened to you?' cried Sarah. 'Let me help you in.'

Her sister staggered forward and almost collapsed into Sarah's arms. Sarah caught her, and hugged her, wrapping her arms around Melanie's frail body, clutching her tight. She kissed her sister on the forehead, covering her face with hot tears. 'I thought I'd lost you,' she said. 'This time, I thought it was the last.'

'Hey, sis,' said Melanie with a weak smile. 'You can't get rid of me that easily. I always come back, even when you think I'm lost. Besides, I had a knight in shining armour to save me.'

Behind her on the steps that led up to the house stood a dejected-looking teenage boy Sarah had never seen before. The boy wore ill-fitting clothes and an expression of inconsolable grief. His hair was the colour of straw, and was styled like a haystack. He lifted his chin to look at her and she saw immediately that his eyes were ringed with red.

She turned away from the boy, her face burning. Melanie never brought strangers back to the house. It was one of the unwritten rules that held Sarah's life in place. Melanie knew how badly she reacted to anyone new. 'What is he doing here?' she hissed.

'This is James,' said Melanie. 'He rescued me. Without him, I'd be dead now.'

The boy stood glumly on the steps, his shoulders stooped, his face like misery itself.

'Are you bringing him inside?' whispered Sarah.

Melanie shrugged weakly. 'He has nowhere else to go.' She clutched at Sarah's arm for support. 'He's just a boy. Can he stay with us? Please say he can.'

Sarah gripped her sister tightly to support her. This was no time for an argument. Melanie needed her, and the boy lurking outside obviously did too. She would just have to deal with it somehow. 'Come on in, James,' she said, looking at the wall, not able to turn her eyes toward him. 'I'm sorry if I seem rude, but I'm not very good at meeting new people.' She flicked her gaze over him quickly as he hobbled up the steps. There was nothing to be afraid of. He was just a young man who had been through some kind of trauma. Just a boy, not even a man. And a skinny, bedraggled-looking one at that. 'You two look as bad as each other,' she said. 'Should I call an ambulance?'

'No,' said Melanie quickly. 'We're okay, we just need to rest.'

'Come inside and let me examine you,' said Sarah, letting Melanie lean her weight against her. She didn't weigh much more than a child. 'You've lost pounds. Haven't you been eating?'

Melanie tried a weak smile. 'You can never be too thin, huh?'

'So they say.' Sarah had never had that particular problem herself. She had always been big-boned compared with her sister, and now Melanie had withered away to almost nothing. She helped her to a chair in the hallway and looked back at James.

The boy hadn't moved, just stood in the entrance. A tear ran down one dark-stained cheek. He didn't look malnourished like Melanie, but there was a desperate wretchedness to him that was just as worrying. He looked like he might drop dead with sorrow.

'Come on in, James,' said Sarah. 'I'll make you a nice hot cup of tea.' It was what she did best. Look after the sick.

The boy shook his head, his sandy thatch sweeping his forehead, his face turned down to his shoes.

'James doesn't drink tea,' explained Melanie.

'Coffee then, or perhaps something stronger?'

Melanie laid a fragile hand on Sarah's arm. 'Nothing for James. No food or drink. He just needs rest.'

Sarah nodded. Still not looking at him, she said, 'I'll

make up the guest room for James.' Guest room was a joke. When had they last had a guest at the house? When had Sarah last spoken to a stranger, other than a few words to the postman, or some delivery guy? When James didn't respond, she added. 'He can sleep, or take a shower, or whatever he likes. I expect he'll feel better after some rest. I expect you both will.'

Leaving Melanie slumped in the hall chair, she stepped gingerly over to where the boy still stood and slid her gaze cautiously in his direction. If she was brave, she could do this. He was just a boy, not a monster. She reached out a timid hand to him.

He lifted his face, gazing at her hand as if he had no idea what it was. She gave him a tentative smile, but his eyes stayed blank and expressionless. She realized then just how damaged and unthreatening he was. Gently, she took his hand in hers and led him inside. 'Come with me, James. I'll look after you.' She smiled down at her sister. 'You too, Mel. You know that looking after people is what I'm here for.'

Chapter Fourteen

Hammersmith, West London, New Year's Day

They were on the road again at last and Chris Crohn could hardly believe it. The hire car was a gleaming black SUV exactly like he'd envisaged. Tinted windows, integrated satellite navigation, the lot. The only features it lacked were built-in machine guns and flame throwers, but the car rental company hadn't offered those as options.

The only trouble now was Seth, as usual. His friend tossed his long hair out of his eyes as he wrestled with the gear stick.

'I thought you knew how to drive,' Chris accused him.

'I do,' said Seth. 'But this car is twice as big as my old one, and I don't know what half the controls are for.'

So far Seth had stalled the car twice driving out of the parking area, opened the sunroof by mistake while setting the climate control, and told the navigation system to direct them to Hereford Road in London instead of the small town of Hereford in the west of England.

'Remind me again why we're going to Hereford?' said Seth.

'Because it's the wilderness,' said Chris. 'No one lives there.'

'That can't be literally true,' said Seth.

'No,' agreed Chris, as the navigation system instructed them for the tenth time to make a legal U-turn. 'But it's one of the least populated areas of England. It'll be a good base.'

'Can't you turn that thing off?' asked Seth.

Chris studied the dashboard through his thick lenses. He prodded the touchscreen control panel and cancelled the directions. The navigation system fell silent at last. 'That wasn't difficult,' he said. 'Maybe I could drive this car myself with a little practice.'

'You don't even have a driving licence.'

'Once the apocalypse comes, I won't need one,' said Chris darkly. Seth went silent. Mentioning the "A-word" always sent him into a sulk. In the old days, Chris had never been any good at getting people to do what he wanted, but now it seemed that manipulating Seth was as easy as programming a computer. And if Chris could learn *people skills*, he could surely learn to control a vehicle.

They drove along for a while in silence, Chris studying the car's handbook to get an overview of its key functions. It really didn't look that hard at all. The only problem was that the car was a physical object, and Chris preferred dealing with things that he couldn't touch. He and the real world didn't always see eye to eye.

At least they were on the move now, although the going was slow. The police had advised motorists to stay home unless their journey was absolutely necessary, and the result was that half of London had taken to the roads. All the major routes out of the capital were heavily jammed, and they were struggling to push through the congestion.

'I wish I could have brought my vinyl collection,' mused Seth. 'I miss it already.'

The car didn't even have a CD player, only a wireless connection for digital music. The world had gone virtual in the past few years. But soon everything that had been digitized would vanish forever. Chris found his mood turning melancholy just when he should have been glad.

'What else will you miss?' he asked his friend.

'So many things. Cappuccinos, selfies, texting, emojis, animated GIFs. All those things will be gone, right?'

'Right. Yeah.' A silence hung over them as they considered the full ramifications of the situation.

'There'll be plenty that I won't miss though,' continued Seth. 'Like Twitter trolls and laggy Wi-Fi. What about you? What will you miss?'

It was an excellent question, but too awful to truly consider. Everything Chris loved was destined to disappear when the Information Age came to an end. Nothing would be saved. He gazed out of the car at the raindrops making trails down the outside of the windows. The traffic was coming to a complete halt, and the sky was already beginning to darken. They would need to make it out of the city before the curfew began at midnight. Would the army really make mass arrests, or perhaps even shoot civilians? If the authorities were serious about stopping the apocalypse, they would need to take extreme measures. Even the curfew would do little to stop the werewolves from spreading. Like a virus infecting a host, or a cancerous tumour bringing about its own ultimate demise, the spread of the condition was a mathematical certainty. Soon the modern world would be swept away, and Chris would have to learn to survive in an age for which he was totally ill-suited and woefully unprepared.

'I'll miss the abstract,' he said at last. 'Words, symbols, codes, numbers. All the things that don't exist in the real world.'

Red lights from the car in front cast a gloomy glow over them, and Seth slipped the car into neutral. 'Those things will still exist,' he said. 'As long as you remember what they are, you can keep them for as long as you like.'

That was true enough, Chris supposed. 'We've still got the Japanese origami book I gave you for Christmas,' he told Seth. 'That's something, isn't it?'

'Yeah,' said Seth. 'I never thanked you for that. I'm sorry.'

The traffic began to crawl slowly on again through the rain. They had been driving for two hours already, but had only just joined the A4 heading west out of Hammersmith. The A4 followed the route of the ancient road connecting London to the west of England in pre-Roman times. The west had always been steeped in history and myth, a place of magic and mystery, of pagan worship and legends of King Arthur and the Isle of Avalon. The Neolithic sites of Stonehenge and Glastonbury Tor dated far back beyond the Roman settlement of England, into the mists of prehistory. It was perhaps appropriate that they were headed that way, leaving civilization behind, and returning to a simpler, more savage age.

The car picked up a little speed as the greater part of the traffic turned off the A4 and onto the motorway. Chris had insisted that they stay on the A4, following the old road. The old ways would be best from now on. He thumbed idly through the pages of the origami book as they pushed on through the rain and the lines of cars. 'What did you think of the book?' he asked.

Seth shrugged. 'I never got around to reading it,' he admitted. 'Maybe there'll be time for that when the apocalypse really kicks off.' It was the first time he'd used the "A-word" since this whole thing had started. That was good. It was a sign of growing acceptance.

'Yeah, maybe,' said Chris. 'Maybe there'll be time for things like that.'

Chapter Fifteen

St George's Crescent, Kensington & Chelsea, London, New Year's Day

Doctor Helen Eastgate watched the news images flicker on the screen of her laptop. Carnage in central London overnight. Police battling with rioters. Crowds running from rampaging wolves. The official death toll rising steadily as the day went on. She felt horror as she watched, but also a grim sense of satisfaction. Her suspicions had been right all along. Werewolves were real, and they were here in London.

It was hardly something to be pleased about, but for Helen these events changed everything.

She had observed her student Leanna Lloyd closely for weeks now. It had been terrifying at first, knowing that a werewolf was working in the lab right alongside her and her other students. Her instinct had been to run, to scream, to call for help. But Helen was first and foremost a scientist. Her role was to study, to gather data, to test hypotheses. Who was better placed than her to study these creatures, to find out how they behaved? As far as Helen could tell, Leanna was some kind of ringleader. The opportunity to observe her at close quarters was too good to miss.

It helped that Leanna was so cold and distant. She didn't interact socially with staff or students unless there was something she wanted from them. She had no friends at the university. She made no small talk. No genuine feeling animated her face, only simulated emotions intended to manipulate and deceive. Leanna's crystal blue eyes remained dead at all times, and if a smile ever formed on her ruby red lips, Helen felt her skin crawl with disgust. She had long since stopped thinking of Leanna as human. Better to see her for what she truly was. A monster wearing a woman's mask.

She hadn't embarked on her surveillance casually. At first she'd considered going to the police and telling them everything she knew. But that would have been a colossal waste of time. A werewolf in London? She would have been laughed at for sure. She'd had no evidence that werewolves existed, except for Professor Wiseman's papers and copies of his research notes that she'd managed to get from the publishers of the journal. But Wiseman had been dismissed as a crank. His findings would convince no one.

But things had changed. After months of *Beast* sightings and gruesome *Ripper* murders, werewolves had finally appeared on the national news. The authorities would have to take her seriously now. She had amassed a good deal of evidence. She knew about Leanna, and the two other students who lived with her, Adam Knight and Samuel Smalling. She'd pieced together some of Leanna's research work too. She would pass her information directly to the security services. This was too big for the police to handle.

She closed her laptop and put it into a rucksack ready

to take with her. Most of the data she'd collected about Leanna was stored on the device, but she had other material in her office at the university. The more she could hand over to the authorities, the more likely they would be to take her seriously. Best of all would be the sample of Leanna's DNA she had gathered. The DNA was irrefutable proof that a new non-human species existed.

She threw on a coat and hat and stepped out into the winter evening, the laptop safely tucked into her rucksack. Her tiny basement apartment in Chelsea was her refuge against the cold and the dark and she was loathe to leave it. Reluctantly she locked the door behind her and darted up the stone steps to street level. Back home in Australia her family had thrown barbeques at this time of year, and she and her little sister had played in the back yard in nothing but shorts and a thin top, spraying each other with water from a hosepipe to cool off. It was ten years since she'd left her home, and she'd never stopped missing it. People had told her she'd get used to the cold and damp of the British winter, but they'd been wrong. She hated it more and more as the years passed. She couldn't imagine growing old in London. One day she would decide she'd finally had enough of the weather and would return to the southern hemisphere. One day soon, perhaps.

The January air was thickening with swirling mist, and she wrapped her scarf tightly over her face. She hesitated for a moment, torn between heading for the university to collect the extra information and going back inside to call the security services. She had told nobody about what she knew. If something were to happen to her, the evidence she had collected would be lost. Perhaps it would be wiser to go back inside, to the warmth and the safety.

But no. The root of her doubt was fear, pure and simple. Fear, like superstition, was a primitive force that fed off the cold and the dark. Helen had spent her life resisting such forces, arguing for rationality over emotion. Now was the time to face down her fear. Besides, the greatest risk of all was that the authorities would refuse to believe her. *Show me the evidence*, she always told her students. *Extraordinary claims require extraordinary proof.* Her own words rang loudly in her ears. She needed to gather all the evidence she could, to make her case as strong as possible. If she could show them everything she knew, they would have no choice but to believe her. She pulled her hat over her ears and set off at a brisk pace.

The route to Imperial College was one she had walked hundreds of times, thousands probably, and her feet knew the way for her. The mist grew thinner as she headed north away from the river, and lights from cafes and restaurants threw a warming glow across her path, but the area was strangely deserted. Normally the streets around Sloane Square bustled with activity, but this evening few people had ventured out. Some of the shops and restaurants were sealed up with steel rollers, and Helen guessed that wasn't just because it was New Year's Day. In the distance a police siren blared out, a brief echo of the troubles that had spilled onto the streets of London the previous night. The new curfew would begin later tonight, and she would have to be back in her apartment by then, or better still, showing all her evidence to an official at the security services.

The reminder stiffened her resolve and she hefted her rucksack firmly onto her back, feeling the reassuring weight of the laptop inside. She thrust her hands into her pockets and ploughed on. She walked quickly, avoiding making eye contact with the one or two hardy people who passed her. Trails of mist appeared in front of her again as she passed the Victorian brick-and-tile edifice of the Natural History Museum, the tops of its towers lost in the thickening fog.

The sight of Imperial College emerging from the damp and murk had never felt so welcoming, and she almost ran to the brightly-lit entrance of the new Biomedical Institute and up the stairs to her office. It was only as she fished her keys out of her bag and fumbled them in the lock that she realized how much her hands were shaking.

She closed the door to her office and leaned back against it, switching the lights on and waiting for the fear to recede. Her job now was simple. Gather the evidence. Return to her apartment. Make the phone call.

In under a minute her breathing had returned to normal. She made her way over to her desk, stepping around the heaps of papers and books that filled much of the floor, wishing as usual that she could be a tidier person. Her foot caught one of the teetering piles, and papers spilled over the floor, scattering knowledge carelessly. Helen cursed herself for her lack of organization. If she'd been better organized, she would have kept all the information at home, and wouldn't have needed to return now to fetch it.

The office safe was tucked away beneath the desk, and she keyed in the combination as quickly as she could. Inside were printed copies of Professor Wiseman's notes and photographs that she had sweet-talked the editor of the journal into sending her. She gathered them up and dropped them into her rucksack, where they snuggled down next to the laptop. A brown paper envelope at the back of the safe stored a sample of Leanna's DNA, and she added that to the rucksack too. Of all the evidence she had gathered, that was perhaps the most explosive, the one piece that was guaranteed to convince another scientist that her story was true. A simple brown envelope containing a single strand of human hair. Its genetic code held more information than all the books and papers scattered about this office.

It had taken perhaps one minute to transfer the contents of the safe into her rucksack. She wondered now why she had been so afraid to come. It had been the dark that had frightened her. Just the dark. Night fears that vanished as soon as an electric light was switched on. Quickly she closed the safe and left her office, locking the door behind her. She was about to head back down the stairs when she noticed a light from the genetics lab where Leanna and the other students worked.

There shouldn't have been anyone here at this time. New Year's Day was an official holiday, and the university was closed. Most of the students were away, still not back after the Christmas vacation. The light coming from the lab was dim, probably from a computer screen. Perhaps an experiment had been left running over the holiday period. If anyone had left something running, it was probably Leanna. Helen should leave it and go, but now that she had conquered her fear of the dark, it seemed that curiosity had got the better of her. She had never been able to resist its powerful lure. Curiosity was the path to knowledge, and knowledge displaced ignorance, just as light conquered the dark.

She peered through the glass window of the lab. As she'd suspected, the light came from the screen of a computer connected to a DNA sequencer. The desktop machine was one of many, arranged in a long row of metal boxes about the size of microwave ovens, each one capable of analyzing an entire human genome. All of the machines were switched on and running, the results of their analysis appearing on the screens next to them, gene by gene, nucleotide by nucleotide.

Helen glanced around cautiously, listening for the slightest sound that might indicate someone else was present. The building was empty. There was no one in the lab. She pushed the door open and went inside.

Chapter Sixteen

A secret military location, North London, New Year's Day

The convoy sped along the road at high speed, the Prime Minister riding in her usual car, a black Jaguar XJ Sentinel. The triple-glazed windows of the car were made from darkened and bullet-proofed polycarbonate glass, making it hard to see clearly in the gloomy dusk that had already closed in on the city. In any case, the PM had more than enough documents to keep her attention firmly within the car.

The vehicle had been modified extensively for Prime Ministerial use, with 13mm explosive-proof steel armour plating, bullet-proof titanium and Kevlar lining in the cabin, and seals against biological and chemical attack. A pair of unmarked Range Rovers escorted the Prime Ministerial car, front and back. They were manned by officers from SO1 Protection Command armed with Glock 17 pistols. Motorcycle outriders rode ahead, their blue lights and sirens clearing a path through the London traffic.

None of that knowledge gave the PM much comfort. The crisis she faced now was one of the gravest faced by any leader. The public didn't know the half of it, however much guessing and speculation the TV networks and newspapers engaged in. *It is as bad as they fear, worse than I could have believed.* In such times, a leader must have broad shoulders and show a brave face, but the burden of leadership weighed heavier now than at any other time since she had come to office. Difficult decisions had already been taken; harder ones lay ahead. She would not change her place with another though, however difficult the challenge. That was not her way.

Her greatest fear was not being remembered as the Prime Minister who brought the army onto the streets of Britain and imposed a curfew. It was that she had not gone far enough to ensure that this strange new threat was defeated.

The convoy swung off the main carriageway and down an unsigned road lined by a twelve-foot concrete wall topped with barbed wire. Security cameras fixed to metal poles observed the cars' progress as they followed the road around a gentle curve, and the tops of fortified watch towers could be seen jutting above the wall. After a short distance the leading Range Rover turned sharply right and paused briefly as a solid steel gate slid slowly to one side, allowing it to enter. The PM's car followed closely.

Once inside the gate, bright area lighting from the watchtowers lit the way, and the car drove up to the single building situated within the grounds. The building was almost featureless – a low brick structure with a flat roof, no windows, and just a pair of brutally-clipped shrubs to mark the main entrance. Uniformed soldiers stood to attention outside, and the PM recognized the bull-necked form of General Sir Roland Ney, Chief of the Defence Staff, standing stiffly in front, his row of medals shining brightly under the lights, his gunmetal eyebrows knotted together beneath his sharply peaked cap. *Good.* The General was nothing but efficient, and the PM had no time now for anything other than utmost efficiency. Nevertheless, she paused for a moment before leaving the car to remind herself of the General's other qualities. *He has a reputation as a ruthless man too.* She feared she may also have need of that.

The General saluted her as she emerged from the car, then spun on his heel to escort her inside the facility. 'Have you visited the hospital before, Prime Minister?' he enquired.

The building was sparsely furnished and primitive, like something left over from the Second World War, the floors made from battered linoleum, the ceilings low and oppressive. Tangles of pipes and cables snaked along walls that had been splashed with paint in sickly hues.

'No, I'm afraid not.'

'Not many people have,' he remarked. 'We try to keep a low profile. This is the last of the United Kingdom's military hospitals. All of our other hospitals were closed or turned over to the Ministry of Defence at the end of the Cold War and are now operated by civilian personnel.' She sensed the disapproving tone in his voice. 'Your predecessor wished to do the same with this facility,' he said. 'But fortunately for us he was unable to complete his legislative programme before his unexpected departure.'

'Not so fortunate for him,' commented the PM.

'Perhaps not. But let us be grateful that the hospital survives, even in its woefully under-funded state.'

'Noted, General. I will see what I can do.'

An incline of his head was all the acknowledgement he gave her. *More than efficient, positively spartan in his habits. I like him.*

A retinue of SO1 officers and military personnel had followed them into the building and they swept along in the wake of the General's rapid strides. The PM had to half-walk, half-trot to match his pace, but she didn't ask him to slow. Her impatience to see this *thing* for herself had become irresistible.

The General opened a door that led to the top of a flight of steps. 'We go down one level here,' he commented. The concrete steps descended steeply underground to a corridor that felt more like a tunnel. The ceiling was lower than ever, the pipes and cables more thickly tangled than above ground. The General strode quickly past a series of doors marked with biohazard warnings.

They turned a corner and came to an abrupt halt outside a closed door marked *Autopsy Room One*. A long horizontal window allowed them to peer inside. The room visible through the glass panel was brightly lit, more modern in appearance than what she had seen so far of the hospital, and painted starkly white. A bank of small metal doors lined the back wall, and in the centre of the room stood a metal table, brightly lit by surgical lighting overhead.

A group of people dressed head to foot in white medical overalls stood around the table. Each wore white boots and gloves and a clear plastic helmet with face masks beneath. But the PM's attention was drawn to the body of the creature lying on the table in the middle of the room. Stretched out, it measured perhaps seven feet long, heavily muscled, and clothed in thick black fur from head to tail. A large monitor screen suspended from the ceiling on metal stalks displayed a close-up image of the animal's head. Its long snout was clearly visible, and there was no doubt that this was a wolf, despite its enormous size. Savage canine teeth protruded from its jaws.

She raised a hand involuntarily to her mouth. So this was the monster that had emerged from humanity's darkest folk memories and fairy tales, the creature that had dared to enter the modern world where it so clearly did not belong.

Any residual doubts she may have held were wiped from her thoughts now that she had seen the creature for herself. It was a werewolf.

Chapter Seventeen

*Electric Avenue, Brixton, South London,
New Year's Day*

The violence began as soon as darkness fell. Ben, Mr Kowalski and Mr Stewart started their patrol at dusk, and within ten minutes of walking the streets, the sirens of distant emergency vehicles began to punctuate the night. A thick fog had descended too, deadening all sound and wrapping them in a cold blanket that made it hard to see more than a hundred paces. Ben turned up the collar of his coat and thrust his hands deep into his pockets.

'Trouble is starting already,' muttered Mr Kowalski from under his moustache. 'Will be worse than last night, probably. But this time we are ready.' He reached a heavy hand inside his coat and brought out two steel knives secured in leather pouches. The tops of the blades glinted dimly in the eerie half-light of the fog. 'Here,' he said, offering one to each of the two men.

Ben frowned. 'I thought we agreed. Ms Ali said no knives.'

'She say no. I say yes. What do you say?'

Mr Stewart held out his hand and the Polish shopkeeper placed the handle of one of the weapons in his meaty palm. He wrapped his strong fingers tightly around it and slid it under his jacket. 'This will give the bastards something to think about,' he growled.

The remaining knife was offered to Ben. He hesitated, then shook his head.

Mr Kowalski shrugged and hid the knife away. 'You are good with fists?' he asked.

'I've never had the chance to find out,' said Ben.

'Then just hope that you are good,' said Mr Kowalski darkly.

Ben's misgivings about this endeavour were growing with each moment, but it was too late to turn back now. 'Where are your sons?' he asked Mr Kowalski. 'Are they out on patrol?'

'Later. For now, they guard shop.' He grinned. 'Looters will get nasty surprise when they come tonight.'

'Let's hope they don't come.'

'Oh, they will come. But this time, we are prepared.'

Ben didn't want to ask what kind of preparations Mr Kowalski's sons might have made. But he had to admit that the Polish man was probably right. Trouble was coming, and they needed to be ready for it. He wondered if he should have accepted the knife. But on balance, he was probably better off without it.

Mr Kowalski strode off down the road, Mr Stewart at his heels. Reluctantly, Ben followed. Being left behind would be even worse than going with them.

Another siren cut through the clammy night. This one was closer and sounded like it was coming straight toward them. The wailing sound grew louder, sawing at Ben's head, and a blue flashing light emerged out of the fog not far away. The police car swept past at high speed and disappeared into the murk. They had no way of knowing where it was headed, but at least it hadn't stopped. The emergency was elsewhere.

The two men in front turned down a residential side street and Ben followed them. The fog grew thicker as they headed toward the river, swallowing the light from the streetlamps and shrinking their world to a small and ever-tightening circle. The only sound was the muffled tap of their own footsteps, and the other men's heavy breathing.

Mr Stewart turned back to look at him. 'So what's this act of heroism Ms Ali talked about?'

Act of heroism. He wished that Ms Ali had never mentioned it. Now it just seemed to give him more to live up to. 'There was an incident at the school where I teach,' he said.

'So you're a teacher?' Mr Stewart snorted contemptuously as if this was the worst profession a man might have. 'Since when did a school teacher ever get the chance to be a hero?'

Ben felt his anger rise at the needless provocation. 'The school's headmaster attacked two of the girls. Another teacher and I tackled him and took him down. But really, I'm no hero.'

'What happened to the girls?' asked Mr Stewart. 'Did you save them?'

Ben's mouth went dry as he relived the memory. 'We managed to save one of them. The other was ... killed.' He had almost said *eaten*. It was the truth, but saying it was too horrible. The headmaster, Mr Canning, had still been eating the girl when Ben had arrived to confront him.

'You're right, then,' said Mr Stewart dismissively. 'You're no hero. You let her die. You were too afraid to save her.' He turned his face away, leaving Ben staring angrily at his back.

At the end of the street they turned left again, into a busier road. A row of shops clustered together, mostly fast-food outlets and a cafe. The cafe was closed, but a pizza place and a Chinese takeaway had some customers inside. Mr Kowalski went into each restaurant, shaking hands with the owners and exchanging a few words, checking that all was in order.

'Is good,' he announced, stepping back onto the pavement. 'No trouble yet.' He paused and looked into Ben's face, studying him with darkened eyes. 'You saved life of one girl?' he asked.

Ben nodded, afraid of hearing the Polish man's judgement. Now he thought about it he wondered if he really was the hero people had made him out to be. As Mr Stewart had pointed out, one girl had died, and it was Rose Hallibury who had stabbed Mr Canning in the eye with her pen. Ben had done little more than create a distraction, now he thought about it critically. The prospect that both these men would brand him a failure seemed suddenly terrifying.

Mr Kowalski looked deep into his eyes as if seeing the event play out, and weighing his performance. 'Sounds to me like you are hero,' he said at last. He swept his gaze toward Mr Stewart and then back to Ben. 'You were scared?' he asked.

'Yes,' admitted Ben. Terrified, although somehow he had managed to push the fear away, otherwise it would have paralyzed him.

Mr Kowalski nodded, as if he knew exactly how Ben had felt. 'Every hero is scared. But is hero anyway.' His next words were harsh and he directed them at Mr Stewart. 'Man who is not scared is not hero. Man who is not scared will soon be dead man.'

Mr Stewart snorted with contempt, but the Polish man grabbed his shoulder and drew him closer. 'Only a knife feels no fear. Don't let knife make you stupid.'

Mr Stewart glared angrily at him for a second, then shrugged him off and strode quickly away along the pavement. Ben and the shopkeeper followed in his wake.

The fog became ever thicker as they walked, and Ben

was glad of his warm coat. He quickened his pace so as not to lose sight of Mr Stewart. Mr Kowalski stayed beside him, seeming to move with ease through the night, as if it were his natural habitat. Ben found it hard to imagine that the Polish man could ever show real fear. He was glad to have him beside him.

After a minute they caught up with Mr Stewart, who had stopped for some reason.

Up ahead, a group of young men emerged from the billowing fog. Ben made out four shapes, most likely youngsters out to buy food from one of the fast-food restaurants, or heading to a nearby pub or bar. But Mr Kowalski wasn't taking any chances. He stopped the men and held up a flashlight to their faces.

The young men were masked, wearing scarves over their mouths and noses, just their eyes peeping out over the coverings. 'Hey, what are you doing?' demanded one, holding a palm to his face as the shopkeeper dazzled him with the beam of light.

Mr Kowalski continued to shine the light in their eyes. 'Where you going?' he asked. 'Why you cover your faces?'

The youngsters backed away. 'Ain't going nowhere,' said the one who had already spoken. 'And everyone's wearing face masks now. Ain't you heard? There's a virus out there.'

'Yeah,' said one of the other youths, taking a step forward. 'Turns you into a wolf, yeah?'

The Polish man swivelled the light toward him and the youth fell back a step, covering his eyes. 'You better go home, son. Is not safe on streets. And masks won't save you from wolves.'

The youngsters eyed each other uncertainly. 'Keep your cool,' said the first one. 'We ain't causing no trouble. We'll go, okay? But you should get yourselves some masks too, before it's too late.' The four of them turned and sloped off, back the way they had come. Mr Kowalski watched them go.

'Hey,' said Ben. 'I thought we were supposed to be protecting the community, not terrifying everyone.'

'Better if they are terrified,' muttered Mr Kowalski. 'Then they stay safe.' He headed off down the road again, Mr Stewart in his wake. With a sigh, Ben followed them.

The fog began to thin a little as they moved away from the river and back toward the High Street. They were approaching another line of small shops when they heard an engine gunning. Mr Kowalski held up his hand for them to wait. A car sped past them, brakes screeching as it reached the corner with the High Street. A high-performance car, shiny black paintwork gleaming as it emerged from the mist. The car veered to the side of the road, its wheels crunching against the kerb, then lurched back on course, accelerating rapidly, its engine screaming under the stress.

It rounded the corner and crashed straight into one of the shop fronts on the High Street. Glass smashed and an alarm began squealing its distress call.

'Ram raid!' shouted Mr Kowalski.

The front of the shop was protected by steel rollers, but the car's impact had left a sizeable dent in the metal. The car reversed back a few feet, its tyres squealing, then rammed the shop window again, making the steel shutters buckle even further. The car reversed out into the street accompanied by the scream of metal tearing against metal as it ripped the shutters apart. The steel rollers that covered the shop windows were now twisted out of all recognition.

The doors of the car flew open and two men jumped out, hooded and masked. They ran toward the shop entrance.

'Come on,' said Mr Kowalski. 'We end this now.'

Chapter Eighteen

A secret military location, North London, New Year's Day

'I think it best if we do not enter the autopsy room,' the General told the Prime Minister. 'We can communicate with the medical staff via an intercom.' He indicated the grille of a speaker, and a microphone fixed to the wall below the room's glass window. 'The doctor in charge of the post mortem is Colonel Michael Griffin. He's one of our most senior and experienced medical officers. Colonel Griffin is –'

The Prime Minister cut him off with a sharp nod. 'I've read his file.' It had come out more abruptly than she'd intended. The shock of seeing the creature in the flesh had affected her more than she cared to admit. 'Your briefing notes were extremely thorough. Thank you, General.'

She had seen the Colonel's photograph in the notes she'd studied in the car. A good-looking man with prematurely greyed hair, startling blue eyes, a firm jaw and the hint of a bewitching smile on an otherwise stern face – an archetypal military hero.

She peered through the glass at the man in the room beyond, searching for recognition of those fine looks. But beneath the face mask and plastic helmet, the man on the other side of the glass window who acknowledged her with a raised hand could have been anyone.

His file suggested that he was far from just anyone, however. Qualified as a doctor at the University of Cambridge, and trained as an officer at the Royal Military Academy in Sandhurst, he had been a high-flyer from an early age. He had served in Iraq as a combat medic with the Royal Army Medical Corps and then commanded a field hospital in Helmand Province in Afghanistan, where he had been decorated with a Military Cross. He had been promoted to the rank of Colonel at the age of just thirty-nine.

Those were the cold facts, but if the PM had learned anything during her years in public office, it was that written briefings were no substitute for a face-to-face encounter. Staring through the glass pane at the man clad from head to foot in white overalls, his face concealed by a mask and helmet, she wished more than anything that she could see the expression on that face, and thereby know the man who wore it. She would have to settle for hearing his words and watching his body language instead.

The voice that came from the intercom was deep, but warm; professional in tone, but with a trace of a country accent. 'Good evening, Prime Minister.'

'Good evening, Colonel Griffin. Please give us your assessment of the creature.'

The Colonel adjusted the camera positioned over the post mortem table so that the head and shoulders of the wolf were fully visible on the overhead monitor. 'Can you see that?' he asked.

The PM nodded. The creature's snout, eyes and ears were uncannily like those of a German shepherd or a

Husky, but the animal stretched out before her on the metal table was two to three times the size of any similar dog.

Colonel Griffin began to speak briskly into his microphone, his voice smooth and precise. 'The subject was found dead at approximately 1:30am this morning by armed police patrolling the area close to the Battersea riots. Police officers secured the site and a forensic team was brought in to sweep the area. Initially the police wanted their own pathologist to conduct a post mortem examination, but General Ney received word of events and requested that the military assume charge of the investigation.'

The PM nodded again. She had approved the General's request herself in the early hours of the morning.

'The cause of death was internal bleeding due to tearing of the blood vessels connected to the left kidney. This was caused by a single abdominal ballistic wound.' The Colonel picked a small metallic object from a tray and held it up to the camera. 'A round from a Glock nine-millimetre pistol, as used by the special police.' He let the bullet fall back into the tray with a soft clink.

The Colonel moved the camera round so that the monitor behind him displayed the location of the bullet wound in the animal's belly. 'The blood loss was heavy, and the creature would have died within minutes of being shot, which is consistent with the times recorded in the police reports. The subject had also sustained an injury to its hind legs, perhaps when jumping over a wall. In addition, the front claws of the creature were blooded.' Griffin panned the camera to show the ferociously curved knife-like talons of the beast, enlarged several times on the big screen. He looked up at the PM. 'Human blood,' he added.

'What is it, exactly?' she asked, 'The creature, I mean. If that's not a stupid question.'

'Not a stupid question at all. The answer is that I don't

know for sure. The creature is male, and appears to be youthful. Before it was killed it was in a good state of health, although steel pins in one of its legs indicate previous historic injuries.'

'What?' The PM interrupted him. 'Steel pins? Please explain.'

'The steel pins are of the type commonly used to repair broken bones after severe fracture. I have sent them away to see if we can identify their make and date of manufacture. It may be possible to discover where and when they were used.'

The General leaned toward the intercom. 'Colonel, are you saying that this creature, this *wolf*, has received medical treatment?'

'Quite so, General. But may I correct you in one important regard. This animal may look like a wolf, but it is most definitely not a wolf. Anatomically there are very clear differences.' He swung the camera again, this time zooming out to show the whole of the beast. 'The spinal structure and rib cage are roughly identical to that found in wolves and dogs, however the tail bone is missing entirely, and the tail that you see here is almost certainly without any real function.' The camera zoomed in on the tail, and the Colonel flapped the loose appendage up and down to demonstrate. 'The bones that make up the front and rear legs are approximately what we would expect to find, but the metacarpal, proximal, medial and distal bones in the paws are quite out of proportion.

'There are other notable differences. For example, wolves have claws.' The Colonel shifted the camera again to show the vicious front paws. 'This creature has talons, similar to those of a bird of prey. They are large hooked claws, used to stab and kill its prey.' The Colonel zoomed in on the razor-sharp talons, still reddened with blood.

'Other differences – wolves don't have sweat glands, except in the nose. This creature has sweat glands in its skin, like a human. And if this is a wolf, it is the first to possess opposable thumbs.' He moved one of the front toes to indicate how it rotated.

'Opposable thumbs?' queried the Prime Minister with a frown. 'Like humans have?'

'Indeed. Exactly so. But that is far from being the most intriguing aspect of the skeleton.' The Colonel picked up a remote control and pressed a button. The view on the overhead monitor switched to an X-ray image.

'What are we seeing now, Colonel Griffin?' asked the PM.

'An X-ray of the creature's skull, Prime Minister.'

'But surely that is a human skull.'

'It is certainly not what we would expect from a wolf,' confirmed the Colonel with a trace of irony. 'Nevertheless, this is the bone structure of the creature you see before you.' He switched the view on the screen back to the camera and moved it to show the animal's head. 'If you look closely you can see that all is not quite as it appears. First of all, the creature's head is disproportionately large for a wolf. That is due mainly to the fact that it has a brain identical in size to a human. A normal wolf skull has a projecting maxilla, or jawbone, that supports the nasal bone and sinus cavity. In this creature, by contrast, the upper jaw is flat, like a human jaw. This creature's snout is supported by cartilage, not bone. You might almost think of it as a mask, or a disguise.'

'A disguise?' demanded the General, knitting his eyebrows together in a frown. 'Disguise for what?'

'A disguise to hide the fact that it began its life as a human being.'

The General's booming voice was suddenly hushed. 'How can that be possible?'

'How, I cannot say, sir. But the subject's core anatomy is human. The wolf appearance is largely superficial. Genetic analysis confirms it. The subject's DNA is almost entirely human.'

The corridor and the adjacent room fell silent. All those

present stared in mute disbelief at the image of the wolf head on the overhead screen, the wolf that was not a wolf at all.

The PM's head was buzzing, but she was determined to get to the root of the matter. '*Almost* entirely human?' she queried. 'In what way does the DNA differ?'

'The genes of a dog or wolf are divided into thirty-nine chromosomes. Humans have roughly the same number of genes, but spread across twenty-three chromosomes, and only around three quarters of the genes are exactly the same in dogs and humans, so it's a simple matter to tell the two species apart. The creature here has twenty-three chromosomes, just like humans, but its genes are ninety percent human and ten percent canine. My conclusion is that it was born human, but something happened to change its genetic makeup. The result, as you can see, is a hybrid species; something completely new to medical science.' The Colonel nodded to the General to indicate that he had concluded his analysis.

'What could have happened to cause this?' asked the PM. 'Some kind of genetic engineering? Is such a thing possible?'

'Certainly not to my knowledge,' said the Colonel. 'I am not aware of any research teams that have attempted modifications on this kind of scale, even to plants or primitive animals. Certainly not on humans or higher animals.'

'A rogue team, then, operating in secret?'

'I cannot rule that out of course, but it seems extraordinarily unlikely. The changes to the DNA structure are decades ahead of anything that is currently possible even in the most advanced laboratories.'

'Then what?'

For the first time, the Colonel seemed to lose his confidence. He spread his hands in a gesture of defeat. 'I'm sorry,' he said. 'I honestly don't have the slightest idea.'

Chapter Nineteen

Department of Genetics, Imperial College, Kensington, London, New Year's Day

Helen entered the genetics lab and crept over to the nearest computer screen. As she'd suspected, it was one of Leanna's "secret" experiments.

Leanna was always running experiments late at night when she thought no one else was watching. But Helen watched. Nothing slipped past Doctor Helen Eastgate. Over the weeks and months, she'd become very familiar with Leanna's painstaking work, always so meticulous, always so carefully hidden from view. Leanna's formal studies at the university were simply a front for her own private research.

But Helen could keep secrets too. She'd waited patiently to collect samples of Leanna's own DNA. Stray hairs, so fine and golden, almost invisible when left behind on work surfaces. They had revealed their secrets under Helen's scrutiny.

The paper that Professor Wiseman had written claimed that genetic changes were at the root of the condition he had named lycanthropy. Helen had imagined a scattering of altered genes, but the first time she'd analyzed Leanna's DNA she had been shocked beyond measure. Leanna Lloyd was a living miracle. It was a wonder that she could still be alive with chromosomes so utterly changed. Wiseman's paper had outlined the nature of the changes in general terms, but seeing them for herself in the harsh light of the computer screen had been utterly different to reading about them in a scientific paper. Leanna's secret was written throughout her entire body at the cellular level. She was no longer human. No longer remotely human. A chimpanzee was genetically much closer to being human than Leanna. Some process had altered her genes beyond recognition.

The rogue DNA in her chromosomes appeared to be canine in origin, presumably a selection of wild wolf genes. Wiseman had documented the way those alien genes were transferred to their human host. A virus.

Knowing what she now knew, Helen no longer found the idea so strange. It was, after all, precisely the mechanism that she used in her own scientific research to manipulate genetic material in the laboratory. Viruses had evolved over billions of years to invade living cells and insert their own DNA into the host cell nucleus, tricking their victims into manufacturing more copies of the original invader. It was only a small step to imagine that a virus could transfer genetic material from one animal host to another. And while scientists had spent decades working to develop the technique for use in curing genetic conditions, nature had already perfected it, unknown to them all. It would be funny, if the consequences weren't so dire.

Helen peered at the computer display that lit up the dark laboratory with its bright white light. The gene sequencer had already completed its DNA analysis and was displaying its results on the screen. Helen frowned. She had seen a lot of DNA sequences in her time, including Leanna's rogue DNA with the wolf genes present. But not like this. This wasn't Leanna's DNA, it was even more exotic and alien. The familiar twenty-three chromosomes of the human genome were present, but full of anomalies and defects. The creature with this genetic makeup was even less human than Leanna.

Perhaps this was some failed experiment, a glitch. Helen moved to the next screen and felt her pulse speed up. This one had also finished. The results were even stranger than the first. The DNA profile on the screen was the blueprint for a monster. Could an organism with this kind of mutant DNA even survive?

The changes here were vastly beyond anything she had imagined. She was looking at an entirely new kind of species. If such a creature was capable of surviving, Helen couldn't begin to guess what its abilities might be.

A female voice behind her broke her chain of thoughts. 'Doctor Eastgate, what a surprise.'

There was no mistaking that disquietingly familiar voice. Helen felt suddenly cold again. The fear that had crept up on her earlier had come back even stronger than before. She turned slowly, the backpack containing her laptop, papers and genetic sample suddenly weighing heavily on her shoulders. She ought to have gone when she had the chance.

Leanna stood in the doorway, her blue eyes sparkling and her blonde hair shining even in the semi-gloom of the darkened laboratory.

Helen stared back at her wide-eyed. Her hands began to tremble with a violent shaking that she couldn't control. She hid them in her coat pockets to hide her fear.

'Curiosity killed the cat,' said Leanna lightly, nodding to indicate the computer display that Helen had been studying.

Helen fought to keep her voice calm. 'And it killed

Professor Wiseman too, I presume,' she accused.

Leanna entered the lab and closed the door behind her. 'Not curiosity, no. I killed him myself. And then I ate him.'

Helen felt her gorge rise, terror threatening to overwhelm her senses. Fear was the enemy now, as much as this monster disguised as a young woman. Any pretence at secrecy was over, and she had no doubt that Leanna was here to kill her. 'So, what happens now?' She cast her eyes around the lab, hoping for some kind of lifeline. There was only one exit however. No way out other than past Leanna. And no one else in the building to come to her rescue.

Leanna smiled a cold, cruel grin. 'What do *you* think will happen?'

Helen thought quickly. 'I think the police will be arriving here any second. I called them before I came. They know all about you. I've been reporting back to them for weeks.'

Leanna stared at her silently for a moment. Then she threw her head back and began to laugh. 'I don't think so. You're a terrible liar, Helen, didn't anyone ever tell you? Too focussed on discovering your precious truth to know how to tell lies. The police have plenty of other things to keep them occupied this evening. They aren't coming to save you. And soon the curfew will begin. I think we have this place to ourselves tonight, just you and me. So if there's anything you want to say, any famous last words, I suggest you unburden yourself now.'

Helen backed away, putting more distance between herself and Leanna. The girl looked harmless enough, but Helen wasn't fooled by her surface appearance. She had seen the genetic profile that lurked in each cell of her body. She had read about the so-called *Ripper* murders in the newspapers. And she had watched the news footage of wolves prowling London streets, displaying claws and fangs as deadly as sharpened blades. Leanna may be in human form right now, but Helen knew that she was capable of extreme violence. She scanned the worktops of the benches as she retreated, searching for something, anything that could help her escape.

'Nothing to say?' asked Leanna. 'How disappointing. I suppose we'll just have to say our last good-byes then.' She took a step forward, advancing as Helen continued to move backward.

'What about Professor Wiseman?' demanded Helen. 'What were his last words?' She needed to keep Leanna talking. Anything to stall her and buy more time.

Her question had obviously hit Leanna's weak spot. The girl scowled, her face contorting in anger. 'Wiseman was a fool, the biggest fool of all. Do you know what he said to me? Can you imagine? At the very moment of his death?'

'Tell me.' Helen cast her gaze from left to right, searching for something she could use to defend herself.

'He told me it was all his fault. He said he was sorry for what he'd done. He said he forgave me.' Leanna sneered. 'As if I wanted his forgiveness. As if that could possibly make any difference to the outcome. Wiseman was weak. He deserved to die.' She sprang forward a step, closing in on Helen. 'The weak will always die at the hands of the strong. He was a biologist, he should have understood that. You should know that too.'

Helen took another step backward and felt the solid edge of a workbench against her back. She had reached the far end of the laboratory. There was nowhere else to go. 'Wait,' she said. 'I can help you.'

Leanna laughed again. 'Help me? Do you really think so?'

'Of course. I'm a genetic scientist. I have all the resources of the university available. We can work on this together. I've seen your experiments. I know what you're trying to do.'

Leanna kept walking forward, unhurriedly. 'Really? So tell me, what am I trying to do?'

'Develop a cure. Restore your original DNA. Become human again.'

Leanna burst into laughter again, louder than ever. The cruelty of the laugh was like a slap to Helen's face. 'Change me back? So I can be like you?' Her laugh died in her throat, as suddenly as it had begun. 'Why would I want to be human again? So I can be weak? So I can know fear, and hunger, and disease? You think I would want that? You think this is some kind of curse? Becoming lycanthropic was the most wonderful thing that ever happened to me.' Leanna's voice was as cold as her crystal eyes. 'Lycanthropy isn't a sickness. It's nature's gift. Who would want to be human when you could be lycanthropic?' She jumped up suddenly, springing several feet off the floor onto the top of a workbench. 'Could I jump like this if I was human?' She picked up one of the DNA sequencers and hurled the machine toward Helen. 'Would I be this strong if I was still human?'

Half a million pounds worth of scientific equipment tumbled in Helen's direction. She rolled to one side just before the machine crashed into the wall behind her.

Leanna leapt back down to the floor, her face alive with pleasure for the first time since Helen had known her. 'Could I smell the fear on your skin if I was only human?' she asked, wrinkling her nose to sniff the air.

Helen crouched where she had rolled, panting breathlessly. 'What do you want, then?' It was all she could think to say.

Leanna continued to walk closer, casually, as if she had just flicked a ball of paper, not flung a forty-pound weight halfway across a room.

'Like I told you when we first met, I'm an idealist, a dreamer. I want to make the world a better place. I don't just want to cure disease. I want to free humanity from all weakness. I want to give us superpowers. I want to free us from the curse that has always haunted us. Human suffering.'

'You're mad.'

'Oh no. I'm not mad. I'm a wolf. You see, lycanthropy is a fast track for human evolution. It culls the weak and gives unimaginable powers to the strong. It will transform the world in ways that people like you are too blinkered even to imagine.'

Helen knew she was talking to a monster, but she decided to try one last appeal to the fragment of humanity that surely must exist, locked somewhere within the wolf. 'You speak of idealism. You must understand that you're creating a new species of predator that hunts and feeds off humans. Stop now, before it's too late. I can help you with your ideas, but you must become human again.'

Leanna's look of pleasure turned to anger. 'Human? Why? You humans have no claim to the moral high ground. Humans eat other animals, just like dolphins eat fish, and lions eat antelope. The only rules of nature I know are that predators eat prey and the strong rule the weak.'

She snarled then and came for Helen. She moved with incredible speed, covering the distance between them in seconds. Helen threw herself to one side and crashed painfully into a workbench. She almost tumbled to the floor, but managed to stagger around to the other side of the workbench just as Leanna's fingernails whipped in front of her face.

Leanna smiled, and Helen had the feeling that the girl had allowed her to escape, like a cat playing with a mouse. The bench between them was fixed securely to the floor, but Helen was under no illusion that it provided a safe barrier. She had already seen Leanna jump onto the other bench. She could leap this one too in a second, if she wanted to. But she didn't, yet.

'You can't get away from me,' said Leanna. 'But don't stop trying. This is fun.'

Helen backed away and moved along the far wall of the lab, searching for a tool or a piece of equipment she could use. Experimental apparatus was stored on shelving along the wall. She was always lecturing her students on how dangerous lab work could be. Surely there was something dangerous here, when she needed it?

Leanna circled her, prowling around the edge of the room, like a lynx. 'Do you know how much I've longed for this moment?' she asked. 'You're such an interfering busybody, always poking your nose in where it doesn't belong. It's high time you got what you deserve.'

Helen scoured the shelving for something she could use. Her hand seized on a hypodermic needle and she gripped it tightly.

Leanna had seen her do it. 'Ah, yes, about time. A weapon. That's what made humans the apex predators, after all. Let's see you use it, then.' She ducked low behind a bench and disappeared from view.

Helen swept her gaze from left to right, seeking a glimpse of the girl. She felt panic rising. Fear flowed through her limbs, sapping the will to move. She clutched the needle, craning her neck for a glimpse of movement, listening for the slightest noise that would tell her where Leanna had gone. A chair crashed over to one side and she flicked her eyes to it, just in time to see the girl appear. Helen lifted the needle in front of her and held it out protectively.

Leanna flew at her, springing like a wolf, her arms outstretched. Helen thrust with the sharp needle but Leanna's hand reached out and brushed it aside, swatting it out of her grasp.

Helen stumbled as the girl landed on her, but managed to jerk herself sideways at the last moment, tumbling over a nearby chair and crashing to the floor beside it. She landed awkwardly, her shoulder taking the brunt of the fall, and a jolt of pain shot through her arm and down her spine. She lay there stunned, unable to move, her breath coming in ragged gasps.

Leanna had landed neatly on her feet a few yards away.

Her eyes flashed in angry brilliance. 'A human without a weapon is a pathetic creature, you know. An easy kill. And now I'm bored. It's time to end this.' She walked toward Helen, her fingers curling and uncurling in anticipation.

Helen scrabbled away from her along the floor, until her back collided with the genome analyzer that Leanna had thrown earlier. She had backed herself into a corner. Now she would die, and the knowledge that might have helped to save the world would die with her.

Leanna crouched lower as she advanced, almost dropping to all fours. She opened her mouth to reveal neat white teeth in two perfect rows. Saliva dripped from her tongue.

Helen pushed herself back to her feet, instinctively seeking to distance herself from her foe, but there was nowhere left to go.

Leanna crept forward, blocking the only exit and closing the gap between them inexorably.

Helen fumbled on the bench behind her, desperately pushing away test tubes and plastic beakers as she searched for some last hope. Finally her fingers closed around an object and she picked it up. A glass vial with a yellow hazard warning sticker. Concentrated sulphuric acid. She hurled it in Leanna's direction.

The glass vial struck the side of Leanna's head and shattered, covering the girl's face with clear liquid. Leanna shrieked. Immediately the acid began to react with her skin. She threw her hands to her face and doubled over, screaming in pain. The acid burned into her flesh with a fizzing noise, making her skin bubble as it dissolved the exposed soft tissue layers and began to bite deeper.

Helen didn't stop to see how far the acid would burn. She ran from the lab as fast as she could, covering her ears to shut out the piteous wailing that followed her.

Chapter Twenty

Bath Road, West London, New Year's Day

Chris Crohn found his mood lifting as the day wore on. Perhaps it was because they were nearing the edge of the city; perhaps lack of sleep was producing a surge of adrenaline. 'This is Civilization 2.0, Seth. The old ways no longer apply.' He gestured at the mass of unmoving cars in front of them. 'These people already get it. People like us. Leaving the old world behind, heading out into the wilderness and bringing with them nothing more than what they can carry. We're like the pioneers that crossed America, in search of a new life in the west.'

'Or maybe they're just heading home after a New Year's party,' said Seth. 'Either way, we've been stuck in this traffic jam for over six hours now. We need to find a way to get off this road.'

Seth could be such a source of negativity. Chris ignored him. 'The operating system of humanity has been updated, and we're the early adopters. Obsolete rules have been torn up, shredded and bagged for recycling. The rules that will replace them are as yet unwritten. We're at the cusp, Seth, people like us. We are the future.'

Seth stared gloomily at the road ahead. 'If this is the future, I preferred the past.'

'I know you did. Me too, in many ways. But life was hard then for people like us. All those arbitrary social rules to follow, elaborate rituals, arcane interpersonal subtleties that we could never hope to grasp. This transition will be a cleansing, a burning of all that. In the future, the only rules we'll need to learn will be the rules of survival.'

'Chris, when did you last eat?'

'It must have been at breakfast time.'

'I think you may be getting low on sugar.'

It was possible. The thought of food had been far from his mind and he was feeling a little lightheaded. For despite the tedium of sitting in an endless line of traffic, he had found the day exhilarating. It was like the time he got his first smartphone, working out how its tiny, primitive operating system could be hacked, how he could modify it to make it do what he wanted. The adventure of discovery, of exploring unknown frontiers was the stuff that made existence worthwhile. 'It's the thrill of the new, Seth. It's what we need to let us know we're still alive.'

'If you want to stay alive, I suggest you break out some of those energy bars. I'm starving too.'

Seth was right. He'd allowed himself to start dreaming. In order to survive, he would need to focus tightly on essentials, and not get distracted. Details would make the difference between life and death from now on.

He undid the seat belt and reached around to grab the box of snacks they'd stowed on the rear seat. He snatched a couple of cereal bars and some energy drinks for himself and Seth.

'How far have we come?' he asked.

Seth studied the on-screen map on the dashboard.

'We're not far from Heathrow Airport now, so I guess we've travelled just under twenty miles. We could have come here on the train in less than an hour.'

'The trains aren't safe,' Chris reminded him. 'I already explained that.'

'We could probably have walked it.'

'Not with all our gear.' They had spent the last of Chris's money buying food and essential survival equipment, filling the back of the car with an assortment of stuff. The money was all gone now, but Chris didn't think they'd need it in the future.

'How far were you hoping we could travel today?' Seth asked.

Chris shrugged. 'I don't know. I hadn't really planned. I was so desperate to get on the road, I hadn't properly thought about our route.' It was unforgivable really. He'd had plenty of time to plan, and while he'd spent ages deciding on their ultimate destination, picturing himself as a wasteland warrior fending off werewolves, he'd given scant thought to some of the details. 'I've let you down, Seth. I've got to get the details right in future.'

The sense of elation that had gripped him earlier had dissipated, to be replaced by an overwhelming sense of dread. He cast his gaze over the sea of red brake lights from the cars stretched out in front of them as far as he could see. When midnight came, the curfew would begin. Would the soldiers really try to arrest everyone trapped here? And would they use force if people resisted? If they did, the sea of red would quickly become a sea of blood.

Chapter Twenty-One

Electric Avenue, Brixton, South London, New Year's Day

The building that the ram raiders had driven into was a pharmacy. Ben could see its neon cross sign glowing an eerie green through the fog. Two masked men ran from the wrecked car and entered the building, slipping through the gap that the car had torn between the metal shutters.

A security alarm blared out in the silence of the night, but the thick fog dampened its cry. Ben hoped that the security system would automatically alert the police, but he had no way of knowing if it would, or how long they would take to arrive.

'I'll phone the police,' said Ben. 'And let Salma Ali know what's happening.'

'There's no time for that,' said Mr Stewart. 'Someone else will call the police.'

'They are two. We are three,' said Mr Kowalski. 'We

can take them.'

'Let's do it,' agreed Mr Stewart.

'We should wait for help to arrive,' said Ben, but the two other men had already crossed the road toward the pharmacy. He hesitated, then hurried after them.

Mr Kowalski entered the shop first, squeezing his way between the ripped steel rollers that had protected the shop windows. A steel blade glinted in his hand. Mr Stewart drew his own knife from his jacket and followed him inside.

Ben lingered outside. He had no experience of this kind of thing. What if the masked men were armed? They might well be. They might even have guns. He had nothing, and with hindsight that seemed stupid. If they attacked him with weapons, how could he hope to defend himself?

Shouts emerged from the pharmacy. It sounded like a fight had broken out, but Ben could see nothing through the metal window blinds. He squeezed his hands into fists, readying himself in case one of the raiders emerged, wondering if he should wait outside or join the others.

More cries came from inside. He recognized Mr Kowalski's thick Polish accent and Mr Stewart's voice too. The higher-pitched shouting of younger men cut across the other shouts. He couldn't tell which side was winning the fight.

Coward. He was no use to anyone out here. He imagined what Mr Stewart would have to say to him if he did nothing to help. He still hadn't even phoned the police, but there was no time for that now. He had to do something. Reluctantly, he bent low and forced himself through the narrow gap between the metal rollers.

The shop was not a large one, and was unlit inside apart from the faint glow from a display cabinet stocked with beauty products and a larger-than-life backlit image of a woman with perfect skin. Four dark shapes grappled with each other amidst a sea of spilled bottles, plastic jars and brightly-coloured pills.

He stepped gingerly across the scattered debris to the two nearest men. Mr Stewart had one of the masked youths pinned to the floor, his knife held in one hand. His opponent's knife had fallen to the floor. The man was fighting back, trying to wrestle the weapon from Mr Stewart.

'Grab the knife!' yelled Mr Stewart. 'Stick it in him!'

Ben stared at the dropped weapon in shock. He wasn't about to stab an unarmed man, whatever the situation. He stood frozen for a moment, unable to act.

The young man twisted in Mr Stewart's grip and threw the older man off him. He struggled to his feet and lunged for the knife.

It was just what Ben needed to break him out of his paralysis. He kicked the knife across the floor out of harm's way and threw himself on the masked raider. The man went down under his weight and crashed to the floor with a sharp cry. Ben grabbed hold of his wrists and held him down.

Mr Stewart appeared a second later, kneeling down on one of the man's arms and pinning him to the floor. Now the prone man was helpless. Mr Stewart brought the tip of his blade to his neck. 'Don't move a muscle, or you're a dead man,' he snarled.

On the other side of the shop, Mr Kowalski seemed to have his own assailant under control. The second youth lay face down, his head twisted to one side, his arms held tightly in the Polish man's strong grasp. 'You've broken my arm!' screeched the would-be burglar. 'You've broken my fucking arm!' In response, Mr Kowalski twisted his knee into the man's back, making him squeal with pain. He clearly didn't need Ben's assistance.

Neither did Mr Stewart, who now held the other youth immobile, his knife held against his throat.

Ben stood up and dusted himself down. There didn't seem to be anything left for him to do.

A moment later the rising-and-falling sound of a police

siren began to warble in the distance and before long, blue flashes outside indicated that the police had arrived. Two uniformed officers pushed their way into the shop past the battered steel shutters. They looked from Ben to the men on the floor and back to Ben again. 'We have a report of a break-in,' said one of the police officers.

'We caught these men trying to steal from the shop,' Ben explained.

'And who might you be?'

'Ben Harvey, Neighbourhood Watch.'

'Anyone hurt?'

Ben pointed to the youth that Mr Kowalski had immobilized. 'I think that man's hurt his arm.'

'He fucking broke it,' wailed the youth through his mask. 'That's assault, that is.'

Mr Kowalski shrugged. 'Is accident. These men are criminals. Caught red-handed. We make legal citizen's arrest.'

The other police officer laughed. 'It looks like you guys handled the situation well enough. I think we can take over from here.' He bent down and cuffed the two men lying prone on the floor. The one with the broken arm cried out again as the handcuffs went over his wrists. The police officer and his colleague dragged the men to their feet and ushered them toward the exit.

'Wait,' said Ben. 'Don't you want to take statements from us?'

'I don't think that will be necessary, sir. I think these men got the treatment they deserved. Given the current emergency, we've been told to go easy with the paperwork until things calm down again. Thanks once again for your help.'

Ben watched the police leave. He could hardly believe that they'd gone with barely any questions asked. They didn't seem to care that one of the burglars had been assaulted. They hadn't even said anything about Mr Stewart's knife, even though it had been clearly visible to everyone.

Mr Stewart slid the knife back inside his jacket and Mr Kowalski picked up the knives the two thieves had left behind. He stowed them inside his grey coat. 'Is good work,' said the shopkeeper, grinning. 'We will not see those two again.'

Mr Stewart smiled nastily. 'That one with the broken arm certainly won't be taking part in any more ram raids for a while.'

Ben nodded. It was hard to argue with that logic. He still wasn't sure how much contribution he'd made to the arrests, but at least he hadn't lingered uselessly outside while the other men did the dangerous work. He'd been there when it mattered, and even Mr Stewart couldn't say that he hadn't.

Mr Kowalski gave him a hearty slap on the back. 'Was good for first time,' he said encouragingly. 'Next time we do even better.' He held out a hand. In his palm was the knife he had offered earlier. Ben eyed the weapon nervously.

The Polish man thrust his hand closer, urging him to take the knife. 'Next time you come prepared,' he insisted.

Ben stared at the steel blade in its leather sheath a while longer, trying to decide what to do. He had never carried a knife in his life, and didn't know how to handle one. He probably wouldn't use it even if he got into another fight. But it would be there if he needed it. He hesitated another second, then took the knife from Mr Kowalski and slid it into the inside pocket of his coat.

It hardly felt like he'd made any decision at all.

Chapter Twenty-Two

Bath Road, West London, New Year's Day

Chris watched as the soldiers went from vehicle to vehicle, questioning each of the drivers in turn, examining documents, searching some of the cars, occasionally forcing their occupants onto the roadside at gunpoint. He braced himself for the sound of shots being fired, but so far there had been none.

'What do you think they're doing?' asked Seth. 'They can't arrest everyone. Are they looking for rioters?'

'It's not rioters they should be worried about. It's werewolves.'

The troops had dogs with them too, and they were searching the cars, sniffing the occupants. If the dogs barked at them, the people were marched into armoured cars and driven away. An entire family had been taken off, the mother screaming at the soldiers, the children in tears. Could they really have been werewolves? It seemed that the army was taking no chances, and Chris was pleased to see it. There was still a possibility that prompt and decisive action might be enough to nip the threat before a catastrophe unfolded.

'They should put them all in quarantine,' said Chris. 'Everyone that the dogs identify. They have to stop the infection while they still can.'

'What?' said Seth. 'Imprison whole families and children just because a dog doesn't like the way they smell? That's sick.'

'No. If they don't stop the spread of the disease, every family will end up dead. It's a mathematical certainty.'

'Let's hope the dogs don't think you smell weird, then,' said Seth.

Chris gave his armpits a quick sniff. They were a bit rank, to be honest. Thankfully the air conditioning in the car was very efficient.

A soldier rapped loudly on the glass of the driver's door and Seth wound the window down. Damp, freezing air entered the car. The soldier shone a flashlight inside. 'Do you have a driving licence or other form of ID?' he demanded.

Seth showed the man his licence, and Chris gave him his passport. The soldier studied them carefully, shining the light into each of their faces in turn. 'Please state your reason for travel.'

'Evacuation,' said Chris.

'We're heading west,' added Seth. 'Away from London.'

'And what is your intended destination?' asked the soldier.

'The wilderness,' Chris told him.

'Herefordshire,' clarified Seth.

The soldier thumbed through the documents again, then shone his light into the back seats of the car. He frowned at the cardboard boxes piled high there. 'Get out of the car,' he said, holding on to their documents. 'Now,' he growled.

Reluctantly Chris opened the passenger door and

stepped out into the cold night. The soldier herded him and Seth away from the vehicle and over to the roadside. Two more soldiers joined them, rifles slung over their shoulders. Another soldier was bringing the dogs.

'Search this vehicle,' ordered the first man. He pointed his rifle at Chris. 'Over there, now!' He gestured at the grass verge next to the road. 'Kneel down, hands behind your heads!'

Chris got to his knees, his trousers squelching in the cold mud. He'd left his jacket inside the car, and his thin T-shirt flapped and snapped in the freezing January wind. Another detail he'd got wrong. He glanced sideways at Seth's turtleneck jersey with envy.

The troops pulled boxes out of the car and dumped them in a heap, rifling through the carefully-packed supplies and upending them into the road. The dogs scrabbled inside the vehicle, sniffing everywhere, tails twitching with excitement.

'Please don't break anything,' said Chris.

'Just shut up,' hissed Seth. 'You've already got us into enough trouble.'

'Sir, look at this.' A soldier was lifting equipment out of one of the boxes. 'Weapons. Knives, axes, metal poles. What are these?' He lifted out a pair of short wooden sticks connected by a metal chain.

'Nunchucks,' replied his colleague, chuckling. 'As used by Bruce Lee in the movies. They're almost useless in real combat.'

'They're not,' said Chris indignantly. 'You just have to know how to use them properly.'

A boot in the back of his head pitched him face forward into the mud. 'Bring the dogs over here,' said the soldier behind him. 'Let's give these sons of bitches a good sniff.'

Chapter Twenty-Three

West Field Terrace, South London, waning moon

Rose Hallibury lay awake, staring at the ceiling of her bedroom, a cold sweat beading her forehead. Light from the streetlamp lent a dull glow to the room. She swept her gaze rapidly around the dark space, picking out the desk, chair and the bulk of the wardrobe in the semi-blackness. Her heart hammered in her chest and she was panting breathlessly. Her dream had come again, worse than before.

The dream had first visited her soon after she'd witnessed the attack at the dog kennels. In the dream, the men in the leather jackets had done their evil work with their hammers, knives and bats, killing the dogs and leaving her curled up in a ball. Then the dogs had come for her. The dead creatures, battered and bloody, had risen to their feet, their eyes glowing red and cruel. They were no longer frightened; they were angry. Angry with her. 'You let them kill us,' whispered the dogs. 'We trusted you, and you let us die.' The dogs had savaged her then, and she'd awoken, breathless in the night.

The second dream had been even more terrifying. She'd been back at school, the headmaster's hands around her throat like claws, his teeth snapping at her neck. She'd turned and stabbed him in the eye with her pen, but he hadn't died. Instead he'd smiled at her, a sick gloating grin. 'You'll be sorry you did that, Rose,' he whispered, as the blood gurgled from his empty eye socket, the pen sticking out like a spear. 'I'll make sure you're sorry.'

His words still rang in her ears. She'd heard them clearly, as if he were in the room with her right now. She switched on her bedside light, but there was no one there. It had been a dream, nothing more.

But she wasn't so sure. The dreams had shown her more than just the past. They'd given her glimpses of the future too. A terrible future, filled with pain and suffering and death. A burning city, soldiers shooting at will, wild animals roaming the streets, tearing at victims. And worst of all, her parents and her little brother, Oscar, lying dead in the gutter, their bodies twisted and broken.

Some of the visions were already coming to pass. Soldiers on the streets; burning buildings; wolves. She had seen it first in her mind's eye, and now it was happening for real.

A tear rolled down her cheek, and she wiped it away fiercely. Weakness wouldn't serve her now. She needed to be strong, stronger than she had ever been before. She wouldn't let the visions come true. She would not allow it.

Chapter Twenty-Four

Upper Terrace, Richmond upon Thames, West London, waning moon

A day had passed since Melanie had returned home, and Sarah was growing ever more anxious. Mel was a dreadful patient, not allowing Sarah to tend to her wounds properly, refusing to eat proper meals, constantly saying that she just wanted to be left alone. And she positively forbade Sarah to call for a doctor. It was just like Mel to be difficult. She had always had a strongly independent, defiant nature. But she had never shut herself away like this before.

Usually her sister adored being fussed over. As a small child she'd once had a nasty ear infection and had loved being the centre of attention for a week. It had made Sarah jealous until she caught the illness too and realized how horrible it was. But Melanie was willing to endure any hardship if it meant she could be the main event. Her current refusal to be looked after was both uncharacteristic and worrying.

Equally worrying, despite Sarah's continued questioning, Mel refused to say where she had been during the time she'd been missing. She wouldn't discuss James either, other than to repeat again that he'd rescued her.

'From what?' Sarah demanded. 'From where?'

'Ask him yourself,' said Melanie, knowing full well that Sarah could barely bring herself to speak to their new guest.

At least James was no trouble. He stayed in his room, never coming out, not even appearing downstairs for meals. She had taken some tea and bread up to him the first day. She'd stood outside the guest room, knocking on the locked door, but James hadn't emerged or even acknowledged her. She'd left the food and drink on a tray outside his room, but today it was still untouched. She hadn't seen him since he'd first arrived, and only occasional sounds like the creak of the floorboards as he moved around the room convinced her that he was still in there.

A couple of times during the night she'd heard loud sobbing coming from his room and had knocked again on his door, but he hadn't replied. Only once had she seen him, creeping quietly to the bathroom. He'd averted his face from her quickly when he saw her, but not before she'd seen the red eyes and tear-stained face that showed he'd been crying again.

So it was a surprise when she heard him coming down the stairs in the early hours. She had stayed up late, tending to Grandpa, who no longer seemed to distinguish between day and night, and might eat or sleep at any time, or not at all. The old man had drifted off eventually, and Sarah was sitting quietly by the TV, watching the latest events unfold on the news. She started up when James appeared, opening her mouth to greet him, then quickly closed it again, as the words turned to dust in her open mouth. She turned her face away, embarrassed and ashamed by her inability to speak to him.

James stood in the doorway, seeming afraid to enter. An awkward silence filled the room for a long while until James broke it, saying, 'I should leave. You don't like me staying here. You want me gone.'

'No, no,' said Sarah, forcing herself to say the words aloud. 'It's not that.' She felt terrible that James had jumped to that conclusion. But really, how could he think otherwise? She knew just how bad her behaviour must seem to other people. It had been years now since any guests had come to the house. Melanie had stopped bringing people home when she realized that Sarah just couldn't handle them anymore.

'What then?' he asked. 'Is it something Melanie told you about me?'

She looked up at him, forcing herself to make eye contact with him very briefly. He still looked terrible. The time he'd spent in his room had done him no visible good. Hardly surprising since he hadn't touched any of the food or drink she'd made him. He hadn't showered or changed clothes either, as far as she could see. The tear tracks on his cheeks looked fresh, and his eyes seemed even more sunken, more ringed with black than when he had first come to the house.

'My sister hasn't really told me anything about you,' she said. 'But this isn't about you. It's about me.'

'How do you mean?'

She took a deep breath and stared at the wall. 'I'm not very good at meeting new people. In fact, that's something of an understatement. I have an extreme pathological form of shyness. The condition I suffer from is called anthropophobia. I don't suppose you've heard of it? It's quite rare.'

'Anthropophobia,' repeated James. 'That must be a Greek word. Fear of other people?'

'Hey, you're good,' said Sarah, forcing a tiny smile onto her lips. She glanced toward him, then turned her gaze to the floor. She found that she could speak to him as long as she didn't look at his face. There was something reassuring about the boy that made her want to open up to him, despite herself. 'It started when I was a teenager, perhaps even earlier. Perhaps I've always been this way. I was awkward with other people, worried what they would think of me. I think it was because I had such a wonderful sister. Everyone always loved Melanie. She charmed them, made them feel good about themselves. She had so many friends, and she was thin and beautiful too. I knew I could never be like her, so I guess I gave up on life altogether. I developed an eating disorder. I hated the way I looked, the things I said. Gradually I withdrew from other people. I had fewer and fewer friends. Eventually I stopped going outside completely. The only people I ever speak to now are Melanie and Grandpa.

'It's not worked out so bad, really,' she continued. 'Melanie and I make a team, of sorts. She does the things I can't do. She deals with the outside world and brings home money.' She stopped for a moment, hoping James wouldn't ask how Melanie earned her money; that she wouldn't have to tell him about the men she seduced and stole from. 'And I do the things Melanie can't. I stay home and care for Grandpa. So, together, it all works out.'

She looked up and saw that James had covered his face with his hands. That was good. If he didn't look at her, maybe she could be okay with him. In fact, it was a relief to speak about her condition at last, to someone who seemed to understand a little. Melanie had never understood. She was able to accept Sarah, but would never really understand her.

James kept his hands over his face. 'It all worked out until now,' he said glumly. 'Until I arrived and drove a wedge between you and Melanie.' He began to sob quietly, his shoulders rocking gently. 'Everything I touch I destroy,' he said. 'Anyone I care about gets hurt, or worse. I should have just killed myself when I had the chance.' He broke down completely then, racked with a desperate sobbing, a noise like a wail escaping from his open mouth.

Sarah sat watching him, wondering what to do. Melanie would know. She was so good with people. Or was she? Maybe that was only half the story. Melanie could be selfish too. She kept a foul tongue in her pretty head. She grew bored with people quickly and lashed out without thinking. She fled from situations she couldn't handle. She created messes and left them for others to clean up. Would Melanie really know how to deal with this?

Sarah stood cautiously and edged across the room, slowly closing the gap between herself and James. She reached out a hand and touched his shoulder, feeling the agony that shook his body in violent spasms. Her other hand lifted itself unbidden to touch his arm, and she gripped him as he cried, feeling the warmth of another human being under her hands for the first time in years.

After some minutes he quietened, and his body ceased its shaking. He lifted his chin and looked up at her. She forced herself not to turn away. There was nothing to fear. He was a boy, just a harmless boy. She waited until he had stopped crying completely before she took her hands away from him.

Chapter Twenty-Five

Brixton Hill Police Station, South London, waning moon

Liz went into work early the next morning. A good night's sleep and a hearty breakfast of fried bacon and sausages cooked by her father, and she was feeling much more herself.

'You're looking better, love,' her father said. 'Apart from your eyes. Are they still hurting you?'

'It's just tiredness,' she said, pulling on her sunglasses so he couldn't see the yellow tint. They'll be better in a few days.' She gave Mihai a hug and headed off to report for duty.

Dean arrived at the police station the same time as her. He gave her a big grin. 'It's good to see your lovely face,' he told her. 'Just what I need on a beautiful day like today.'

'Yeah,' said Liz. 'I wish I could say the same for you.' The dark bruises on his forehead looked even worse than when she'd last seen him. 'You should really be at home.

Or better still, back at the hospital.'

'I'd just be clogging up a bed,' he said. 'I can't bear being useless.'

When they went inside there was a letter waiting on Dean's desk. He picked it up and read it with dismay. 'Oh,' he said, the broad grin vanishing from his face. 'It's from the Chief Superintendent. He wants to see me in his office.'

The Chief Super didn't normally send personalized letters, and when he did they meant important news – sometimes good, but more often bad. 'Maybe a promotion?' suggested Liz optimistically. 'Or a commendation for bravery?'

'More likely a reprimand for getting into such an awful mess on New Year's Eve.' He went off to the Chief Super's office, a glum look on his face.

She made a cup of tea for them both and started working on her report of the New Year's Eve events. The part where she had saved people from a burning vehicle was straightforward. The bit where she had transformed into a monster and savaged a bunch of rioters would require some creative writing.

She was sitting with her fingers poised over her computer keyboard when Dean returned from the meeting with the Chief Superintendent. She glanced nervously at his face and was relieved to see that his grin was back. 'What was it, then?' she asked. 'A big fat pay rise?'

'Not exactly. At first I thought I was in trouble over what happened during the riots. You know – the way we got separated from the others. But in fact the Chief was full of praise – for me and you too. But that's not what he wanted to speak to me about.'

'What then?'

'It wasn't anything to do with the riots. Or rather it is, I suppose.'

'Dean! Stop being so cagey. What did he say?'

'He's speaking to all the Authorised Firearms Officers

in the borough. There's a new policy in place as of today. All Firearms Officers will carry weapons routinely until the current crisis is resolved. And even better news – he wants us out on patrol as much as possible, so you can scrap that report you're writing and come with me. We're hitting the streets! Come on, before he changes his mind.'

She grabbed her jacket and followed him out of the office. She was relieved that she wouldn't have to file her report, and it would be good to get out on patrol again, but the fact that Dean would be carrying a gun did nothing to put her at ease.

Like most British police officers, Liz had never been trained to use a gun. She had never wanted the life-or-death responsibility of handling one. But Dean was an Authorised Firearms Officer and was qualified to handle weapons if the situation required it. That happened very rarely and could only be authorized by a senior commander. The fact that the Chief Superintendent felt the need for Dean to begin carrying a gun at all times made the gravity of the current situation even more apparent.

Dean led the way to the station's secure armoury. The officer there issued him with a pistol and a holster, and also an assault rifle. 'Sign here,' said the officer, and Dean scrawled his messy signature on the paperwork.

Liz must have looked apprehensive, because Dean gave her a reassuring smile as they walked out to their patrol car. 'We'll be safe with these bad boys,' he told her when they reached the car. He showed her the pistol. 'A Glock 17 semi-automatic. It's a self-loading 9mm handgun with seventeen rounds. I'll be carrying this at all times from now on.' He slid the handgun back into its holster. Next he showed her the assault rifle. 'This beauty is a Heckler & Koch G36C semi-automatic carbine. It's for more serious action.' He opened the boot of the patrol car and secured the rifle inside. 'Let's go,' he said.

She got into the car and sat in the passenger seat next

to him. He could tell she was still nervous about the weapons. 'Look,' he said reasonably, 'if you'd had a gun with you when Dave Morgan was attacked by the *Beast*, he wouldn't be dead now.'

She nodded uncertainly. With a gun in her hand she could have shot and killed that creature before it had even attacked. Dave Morgan would still be her partner, instead of Dean. And Dave's widow and daughters would still have a husband and a father. But knowing what she now suspected – that the *Beast of Clapham Common* was actually a human transformed into a monster – she couldn't be certain that she'd ever have pulled the trigger.

Chapter Twenty-Six

West Field Terrace, South London, waning moon

Rose's father returned to work after the Christmas and New Year holiday. It had been good having the whole family around over Christmas, especially after all her horrible experiences, and she'd felt safe knowing that he was home and not in any danger. Now, after her nightmare, she felt a cold stab of fear waving goodbye to him when he set off by car after breakfast.

But to her surprise and relief, he was back home again within an hour of leaving. 'It's mad out there,' he complained. 'Total gridlock. The police have told people only to travel if their journey is absolutely necessary. But what is that supposed to mean? Is going to work absolutely necessary? Or has that become optional, now?'

'I don't know, love,' said Rose's mum. 'They're just trying to bring some order to the chaos, I expect.'

'I'm sorry,' he said. 'I didn't mean to get cross. It's just that the army seems to be causing most of the chaos. They've put up barriers and checkpoints on all the major routes. It would have taken me hours to get to work, so in the end I just turned around and came home.'

'What about public transport?' asked Rose. 'Could you take the bus or the train?' Not that she wanted her dad to go to work at all. She was relieved when he shook his head.

'According to the travel reports on the radio, the buses are having the same problems with congestion, and half of the underground train stations have been closed too. I'll call my boss and tell him what's happening, and see if I can get some work done from home.'

'What about the curfew last night?' asked Rose. 'The soldiers didn't shoot anyone did they?' The memory of soldiers shooting people in her dream still haunted her.

'No,' said her dad. 'Of course not. They arrested some people, but so far they haven't needed to use their weapons.'

So far, thought Rose. Yet in her dream, they already had. She had seen how it would be.

'We should stock up on food,' said her mum. 'It would be a good idea to make sure the cupboard and fridge are both full, just in case. And I need to get more medication for Oscar too.' Rose's younger brother, Oscar, suffered from cystic fibrosis. He needed various medicines to stop him becoming seriously ill.

'I'll come with you,' said Rose. She'd been cooped up far too much recently, and it would be good to get out of the house again. She was determined not to let her dreams frighten her. Getting outside would be the best way to stay strong. She grabbed her coat and scarf and headed out with her mum.

Usually they shopped at the big supermarket about a mile away, but with the traffic being so bad, her mum decided to head to nearby Electric Avenue instead. It was a bustling part of town, full of small independent traders.

The street had been a flash point for race riots back in the 1980s and had lent its name to a famous song, but these days it was the thriving heart of trendy multicultural Brixton. 'It'll be just like how my own mother used to shop when I was a girl,' joked her mum. 'She used to go to the butcher and the baker every single day.'

'And the candlestick maker too?' suggested Rose.

'Let's hope it doesn't come to that,' laughed her mum.

But when they got to Kowalski's Polish supermarket it was more like life during wartime. The shopkeeper's son stopped them as they walked through the door and handed them a basket. 'How many people are in your household?' he asked.

'Four,' replied Rose's mum, surprised by the question. 'Why?'

'You can only buy six items for each person,' he told her, handing her a piece of card with a large number '4' written on it in green.

'Only six items each?' she demanded. 'You must be joking. How are we supposed to manage with that?'

'I'm sorry,' said the young man. 'We don't know when we'll be able to re-stock. I suggest you come back again this afternoon if you need more. My father might have been able to get more supplies by then.'

They bought what they could. The shop had already been emptied of bread and fresh milk, and the only fruit and vegetables remaining looked old and bruised. In the end they had to choose mostly tinned and boxed goods. 'At least this stuff will keep,' said Rose.

The prices were much higher than at their normal supermarket too. Reluctantly her mum handed over her credit card to the man at the checkout, but he pointed to a sign that stated, *Cash only, thank you*. 'No cards? Really?' she asked indignantly, searching in her purse for some money. 'And I can't believe how much you're charging for basic foods.'

The man, who Rose knew as the shopkeeper's other

son, shrugged indifferently. 'Supply and demand,' he said. 'One week from now, you'll look back and think this was cheap.'

'How rude,' said her mum once they had left the shop. 'I won't be going back there unless I have to.'

But when they reached the pharmacy at the corner of the High Street a nastier shock awaited them. 'Oh my God,' said Rose, staring at the twisted steel shutters that had once protected the shop entrance and windows. The car that had been used to smash into the shutters still stood abandoned, its wheels up on the pavement, blocking the route to pedestrians. It looked like someone had set the car alight, and it was little more than a burned-out wreck. A makeshift sign on the door of the pharmacy read, *Closed until further notice.*

Her mum had turned even paler than usual. 'How are we going to get your brother's medication?' she whispered.

'We'll just have to find another pharmacy,' said Rose. She took hold of her mother's hand. 'Come on, let's go looking.'

Chapter Twenty-Seven

Cabinet Office Briefing Room A, Whitehall, Central London, waning moon

'Well,' said the Foreign Secretary, his voice heavy with irony, 'Britain is leading the world once again. At least in the number of werewolf killings.'

The Prime Minister glared at him over her half-moon glasses. This was a time for the utmost seriousness, not flippant remarks. She needed people around her she could rely on. Anyone in this room who didn't carry their weight would have to be replaced. She wondered how many of these men and women she could really trust. Even in times of crisis, politicians were always on the lookout for advantage and political capital. She needed allies, not loose cannons.

The man had a point though. London really did seem to be the point of origin of this epidemic. The city was a month or two ahead of other world capitals in terms of the spread of the disease, or whatever it was. The New Year's Eve attacks had been far more numerous in London than in any other city, although other countries had reacted very differently in response to the crisis.

'How many killings in other countries?' she asked. 'Give me the breakdown by country.'

The Foreign Secretary's Principal Private Secretary had the information on hand. 'In the UK, as you know, the total number of deaths directly attributable to' – he paused and cleared his throat – '*werewolves* is estimated to be between fifty and one hundred. That includes all known incidents dating back several months. Deaths due to last night's rioting, arson and other violence is of the order of sixty-five, and the number of people killed by armed police currently stands at three, for a grand total somewhere in the region of one hundred and fifty. The number of injuries runs to many hundreds. I'll provide you with a more accurate estimate as soon as I have reliable figures.'

The PM nodded grimly. The phrase *currently stands* reminded her of the consequences of her orders. But the alternative might be even more dreadful.

The principal private secretary continued. 'In Russia, numbers are difficult to pin down, as the government has declared a state of national emergency and has expelled all foreign journalists. Our Ambassador in Moscow estimates that while the number of werewolf killings may be relatively low, the authorities have used the emergency to impose a large-scale crackdown on suspected militants across the country. As many as five thousand individuals are reported missing. They may have been killed or merely imprisoned.

'The situation in China is similar, with political dissidents being rounded up in significant numbers. As for deaths due to werewolves, it is impossible to put forward any reliable number.' The Secretary referred to his notes. 'In the United States, werewolf attacks have been reported in the cities of New York, Boston, Chicago, Philadelphia and Atlanta, with the total number of confirmed fatalities currently at twenty-two.'

'Nothing on the west coast?' asked the PM.

'As of yet, no. However, riots have spread throughout the country and police have shot dead more than three hundred people. Overnight curfews have been imposed in the cities of Los Angeles and Washington DC. We are in close contact with the Department of Homeland Security and are exchanging information that may be of mutual benefit.'

'What about Europe?'

'Most European capitals have experienced suspected or actual cases of werewolf attacks, but not on the same scale as the UK. Romania is of particular interest, as many of the reported attacks date back at least a year. In fact, members of the public are coming forward claiming that werewolf attacks have been an open secret in the country for decades, although the government has dismissed such claims as superstition and hysteria.'

'Hysteria,' mused the Foreign Secretary. 'So it wasn't invented in Britain after all. Just another ghastly foreign import.'

'Foreign Secretary,' warned the PM sternly. 'If you have nothing positive to contribute to this discussion, I would be obliged if you could keep your thoughts to yourself.'

He opened his mouth to make some clever retort, but closed it again when he saw the look in her eyes. She would need to replace that man, and soon. The middle of a crisis wasn't the ideal time to dismiss a colleague, but she had simply had enough of his snide comments. This would be the last COBRA meeting he attended. She had already chosen his replacement.

'Tell me about the state of the overnight curfew,' she told the Home Secretary.

'I am pleased to report that this was carried out as planned, Prime Minister,' replied the grey-haired man seated to the left of the Foreign Secretary. 'Troop movements proceeded largely without a hitch, and the curfew was imposed from the hour of midnight as intended. The troops set up roadblocks and conducted searches of vehicles, and detained three hundred and fifty-eight suspects. There were only two reported injuries, and no rounds were fired.'

The Home Secretary was always professional in his approach. She had often thought him dull, but now she was thankful for his colourless face and his factual, precise reporting.

'In addition to the overnight curfew,' he continued, 'police numbers have been strengthened. All police leave has been cancelled and officers are being re-assigned from desk duty to active patrol. All Authorised Firearms Officers have been issued with firearms and will carry them until further notice. Their objective will be to contain any further outbreaks of violence and disorder before it can spread.'

'Good.' The PM badly needed some good news. If they could contain the public disorder and rioting, they stood a chance of defeating the threat from the werewolves, before the disease or whatever it was could spread. 'Do we have any idea why Britain has been so badly affected by this outbreak?' she asked.

The Foreign Secretary raised one eyebrow but said nothing. The Home Secretary shuffled through his briefing notes but seemed to have none that might address the question. The other ministers present looked to their principal private secretaries, but no explanations were forthcoming.

A deep gravelly voice from the end of the table answered her. 'Prime Minister,' said the Director-General of the Security Service, MI5, 'I believe I may know someone who can help us with that.' The Director-General had the look of a retired prize-fighter. He leaned back in his chair, pushing his wiry glasses to the bridge of his nose with thick stubby fingers. 'If you will allow me, I would like to introduce you to Doctor Helen Eastgate.' He motioned to his secretary, who opened the door to the briefing room.

A young woman entered. She was in her early thirties, with curly blonde hair that had been pulled into a twist but was already starting to escape from the band that held it. She wore a well-tailored suit, but her blouse was misbuttoned, and she tugged at her jacket, as if she was unused to wearing anything so formal. She peered with curiosity at the rows of grey faces and grey suits that greeted her entrance. The PM was reminded of the day she had first entered Parliament, a young woman self-conscious amongst so many grey old men. Times had changed, and the room now held almost as many women as men.

'Doctor Eastgate is a lecturer in infectious diseases at the Department of Genetics, Imperial College, London,' explained the Director-General. 'I believe she has information that will be of interest.'

The new arrival stepped forward. 'Thank you for agreeing to hear me, Prime Minister,' she said in a gentle Australian accent. 'I'm actually a molecular geneticist.' Without being offered a seat, she sat down next to the Director-General, who seemed vaguely taken aback by her directness.

The PM nodded encouragingly, concealing a smile at Doctor Eastgate's behaviour. The woman's confidence and her willingness to contradict the Director-General of the Security Services on a point of detail were more than enough to outweigh her untidy appearance. The PM herself had been no stranger to wardrobe calamities when she'd first been elected to office. Whatever her looks, the young woman's voice exuded credibility. 'And what information do you have to tell us, Doctor Eastgate?' she asked.

The woman's voice rang clearly across the meeting room. 'The identity of the ringleaders of the werewolves.'

Chapter Twenty-Eight

Holland Gardens, Kensington, London, waning moon

Adam slipped into the meeting room in the new house five minutes late, in calculated defiance of Leanna's authority. The way she assumed command at every opportunity was increasingly grating. But he was disappointed to find that she wasn't yet there. That was unusual. Leanna was usually punctual to an annoying degree.

Instead, Warg Daddy and one of his cronies sat at the table, both wrapped in black leather jackets and dark sunglasses. A ridiculous affectation. Adam wore tinted glasses himself when he raced under the bright floodlights of the track at the University Athletics Park, but even with the photosensitivity brought on by lycanthropy, he had no need of them in normal indoor lighting.

He slouched over to the meeting table and took his place opposite the two men.

Warg Daddy's stupid bald head looked like a misshapen billiard ball and his thick black beard gave him the look of a modern-day buccaneer. Had these so-called *War Councils* been his idea? They sounded like the kind of thing the pompous jerk might have invented. *Leader of the Pack,* he called himself. Jerk.

Warg Daddy pointedly ignored his arrival, not even turning his head in his direction when Adam sat down.

Whatever. Adam could ignore Warg Daddy just as easily. He turned his attention instead to the stranger sitting next to him – a huge ginger-haired man, even taller than Adam himself, and broad-shouldered with it. The wolf tattoo on his thick neck was identical to Warg Daddy's, showing that he was another of the Wolf Brothers, and just like his leader, he stank of engine oil and sweat. This must be Snakebite. Adam wondered why Leanna was so keen for him to come to the meeting.

He was an ugly bastard, his hair straggly and unkempt, reaching to his shoulders, a buzz of fiery stubble crawling over his face like sandpaper. His huge fists curled into tight balls on the table, a wash of prickly red hairs visible on the backs of his hands. And just like Warg Daddy he wore shades indoors.

The stranger turned his face toward Adam, removed his dark glasses and stared unnervingly straight at him. Adam stared back, unwilling to look away first. He suddenly wished he was wearing sunglasses himself. He felt naked and exposed under that relentless gaze. The stranger stroked his red beard thoughtfully and replaced the glasses on his ugly face, blacking out that measuring stare. Adam turned away in relief. So far nobody had said a word, and already he felt thoroughly humiliated.

Where was Leanna? The other two gave the impression they knew the answer, but Adam was damned if he was going to ask. Instead, he looked around the conference room, taking in the opulence of his new surroundings. They were in a basement room of the new house that the

Wolf Brothers had found. The room was extravagantly furnished, with smooth granite floors that shone like mirrors, crystal chandeliers hanging from the ceiling, and a grand piano in one corner. One wall held a TV screen bigger than any he had ever seen, and the wall facing him was sheer glass. Through the glass he could see an underground garage where a gleaming Aston Martin and a Bentley were parked next to the Wolf Brothers' motorbikes.

How the hell had the Wolf Brothers managed to get hold of such luxurious accommodation at short notice? It was seriously impressive, although Adam would never give Warg Daddy the satisfaction of knowing that.

He stretched his long athletic legs under the marble table and leaned back defiantly in his chair, tipping it onto two legs. He balanced there for a minute, rubbing the faint scar on his nose that marked the spot where Leanna had once bitten him into submission, back in the mountains of Romania. As he did so, Leanna made her entrance.

He jumped to his feet when he saw her, shocked by her appearance.

She was dressed immaculately in a kind of business suit, her lips bright with crimson lipstick, her long blonde hair brutally tied back and anchored in a complex twist. But the right half of her face was covered with thick bandages. She walked slowly, one hand against the wall for support, her steps slow and uncertain. Even Warg Daddy looked appalled by the sight of her, and Snakebite got out of his chair and took a step toward her.

She raised a blistered and reddened hand to stop him. 'I don't need help,' she snapped. 'I can manage by myself.' Slowly she made her way to the head of the table and sat down.

'Oh my God,' said Adam. 'What happened to you?'

She said nothing in reply, but fixed him coldly with one blue eye. The other eye was hidden by the cloth that bound her head.

'What happened?' he repeated. 'That looks like a chemical burn. Do you need medical treatment? You look like you ought to be in a hospital.'

'Don't be a fool, Adam,' she snapped, her voice as cold as ice. 'I can't go to a hospital. I treated myself perfectly well, as you can see.'

'But, what –'

She cut him off before he could ask his question a third time. 'I don't want to talk about it. It doesn't concern you. We have other matters to discuss.'

He stared back insolently. Whatever had happened to her, she clearly wasn't willing to accept any help, or even to discuss it. Adam didn't care. She could suffer in silence if she wanted to. She made him suffer enough.

Her crystal blue eye stared coldly back at him, seeming to read every thought in his head. He turned away and found that Warg Daddy and Snakebite were also staring in his direction. Dammit! It should have been him sitting in Warg Daddy's chair as Leanna's lieutenant, or better still, in charge of this entire operation. He had been one of the three original werewolves, the second in fact, after that idiot Samuel, and before Leanna herself. Now he'd been side-lined and these upstart Wolf Brothers were trying to push him further down the tree, as if they expected him to just submit to it. There was only so much humiliation that he could take.

Leanna broke the awkward silence. 'Let's get this meeting started.'

Straight to business, thought Adam grudgingly. He admired Leanna for that, at least. There was never any bullshit when she was in charge, he would be the first to admit it.

'You already know Warg Daddy of course,' she said to him. She nodded to the man at her side. 'Let me introduce Snakebite, Warg Daddy's second-in-command.' She turned to the man with the ginger beard. 'Snakebite, this is Adam Knight. He was with me in Romania, with Professor

Wiseman and Samuel Smalling.'

The red-haired monster lifted a hairy hand. 'Good to meet you, Adam. I've heard a lot about you.'

Adam glared at the hand for a moment, before reaching out to shake it. The huge fist closed tightly, almost crushing his fingers in its grip. 'Hi,' he managed.

Snakebite nodded his head, weighing the word carefully as if Adam had made some profound pronouncement, before eventually releasing his hand.

'So, Warg Daddy, you found us a house, just like I asked,' said Leanna.

Warg Daddy looked pleased with himself. 'It belongs to a Russian billionaire. It's designed to be private and secure. You've seen the size of the place. High hedges screening us from the road, underground parking, security cameras all around. The neighbouring houses are currently empty, apart from skeleton staff. This house is perfect for us.'

'What about the owner?'

'Away. The family was here for a week just before Christmas. They won't return for several months at least.'

'How do you know?' asked Adam.

'We questioned the security guard and the maid. We made sure they weren't lying.'

'What did you do with them?' asked Leanna.

'Dead. They won't be talking to anyone again.'

'Any other staff?'

'Not while the house is empty. We have the place to ourselves.'

'Good,' said Leanna. 'Excellent work, Warg Daddy. And you too, Snakebite.'

Warg Daddy's face didn't change at the praise. Snakebite's head tilted forward, almost imperceptibly.

Leanna switched her attention to Adam. 'What about you, Adam? Your job was to locate James.'

'Sure,' he said. 'I'm on to it.'

'What progress have you made?'

He shrugged. 'I watched James' house, but it's obvious

that he doesn't live there anymore. I called in, pretending to be someone who knew him, but his father said they'd heard nothing from him in weeks. He was telling the truth, I'm sure. No one has any idea where he's gone.'

He thought she would interrogate him for details, reprimand him for his lack of progress, but she simply nodded absent-mindedly and said, 'Keep watching anyway. I want him found.' It was as if she had something else on her mind, presumably whatever or whoever had caused the injury to her face.

Her next statement surprised him too. 'The purpose of this War Council is to decide our future strategy,' she announced. 'Let me hear your ideas.'

Adam blinked in astonishment. It was unlike Leanna to ask for suggestions. Usually she just gave orders. He opened his mouth to speak, but Warg Daddy beat him to it.

'We attack,' rumbled the big man. 'Hit hard. The Wolf Brothers are ready to fight. I say we pick out some key targets and take them down.'

Adam shook his head. 'The Wolf Brothers are … how many? Nine? How do you think you stand a chance against the British Army?'

Warg Daddy flexed his muscles. 'We adopt guerrilla tactics. We choose vulnerable targets, strike hard, then disappear into the night. It's like Iraq, Afghanistan. The army can't deploy heavy weapons in a city like London. We have the advantage.'

'You just don't have the numbers, or the capability,' said Adam. 'Listen, the spread of the disease is a mathematical certainty. We don't need to do anything stupid and reckless.'

'So we do nothing?' growled Warg Daddy.

'We let the condition spread naturally. Lycanthropy is like any communicable disease – once it reaches a critical point, it spreads through the population exponentially. No one can do anything to stop it. We're probably already past the tipping point already.'

'No,' said Leanna. 'The tipping point is some way off. The balance of power still lies with the humans. And now that the authorities finally understand the threat we pose, we are at our most vulnerable. This is the moment of greatest risk.'

'Right,' agreed Warg Daddy, thumping the table with his fist. 'We need to attack, now.'

'No,' said Adam in frustration. 'The police and the army already have their hands full dealing with the vigilantes and rioters. People are taking to the streets, demanding that the government does more to stop the violence. More vigilantes will come out tonight, and looters and gangs too. The authorities will crack down hard. We just need to lie low for a while and let them do our work for us.'

Leanna nodded. 'You think that civilization will begin to crumble by itself?'

'The cracks are already showing. Let's see how wide they grow.'

Warg Daddy rubbed his head. 'I think …'

Leanna cut him off abruptly. 'Don't think.' She smiled at him then, to soften the blow. White teeth between red lips. 'Leave the thinking to others.'

Snakebite had been listening in silence. Now he said, 'There's one thing I don't understand.'

'Not now, Snake,' said Warg Daddy. 'I'll explain it to you later.'

Leanna ignored Warg Daddy's comment. 'What is it you'd like to know?' she asked Snakebite.

The big man leaned forward, spreading his huge hands over the marble table. 'What causes the condition to spread? Why has it never happened before?'

'Don't ask stupid questions,' grumbled Warg Daddy. 'That's obvious.'

Leanna smiled sweetly at him. 'Perhaps you'd like to explain it then, Warg Daddy?'

He flashed an irritable look in her direction. 'It's like any disease, isn't it? Like the Black Death. It just comes from nowhere and infects everyone.'

'Yeah,' said Snakebite. 'But why? Why does that happen? Why now, and not before?'

Adam stared at the red-bearded man opposite him. It was a very good question. Simple, yet profound at the same time. And Warg Daddy clearly had no idea how epidemics worked. 'It's like this,' said Adam, finding himself eager to explain, despite his earlier misgivings about Snakebite. 'To become an epidemic, a disease has to spread easily from one person to another. Lycanthropy doesn't spread very easily at all, compared with diseases like smallpox or malaria. The genetic mutations that cause lycanthropy are carried by a virus. And that virus can only be passed on via a bite or a scratch or a blood transfusion. It can't spread through casual contact, so it's not highly contagious. That's why it's hard for a lone werewolf living in an isolated community to spread the disease without being discovered and killed. So historically all outbreaks of lycanthropy have been very limited. That's why people speak of it as a legend, rather than a known disease.'

Snakebite nodded in understanding. 'But in a big city like London …'

'That's right,' said Adam. 'In an urban setting where the population density is high and carriers of the condition can attack victims without being discovered, the condition can begin to spread. That's what's happening now, and it's why no one can stop it.'

'What about a cure?' asked Snakebite. 'Or a vaccine?'

'No vaccine or cure exists,' said Adam. 'The condition is so different from any previously known disease it will be impossible to find any effective medical intervention in a useful timeframe.'

Snakebite nodded. 'I get it now.'

Warg Daddy rubbed his bald head with his thumb. This discussion seemed to be making his head hurt. 'So what do we do?' he asked.

Leanna gave Snakebite an encouraging smile. 'I invited you to this meeting to hear your opinion,' she said.

Snakebite stroked his fiery beard thoughtfully. 'One day we will need to fight, like Warg Daddy says. But not yet.' He looked at Adam. 'But if we do nothing, the disease may not spread fast enough. There's a tipping point when the disease can no longer be stopped, but we haven't reached it yet. And so we need to spread the disease, spread it as widely and as quickly as we can.'

Warg Daddy regarded Snakebite with a puzzled frown on his face. 'How do we do that?' he asked.

Leanna twitched the corners of her mouth into a smile. Two rows of sharp white teeth poked between blood red lips. 'The fun way,' she said. Her blue eyes remained as cold as ice.

Chapter Twenty-Nine

*Upper Terrace, Richmond upon Thames,
West London, waning moon*

Melanie lay in her bed, resting on her right side. Since the madman with the cricket bat had hit her and tied her up, she had grown very used to spending her days lying in bed. At least now she was back in her own bed and was no longer tied to it. Her left side was still too sore to put any weight on it however. She breathed shallowly, trying not to move her head. If she turned it more than a fraction, the pain struck her again like a bolt of lightning.

She had slept fitfully since getting home. Sarah had given her painkillers but they only partially numbed the pain. Pale January light leaked through a gap between the curtains, and the light made her head throb. She was too weak to get out of bed and draw them closed. Even lying still doing nothing was a struggle. The pain was almost too great to master, but after a while she developed an uneasy truce. She could endure it, as long as she didn't try to open her eyes. The pain and the sunlight together were a force too strong for her.

She heard footsteps coming up the wooden stairs and tiptoeing across the landing. Someone stood outside her door. Sarah probably, come to feed her, or tend to her again. Melanie loved her sister dearly, but she hated being dependent on her. She would send Sarah away rather than admit to being helpless. She waited silently, hoping that her sister would go.

A sudden knocking on the bedroom door sounded like thunder and set her head throbbing more than ever. 'Go away,' she said, not opening her eyes. 'I don't need anything.' The knocking came again, loud and insistent. Melanie said nothing. Talking hurt too much.

The door handle turned squeakily and she felt air move as the door opened. 'Leave me alone, Sarah. I need to rest,' she said, her eyes still closed.

'It's not Sarah,' said a voice. 'It's me.'

James. What was he doing here? 'Go away,' she said. 'I'm too tired to talk.'

She heard the door close again, but James hadn't left. The floorboards creaked as he came closer to her bed. 'You're hurt,' he said.

'Tell me something I don't know.'

'No, I mean, you're injured. You're still bleeding.'

She touched her hand to her left side, where blood still trickled from her skin if she shifted suddenly. 'I'm okay. I'm healing. I just need rest.'

He came closer until his presence blocked out the light from the window. 'I can smell the blood,' he said. 'I could smell it from downstairs.'

Melanie opened her eyes slowly and looked up at him. 'That's a useful talent. Everyone should keep a tame werewolf around the home, don't you think?'

James looked hurt. 'I only want to help,' he said. 'Shall I ask Sarah to come and change the dressing?'

'No,' said Melanie. 'I can't stand her fussing. She just wants to help me too. I hate it.'

'She cares for you,' said James. 'She's your sister.'

'My wonderful selfless sister, always helping others. So much nicer than selfish me, don't you think?'

He sat down in a chair at her bedside. 'No, I don't think that. Why would you think it?'

'Because it's what everybody always says,' said Melanie. 'We're twins, so everyone's always comparing us. I was always the pretty one, going out and having fun. So Sarah had to be the serious one, staying in and helping others. Don't think I didn't know what they said behind my back.'

'What?' said James.

'That I'm a selfish bitch.'

'Did you hear them say that?'

'I didn't need to. I know it's true.'

'You can't just hide away up here forever,' he said.

'Don't tell me what I can or can't do in my own house,' she snapped. 'You're a guest here, remember.' She could tell by his expression that she had stung him with her words, and that had never been her intention. The words just came out wrong sometimes. She softened her voice. 'Look at my face,' she said, holding her bruised and damaged skin up for inspection. 'How can I go out like this? Who would want to look at me now?'

'Beauty isn't just skin deep.'

'Mine is,' said Melanie stubbornly.

'There's beauty inside too. It's inside everyone.'

'No, only people like my sister have beauty on the inside. My inside is horrible and selfish. No one wants to see it. Not even me. Besides, how can I just go back to my old way of life? Look what's happening out there. The world is ending. How many men would want to go on a date with me when the world is ending?'

'Most of them, I imagine. But that isn't the point. You don't have to go back to your old way of life. You're free to do whatever you want. It's me who's the real outcast,' continued James. 'I can't ever go home, or even show my face outside. I'm a murderer. A monster. A beast. I even betrayed my own kind, so I can't go back to the other werewolves. Not that I'd want to. They were all horrible. Apart from Samuel, you're the only person who's ever accepted me for what I am.'

'And Sarah too. Never forget about good old Sarah.'

'She doesn't know I'm a werewolf.'

'Don't tell her. She's scared enough of you already.'

'I know. I'm trying to keep out of her way.'

'That's a good idea. Let's all keep out of each other's way. We're all broken people in this house. A selfish bitch, a woman who's terrified of strangers, a grieving werewolf, and an old man who can barely remember his own name. I would laugh if it didn't hurt so much.'

James ignored her. 'You don't have to stay broken,' he said. 'You made me a promise.'

'A promise?'

'When I rescued you from that madman, you promised to become a better person, to put other people first.'

Melanie scowled at him for reminding her. 'You tricked me into making that promise. I thought it was a dream. I thought I was talking to my own conscience.'

'I didn't trick you. You fooled yourself.'

'I'd have said anything to stop a wolf from killing me.'

James seemed hurt by the reminder that he had nearly killed her. 'It was more than that,' he insisted. 'You meant something. And a promise is a promise.'

'Words mean nothing,' said Melanie. 'They're just hot air. Anyone can say them.' But she was fooling herself again now. She had meant her promise, and they both knew it.

James said nothing, but got up from the chair, letting the light from the window fall on her face again.

She closed her eyes to block out the pain.

He walked quietly to the bedroom door and opened it. Before the door closed, she heard him say, 'You *can* change. You must. For your own sake. For all our sakes.'

Chapter Thirty

West Field Gardens, South London, waning moon

'Do you like this dress best, or the other one?' asked Aasha.

'This one,' said Drake. He lounged back on her bed, his aching shoulder supported by pillows, enjoying the smell of her perfume, admiring the amount of smooth coffee-coloured skin her dress revealed. His knowledge of women's fashion was close to zero, but that didn't stop him having a strong opinion about which dress she should wear. The rule was simple. The more flesh on display, the better. He didn't understand why girls had to think so hard about it.

Aasha admired her looks in the mirror. She turned one way, then the other, then back again, flicking her glossy black hair over her bare shoulders. She seemed to enjoy looking at her body just as much as he did. 'Why do you prefer this dress?' she asked.

There was a trap in the question, Drake could sense it. 'It makes you look beautiful,' he said.

'And the other one doesn't?' she asked mischievously.

'This one makes you look even more beautiful.'

Aasha laughed. 'You just like the way it shows off my cleavage.'

'Yeah,' he admitted. 'Why wouldn't I?'

'You're a bad boy,' she teased. 'And I'm a nice Sikh girl from a good family. I shouldn't allow you into my bedroom. I'm afraid of what you might do to me.'

'What would you like me to do?'

'I'll tell you,' she said, coming closer to the bed. She leaned over him, letting him see even more of her body. 'I want you to take me out tonight.'

'What?' said Drake. That hadn't been what he'd expected, but since he'd started to spend time in Aasha's company he was learning to expect the unexpected.

'I hate being cooped up in this house. I want to wear this dress somewhere fun. I want to go out and have a good time, not hang around here.'

'I can show you a good time right here,' he said, reaching out to touch her.

She slapped his hand away.

'Ouch,' he cried. Her slap had actually hurt him. 'Mind my bad arm.'

Aasha ignored his complaint. 'It's time we had a night out. Just you and me.'

'You know what your mum said,' said Drake warily. 'You're grounded. No way is she going to let you come out with me.'

'I thought you were a bad boy,' said Aasha. 'Not a goody-goody like my little brother.'

'I am,' he said.

'Well then,' said Aasha, as if that settled things. 'I'll sneak out without my mum knowing. Vijay can cover for me if she asks. She always believes everything he says.'

'Where do you want to go?'

'Somewhere I can wear this dress.' She walked over to her dressing table and opened a box. Her slender fingers drew out a pair of gold earrings, and she put them on. 'Do these go with the dress?'

He shrugged. 'Yeah, sure,' he said. 'They're nice.'

'They aren't really,' said Aasha. 'They're just cheap junk. A real boyfriend would buy his girlfriend nice stuff. Expensive stuff.'

Drake sighed. 'You know I ain't got much money.'

'Not much of a boyfriend then, are you? A real boyfriend would get some money. From somewhere.'

'Where from?'

'From wherever he could grab it.'

Drake turned away from her in dismay. Being with Aasha was the most exciting experience of his life, but she was always pushing him, pushing him further than he wanted to go. Sometimes he felt like he should turn his back on her and run far away. But how could he do that? How could he run away from such intoxicating beauty? This must be what the songs talked about when they said that love hurt. He had never really understood that before.

'What's wrong?' demanded Aasha, her hands on her wide hips. 'Not scared are you?'

'No.'

'You are scared. You're like my kid brother. He's scared of everything.'

'I'm not.'

'You are. You're just a kid like him. I'm two years older than you, I should never have agreed to be your girlfriend.'

Drake got to his feet, a mix of fear and anger animating him. He stood tall, towering several inches over her, even though she wore heels. 'I'm nothing like Vijay! I'm taller than you. And stronger too.' He gripped her arms tightly with his hands, ignoring the pain in his injured shoulder. He had to suppress a strong desire to slap the stupid cow, to teach her a lesson.

Aasha seemed to sense his desire. She raised her face to

his. Her eyes shone. 'Big strong boy. Are you gonna hit me then?' She turned her cheek toward him. 'Slap my face. Or are you too scared even to hit a girl?'

He released her from his grip and stood confused. 'I ain't gonna hit you,' he said, his hands by his side.

'Then steal for me, instead. Prove you're not afraid of anything. Show me how bad you can be, and I'll show you just how good I can be.'

Chapter Thirty-One

King's College Hospital, Lambeth, South London, waning moon

Chanita knocked nervously on the door of the Medical Director, Doctor Brookes. This was going to be a tough encounter, but she had never shied away from difficult conversations. Years spent working as a nurse in the hospital's Emergency Department had given her plenty of practice at delivering unwanted messages.

She had no doubt that Doctor Brookes would be reluctant to hear what she had to say. He would probably try to placate her with empty words, but Chanita was resolved to stay until he agreed to take action.

She blamed the Medical Director for the death of Doctor Kapoor. She was missing Doctor Kapoor terribly. He had been a fine doctor and a man of great principle. The two of them had forged a strong bond. Now he was gone, and she felt that a part of her had been taken with him. If only Doctor Brookes had agreed to Doctor

Kapoor's request for additional resources, he might never have been attacked and killed by that patient.

To his credit, the Medical Director had acted swiftly and decisively following Doctor Kapoor's death. It was obvious that the Emergency Department had been operating well beyond its capacity. Doctor Brookes had brought in extra resources from other departments, cancelled non-urgent operations, and established a ward dedicated entirely to bite and scratch cases. Immediately after the New Year's Eve chaos, he'd declared a Black Alert, meaning that no more emergency beds were available. Anything that wasn't a Level 1 trauma – wolf bites, gunshot wounds, car crashes, and so on – was being rerouted to one of the city's other hospitals, and that had taken some of the immediate pressure off the department.

He'd gathered a specialist team of nurses too, and put Chanita in charge of them. That had led to some resentment, as Chanita wasn't the most senior nurse on the team. But she was the one with most hands-on experience of the syndrome. That's what they were calling it now. Not a disease, but a syndrome. No one knew exactly what it was, or where it had come from. But they knew what it could do.

But the Medical Director still hadn't gone far enough. Doctor Kapoor wasn't the only person in the hospital to have been attacked by one of the bite patients. And there were rumours that several of the treated patients had run amok after being discharged, attacking and biting victims themselves. The practice of discharging patients back into the community would have to stop, but Chanita couldn't make that call. She didn't even know if the hospital had the authority to detain people against their will. Only Doctor Brookes could make the necessary decision. She had spent the past hour assembling a case for detaining all treated bite patients in indefinite quarantine, and had rehearsed her argument a dozen times. She knew she was right. She just needed to convince the doctor.

She knocked again on the door, louder this time.

'Come in,' said a gruff voice.

She took a deep breath and smoothed down her uniform before entering the Medical Director's office.

Doctor Brookes sat in his usual place behind his desk, his thinning hair looking greyer than ever, his face white and lined with fatigue. Opposite him sat a man in military uniform. The stranger was much younger than Doctor Brookes, very tall and slim but with broad shoulders. His skin was tanned but smooth, framed by short, silver-blonde hair. What most caught Chanita's attention though was his sapphire blue eyes, and she found herself staring into his face, her jaw slack, her well-rehearsed argument temporarily forgotten.

The man's mouth suggested amusement at her startled look, and he jumped to his feet with a fluid, easy movement and half-bowed to her, like a knight to a lady.

Doctor Brookes looked at her grimly, as if he had just received terrible news. 'Chanita, I'm in the middle of a meeting with Colonel Griffin.'

The Colonel waived the doctor's objection aside. 'I think we'd just about finished here, Doctor Brookes. In fact Chanita was the next person I intended to speak to. Why don't we tell her the news right away? We can wrap up any outstanding business later.'

Doctor Brookes indicated for her to sit. It seemed like he had very little choice in the matter. 'Colonel Griffin has just been appointed as the hospital's new Medical Director,' he explained. He held up a sheet of paper. 'The Prime Minister herself has appointed him to this role.'

Chanita raised her eyebrows. 'Medical Director for the Emergency Department?' That would mean that Doctor Brookes would lose his role.

'For the entire hospital,' said the doctor, as if he could only half believe what he was saying. 'It seems that from now on this hospital will treat bite and scratch cases only. All other patients will be transferred to other hospitals, or discharged.'

'This is a temporary measure,' said Colonel Griffin. 'Just as long as the current emergency continues. Afterwards, everything will return to normal, and I will be gone.' He smiled at Chanita, a sparkle in his blue eyes.

The smile encouraged her to be brave. 'A soldier as Medical Director?' she enquired. 'A curious appointment.'

The Colonel laughed. 'I thought so too, but these are strange times, are they not?'

She nodded. 'So the entire hospital is to become a centre for treating the syndrome? Do you plan to bring patients here from other hospitals too?'

'That's right. We'll establish a specialist centre of expertise, building on the success of your team here.'

Chanita hesitated. This was the moment for her to argue her case. 'We've had some limited success in treating the patients,' she admitted. 'But we don't yet have a cure. We don't even have a definitive test for the disease. We can't be sure that the patients we discharge are fully recovered.'

'Go on.'

'So can I ask what you plan to do with the patients after they've been treated?'

'What do *you* think we should do?' asked the Colonel, watching her face closely.

'Keep them here,' said Chanita quickly. 'In quarantine. It's too dangerous to let them leave until we understand more about how the condition evolves and spreads.'

Doctor Brookes frowned. 'I don't think that's feasible, Chanita. Resources are already stretched to breaking point. And this is a hospital, not a prison.'

But the Colonel was studying her intently. 'Your concern is that discharged patients might spread the disease among the population?' he asked.

'Precisely.'

Colonel Griffin gave her another of his smiles. 'My thinking exactly. Until we fully understand the nature of this new syndrome and its infection pathways, our only hope of containment is to make this hospital into a secure quarantine facility and establish strict biosafety conditions. If we can contain the disease sufficiently we might even be able to stop its spread without any further action.'

Doctor Brookes protested. 'You can't simply keep patients in the hospital against their will.'

'Actually,' said the Colonel, 'with the emergency powers I've been granted by the Prime Minister, I think I can. In fact, I think that's precisely why she put me here.'

Chapter Thirty-Two

Brixton Village, South London, waning moon

Salma Ali was pleased with the way the night patrol had arrested the ram raiders on the first night of the Watch. 'You did very well,' she said to Ben and Mr Stewart the following morning. 'You kept our community safe from harm.'

Ben felt awkward accepting her praise. He had kept waking during the night, wondering if he had done the right thing. Should he have called the police instead of getting involved in the fight? Or should he have joined in sooner? Above all, should he have agreed to carry a knife? 'I'm still not sure if we did the right thing,' he said. 'Maybe we should leave this in the hands of the police. They turned up quickly enough last night.'

'You think so?' sneered Mr Stewart. 'If we hadn't acted when we did, those thieves might have got away.'

'Perhaps,' admitted Ben. 'Still, one of those men ended

up with a broken arm. How can that be right?'

'One thing I've learned during my years as a lawyer,' said Salma Ali, 'is that there's really no such thing as right or wrong. There's only win or lose.' She smiled at Ben engagingly. 'Anyway,' she continued, before he could respond, 'today I have a completely different task for you both. One that won't involve any kind of violence. It's clear that in order to help our community we need to find out more about our residents – names, addresses, telephone numbers and so on. I'd like you both to go door-to-door, asking people to complete one of these forms.' She picked up a neatly-stacked pile of paper from her table and handed them to Ben. 'With this information we'll be able to plan better, whatever happens in the days to come.'

'What are you expecting to happen?' he asked.

'I really don't know, Ben. But we have to prepare for the worst. You know yourself just how stretched police resources are at present. My contacts in the criminal justice world tell me that under the new emergency powers introduced by the government, the police will be responding only to the highest priority situations, and will be aiming simply to arrest suspected criminals and put them into custody. The normal judicial processes have been suspended. That means we're largely on our own as far as day-to-day law enforcement goes. And that makes the role of the Neighbourhood Watch even more vital.'

He studied the printed forms she had given him. 'There are a lot of questions here,' he remarked.

'That's right. We need to find out how many people are in each house, get a list of their names, how old they are, if they have any special needs, whether they go out to work, or whatever.'

'Why do you need all that information?'

'So we can do our job better. The more we know about our neighbours, the more we can help them.'

'What if people don't want to give us this kind of

information?'

'Then maybe we can't help them so much. We only have limited amounts of manpower, time and other resources available to us. If people won't give us what we want, maybe we can't give them what they want.'

'You're saying you'll refuse to help people if they won't fill in these forms?'

She smiled at him again. 'No, of course not. But we can only operate effectively and efficiently if we have the right information.'

'We're supposed to be helping people, not spying on them.'

'We are helping them, Ben.'

'But you don't deny you're spying on them too?'

She sighed. 'We're not doing anything illegal, Ben. We're just watching to make sure everyone's safe. That's what the Neighbourhood Watch scheme is all about.'

'What if I don't want to join in with your scheme?'

She held up her hands. 'It's your choice. I can't force you. But it won't be me you're letting down. It'll be your neighbours. The young, the sick, the elderly. They're the ones who need your help, Ben. They really do.'

Mr Stewart was pacing the room impatiently. 'Can we just get on with it? Or is mister smug teacher going to skip this job too?'

'I didn't skip any job,' snapped Ben. 'Don't ever suggest I did.'

'Please, gentlemen,' interjected Salma Ali. 'Let's all work together on this.'

Ben glared at the other man. 'Come on then,' he said. 'Let's get on with it.'

As soon as they were outside, Mr Stewart said, 'I don't know what you're so fussed about. I'd have thought this job would be just right for you.'

'How do you mean?' asked Ben.

'Nice easy work, filling out forms. That's the kind of thing teachers are good at, isn't it?'

'What is your problem with teachers?'

Mr Stewart shrugged. 'Let's just say I don't have many fond memories of my school days.'

'That's hardly my fault,' said Ben. 'Maybe you should have made more of the opportunities. Anyway, what do you do for a living?'

'What difference does it make?' demanded the other man.

Ben wanted to shake him in frustration. 'None,' he said. 'I don't actually care what you do. I was just being polite, but I don't know why I bothered.'

'Being polite won't help you next time we get into a fight,' sneered Mr Stewart.

'Right,' said Ben angrily. 'Have it your way.' He had been about to suggest they call each other by their Christian names. All this *Mr Stewart, Mr Harvey* nonsense was starting to irritate him. But it seemed that the other man was simply going to rebuff any attempt at friendship.

He walked crossly up to the nearest house and rang the doorbell.

An elderly woman answered the door and seemed pleased to have visitors. 'Come in,' she said. 'I don't often have such nice-looking young men call at my door.'

'We can't stop,' said Ben apologetically. 'We have the whole street to cover. Can we leave this form with you and call back later? If you have any problems answering the questions, we can help you when we come back.'

The next few houses were straightforward too. Once Ben explained who they were and what they were doing, people seemed happy to help. They were also keen to find out if he had any news for them, but he didn't really know anything they hadn't already seen on the TV themselves.

The next door was answered by a middle-aged man wearing casual trousers and a shirt. He gazed suspiciously at the two men on his doorstep. 'How can I help you?' he asked.

'Hi,' said Ben. 'We're from the Neighbourhood Watch

scheme. We're just conducting a preliminary assessment of the local community, and we'd be grateful if you could fill in this form with your personal details.'

The man took the form and studied it carefully. He frowned. 'Why do you need this information?'

'We're trying to build a snapshot of the local area,' explained Ben. 'We need to find out who lives where, who needs help, who has skills that we can use, that kind of thing.'

The man began to read some of the questions aloud. 'Medical conditions? Ethnicity? Religion? Why would you possibly need to know my religion?'

Ben hesitated. He had wondered the same thing when he'd first read the questionnaire. 'Look,' he said. 'Just answer the questions you feel comfortable with. Leave any that you'd rather not answer.'

'I don't feel comfortable with any of these questions. I don't even know who you really are. Show me your ID.'

'I'm sorry,' said Ben. 'We don't have ID cards. Only the Neighbourhood Watch coordinator holds an ID card. She's been authorized by the police. In fact she's a lawyer. Do you know her? Salma Ali. She lives just a few doors down.'

'Why don't you send her round then?' suggested the man.

'Well perhaps we will,' replied Ben. He would be quite happy to pass all the grumpy neighbours to Salma Ali to deal with.

Mr Stewart wasn't so easily deflected however. 'Hey,' he said, taking a step toward the man. 'It's only a piece of paper. Why don't you just do what we asked?'

'I beg your pardon?' said the man. 'What are you, some kind of private militia?'

Ben opened his mouth to soothe the situation, but Mr Stewart pushed past him. He advanced aggressively until he was staring the homeowner in the face. 'Look, we're here to protect the community, and we're just asking for a little information. We can't force you to cooperate with us, but if you've got something to hide, we can draw our own conclusions.'

'I can hide whatever I like from you,' said the other man, raising his voice in anger. 'You have no authority to poke into people's private lives. But if you claim to be making the area safe, let me tell you that my daughter has been attacked three times in as many weeks, and you clowns have been entirely useless in protecting her.'

'Mr Harvey?' said a voice from inside the house. 'Is that you?' A teenage girl appeared behind the man. Ben recognized her immediately. Her bright red hair and pale, freckled face seemed to light up the dim hallway.

'Rose?' he said. 'Rose Hallibury?'

The man in the doorway – Rose's father presumably – turned to her in surprise. 'Do you know these men?'

'I know one of them,' said Rose. 'It's Mr Harvey, the teacher from school.'

'The one who rescued you from the headmaster?'

She nodded.

Her father turned back to face Ben. The anger that had animated his face had gone. 'I owe you an apology, Mr Harvey. If you'd said who you were …'

'You know these people?' interrupted Mr Stewart. He seemed put out that he'd been robbed of his opportunity for a confrontation.

'I know them,' confirmed Ben, relieved that Rose's appearance had calmed the situation down so quickly. 'Don't worry. They're with us.' That seemed to placate Mr Stewart, but Ben felt a cold wave creeping up the back of his neck. It had come to this, already. People were with you, or they were against you.

'I'm Richard Hallibury,' said the man. 'Rose's father.' He reached out a hand to shake Ben's.

Ben seized it gladly. 'Ben Harvey. Pleased to meet you.' He turned his attention back to Rose. 'How are you?' he asked.

'I'm good,' she said. 'What about you? I didn't see you after the police took Mr Canning away from school. Did you have to go to the hospital?'

'Just for a few hours,' said Ben. 'I'm fine now.' He didn't mention the killer headaches and the lingering effects of concussion. He hoped that the stitches in his forehead wouldn't give him away.

Another person appeared in the hallway behind Rose. A younger boy, in a wheelchair. 'What's up?' he asked.

'It's Mr Harvey from school,' said Rose. 'He's in the Neighbourhood Watch now.'

'Cool,' said the boy. 'Is that like the vigilantes?'

'No,' said Ben firmly. 'Absolutely not.' But the question had shone a spotlight right at the heart of his concerns.

Chapter Thirty-Three

King's College Hospital, Lambeth, South London, waning moon

Colonel Griffin wasted no time in establishing his authority in the hospital. Within an hour of his arrival he had called for a general meeting of all staff, and Chanita was eager to hear what he had to say. Change certainly needed to happen, and from what she had seen already, the Colonel wouldn't shy away from the tasks that needed to be done.

The rumour mill in the corridors and staff rooms was operating at fever pitch, and the announcement that a military man had replaced Doctor Brookes as Medical Director was generally going down badly. From anaesthetists and surgeons down through nurses, porters and even the catering staff, everyone Chanita spoke to had severe misgivings. The Colonel would face a tough time winning them over, but she already knew that she would give him her full support. She wondered if the Colonel would be able to work the same magic that he had already used to win her around.

They gathered together in the hospital's dining room at noon, as requested. The atmosphere in the hall was rebellious. Nurses grumbled about being taken away from their patients, and one junior doctor wondered aloud if the new man would have them all marching up and down and saluting.

Colonel Griffin entered the room at twelve o'clock precisely and bounded up onto a dining table to address his audience. He stood confidently, wearing the trace of a smile, looking around the hall in a relaxed manner, quite unlike the overbearing warrior-figure that many had dreaded. Chanita could tell from the reaction of those closest to her that the new arrival's youthful good looks were already creating a strong impression. The mood in the hall had shifted even before the new Medical Director had opened his mouth.

The Colonel wasted no time getting to the point. 'Hello, my name is Colonel Griffin, and I'm replacing Doctor Brookes as Medical Director with immediate effect. I know what you're all thinking. Who the hell is this guy dropping in and taking over? Am I right?'

A murmur of agreement rumbled through the hall, and Chanita detected some anger in the crowd.

'I see some of you staring at my uniform, and not liking what you see,' he continued. 'Well, underneath this uniform you'll find a medic. I'm a doctor first, a soldier second. My job isn't to tell you what to do. It's to give you the tools and facilities you need to carry on doing the job you're already doing. I'm here to empower you, so that you can get on with what you do best. Treat patients. Make people better. I'm going to be listening a lot more than talking, and you can come and see me any time. Bring me problems, suggestions, questions. I want to hear what everyone has to say, and I don't want to get in the way.'

The doctor paused to scan the faces in the hall. 'But

there are going to be changes,' he said. 'The main change is that this hospital will become London's dedicated centre for treating bite and scratch victims. All cases of the new syndrome, or anyone showing symptoms, will be brought here for treatment. Secondly, I will be imposing strict quarantine conditions. That means that no one will leave the hospital – patients or staff – until the current crisis is over. Let me repeat that, in case there are any doubts – starting today, no one will leave the building for any reason, until I declare an end to the quarantine.'

Now the anger in the crowd bubbled over. Doctors and nurses began shouting in protest.

The Colonel calmed the protests with his hands. 'In view of this, only those staff who wish to volunteer their services will be asked to remain. Anyone who wishes to transfer to other hospitals will be free to leave. But those who agree to stay must comply with the quarantine rules. That means they will sleep, eat and work at the hospital until I deem it is safe for them to go home. I understand that this is a lot to ask, but I would like you to make your decision within the next hour, so that we can implement the necessary biosafety protocols as soon as possible.'

Chanita scanned the faces of the doctors and nurses around her. It was hard to say how they felt about the prospect of indefinite confinement within the hospital, but the anger and resentment she had detected earlier seemed to have dissipated.

The Colonel began to speak once more. 'I've worked in civilian hospitals, just like this one, and in field hospitals in the middle of conflict zones. Believe me when I say that the way the current situation is developing, this hospital is going to be in the middle of a new battleground. Events like the recent rioting will be the new normal, and we need to be ready to deal with that. But don't worry. To relieve pressure, all patients not suffering from bites or scratches will be transferred to other hospitals. Our focus here will be entirely on treating and caring for patients with the new condition. And to keep the hospital safe and secure, soldiers will be brought in to provide round-the-clock protection.'

Colonel Griffin softened his last pronouncement with a boyish grin and a flash of his blue eyes. 'I'm going to stop talking now and let you get back to your work. Anyone who wants to leave, please be sure to be out of the hospital before the quarantine begins in one hour. Those who wish to stay, I'm happy to welcome you aboard.'

Chapter Thirty-Four

*Upper Terrace, Richmond upon Thames,
West London, waning moon*

Thousands of people were marching across Grandpa's television screen, chanting and waving banners, and he scowled at them in annoyance.

Sarah did her best to soothe him. 'Look at all those people, Grandpa. They're marching in Trafalgar Square.'

It was a beautiful sight. The buildings around the perimeter of the Square shone brightly in the dim light of the winter afternoon, and an enormous Christmas tree stood at the centre of the Square, almost as tall as the stone pillar of Nelson's Column. The carved features of the Admiral himself stared down at the people milling below, many of them carrying burning candles as if they might suddenly start singing Christmas carols.

'Do you remember taking me and Melanie to Trafalgar Square when we were little girls?' she asked, hoping to stir some kind of memory in the old man. 'You showed us the paintings in the National Gallery, and we ate sandwiches by the fountains next to Nelson's Column.'

'I remember,' said Grandpa. 'Melanie was always such a pretty little girl.'

'Yes, she was,' agreed Sarah. Everyone had always said so, for as long as she could remember. They never said the same about Sarah. They looked for other words. *Clever. Polite. Well-behaved.* Never pretty. Sarah would have given anything to be pretty like her sister, instead of polite and well-behaved or even clever, but nothing she did with her hair or her clothes made any difference. She would never be a pretty girl.

'Look at them,' complained Grandpa from his bed. 'Long-haired hooligans and trouble-makers, the lot of them. Don't they know there's a war on?'

'It's not a war, Grandpa,' said Sarah patiently. 'It's a national emergency.' That's what the Prime Minister had said when asked, and that was still the official position, although it was beginning to feel rather like wartime with the overnight curfew in place and soldiers establishing checkpoints all around the city.

'What are the soldiers doing, then?' asked Grandpa. 'There must be a war, if there are soldiers on the streets.'

'The soldiers are there to keep order,' she explained. 'That's why the people are marching. They're protesting against the soldiers and the midnight curfew. They're going to defy the curfew and occupy the Square all night.'

'They should learn to be more grateful,' said Grandpa.

The TV was on permanently now in Grandpa's room, and Sarah controlled the remote. She flipped between the various news channels, always seeking out some new nugget of information, some interview she hadn't already watched a dozen times, some clue that the nightmare might be coming to an end. But at every bulletin, the news remained the same, or took a turn for the worse.

She flicked through a few channels now to see if she'd missed anything, but the protest in Trafalgar Square was the main item of interest. When she switched back to the live broadcast she saw that a group of young men and women had climbed atop the great bronze lions that flanked the base of Nelson's Column. They unfurled banners that read *End the curfew* and *Impeach the Prime Minister*.

The camera zoomed in on the protesters. Guy Fawkes masks covered their faces, and they held flaming torches that spluttered brightly in the late afternoon shadow that had fallen across the Square. The protesters shook their fists and punched the air, shouting their slogans amidst the din of the crowd.

The TV switched to another camera angle, showing a line of police officers struggling to contain the protesters as they surged in a wave, pushing against riot shields and shouting into the faces of the officers. The police stood their ground, faces grim, arms linked to hold back the mass of the crowd.

'I don't think they're going to be able to hold their position much longer,' said the correspondent on the scene. 'After the scenes of carnage on New Year's Eve, the Police Commissioner has vowed to act with restraint and to permit peaceful demonstrations, but the marchers are taunting the police and trying to provoke them into action. There's a significant hardcore of protesters here, seeking violent confrontation with the authorities.'

As Sarah watched, bottles and other missiles began to appear in the air above the masses in the Square. Some landed behind the police line, some crashed into riot shields. One hit a young woman in the face, and the camera switched eagerly to show the blood running from a gash in her forehead. The crowd was pushing violently now, struggling to force a gap in the police line and break through. Voices began to chant, 'End the curfew,' as the disorder grew.

'Disgusting,' said Grandpa from his bed. 'They should shoot the lot of them.'

More bottles flew through the air, and this time they were joined by flaming torches too. A burning bottle struck the ground behind the police line and a sheet of flame swept across the flagstones, setting fire to the clothing of the nearest officers.

The police line broke in an instant and the crowd surged forward like water flooding a breached dam. Within a minute the Square had descended into chaos, with masked and hooded figures running everywhere, kicking and striking at the police from all directions. The rhythmic chanting of protest had switched to battle shouts and cries.

'Oh no, look at the tree,' said the reporter on the ground, and the image switched to the giant Christmas tree that stood in the middle of the Square. The tree must have been a hundred feet tall, decorated from top to bottom with bright ropes of light, and crowned with a star. A group of men stood at its base, pushing at the trunk. The tree tipped from side to side as the men heaved. With each sway, the bright star at its tip swung further. Eventually the tree leaned far over to the side and didn't stop. The star crashed to the ground like a shooting star, bringing the mass of the tree with it, clearing a wide arc of people who just managed to jump clear in time. The lights of the tree went out with a loud pop and the Square grew abruptly darker.

Sarah looked on, transfixed. There was a beauty to the scene, an order amidst the mayhem. Viewed from afar the people were like ants, all individuality removed. They danced together in a complicated waltz, spontaneous patterns emerging from out of the pandemonium. The dancers shifted and the patterns broke up, only to be replaced by new and ever more complex structures. Bursts of light flickered on and off, like a coded message.

The camera zoomed in again and the illusion was shattered. At close quarters there was no dance, no pattern and no beauty; only anger, violence and bloodshed. The police had pulled back into a tight circle, closing ranks to protect each other, but some had stumbled and fallen. The crowd swept over the fallen officers, crushing them underfoot without pity or mercy. Those who remained on their feet struck at their opponents with batons and shields. The protesters fought back with baseball bats and other improvised weapons. Burning missiles flew through the air, spreading orange fireballs wherever they landed.

Afternoon shadow had given away to nightfall now, and the glow of burning fires and torches studded the Square like a candlelit vigil.

Suddenly a crackle of gunshots cut across the noise of the fighting. The voice of a reporter could be heard, yelling into his microphone. 'Did you hear that? Can you hear it? I don't know where it's coming from.'

The scene switched to an overhead view from a moving helicopter. The camera swung widely, the light was poor, but there was no mistaking what was happening.

'The army seems to be moving into the Square from all sides,' said the anchorman back in the studio. 'Soldiers are advancing from all directions. They're firing into the air.'

A few warning shots had been fired, but as Sarah watched, the protesters rushed forward in response, hurling missiles at the soldiers, attacking them with a variety of weapons. The soldiers held their ground, but the crowd had become a mob. More petrol bombs exploded and suddenly the troops were firing again. This time their rifles were turned on the crowd. Guns fired indiscriminately as the soldiers fought for their lives. Protesters fell to the ground and lay still, apparently dead.

Abruptly the scene switched back to the studio and the shocked face of the anchorman. The reporter's voice continued to relay the news from the scene. 'The soldiers have come under attack and are moving forward in response, firing at close quarters. The number of casualties on both sides is growing by the second. I can't believe this is happening.'

The scene switched again to show crowds of

bystanders rushing from the Square in panic.

'Turn it off,' said Grandpa. 'I'm tired of this show. When can I have my usual shows back again?'

Sarah gripped his hand tightly. 'I don't know, Grandpa. I don't know if they're ever coming back.' She pressed the mute button on the remote control and they continued to watch in silence. It was easier that way.

Chapter Thirty-Five

Brixton Village, South London, waning moon

When Ben and Mr Stewart had finished their round of the area, they returned to Salma Ali's house with the completed questionnaires. 'This is what we managed to get,' said Ben, handing the pile of papers over to her. 'Some people were out, and a few refused to cooperate.'

'That's to be expected,' she said. 'I'll try again myself with the difficult ones. I find that I can usually persuade people to do what I want without too much trouble.'

'Good,' said Ben. From what he'd seen of Salma Ali's persuasive skills he didn't doubt it for one moment.

'Well,' said Mr Stewart, 'I'll be off then. I'm on patrol again tonight.'

'Thank you for your hard work, Mr Stewart,' said Salma Ali. 'Ben, would you mind staying on? I have something to say to you.'

'Sure,' he said. 'But I need to get ready for the night patrol too.'

'Don't worry about that,' said Salma, smiling. 'I have something else in mind for you.' She waited until Mr Stewart had left, then laid a delicate hand on Ben's arm. 'Please take a seat.'

He sat down awkwardly. Salma Ali was a very pretty woman, but if she was about to suggest anything of a personal nature, he wasn't sure that he was ready for a new relationship. He still hadn't got over the last woman he'd dated, and wasn't sure if he ever would. Women like Melanie Margolis were few and far between. In fact, now he thought of it, there was no woman quite like Melanie.

Salma seemed to have anticipated his thought process. 'Don't worry,' she told him. 'I'm not about to seduce you, despite the fact that you're a very attractive man.' She grinned impishly at him. 'I can tell that you're a little nervous around me. I'm used to that. Most men still aren't comfortable with powerful women getting what they want. But I can assure you that I never allow my personal feelings to intrude into the workplace.'

'Okay,' said Ben, relieved. 'What then?'

She leaned back in her chair. 'One of my little birds told me how you'd diffused an awkward situation today. A situation that could very easily have become violent, or so I'm told.'

He wondered who her little bird might be, and how many of them she had. 'Mr Stewart and one of the residents had a disagreement about the questionnaires,' he said. 'That's all.'

'And you expertly calmed both sides.'

'I didn't really do much,' said Ben. 'It turned out that I knew the girl who lived there, and she recognized me.'

'The girl you so bravely rescued from the killer headmaster,' continued Salma Ali. 'And there's no need for you to be modest. You've proved your worth on several occasions already. I can't ignore your talents any longer.'

He started to say again that it had been nothing, but she held up her hand to stop him. 'No false modesty, please. The fact is I need people like you, Ben. I need all kinds of people. Even goons like Mr Stewart have a part to play. But people like you are rare. There's a lot to organize if we're going to keep our residents safe in the coming days and weeks. Most people don't know the half of it. The news isn't reporting what's going on behind the scenes. My contacts in the police and in local government are telling me what's really happening out there. It's going to get a lot worse, Ben. A lot worse. We need to prepare for total war.'

'Total war?' said Ben, raising his eyebrows. 'That's an exaggeration, surely?'

She shook her head. 'Already the police have pulled out of most day-to-day policing. They're no longer working to bring criminals to justice. They only have the resources to react to the worst of the violence. People are being locked up and held without trial, without even proper legal representation. The army is handling the most serious violence and disorder, but to do that the soldiers are putting up roadblocks, shutting down whole parts of the city. There's been serious violence in Trafalgar Square this evening apparently. People are staying home from work and the economy's already starting to crash. In a matter of days, food and other essential supplies will begin to run out. That's why I asked you to gather the questionnaires today. We'll need to coordinate with people like Mr Kowalski, to help maintain the supply of food, medicine and other essentials. To do that we need to move beyond just running night patrols, and start being pro-active. That's a lot of work, some of it dangerous. We'll be competing with other groups to get hold of the necessary supplies. I need a deputy to help me, Ben, and I want that to be you. What do you say?'

Chapter Thirty-Six

The Tarnished Spoon, South London, waning moon

No one would ever claim that The Tarnished Spoon was the finest pub in London, but it had suited Warg Daddy well enough over the years. Beer was beer, after all, and the Spoon's landlord was always happy to take money from hairy bikers, even if they got a bit rowdy on a Friday night. He was happy to take money from anyone in fact. Money was money, there was no denying it.

On a hot summer's night, the pub's back yard was a pleasant place to sit and drink and watch the sun go down, but in January no one sat outside, especially on a night like tonight when the mist was rolling in from the river, and the wooden benches out back dripped with cold droplets of water. Still, it was a good place to wait, especially now that Warg Daddy had no use for beer. The only drink that passed his lips these days was the slick elixir of human blood.

Light and noise spilled out into the yard as the back door of the pub opened, and a man reeled out, clutching a beer bottle in his fist. Warg Daddy recognized him immediately. It was Weasel, one of the Spoon's regulars, and he owed Warg Daddy beer money. There was little chance of that debt being repaid. Weasel never had any money, unless someone had taken pity and lent him some. But maybe Weasel could pay his dues another way. Leanna wanted the condition spread as widely as possible, and even low-life scum like Weasel were good enough for biting.

The man clutched at a wooden table to steady himself as he lurched out into the cold air, his feet crossing under him to almost trip him up. He gripped the table tightly to steady himself before bringing his attention to focus on Warg Daddy standing at the nearby bench. Behind him, the door of the pub swung closed, sealing the sounds of laughter and music inside. A hush descended on the yard.

'Hey, Warg Daddy,' called Weasel, his breath forming clouds in the winter night. 'Long time, no see.' He took a swig from the bottle, but to his apparent puzzlement it was empty. He tipped the bottle upside-down to check that there was no liquid left inside, before tossing it aside with a shrug. 'Buy an old friend a drink, would you?'

Warg Daddy beckoned to him. 'Come with me,' he said quietly. 'I have something to show you.'

'Yeah? Wozat?' breathed Weasel. He rubbed his hands together and stumbled forward, following Warg Daddy into the darkened depths of the yard where the shadows waited. 'A few coins to share? Or a bottle of something to keep an old friend warm on this cold night?' He grinned hopefully, a toothless grin that did nothing for his looks.

'I wasn't thinking of that,' snarled Warg Daddy.

'No?' said Weasel, the smile dying on his lips as he noticed the Wolf Brothers lurking in the shadows. He nodded warily in their direction, greeting some by name.

'That you over there, Snakebite? And you, Slasher? Meathook, too? All the boys are here, then.'

The Brothers fanned out around him, blocking his exit.

'What you got for me then?' asked Weasel, nervously.

Warg Daddy stared at him, expressionless. 'A sack over your head,' he said. 'A rope to bind you.' The Brothers closed in on him from all sides. Snakebite showed him the cloth sack. Slasher pulled out the length of rope and twisted it in his hands, snapping it taut.

Weasel's eyes widened, taking in the implements, before roaming uneasily around the ring of men, searching for an exit. Finally he returned to Warg Daddy. 'Having a little joke with a friend, eh, Warg Daddy? No harm in a joke, I say. I likes a joke as well as the next man, that I do. No need to scare the shit out of a man, though. No need at all.'

Warg Daddy laid a firm hand on the man's collar. 'You're coming with us now, Weasel. And quietly, with no bother. It'll be better that way.'

Bring them to me unharmed, Leanna had instructed him. *Alive and undamaged. We will need to care for them when the fever takes them.*

Slasher snapped the rope tight again, while Snakebite flapped the sack menacingly.

'What if I don't want to?' asked Weasel. 'You know, I just remembered I left my jacket inside the pub.' He started to move back toward the building, but a wolf-tattooed arm shoved him back.

'We don't have to hurt you,' said Warg Daddy. 'But we'd be happy to do some hurting if it comes to it.'

Snakebite threw out a meaty hand and grabbed at Weasel's grubby collar, twisting it tight around the man's scrawny neck. 'Might be we'd like to do some hurting,' he said. 'Might be that hurting people can be fun.'

There was a murmur of agreement from the other Brothers, a general nodding of heads.

Weasel peered at them with his beady eyes. He looked

like a man who thought that hurting might be no fun at all.

'Better to come quietly,' concluded Warg Daddy. 'All things considered.'

Weasel threw up his hands in a gesture of submission. 'Sure, yeah. Whatever you guys say. I'll do it. Nobody wants to get hurt, do they? Not me, leastways.' He flicked his eyes around the group of men, panic evident in the way his eyes flashed from one towering figure to the next, probing for a gap in that looming wall of muscle and black leather.

Warg Daddy sighed. He knew Weasel well enough to guess what was going to happen next. It was all so unnecessary. Warg Daddy had put forward a good case for compliance. There was really no need for hurting. Hurting would lead to damage. And if Weasel got badly damaged, Leanna wouldn't be happy. Not happy at all. He rubbed the top of his head with his thumb, rubbing away at the problems that made his head ache so much, hoping for things to turn out well, but expecting them to go badly.

He didn't have long to wait. Weasel lurched suddenly and dodged around Meathook, making a mad dash for it. He was surprisingly quick for a drunk and had obviously picked his escape route with some care. He hadn't chosen wisely however. Meathook might have been the shortest man in the circle but he moved quickly and was a vicious bastard. A single right hook from his rocky fist knocked Weasel backward, stunned. He followed up with a slash of sharp nails across Weasel's ugly face, whipping droplets of dark blood into a whirl. Weasel froze in shock, a move that guaranteed Meathook's next blow hit him with full force in the solar plexus, folding him to the ground with a sound like a sack of flour bursting open.

Warg Daddy scowled in irritation. It was already too late to do a thing. The Brothers moved in as one, kicking the raw crap out of Weasel, pummelling him with steel-toe boots, kicking till the blood sprayed over their trousers and gore spilled out onto the cold paving slabs of the yard.

They were like that, the Brothers, too keen by half once the violence got started. He would have to speak to them about it later. He was Leader of the Pack, after all. But for now, events would have to take their course.

They fell on the prone body, tearing at flesh with sharp teeth, slurping blood from severed arteries, ripping out organs in a frenzy of feeding. He just hoped they would leave his liver well alone. Only a lunatic would try to eat Weasel's alcohol-rotted liver. For now he left them to their fun, wandering over to the enclosing brick wall at the edge of the yard and leaning against it to think through his next moves. In the old days he might have lit up a cigarette or rolled a joint, but none of that stuff did anything for a werewolf. Instead he rubbed his head, soothing his troubles away, seeking a clear path through his problems.

The root of his present difficulty was Leanna. She had assigned him this task of finding more victims, promising they would spread the disease the fun way. But hiding in dark corners with ropes and sacks was no fun at all. His instructions were to bring his victims back to the house unharmed. But why not simply bite them? It would be quicker, easier and so much more fun. But Leanna was adamant. She wanted her test subjects undamaged, unlike Weasel.

After a couple of minutes, Snakebite and Meathook shuffled over to him to report. 'Looks like he's dead,' said Meathook nervously, unable to meet Warg Daddy's stern expression.

Warg Daddy turned his gaze to the tangled mess that had once been Weasel. 'You sure about that?' he muttered. 'You totally sure?'

Meathook shrugged. 'Reckon so.'

Warg Daddy grabbed him and shook him by the arms. 'I fucking knew that already,' he roared. 'What do you think happens now?'

Meathook shrugged again. Warg Daddy had to stop himself from slapping the man to the ground.

Snakebite didn't have to think too long before he found the answer. 'Leanna's going to be pissed off.'

'Too right, she will,' agreed Warg Daddy. He released his grip on Meathook and calmed himself back down. Getting angry never did any good. The Brothers had just demonstrated that all too well. Clear thinking was needed now. There was a solution here, if he could just find his way to it somehow.

'But only if we tell her,' said Snakebite.

Warg Daddy nodded. Snakebite was right. The solution was simple, after all.

'Better to keep this one quiet, I reckon,' continued Snakebite. 'What now?'

Warg Daddy shouldered his way forward, heading down the side alley that led away from the pub and back to the road. The Brothers trailed in his wake, wiping blood from their faces and hands. 'We find another. There are plenty more weasels where that one came from. And let's try not to kick the crap out of the next one.'

Chapter Thirty-Seven

Upper Terrace, Richmond upon Thames, West London, waning moon

Sarah knocked on Melanie's door, taking a tray of food and drink up to her. Her sister lay in bed, the curtains closed, the bed covers drawn up to her chin. She opened her eyes as Sarah opened the door, and peeped over the duvet.

'Are you hungry?' Sarah asked.

'Ravenous,' said Melanie. 'Just tell me it isn't soup.'

'Soup? No, I cooked some chicken and vegetables. Is that okay?'

Melanie pushed herself upright in bed so Sarah could place the tray on her lap. 'That bastard fed me soup every day, like some kind of broth fetishist.' She speared a piece of chicken onto her fork and thrust it into her mouth, chewing it heartily.

Melanie had hardly spoken about her ordeal, and clammed up whenever Sarah pressed her for details. The fact that she had volunteered some information was a good sign. In fact, Melanie seemed much more herself today.

'Well it looks like your appetite's back now,' said Sarah.

'It never went away. I've been hungry for weeks. I must have lost pounds.'

It was true that her body was emaciated. Melanie had never been skinny exactly, just slim-waisted and curvy where it mattered. Now the skin clung tightly to her collarbone, and her shoulder blades jutted out violently when she moved her arms. Her complexion had lost its bloom too, her hair now black as night against her pale face. Her beauty was still there, but she was a haunting ethereal shade of her former self. At least the wound in her side had healed now, and there was no sign of an infection.

She tucked in heartily. 'Mm, this is good. So much better than gooey soup. And there's nothing like coming back to your own bed after you've been strapped to someone else's for the past couple of weeks, don't you think?'

Sarah *did* know what to think, in fact, but she held her tongue. Scolding Melanie about her dangerous lifestyle had never done any good before, and she didn't think it would help now. Melanie would do what she wanted, heedless of what other people said. But there was one thing Sarah couldn't let go. 'You know what you have to do, don't you?' she asked.

Melanie chewed her chicken stubbornly. 'Yes. Make an appointment to get my hair fixed, and then move my social life back into gear as quickly as possible. Do you have any idea how many parties I missed over Christmas and New Year?'

'You know what I'm talking about. That man who abducted you. You have to tell the police what happened. They might still be able to arrest him.'

'No,' said Melanie obstinately. 'We mustn't involve the police.'

'Look, I know you don't want to get into trouble. But even if you did steal money from him, what he did was a hundred times more serious.'

'No,' repeated Melanie firmly. 'I'm not worried about getting into trouble.'

'Then you must tell the police. He might do it to another woman. Men like him follow a pattern. He might kill his next victim.'

Melanie stuffed more food into her mouth. 'Believe me, if I thought he might do it again, I wouldn't hesitate to go to the police. I'm not that selfish, whatever you think.'

'What then?'

'You don't need to worry that he might abduct another woman. I can promise you that he won't.'

'But how can you know that?' pressed Sarah. 'If he's done this once, he's almost bound to do the same again, or worse.'

Melanie finished her meal and placed the knife and fork back onto the clean plate. She glared defiantly at her sister through narrowed eyes. 'No, he won't.'

'How can you be so sure?'

'Because James killed him.'

Chapter Thirty-Eight

Cabinet Office Briefing Room A, Whitehall, Central London, waning moon

The Prime Minister was furious. No, that was an understatement. She had never been quite so angry.

Someone would have to pay for this. Her, obviously. No PM could possibly survive the fallout from the massacre that had taken place at Trafalgar Square. More than one hundred people killed outright, a thousand more wounded. The number of deaths continued to rise, and might eventually reach hundreds. They were all civilians. Anarchists and mischief-makers certainly. Some may have been members of banned organizations. And they had gone looking for trouble, armed with a variety of weapons and initiating the bloodshed by killing a number of police officers. But that didn't excuse the massacre that the entire nation had witnessed live on their TV screens. Heads would roll, and hers would be the first on the block. But she wouldn't be alone. She would make damn certain of that.

She glared around the COBRA meeting room, moving from secretary of state to minister to principal private secretary, waiting for each to lower their gaze before she moved to the next one. The new Foreign Secretary was present, an old political ally and a safe pair of hands in a crisis. But she was under no illusion that an ally could help her now. She needed more than allies; she needed a miracle. Finally her eyes came to rest on the steely stare of General Sir Roland Ney. The Chief of the Defence Staff returned her look, undaunted and unblinking. But eventually he too looked down at his briefing notes.

'General,' she began, keeping her eyes fixed on him. 'I require two things from you at this meeting. Firstly an explanation for this evening's events. Secondly your resignation. I plan to offer my own resignation at the end of this meeting, but I do not intend to go alone.'

A clamour of protest from the others seated around the table greeted her announcement, but she waved it to silence angrily. 'General, your explanation for the behaviour of the soldiers under your command?'

General Sir Roland Ney stood to speak. 'Prime Minister, please may I offer my sincere apologies for any embarrassment I may have caused.'

She could hardly believe the man's insolence. 'Embarrassment?' she shouted back at him. 'This massacre was an outrage.'

The General gave no indication that he shared this view. 'You asked me for an explanation. Permit me to give you one. This nation is in a *de facto* state of war. War has not been declared by either side, but nevertheless, hostilities have been entered. In other countries, war has been made official. Russia was the first nation to make a formal declaration. China followed. They have been joined by Sudan, Somalia, North Korea, Turkmenistan, and Libya. Many other nations have not made an official declaration, yet their actions indicate that a state of war exists.

'In each case there are two sides to the war. The forces of order, and the forces of disorder. I suggest to you that the forces of disorder are many, and that they are already winning this war. They have the advantage in recognizing that a state of war exists. If we do not do likewise, we will lose the war by default.'

The Prime Minister directed a hard stare in the General's direction. 'So what do you suggest? Open conflict on the streets of London? Soldiers firing at civilians? Is that how we win this war, General?'

'If that is what is required,' said the General. 'We have already glimpsed the alternative. Wolves on the streets of London, hunting and killing without restraint.'

'I fail to see how that relates to what happened in Trafalgar Square,' said the PM, her voice icy.

'No nation may win a war against two opponents,' said the General. 'The wolves, or whatever you wish to call them, already number in the dozens, quite possibly hundreds. We do not yet fully understand their nature, nor the rate at which their numbers may grow. But we know the danger they present. They must be stopped immediately, otherwise they may become impossible to defeat. On the other side are the enemies within. We have seen them take ruthless advantage of the situation. Marchers, rioters, looters, murderers, anarchists and enemies of the state. From far and wide they are seizing the moment. They know that this is their opportunity. It is a time of supreme danger to the government. They will not find a better chance to strike. We must take control of the situation decisively and visibly, or else all will be lost.

'That is my explanation. You may do what you wish with it. I also offer you my immediate resignation, as you requested. It has been an honour to serve.'

The General fell silent for a moment, but continued to stand. 'However, I must counsel you against offering your own resignation. At this time, strong government is absolutely essential if the war is to be won. Prime Minister, it is clear that you are the best-suited member of the government to lead the nation at this time.'

He turned to stare at each of the other politicians in the room. 'Prime Minister, you are a giant compared to these others. None are fit to replace you. It would be a catastrophe if you were to step down at this most perilous moment.'

The General sat down again and was greeted with a stony silence. The Prime Minister could hardly believe the man's arrogance, his conviction that his men's actions had been justified. And the notion that she might continue in her position was untenable, ridiculous. She waited for the others in the room to contradict him.

Then the new Foreign Secretary began to clap.

The PM stared at him in amazement. The Foreign Secretary was joined by the Home Secretary, who stood to his feet. Soon the entire COBRA team were on their feet clapping and cheering. They were not cheering for the General she realized, they were cheering for her. Despite everything that had unfolded, maybe even because of it, they wanted her to remain as leader. She had spent her entire political career giving speeches. Now, for the first time in her life, she was utterly speechless.

Chapter Thirty-Nine

West Field Gardens, South London, quarter moon

Vijay was stuck at home, and part of him was glad to be safely out of harm's way, especially with all the trouble that was unfolding in the city. He had only been caught up in one small part of the violence on New Year's Eve, and that had been terrifying enough. Watching the events on TV afterwards he realized that his mum had been right – they could all easily have been killed. And now it was even more dangerous with the soldiers shooting people, and the death toll rising day by day.

But another part of him rebelled against being kept indoors, and that was the part that he had to listen to, no matter how much it frightened him.

What Rose had said to him in the hospital had filled him with anguish. It was obvious that she admired Drake and the way he had beaten that thug with the baseball bat. Aasha too was now totally smitten with Drake, and Drake himself was strutting about like a peacock.

Vijay knew that somehow he had failed his friends, even though he had tried so hard to do the right thing. All his life he had been taught that violence was wrong, that force should be used only as a last resort after all other avenues had been exhausted. But the recent events had cast his thoughts into confusion. It didn't make any difference whether he was wrong or right. He was too weak to matter. The strong did whatever they wanted. They always had. They always would.

He'd followed his sister into town to keep her safe, and in the end he'd done nothing to help her. Others had stepped up in his place. He'd been a fool to imagine that he was strong enough to make a difference. The others were strong. Rose, Drake, and Aasha.

He knew what he had to do next. It was simple. He had to prove that he could be brave like them. He had known it for ever, but now it was more urgent and important than ever before.

The first time he had met Rose at school, almost the first thing she had said to him was that he needed to be strong. He needed to stand up to the class bullies.

He had tried so hard, had even fooled himself for a short while that he had succeeded, but now he saw the truth.

Drake was the brave one. He always had been. And now Drake's bravery had won him the prize he most wanted. Aasha. His sister had always treated Drake like dirt, referring to him scornfully as *Vijay's creepy friend*. But now she was happy to be his girlfriend, despite being two years older than him.

The lesson couldn't be clearer. Vijay needed to be as brave as Drake, and prove it, and then he could be with Rose.

His parents had grounded him, but that didn't matter. He would have to face much bigger challenges than defying his parents if he was going to win Rose's heart. He would have to do something truly dangerous. And nothing dangerous was going to come his way while he was stuck indoors. He would have to defy his parents and venture out.

The New Year was the time for making resolutions, and Vijay resolved to meet the days ahead with courage and fortitude. He would start immediately. He unhooked the sling from over his shoulder and slowly stretched out his arm. The sprained elbow still hurt a little, but it was healing just like the nurse had said. There had been no need for him to be such a baby about it. He would deal with the pain without complaining, for Rose's sake.

He opened the door of his room quietly and tiptoed out onto the upstairs landing. The TV was on in the front room downstairs. His dad was probably watching the news. He could hear the sound of his mum cooking in the kitchen. His grandmother would be sitting in her favourite armchair, sewing or reading, or perhaps having a quiet snooze.

He crept along the landing past Aasha's room. Low voices came from inside. Drake's deep voice and Aasha's too, higher-pitched and louder. It sounded like she was bossing him about. Vijay allowed himself a small smile. He wondered if Drake had any idea what kind of girl he'd taken on. No doubt he would find out soon enough.

He walked quietly to the top of the stairs and hesitated. He didn't want to disobey his parents' wishes. He had always been a good boy. But that was his problem. Too eager to please, like a puppy dog. Too docile. Aasha had always been the rebel in the family. Now he had to find his inner rebel too. He pictured Rose in his mind, drawing the smooth curves of her face, the tight curls of her hair, the willowy form of her body. It was enough to firm his resolve.

Quiet as a mouse, but with the heart of a lion, Vijay sneaked silently down the stairs and out through the front door.

Chapter Forty

Holland Gardens, Kensington, London, quarter moon

Adam turned on the TV to find out what new events had unfolded overnight. He'd stayed up late last night to watch the aftermath of the Trafalgar Square massacre. Everyone was saying that the Prime Minister would have to go. The head of the Army too, probably. Maybe others. With luck the entire government might fall. It was just like he had predicted at the last War Council. Civilization was unravelling before their eyes, and the authorities were doing the dirty work for them.

He flicked to a news channel, fully expecting to see the Prime Minister tendering her resignation. Instead, his own face stared back at him.

The photograph was an old one, taken while he'd been an undergraduate and before he'd embarked on the research trip to Romania. He was wearing his athletics kit, and standing in front of the university running track. The young Adam Knight seemed almost a stranger to him now and it took him a moment to recognize himself. By the time he'd realized it was him, the photo had switched to one of Leanna. A photograph of Samuel completed the trio.

'According to a statement issued this morning by the Security Service, these three individuals – Adam Knight, Leanna Lloyd and Samuel Smalling – are believed to be the ringleaders of the werewolves,' explained the news reader. 'These people are extremely dangerous and should not be approached under any circumstances. The police have set up a dedicated hotline for anyone who has any information relating to these three individuals, and has put hundreds of call handlers in place ready to receive calls from the public. They will be collating, prioritizing and acting on every call received, and hope to place these most wanted suspects under arrest at the earliest possible time.'

Adam continued to stare at the screen in dismay. *Most wanted*. How had the Security Service managed to get hold of this information? His first thought was James. The traitor. He must have gone running to the authorities and told them everything he knew. Leanna had been smart in moving them out of their old house so promptly. Perhaps he had underestimated her.

Then again, if it had been left up to Adam, he would never have allowed James into their circle at all. He had mistrusted him on sight, and had refused to allow Samuel to bring him home. But the others had over-ruled him. It was always the same. Adam knew best, but fools with louder voices had their way. He would have to put a stop to that.

The loudest fool of all was Warg Daddy, and Leanna was a fool to trust him.

Now look at what had happened. His name and photograph were all over the media. Leanna's too.

The news footage switched to a live video showing their old house in Greenfield Road surrounded by uniformed police and forensic teams. 'This is the ordinary house in South London where the three suspects lived,' announced the reporter. 'Anti-terrorist police and special forces soldiers from the SAS entered the house early this morning in a pre-dawn raid. A similar raid was also carried out at a science building at Imperial College, London. However, police have confirmed that so far none of the three suspects has been apprehended.'

They had good intelligence then, but they didn't know everything. If they were searching for Samuel and showing his photo to the public, they obviously didn't know he was dead.

Adam frowned. Perhaps that meant that James wasn't the source of the information after all. But however the authorities had got their intelligence, one thing was perfectly clear. Adam was now as good as a prisoner in his own home. Leanna too. Neither of them would be able to set foot in public until they had secured their grip on power. At least they had somewhere palatial to spend their time under house arrest.

He switched channels to a breakfast talk show. The guests were discussing the current crisis, and the debate was getting heated. People talked openly of werewolves. There was no longer any denial, no references to *Beasts* or *Rippers*. One of the guests even used the word *apocalypse*. *The werewolf apocalypse has begun.* That obviously wasn't the official view of the government. Not yet, anyway.

One of the other guests was a scientist, someone Adam had known slightly when he worked with Professor Wiseman at the London School of Hygiene and Tropical Medicine. The scientist used different words to *apocalypse*. Words like *outbreak*, *quarantine* and even *containment*. Adam snorted with derision. Things had already progressed much too far for containment to be a viable strategy. Appropriate words to use now were *epidemic*, *hysteria* and *panic*.

He flicked through the channels looking for something

to cheer him up. One channel had an interview with a London taxi driver. 'I had a werewolf in the back of my cab the other day,' the man was saying. 'Big yellow eyes and everything. Soon as I saw him I knew what he was. I says to him, *What big teeth you've got, mate.* Know what he says back? *All the better to eat you with.* I ran out that cab as quick as my legs would carry me. You can say what you like about werewolves, but they like a good laugh, they do.'

Adam flicked off the TV. Anyone could see that the situation was now out of control. He'd warned Leanna at the War Council that civilization was unravelling. She had unleashed forces she couldn't begin to understand. The chemical burns that disfigured her face were a reminder of how easily her carefully-laid plans could go awry. She could hold her War Councils and talk about her tactics and strategies, pretending that she was somehow still in control of what was happening, but surely even she must be starting to wonder whether any plan could survive the unfolding chaos.

No, Leanna had badly underestimated the destructive force of the events she had set in motion. Her days as leader were numbered. It was time for Adam to switch sides. The only question was, which side?

Chapter Forty-One

Cyprus Road, South London, quarter moon

'There's something I still don't understand,' said Dean. They were out on patrol, Dean at the wheel of the patrol car, scouring the streets for signs of trouble. So far it had all been quiet.

'What's that?' asked Liz. There were so many things she didn't understand right now that she wouldn't know where to begin with her list of questions.

'On New Year's Eve, what happened after I got hit by that bastard with the iron bar?' Dean indicated the row of stitches that still tied the skin on his forehead together. 'How did you manage to deal with the rest of the gang alone?'

'How do you mean?' asked Liz. She had been hoping to avoid this discussion. The memory of transforming under the moonlight and attacking those rioters was one that she had no desire to share with anyone.

'There were four of them, right? And just you and a

few kids. I was unconscious, so how did you handle the situation on your own?'

Liz swallowed nervously. She hated to lie to Dean. He was her partner. He needed to trust her. But she couldn't tell him the whole truth. 'You took one of them down yourself with tear gas,' she said. He grunted to acknowledge the fact. 'And one of the kids grabbed the cannister and used it on another.'

'Okay,' said Dean. 'That still leaves two.'

She decided to skip the part where she had gone berserk and taken on the rioters with her bare hands, and went straight to the end of the story. 'The *Beast* killed them,' she said. 'When the wolves came, one of them killed the rest of the thugs.'

'And left you and the kids unharmed?'

'Yeah,' said Liz. She had thought that odd at the time, the way the wolf had sniffed at her and then moved on. Now she understood. The wolf had left her unharmed because it had recognized her as one of its own kind. 'The other police officers arrived and started shooting before the wolves could attack us,' she said. It wasn't entirely a lie.

'I spoke to one of the kids when I was in the hospital,' said Dean. 'Vijay. You know him?'

She nodded, afraid of what was coming.

'He told me that you attacked the vigilantes yourself before the wolves arrived. He couldn't be certain of what he'd seen, because he lost his glasses in the fighting, but he said you ripped those guys to pieces. He said you tore at their faces with your bare hands.'

'Ripped them to pieces?' said Liz quietly. 'He said that?'

'*With fingernails like razor blades*, he told me. Those were his exact words. He seemed pretty shaken up about it, actually.'

She showed her short-cut nails to Dean. 'With these?' She forced a laugh, but it didn't seem to convince either of them. 'That's not what happened. Vijay said he'd lost his glasses, right? He probably couldn't see very well. I just used my baton to keep those thugs from harming the kids.'

'You told me that the wolf killed them.'

'It did. The wolf came afterwards. I was just keeping the thugs away, to protect the kids. I didn't really harm them.'

'Is that right?'

'Yeah,' she said, defying him to contradict her.

But he didn't. 'I trust you, Liz. You know I'd trust you with my life, don't you?'

'Yes. I know. And I'd trust you too, Dean. You know I would.'

'I only want to help. So if you need help, just tell me, okay? Any time.'

'Sure.'

He swung the steering wheel then, and the car turned off the road and began to bump its way down a narrow dirt track. She hadn't really been paying attention to where he'd been driving them. Now she looked around. 'Where are we going?'

'There's a place down here. Not a lot of people know about it.'

'What kind of place?' she asked, but he said nothing in reply.

They drove to the end of the track and turned into an open area that might once have been used for parking vehicles. Now weeds forced their way through cracks in the buckled asphalt, and abandoned debris lay scattered around. He stopped the car in front of a large industrial building.

'What are we doing here? This place is deserted.'

'Yeah,' said Dean. 'It's an old factory and warehouse. I used to play here as a kid. This place has been scheduled for demolition for as long as I can remember.'

Liz peered out at the building with curiosity. It was an ugly sight, a stained facade of brick and concrete studded with broken and boarded-up windows. Bushes and even small trees grew up between cracks in the structure. A tangle of rusting pipework crawled up the walls, and blackened chimney stacks teetered high above. The place looked like it was falling apart.

'Come on,' said Dean. 'We're going inside.'

He got out of the car and she followed him with some trepidation. He went first to the rear of the car and removed the assault rifle from its secure location in the boot. 'We'll be needing this,' he said.

'What the hell's going on?' she demanded.

Dean gave no answer. Instead he walked across the asphalt to the front of the old factory. A doorway had been barricaded with wooden boards, but not too securely. It didn't take him long to prise them off, revealing a dark space beyond. 'Come on,' he said, disappearing inside the building.

'Stop being so bloody mysterious,' called Liz. She stood outside for a moment, furious at his behaviour. Then reluctantly she followed him inside.

The interior of the building was dim and she could barely see where he had gone. A disgusting smell assaulted her as she stepped inside, and she covered her nose so as not to gag. There was filth everywhere. Broken bottles, animal bones, human waste. Someone had made this place their home once, but there was no sign of life now.

She could make out the dim outline of a doorway on the wall opposite and she headed through it, trying to catch up with Dean. She passed down a short corridor and then the building opened up to reveal a vast space, almost the size of a football pitch. This must have been the main factory floor, or else the warehouse. It was impossible to tell now. All around them the concrete walls were covered in spray-painted graffiti. The enormous roof structure of metal girders was still intact, but much of the roofing material had fallen in, leaving the space open to the elements. The floor was concrete, but half overgrown with weeds and shrubs. They were still technically inside the building, but it felt more like outdoors.

Dean smiled at her as she scrabbled over a low pile of bricks and concrete blocks to join him in the middle of the open space. 'Sorry to be so cloak-and-dagger,' he said. 'But if I'd told you why we were coming here, you might not have agreed.'

'I still might not agree, when you tell me why we did come here,' she said.

He leaned the rifle against a corroded steel drum in the middle of the factory floor. He picked up some empty glass bottles and arranged them on top of the drum. 'I'm going to teach you how to shoot.'

Liz shook her head. 'No way. I don't need to know how to use a gun. In any case, that's totally against regulations. We'd both lose our jobs if anyone found out.'

'No one's going to find out,' said Dean. 'And I think you *do* need to know how to use a gun. And soon. Times have changed, Liz, and I don't know when they're going to return to normal, if they ever do. There are far worse things that could happen to us now than losing our jobs. And if something awful happens to me I need to know that you can take care of yourself. I need to know that you can take care of Sam and Lily.'

'Nothing's going to happen to you,' she said. It was far more likely that something might happen to Samantha and Lily but she didn't say that aloud. She dreaded to think what Dean might do if his wife or daughter came to any harm.

'We can't take anything for granted,' he said. 'Come on. It won't take long to teach you the basics. Let's start with the pistol.' He slid the gun out of its holster and held it out to her.

Reluctantly she took it. 'Is it loaded?' she asked nervously.

'Sure. It has a fully-loaded magazine. But don't worry. It's perfectly safe to hold.'

'Where's the safety switch?'

He chuckled. 'There's no safety switch in a Glock. But

you can't fire it by accident. Even if you pull the trigger now it won't go off.'

'Okay. So how do I fire it?'

'A Glock will only fire if there's a bullet in the chamber and the gun is cocked. Look at the position of the trigger. If it's right back, like it is now, the weapon is safe. But if the trigger is in a forward position, the gun is cocked and ready to fire. But only if there's a round in the chamber.'

'So what do I need to do to make it ready?'

He showed her a small button on the side of the weapon. 'Press this slide release with your finger and pull the slide back.' He showed her how to do it. 'You can check whether there's a round in the chamber. See?'

He pulled the slide back and the weapon made a satisfying ratcheting sound. She could see that the chamber was empty. He slid it back with a loud click.

'But be careful,' he warned. 'The slide action automatically pulls a round from the magazine, loads it into the chamber and cocks the gun. See how the trigger has moved forward ready to fire?'

She looked. 'So the gun will fire now?' She suddenly felt a strange mixture of fear and power.

'Yeah. If there's a bullet in the chamber, the gun is cocked and you pull the trigger, it will fire. So be careful where you point it, and never put any part of your hand in front of the barrel.'

'What if I accidentally drop it?'

'If you drop a Glock, it won't fire. Only if you pull the trigger.'

'Okay,' she said. 'Let's try it then.'

'Hold the gun with two hands,' instructed Dean. 'That's right. Look through the sights to aim at one of the bottles, and use your right hand to pull the trigger.'

Liz took careful aim, lining up the middle bottle. She squeezed the trigger carefully.

The noise of the gun firing was louder than she'd expected, and she felt the power of its recoil in her arms.

None of the bottles had moved.

'Everyone misses the first time,' said Dean. 'Try again. There's no hurry.'

'How do I reload it?'

'The Glock is self-loading. When you release the trigger it loads another round and cocks the gun, ready to shoot. There are seventeen rounds in a magazine.'

The second shot missed too. 'I think I might need all seventeen rounds,' she said, trying to conceal her disappointment.

'Take your time.'

The third shot missed too, and Liz felt a surge of frustration. She hadn't wanted to shoot the stupid gun at all. But now she had, she was desperate to do it right.

'Keep trying,' said Dean. 'We're here to practise.'

She held the weapon firmly in both hands and aimed carefully. The bottle was dead centre in her sights. She pulled the trigger a fourth time.

The middle bottle shattered.

'I got it!' she cried.

'Feels good?' asked Dean.

'Yeah,' said Liz. She was surprised how good it felt. She felt elated; thrilled. Her earlier worries had all but evaporated.

She tried again and missed. But by the time the magazine was spent, all three bottles were gone and the steel drum was peppered with holes.

'Well done,' said Dean, obviously pleased with the result. 'I'll show you how to swap the magazine for a fresh one, and then we can try out the assault rifle.'

'Okay.' She handed the pistol back and watched as he reloaded the weapon.

He showed her the assault rifle next. 'The G36C is an ultra-short assault rifle that fires 5.56mm rounds. They have more range and stopping power than the 9mm bullets in the Glock. They also stand a better chance of penetrating into a vehicle.'

He let her fire some rounds. The feeling of power was even greater than when shooting with the pistol. *The power of life and death.* By the time she had finished, she was glad to hand the weapon back to him. The feeling of awe had been tempered again with one of dread. After all, who was she to wield such power?

'Just remember,' said Dean. 'You'd only use one of these weapons if you feared for your life, or the life of another. Your goal is to save lives, not to kill.'

She nodded. He had given her a gift, she realized. He had gone out on a limb to teach her something important. She couldn't lie to him any longer. 'Do you want to know what really happened on the night of the riot?' she asked.

'Was it like Vijay said? You went berserk?'

'Yeah,' she admitted. 'I don't really understand how it happened. When the full moon came out from behind the clouds, I changed. Into what, I don't know. I wasn't exactly like one of the *Beasts*. But I wasn't fully human either.'

'What then?'

'I don't know. I felt strong, and time seemed to slow down. I didn't really think about what I was doing, I just acted on instinct. I attacked two of those thugs and left them for dead. And then I changed back to normal. It was all over in seconds. But now I'm scared it might happen again. I'm terrified I might hurt someone I know.'

Dean didn't seem surprised or concerned about anything she'd just told him. 'I guessed as much,' he said. 'Tell you what, I'll keep a close eye on you next full moon. If you start getting hairy I'll tell you.'

'Don't joke about it. It terrified me.'

'Come on, don't be so glum. You went a bit wild. But you didn't completely lose control. You didn't hurt any of the kids, did you?'

'No.'

'So I don't think you'll hurt me either.'

She hoped he was right. But hope wasn't enough. 'If I

do anything weird, promise me you'll handcuff me.'

'Sure,' he said. 'That would be fun. But don't tell Samantha.'

Chapter Forty-Two

West Field Terrace, South London, quarter moon

Vijay knocked on the door of Rose's house and waited. The door opened and Rose stood in the doorway, beautiful and radiant, just as he had pictured her in his mind's eye. 'Hi,' he said. 'I hope you don't mind me calling.'

She looked surprised to see him standing there. 'I wasn't expecting you,' she said.

He wondered if he ought to have sent her a text first, but he had been hoping to surprise her. 'I just wanted to come and see you,' he said. 'I missed you.'

'I thought your mum said you were grounded.'

'Yeah. I am. But I sneaked out of the house when no one was looking.' He waited to see if Rose would be impressed by his bravado.

'Oh,' she said distractedly. 'Was that a good idea?'

The exchange wasn't going the way he had imagined.

'Can't I come in?' he asked, unable to prevent a hint of irritation from creeping into his voice.

'We were just going out,' said Rose. 'Me and mum. We need to try and find medication for my brother. He really struggles to breathe in this cold weather, and if we run out of antibiotics he won't be able to fight off infections.'

Vijay nodded. He had seen Rose's brother, Oscar, a few times, sitting in his wheelchair. Sometimes the boy sat in the downstairs window, looking out, waving at the passers-by. He always seemed to be a happy boy, despite the awful cough he had. Thinking about the difficulties the boy must suffer each day, Vijay suddenly felt ashamed of feeling so sorry for himself. His own problems were trivial compared with Oscar's, and besides there was no better way to cheer yourself up than by helping others. 'I'll come with you,' he said brightly.

'Would you?' said Rose. 'That would be great actually. Then my mum could stay here to look after Oscar and get on with other jobs. I'll just go and tell her.'

Vijay waited proudly on the doorstep as Rose disappeared inside. He had been foolish, as usual. An opportunity to impress Rose had been waiting for him all along, and he had almost missed it because of his impatience. He needed to learn some humility, as Sikh wisdom taught. The lessons of his elders had always seemed so simple in the abstract. Now that he really needed some wisdom, it was hard to find the right path.

Rose appeared again a moment later, wearing a thick winter coat and carrying a shopping bag and a list. 'We tried all the local pharmacies yesterday, but they were closed or out of stock. They told us to try again today.'

'Okay,' said Vijay. 'I don't mind how far we have to walk. Just as long as I can help.'

'Thanks,' she said, giving him a smile. 'I really appreciate it.'

They walked to the nearby High Street, but the pharmacy there was closed. The front of the building had been boarded up with plywood sheets. 'It was worth a try,' said Rose. 'We'll go and check the others.'

They set off together along the main road, heading west toward Clapham. 'What kind of medicines does your brother need?' asked Vijay. The list Rose clutched in her hand seemed surprisingly long.

'Quite a few, actually,' she said. 'Antibiotics in case he gets a lung infection, mucus-thinning medications to stop his respiratory system getting blocked, tablets to help him cough up mucus so it doesn't fill up his lungs, and anti-inflammatories to help with pain relief and prevent fever. He also takes enzyme supplements and steroids, and he's just started a trial of a new drug.'

'Okay,' said Vijay. He'd had no idea that Oscar needed so many different medicines. 'How long before you run out?'

'We have a few weeks' supply of most things. Some more, some less, but I want to stock up as much as possible in case things get worse.'

'Let's hope that the other pharmacies are all open,' said Vijay. 'Do you know what happened to the one on the High Street?'

'It was ram-raided a couple of nights ago. Ben Harvey said there's been at least one robbery every day since the rioting started. And that's just in the local area.'

'Ben Harvey?' queried Vijay. 'Our biology teacher? The one who saved you from Mr Canning?'

'Yes. He's working for the Neighbourhood Watch now. They patrol the area at night, looking out for criminals, keeping everyone safe. My dad's started helping them too, now he can't go to work anymore. He likes to keep busy. He got really cross when he couldn't get into work. Actually, he nearly got into a fight with Ben the first time they met.'

'No way,' said Vijay.

Rose smiled at his shocked face. 'Yeah, but it was just a misunderstanding. They're good friends now.'

'That's good.' It seemed that a lot had happened in the couple of days he had been cooped up at home. He began to wish he'd rebelled sooner, then he could have helped Rose and her family a lot more. 'Are they looking for volunteers?' he asked. 'The Neighbourhood Watch, I mean.' If he volunteered to help out, his mum could hardly prevent him from leaving the house.

'I expect so,' said Rose. 'But they need people to go out at night and deal with troublemakers.' The way she said it seemed to rule Vijay out as a candidate.

'I could do that,' he protested. 'I'm not scared.'

'Well, if you say so,' said Rose. 'You should talk to Ben in that case.'

'I will,' said Vijay, although he wondered if the teacher would allow him to help with that kind of work. His mum would probably kick up a fuss too. 'Do they need volunteers for other kinds of jobs?' he asked.

'Maybe,' said Rose. She stopped walking. 'This is the next pharmacy.'

They went inside. A long queue of people were waiting at the counter, and some of them were getting quite irate, shouting at the pharmacist before leaving empty-handed. Vijay noticed that many of the shelves were empty, or severely depleted. Eventually it was Rose's turn to speak to the pharmacist. She showed him her list but he shook his head. 'We only have a small supply of the anti-inflammatories and steroids in stock,' he said. 'We don't have any of these others. And I don't know when we'll be getting any new deliveries from our supplier.'

'Please,' begged Rose. 'I'll take whatever you have.'

'Okay,' agreed the pharmacist, 'but I can only let you have a week's supply of each. We have to ration all prescription drugs until everything gets back to normal.'

Back outside, Vijay tried to console her. 'Let's hope it will get back to normal soon, like he said.'

She shook her head, tears forming in her eyes. 'Haven't you been watching the news? It's not ever going to get back to normal. It's only going to get worse. The trouble isn't just happening in London. The whole world is falling apart. Australia has closed its borders. Russia and China have imposed martial law. Just look at the curfew and the shooting at Trafalgar Square. That's just the beginning. It's going to get much worse than that before long.'

Vijay was dismayed by the anger in her voice. 'You can't know for certain,' he said.

'I do,' she insisted. 'I saw it all in a dream.'

'Dreams don't always come true,' he said.

'This one already is.'

Chapter Forty-Three

*Upper Terrace, Richmond upon Thames,
West London, quarter moon*

James no longer spent all his time alone in his room. Instead he came out at night to trudge around the house in a pitiable state. To Sarah's relief he rarely spoke, and she was growing steadily used to his ghostly presence. It helped that he made no demands on her. In fact he seemed to take pains to avoid her. Mostly he just slouched in a chair doing nothing, or spent long silent hours in his room, sleeping or brooding, she didn't know what.

He didn't watch the news on TV. He didn't read, or listen to music. He never asked for food or drink and she had no idea how he survived with apparently nothing to eat.

Sometimes she found him late in the evening staring out of the tall windows at the back of the house, seeing nothing or everything in the way the moon cast soft shadows across the terrace. Occasionally she would be disturbed by a muffled scream or cry from his room, but when she tip-toed to his door and knocked, there would be no response. Sometimes when he thought he was alone, she would see him curl his fists in anger, or shake his head furiously. Every day he cried, often for hours at a stretch.

Sarah knew why.

She had read enough psychology books to recognize the symptoms of post-traumatic stress disorder when she saw it.

It was only to be expected, based on what Melanie had told her. James had killed the man who had imprisoned her. Melanie wouldn't say any more about the killing, but however James had done it, it wasn't surprising he was in a state. And Sarah sensed some deeper scar, something that had changed his life beyond all recognition. Something that made him barely able to talk at all. She thought she knew what that was.

He was beginning to show some small signs of improvement. He had started taking daily showers now, although he had given up shaving and was growing a ragged, sandy beard on his chin and neck. Sarah had given him some of Grandpa's old clothes to wear. They fitted him no better than the outfit he had arrived in, and he looked comical in an old man's clothing, but he didn't seem to mind in the least. He didn't seem at all interested in his appearance.

What he really needed was professional counselling to help him deal with his PTSD, but with Sarah being unable to venture out, Melanie being unwilling to, and the whole world falling to pieces anyway, that didn't seem like a realistic option. There was only one way to help James heal, and that was for Sarah to get him to talk to her about his trauma.

That was easier said than done, however. For the first couple of days, it had been as much as she could handle simply knowing that a stranger was living under her roof.

Then they had begun to talk, but you could hardly describe their interactions as conversations. Most of the time Sarah felt that they were each simply talking to themselves, in the presence of the other. Even that had been a big step forward. But the time for a proper conversation was well overdue, and if James wouldn't initiate one, she would have to. And the best way to overcome her fear was to jump right in.

'I know what you are,' she said quietly to him when they were alone together one night.

He was standing by the windows that overlooked the rear garden. His glassy eyes stared out at the dark space beyond. He almost seemed not to have heard her at first. Then, still looking out into the night, he said, 'I don't understand. I don't know what you mean.' But she could see the tremble in his shoulders.

She took a step closer. If he kept his eyes away from her, she could do this. 'You're one of those creatures. You're a ... a werewolf.'

James moved away from the window but kept his back turned to her. 'Don't be silly,' he said. 'How could I be?'

'Mel told me. She said you killed that man.'

The tremble in his shoulders became a shudder and he began to sob. 'She promised. She said she wouldn't tell anyone.'

'We're sisters,' said Sarah. 'Twins. Twins share everything. We can't keep secrets from each other, even if we want to. Please don't be angry with her.'

He continued to cry. 'I'm not angry. Just ... sad.' He turned to her then, keeping his head bowed so she wouldn't have to look at his face. 'So are you going to tell the police? Will you hand me over?'

'No,' said Sarah quickly. 'Of course not. I won't tell anyone.'

'You won't?' he asked in confusion. 'Why?'

She smiled. 'Because you brought Mel home to me. You saved my sister. She trusts you, so I know I can trust you too.' Was it really that simple? It sounded foolish to say it aloud. Childish even. But it was true nonetheless.

'You trust me?' said James in surprise. He had stopped crying and looked directly at her for the first time. 'Even though you know I'm a werewolf?'

Sarah didn't flinch or turn away. 'After Mel told me what you'd done, I remembered that I'd seen your face before. Your photo was on the news after that priest was found dead. It was the first of the *Ripper* murders. I remember thinking that when I first saw your photo on the TV, I thought that the police had got it wrong. The boy in that photo could never have done something so horrible.'

'I didn't mean to do it,' moaned James. 'Something just snapped. I couldn't help it. It was the wolf inside me.'

She studied his face. The boy in that news photograph was hardly visible any more. That was why she hadn't recognized him at first. His hair had grown longer and he now had a beard, but it was more than that. He seemed to have aged a lifetime. Yet underneath the surface changes, the look of stark innocence that had been so striking in the photograph was still there. 'I understand,' said Sarah gently. 'But there's something you still haven't told me. Something you haven't spoken about to anyone. I don't know what it is, but something else has caused your suffering.'

James could no longer contain his tears, and they flowed across his cheeks in rivers. 'Samuel,' he said, in between great sobs. 'Samuel's dead.'

Sarah didn't need to ask more. She had already guessed enough. Slowly, in short steps, she closed the distance between herself and the sobbing boy. She drew as close to him as she dared, as close as she'd been for years to anyone except for Melanie and Grandpa. When she reached her arms around him, he clung tightly to her and she didn't pull back, just let him cry his grief away.

She didn't know how long she held him in her arms.

Her shoulder was wet with tears by the time he eventually stopped crying.

'I'm sorry,' he said. 'I'm sorry for everything.'

'You have nothing to be sorry for,' she said. 'You brought my sister home to me. That's all that matters.'

She held his gaze steadily as he spoke to her. 'You are all I have now,' he said. 'You and Melanie and Grandpa. I won't ever hurt you, I promise. I won't allow the wolf to do you any harm. I'll protect you. I'll keep you all safe.'

'I know you will,' said Sarah. 'You're part of the family now, James.'

Chapter Forty-Four

Holland Gardens, Kensington, London, crescent moon

'Hey!' shouted Adam. One of the Wolf Brothers had stuck out a foot as he walked down the stairs and he had almost gone flying. Only his lightning-fast reactions had prevented him from tumbling down the staircase. He grabbed the banister to stop himself falling, then spun around, furious.

Three of the Brothers stood on the landing, watching him coolly, their faces devoid of expression. He didn't know which ones they were. They all looked the same to him, with their identical black leather jackets and stupid dark sunglasses. All of them bore wolf tattoos on their necks and they slouched around the house in groups, staring at him provocatively.

He glared at them. He wanted to fly at them and rip out their throats, but he'd never be able to take all three.

'Oh, hey, man, did you hurt yourself?' said one of the

three. A short guy. He had a stupid name. Slasher, or Masher, or Basher, or something. They all had stupid names. The guy smirked. 'Sorry, I guess you just tripped over my foot.' He stuck a booted foot out and wiggled it about for Adam to see. One of the others pointed at the foot and made an exaggerated apologetic shrug. The three of them turned away from him and disappeared into one of the middle floor bedrooms. Adam heard them sniggering together as soon as they were out of sight.

He balled his hands into fists. He should go in there and fix this once and for all. How could he share this house with these jerks if they treated him like this? He had put up with enough already. If he took them by surprise, maybe he could take them down before they had a chance to react. No one moved faster than Adam Knight, not even another werewolf.

He bounded up the stairs two at a time, heading for the room, but when he reached the landing another leather-clad figure emerged. Snakebite. There was no mistaking the towering giant with the red hair, even though he dressed the same as the others.

Adam stopped, unable to get around the huge man's bulk.

'Hey, Adam,' said Snakebite, resting a hand like a side of ham on his shoulder. 'You look ruffled.'

Ruffled? Adam wasn't ruffled. He was incandescent with rage.

He tried to push past, but Snakebite's grip held him in place. 'Chill, man, don't go in there. That wouldn't be cool. Anyway, it's time for the War Council.'

Snakebite was right, and Adam felt the fury slowly leach away. He had been a fool to think he could take on three of the Wolf Brothers at once. It was the frustration of being cooped up in the house for days on end, unable to show his face in public. He had so much energy, and no way to release it. Snakebite had probably saved him from a bruising lesson. 'Sure,' he said. 'I was just going to the War

Council now.'

'I'll join you,' said Snakebite.

They walked down the wide staircase to the ground floor, and then down to the conference room in the basement. The house was arranged over four levels, including the basement and its underground parking area. The ground floor was given over to communal space, as well as the private rooms that Leanna shared with Warg Daddy. The middle floor of the house had been taken over by the Wolf Brothers, and Adam had come to dread going there. But he had no choice. His own room was on the top floor, which he shared with the test subjects. Since he was no longer able to step outside the house, and because of his medical background, it had become his job to look after them.

He didn't really mind. The work was easy and it kept him well away from Warg Daddy. The Brothers brought back their latest victims, all tied up and gagged, their faces filled with terror. Leanna would inject them with the virus, and then it was up to Adam to keep them alive during Stage One of the condition. If they survived the initial shock they didn't need much care, just fluids from an intravenous drip once the fever began, and some anti-inflammatories if their temperature rose too high. After a couple of weeks they would move on to Stage Two and could be untied. Adam's main complaint with his job was boredom.

'You were right about us keeping a low profile,' said Snakebite as they entered the meeting room. 'Looks like the humans are doing all the devastation for us.'

Adam nodded, surprised to find Snakebite talking to him, even more shocked that Warg Daddy's lieutenant seemed to be in agreement with him.

The big man with the flaming hair had seemed like an imbecile at first. He asked the dumbest questions imaginable. They seemed to spend half of each meeting explaining things to him. But over time, Adam had warmed to him. They had a lot in common, when he thought about it. Both were number two in their respective groups – Adam answerable to Leanna, and Snakebite always in Warg Daddy's shadow. They were marginalized too by the sexual bond between Leanna and Warg Daddy that was an open secret, though never mentioned.

Snakebite wasn't as stupid as he'd first appeared either, or else he had somehow grown smarter. His questions were naive rather than dumb. Adam was reminded of Professor Wiseman's saying that the only stupid question was the one you didn't ask.

'You were right too,' said Adam. 'About spreading the condition as quickly as possible. On its own, the condition won't spread. Nearly all the victims die. It's harder than I thought it would be to keep them alive.'

'You're doing a good job up there on the top floor,' said Snakebite.

'Thanks,' said Adam. He realized that this was the first time in months that anyone had told him he was doing well at something. He had underestimated Snakebite. The man was no imbecile and he was no thug. He was the closest Adam had to a friend.

'I realize it must be hard for you being cooped up in the house with a bunch of strangers,' said Snakebite. 'Some of the boys like to tease. If you ever have any trouble with them, just let me know.'

'Thanks, I will.'

'You and me, I reckon we need to stick together,' continued Snakebite. 'Just in case Leanna and Warg Daddy decide to trick us in some way.'

'Do you think they might?' asked Adam. Even as he said it he saw how stupid he'd been. Leanna and Warg Daddy wouldn't hesitate to stab them in the back. Neither could be trusted. He suddenly realized how vulnerable he was. But here was the solution. Snakebite. An ally, someone on equal terms. A man he could trust. 'I misjudged you,' he said to Snakebite.

'No hassle,' said Snakebite, grinning. 'It's hard to know who to trust sometimes. But I'm glad we had this little chat.'

Chapter Forty-Five

*South Road, Peckham, South London,
crescent moon*

Ben finished loading the supplies into the back of the truck and slammed the door shut with a loud bang that reverberated around the cavernous interior of the warehouse. The three Serbian men who'd sold them the goods watched him with an air of contempt. One of them spat on the ground, while another chewed gum insolently. The third had his hand inside his jacket pocket, like he was about to pull out a gun. Ben's heart was pounding in his chest, but he tried not to show his fear. He walked quickly to the front of the vehicle and jumped into the passenger seat next to Mr Kowalski and Mr Stewart. 'Okay, let's go,' he said, relieved to be back in the relative safety of the truck unharmed. He locked the passenger door. 'Come on! Let's get out of here.'

Mr Kowalski started the truck and they drove out of the warehouse and back onto the main road. 'Is good haul,' said the Polish man. 'Will keep shop supplied for few days at least.'

Ben nodded and breathed a sigh of relief. They'd done well, this time, following up a contact arranged by some shady character Mr Kowalski knew. Kevin, the man called himself. Ben didn't know if that was his real name. He'd hardly believed a word the man had told him. The guy had some young kid in tow, acting as a kind of henchman, handling the money. They seemed like a pair of characters out of some third world ghetto. Still, whatever the man's name was, he had come up trumps. It was just as well, given the hefty "commission" he'd charged for arranging the deal.

'Where do you think those guys in the warehouse got the food in the first place?' he asked Mr Kowalski. 'Do you think it was stolen?' The three Serbians hadn't given the impression that they were legitimate traders. They'd acted more like gangsters. Their gruff, surly manner had unnerved Ben, and he found himself touching the knife that Mr Kowalski had given him.

The shopkeeper shrugged. 'Is not good idea to ask too many questions. Men like that do not like it so much. Best just to pay money and go home safe.'

'We should be grateful that we got the food,' said Mr Stewart. 'Don't go making trouble.'

Ben said nothing. Trouble was exactly what he hoped to avoid. But the more time he spent negotiating with people like Kevin and his dubious associates, the more he came to expect it. But at least Mr Kowalski was quite capable of taking care of himself, and he kept Mr Stewart on a tight leash too.

When they returned to the shop, Ben left them to unload the truck. 'You two take care of this,' he said. 'I've got some people to call on.'

There were so many people and activities to coordinate, he'd been working almost around the clock. He'd thought that being a teacher was demanding, but his new role as Salma Ali's deputy took even more of his time and energy. Still, for now he was just managing to keep on top of everything. At least his headaches had started to recede, and he hardly needed painkillers anymore. It was just as well. Supplies of even the most basic medicines were beginning to run out.

One of the jobs he had taken on was calling in to check on the most vulnerable members of the community – the elderly, the sick, families with young children, and so on. They were the ones who would suffer most if essential supplies ran out. He was grateful to Salma for having the foresight to gather information on everyone who lived in the area. It had given him a good idea of where the greatest need lay.

The first door he knocked at was the home of the Hallibury family. He had got to know the family well in the past few days. Rose's father, Richard, was a mechanical engineer, and he'd already proved useful fixing cars and broken machinery that the community needed. Rose seemed to have recovered well after all her ordeals, physically at least, although he suspected that she was still mentally traumatized by what had happened to her. Her younger brother, Oscar, had cystic fibrosis and was wheelchair-bound. Ben wanted to check how the family was coping.

Rose answered the door to him, her pale features looking even more wan in the gloomy January light. But she brightened when she saw him. 'Mr Harvey, come on in.'

'Thanks.' He stepped inside and allowed her to show him into the family's front lounge.

Oscar was sitting in front of the TV watching a cartoon, but he turned the volume down when he saw Ben. 'Hey, Mr Harvey,' he said excitedly. 'How are you?'

'Good,' said Ben, smiling. The boy's cheerfulness was infectious. 'But really I came to find out how you were.'

'I'm good,' said Oscar. He coughed, covering his

mouth with both hands. He lowered them and wiped them clean on a handkerchief. 'Excuse me,' he said. 'Sorry about that.'

Ben studied the boy with concern. Oscar was small for his age, and obviously weakened by his condition. He wheezed steadily every time he took a breath. Cystic fibrosis was an inherited condition that caused a build-up of thick, sticky mucus in the respiratory and digestive systems. Oscar's mother had explained to Ben that he was prone to lung infections and had to take as many as fifty antibiotics, anti-inflammatory drugs and other tablets every day to keep the condition under control.

'Are your parents home?' asked Ben.

'They're out, looking for medicine for Oscar,' said Rose. Her brow wrinkled with worry. 'We keep looking, but all the pharmacies are closed, or out of stock. The doctor's surgery is only dealing with emergency cases, and anyway they don't keep drugs at the surgery. Can you help us find medicine?'

'I'll try,' said Ben. His contact Kevin was good at locating food, alcohol and cigarettes, but Ben doubted whether he'd be able to get his hands on medical supplies, especially the kind that Oscar needed. 'I'll ask around,' he told Rose. 'And I'll flag it up to Salma Ali as a priority. If anyone can get help, I'm sure she can.'

'Thanks.'

'And how are you doing?' he asked. 'I mean, how are you feeling, after everything that's happened to you?'

'I'm okay,' she said. 'I guess. I mean, everyone's struggling to cope right now, aren't they?'

'Sure,' said Ben. 'But you've been through more than most.'

'I'm okay,' said Rose. 'Really I am.' But the far-off look in her eyes didn't reassure him.

Chapter Forty-Six

King's College Hospital, Lambeth, South London, crescent moon

'Over here, please,' called Chris to the nurse. 'Can I have some food, please? I'm starving.' He had barely had anything to eat since the soldiers had dragged him and Seth from their car.

The nurse came over to his bed and regarded him with suspicion. 'We don't have any food to give to patients,' she said. 'You lot don't usually accept food.'

'But I'm not one of them,' said Chris. 'Nor is my friend.' He pointed toward Seth sitting in the bed next to him. 'We're not even patients. We're not ill at all. We shouldn't be in a hospital.'

The nurse frowned. 'According to your notes, you tried to bite a soldier when you were arrested.'

'No, that's not true. The soldiers just took a dislike to us. They forced us out of our car, beat us, and took all our stuff. They threw us into prison and then eventually they brought us here. No one will listen to us.'

He and Seth had been passed from pillar to post since being captured by the soldiers. They had been held in individual cells, large secure holding centres containing hundreds of prisoners, and even spent one night on a train, locked inside a freezing cold passenger car. They had been taken to a military base near Aldershot, and then inexplicably returned to London. No one told them anything.

He had begged the commanding officer in the military base to release them, but it had been no use. The officer, a captain, had been indifferent to his pleas.

'You can't just detain us without trial,' protested Chris. 'We have rights.'

'That's where you're wrong, son,' said the captain. 'You have no rights. Now that a state of emergency has been declared, your rights have all evaporated. I'm the one with the rights now. I have the right to detain you here for as long as I desire. And my desire is to lock you up and throw away the key.' He spat on the floor next to Chris. 'I saw what you lot did. If I had my way, you'd be up against a firing squad in the morning, not held here, wasting my time and the time of my men. So I suggest you keep your ideas about rights to yourself, if you want to make the best of your time under my care.'

There was nothing Chris could do. He and Seth had been stripped of all their possessions and left with just the clothes they wore. All the preparations Chris had made had been for nothing. They had even taken his map of the British Isles and Seth's origami book. 'Please don't take them,' Chris had begged, but the soldiers had seemed to delight in making him suffer.

The nurse, Chanita, was examining his medical notes. 'You had a high temperature when you were first brought here, but it seems to be back to normal now.'

'I was just hot,' explained Chris. 'I was panicked about being cooped up with all the werewolves. I thought they were going to eat us. I still do,' he added.

The nurse ignored his last statement. 'And you say you're hungry?' she asked.

'Starving,' said Chris. 'We've hardly had anything to eat for days.'

'I can bring you some food and drink,' she said kindly. 'But I can't offer more than that. We have to keep everyone under strict quarantine. You understand that we can't risk releasing any of the infected patients.'

'I understand that,' said Chris, 'but I'm scared they might eat us.'

'This is a secure hospital under military protection,' said Chanita. She pointed to a soldier standing at the entrance to the ward. 'You're safe here. If what you say is true, then we'll be able to let you go once we've established that you pose no risk.'

'So do you have a way of testing for the infection?' asked Chris hopefully.

'We're working on it,' said Chanita. 'In the meantime, I'll make sure you get food and water and that you come to no harm.'

'Okay,' said Chris. He looked around the ward nervously. Pairs of yellow eyes stared hungrily back in his direction.

Chapter Forty-Seven

High Street, Brixton Hill, South London, crescent moon

Kevin Bailey was feeling pretty pleased with himself. Only a month ago he'd been a wanted murderer, on the run from the police, unemployed, with his livelihood literally going up in smoke before his eyes, and no family either. His prospects had looked bleaker than they'd ever done, and Kevin was no stranger to bleak prospects. Now he was living the life of Riley. He was reconciled with his daughter, had acquired an unexpected grandson, and achieved a kind of security he hadn't known for years, with a thriving business portfolio on the up and up. From where Kevin stood, this national catastrophe was working out very much for the best.

'Give me a hand with these boxes, Kevin,' said Gary the butcher. He was busy unloading packets of cigarettes from the back of the van.

Kevin took a final drag on his cigarette and threw the stub on the ground, stamping it out under his boot. 'Come on, kid,' he said to Mihai, giving the boy a gentle shove in the direction of the van. 'There's work to be done.'

Between the three of them they finished unloading the van in no time. Soon the packets were neatly stacked in the storeroom at the back of the butcher's shop along with the other booty. Cigarettes, beer, bottles of spirits, pharmaceutical supplies and even camping gear. The butcher's shop no longer stocked much meat behind its counter, but in the back room it had diversified into a store for all the goods people wanted most desperately when the apocalypse hit town. The kind of stuff that people were willing to pay good money for, now that shit had finally happened.

'Is too heavy, carrying all this stuff,' moaned Mihai.

Kevin cuffed him lightly on the ear. 'Quit moaning,' he said in a friendly fashion. He knew the boy wasn't lazy. He was a grafter, just like Kevin himself. And smart with it. Much smarter than Gary. But Gary had retail premises and transport, and the business needed him. Plus, local people trusted Gary. Apart from vegetarians, he supposed. Vegetarians probably had no time at all for a butcher. But Kevin had no time for vegetarians either. The salad-eaters would have to make do without ciggies and booze. This was payback time, after so many years when the world had seemed to be turning the opposite way to him. 'You know what this is, kid?' he said to Mihai, waving his arms expansively to take in the stocked shelves of the storeroom.

'Is hard work,' complained Mihai.

'This,' said Kevin, with a feeling of satisfaction, 'is opportunity.' It was the biggest opportunity that had ever headed in his direction, that was for sure. After a lifetime of drawing short straws, he'd got lucky at last. But luck was only part of it. You had to be ready to grab hold of an opportunity when it came your way. Opportunities had passed him by before. He hadn't spotted them quick enough, or hadn't been ready to catch them. But he'd caught this one all right. Caught it and was running with it. He wasn't gonna drop it, no matter what.

'Why we sell cigarettes when people need food?' asked Mihai once Gary had returned to the front of the shop to serve a customer.

'We could sell food,' acknowledged Kevin, 'but food is harder to store, and cigarettes have more margin. We have to follow the money if we want to maximise our profits.'

'I know that,' said Mihai with a scowl. 'Am not stupid. But men who sell cigarettes are very bad men. Is dangerous.'

As usual the kid was right. The Serbians who supplied the cigarettes were a nerve-racking crowd to deal with. They scared the hell out of Kevin. The boss man, Zoran, had been some kind of military leader back in the days of the Bosnian War. Kevin wouldn't have been surprised if the guy had come to London to avoid being prosecuted for war crimes. He had no doubt that Zoran would hurt him badly or even kill him if he ever tried to cross him. But Kevin knew enough about geezers like that to keep his head above water. The rules were simple. Always follow through on the deal you'd agreed, and never try to renegotiate terms at the last minute. Pulling a stunt like that was a good way to get your head blown off, and he had no wish to lose his head, especially not now everything was going so well. 'Don't worry, kid,' he said to Mihai. 'Your Grandpa Kevin's gonna take good care of you. Just listen and learn and you won't get into no trouble.'

The kid had sown a few doubts in his mind now, however. He lit up another cigarette while he thought it through. If things ever turned nasty with his supply chain, it would be better if he had a few more tricks up his sleeve. He had no doubt that he and Gary could take care of themselves well enough in a fist fight, but if one of the Serbians ever turned a gun on them, they'd be toast. Burnt toast at that, and full of holes too. Crumbs, basically.

He'd feel a lot safer if he was tooled up with a shooter in his back pocket, just for emergencies. In fact, now he came to think of it, trading in iron and ammo might just be the next big opportunity for him to follow. His nose was beginning to twitch at the prospect, and Kevin always followed his nose.

Where to get his hands on some guns though, that was the tricky question. It took a couple more smokes before the answer suddenly hit him. From the Serbians themselves. Why had he been so slow to work it out?

Chapter Forty-Eight

Cabinet Office Briefing Room A, Whitehall, Central London, crescent moon

Doctor Helen Eastgate hadn't voted for the Prime Minister. She preferred a more compassionate approach to government. She had been appalled by the way the PM had deployed the army and allowed General Ney to impose a curfew following the New Year's riots. And after the Trafalgar Square atrocity she had been on the brink of handing in her resignation as Special Scientific Adviser to the COBRA meetings. But her views were slowly changing.

The private face of the Prime Minister was no different from her public one. Strong, authoritarian, and unyielding. But now Helen saw glimpses of something softer beneath the hard shell. The more she witnessed the PM wrestle with difficult decisions, the more she began to admire and understand the most powerful woman in the country.

The Prime Minister always listened carefully to both

sides of every argument, probed for facts, and grilled her advisers like an inquisitor, before finally reaching a decision. Her decisions were often made on much less information than Helen would have liked. As an academic, she would have been tempted to await more data, commission a further study, hold off until the evidence was conclusive. But that would be fatal here. The Prime Minister reached her conclusions swiftly, and she owned her decisions. Although Helen still preferred her politicians to wear their hearts on their sleeves, there was no denying that the PM acted with good intentions, and that she was fully aware of the consequences of her actions.

She was grappling with another difficult decision right now. Helen, having heard the arguments for and against, didn't envy her.

'I will not turn this country into Fortress Britain,' declared the Prime Minister. 'The restrictions on movement are already causing real hardship to ordinary people. Supplies of goods are becoming limited. People cannot easily get to work. Businesses are closing and the knock-on effects are in danger of becoming irreversible. I will not extend the restrictions further. That would be a gross infringement of human rights and economically disastrous.'

The Home Secretary held a different opinion. 'But Prime Minister, if we are to contain the violence and apprehend the ringleaders of the werewolves, some short-term sacrifices are necessary. The case for closing our external borders seems crystal clear to me. It is already apparent that the infection originated in mainland Europe.' He indicated Helen's presence at the table. 'Doctor Eastgate's information tells us for certain that the origin point of this disease – ground zero – if you like, was Romania. More Romanian citizens have been implicated in the spread of the disease, and many of the infected patients are in fact foreign citizens.'

The new Foreign Secretary didn't seem any more

sympathetic to the PM's view. 'I must agree with the Home Secretary on this matter, Prime Minister. Refugees are fleeing Russia, the Middle East and countries in Eastern Europe, and heading for Britain. There are already backlogs of refugees in Calais, and reports of disease breakouts at camps close to the French ports. The United Kingdom enjoys a unique position in Europe by virtue of being an island nation. We must take advantage of this natural buffer against the disease, and close the ports immediately.'

The PM glared at them both through steepled fingers. She turned to her military adviser, the old General with his steely face and his enormous eyebrows. 'General, what is your opinion? Must we take this step?'

Helen regarded General Sir Roland Ney warily. Of all the members of the COBRA committee, she trusted the Chief of the Defence Staff least of all. He always took a hardline view and seemed to have little regard for human rights.

The General seemed in no hurry to respond. He appeared to be weighing his options, or else wondering how to word his reply. Eventually he leaned forward. 'Prime Minister, the security policies already in place are yielding results. The curfew, the checkpoints, and the quarantined hospital are containing the infection, or at least slowing its spread. Anything that restricts movement further will only assist and support our existing operations. And it is imperative that we eliminate this threat before the next full moon. I speak as a military adviser, you understand. I cannot comment on other implications of shutting the ports, and I leave that to your civilian advisers.'

The PM seemed to be outnumbered. 'Does everyone here agree with the General?' she asked the meeting in general.

There was a broad murmuring of agreement, and nodding of heads around the table.

The Prime Minister frowned. She crossed her hands and appeared to lose focus momentarily. Helen had come to recognize this as a sign that the PM was about to make a decision. But she didn't make up her mind immediately. Instead she turned to Helen. 'Doctor Eastgate, in your capacity as Scientific Adviser, what value do you think that closing the country's borders would have on containing the spread of the disease?'

Helen hadn't expected to be asked such a direct question. So far she had mainly observed these meetings, occasionally being asked to explain some technical matter. No one had asked her to venture an opinion before now. 'Prime Minister,' she began uncertainly, 'at present we don't fully understand the transmission pathways of the disease. We know it can be passed from one host to another through bites, scratches and blood transfusions. It is quite possible that sexual transmission also exists, but we have no evidence of that. My best guess is that the disease cannot easily be passed by other means, if at all. That means we have a real chance to contain it, but only if we can isolate the carriers of the disease.'

Helen stopped. Somehow her words seemed to be supporting the case put forth by the General. The idea of restricting people's rights to go where they wished was against all her political views. She had emigrated to the UK herself, and had always assumed she would be able to travel freely wherever she wished. Until recently she'd entertained the idea of returning to the hot climate of her home country, but until Australia reopened its borders that was out of the question.

But the scientific case was unassailable, and Helen was a scientist, not a politician. 'Prime Minister,' she continued, 'I agree with the others here. The best way to control the disease is by restricting movement of people as much as possible. We have no definitive way to test patients for the disease, and we know that at least some of those infected are using the condition as a bioweapon, deliberately seeking to spread it. If I were in your position, I would certainly seek to control the borders. At the very least, I would quarantine all those who wished to enter the country.'

The PM looked at her, her expression unchanged. Helen wondered whether her opinion would have any real influence on the outcome. She wasn't even a member of government. By rights, she oughtn't to be here at all, and one or two of the other cabinet members had even remarked on the fact. But she was here at the Prime Minister's personal insistence. For some reason this strong, older woman with so much power at her disposal, and so many advisers to do her bidding, had decided to place her faith in a young Australian she hardly knew.

The PM's eyes glazed over for a fraction of a second, and then she spoke. 'Thank you all for your input. Despite all that has happened, this country remains a democracy. We are answerable to our people. We are not at war. This country has faced many threats, from enemies without and within. Britain is, and always has been, a bastion of freedom. It is the cradle of democracy.

'Foreign Secretary, speak to your counterparts in Dublin, Paris, and Brussels. Inform them that our borders will continue to remain open.'

Chapter Forty-Nine

Holland Gardens, Kensington, London, new moon

Warg Daddy dragged the screaming woman down the stairs and threw her onto the metal-framed bed. Her hands were already tied together behind her back, and Snakebite bound her to the bed frame using some evil-looking leather straps and metal buckles. When she was secured, he pulled the cloth bag from her head and let her take in her new surroundings. She screamed again, and Warg Daddy wasn't surprised. He would have screamed too, if he'd been in her position.

They were in a small basement room of the house, just off the underground garage. Unlike the opulent decor in the conference room and the rest of the building, this room was almost bare, with unfinished walls and a rough concrete floor. Glass vials, syringes and other medical equipment stood on metal shelving along one wall, and assorted surgical instruments were lined up ready for use on a table next to the bed. Leanna called the room her laboratory.

Dungeon, thought Warg Daddy. It looked like a fucking dungeon to him. But if Leanna preferred to call it a laboratory, he would play along. 'She's ready,' he said.

Leanna and Adam were already waiting with their instruments of torture. Leanna's face had healed enough for her to remove the dressing that had covered one eye. The eye was good, but her skin would never heal. One half of her face was reddened and scarred, and her mysterious disfigurement appeared to be permanent. Warg Daddy shivered at the sight. At least Leanna's long golden hair covered some of the burned skin.

Adam passed Leanna a syringe and she went over to the bed. The woman eyed the sharp point of the needle and shook her head desperately from side to side, begging for release. Leanna ignored her. Instead she carefully inserted the needle into her victim's arm and administered the injection.

Warg Daddy watched as the woman gasped, her chest heaving, taking breaths in gulps as if each might be her last. A minute passed. Then her arms began to quiver uncontrollably. She arched her back, her eyes rolled back in her skull, and a hideous screech erupted from her lips. *Anaphylactic shock*. He had seen it enough times now, had endured it himself when he had first become infected with the condition. No matter how many times he saw it, it still creeped him out.

The woman thrashed her limbs violently, straining the leather straps that bound her. Her screaming grew louder and more inhuman.

'Is it working?' asked Snakebite.

Warg Daddy didn't think so. The woman's face was slowly turning red, and her screams died away to an agonising rasp.

'Asphyxiation,' muttered Adam. 'The internal swelling has blocked her airway. She needs an adrenaline shot.' He gave her a second injection, but it didn't seem to make any difference. The woman continued to jerk her limbs in silence. She was clearly choking to death now. There was nothing Adam or Leanna could do to save her. Eventually her arms and legs grew still. 'She's gone,' said Adam at last. 'Just like the others.'

'Dammit!' shouted Leanna, stamping her foot in rage.

'Why didn't we just bite her?' asked Warg Daddy. 'Like you did to us? Why did we have to bring her back here and inject her?' This whole business made his flesh crawl. A werewolf should hunt, not engage in weird medical experiments.

Leanna turned her burned face to him, her blue eyes sparking dangerously. 'You *wanted* to be bitten. You *asked* me to bite you. Do you think *she* wanted to be bitten?' The woman had gone quiet now. All life had left her.

Warg Daddy shrugged. 'I'm not afraid of biting anyone.'

'I didn't say you were afraid,' snapped Leanna, her words like icicles, sharp enough to pierce flesh. 'Don't you understand why we do this?'

Snakebite gave her the answer she wanted. 'It's so you can administer the virus under *controlled conditions* right? To increase the patient's chances of survival.'

Warg Daddy looked at the dead woman strapped to the bed, Adam bent uselessly over her inert body. The conditions didn't look very controlled to Warg Daddy. He'd seen the Brothers exercise more control than this after an all-night drinking session down at The Tarnished Spoon. But Leanna and Adam were medical students. Creepy experiments in underground laboratories seemed to turn them on.

He rubbed his head with his thumb. Life as a werewolf was proving to be tougher than he had imagined. At first it had been a childhood dream fulfilled. He'd gained strength, agility and a range of fantastic superpowers. Becoming a werewolf had been even better than being the leader of a biker gang. In fact, he'd become the leader of a *werewolf* biker gang. Nothing could be better than that.

But then the shadows had begun to creep in. He hadn't noticed at first, he'd been so hyped, but they were growing day by day. The shadows had begun to darken his vision. Brooding forms lurked at the periphery of his eyesight. Dancing figures, dark spots, sometimes even total blackouts. He couldn't bear any kind of bright light and had taken to wearing dark glasses indoors, even at night. Headaches gripped him, but not normal headaches. These were wild and fierce, like demons stomping inside his skull. Some days his head felt like it was being slowly crushed in a vice.

There was no one he could talk to about it. Leanna was no help. She'd been the perfect girlfriend at the beginning, beautiful and sexy, but he never knew if she was going to suddenly flip into evil harpy mode. She could be a cold bitch if the mood took her. Some days she treated him like he was less than dirt. The cruel scars on her face didn't do anything for her looks either. He wondered if she was worth the continued effort.

And now Snakebite was acting weird, like he knew all the answers. Snakebite had always had the slowest wit amongst the Brothers. Warg Daddy hadn't kept him for his brains, but because he was seven feet tall and mean as hell. Now that dumb fucker had started telling him what to do. He ought to smack Snakebite back into place, except that with his crippling headaches, he needed Snakebite more than ever. When thinking was just too hard, Snakebite did the thinking for him. One day Warg Daddy would put him back where he belonged, but for now, he depended on him.

Leanna had flipped into bitch mode again by the looks of it. She turned her wrath on him. 'The test subjects keep dying!' she screeched. 'Almost every single one! Do you know why they keep dying?'

Warg Daddy shrugged. Leanna's words were true. Most

of the victims the Brothers brought back to the house had died, despite Adam's attention. But how was he supposed to know why?

'They're too weak!' screamed Leanna. 'Drunks, drug addicts, alcoholics, low-life scum. Useless, the lot of them. Bring me young, healthy subjects instead!'

He was beginning to tire of this. The work was tricky, and dangerous. Armed police and soldiers were everywhere, and few people roamed the streets at night these days. Tracking down victims and bringing them back unharmed and undetected wasn't half as easy as Leanna seemed to think. 'It's not so easy,' he said. 'We need to find people who won't be missed. The kind that wander around in the dark. On their own, in unsafe places.'

'Bring me people who take good care of themselves. The kind that *will* be missed. Young, fit, healthy, beautiful ones. Humans that are worth changing into werewolves. Ones that may actually survive the change!'

'We'll try harder next time,' he said, lamely. What he really wanted was action. Not all this sack-over-the-head business in back alleyways. Not fumbling in the dark for unwary victims. Not dragging them back to Leanna's lair for her to work her dark magic. Proper action, that's what he needed. The Brothers craved it too. They were restless. Sooner or later, they needed to rumble.

'Maybe there's a better way,' suggested Snakebite.

'Tell me,' demanded Leanna.

'Well,' said Snakebite. 'What about the hospital?'

'What about it?'

'We could attack it.'

Warg Daddy leaned forward, his interest roused. 'What for, Snake? Which hospital?'

'The one where the army are keeping the bite victims. There's a whole new generation of werewolves there. Why don't we break them out?'

Warg Daddy looked hopefully at Leanna. 'What do you think?'

'It's guarded by the army.'

'We can handle that.'

Leanna's eyes narrowed. She was thinking hard. 'The authorities have collected together all the Stage One and Stage Two cases in one place. How convenient. The doctors and nurses are doing our job for us, caring for the infected. For the moment that suits our purposes.'

'But if we can get the patients out, then our numbers will increase,' said Warg Daddy.

'The time to do it will be the next full moon,' said Snakebite. 'The patients will change as soon as we free them. The advantage will lie with us.'

'The next full moon,' echoed Leanna. 'The wolf moon.'

Wolf Moon was the name given to the first full moon of the new year, the first full moon in January. Warg Daddy knew all about it. In some ancient cultures it was called the *Snow Moon* or *Ice Moon*. It was the time when the wolves gathered, when hunger made them forget their usual caution, and they were at their most dangerous.

'We'll do it,' said Leanna.

'We'll have to be careful,' cautioned Adam. 'There's no need to take risks.'

But there *was* a need to take risks. Without risks, Warg Daddy could hardly bear to live.

Chapter Fifty

*Upper Terrace, Richmond upon Thames,
West London, new moon*

I t was time for James to go out. Grocery supplies in the house were running low, and even if he didn't need food, the others did. Melanie was still too weak to venture out of the house, and Sarah couldn't. It had become too dangerous for them in any case.

Before James set out he lit a candle and prayed, kneeling beneath the simple wooden crucifix he had hung on the wall of his room. 'Dear God, please guide me and help me find food for the people of this house. Help me to keep them safe from harm.'

He wanted to add, *not like the way you allowed Samuel to die*, but he resisted the urge. It was not for him to question why God had permitted that to happen.

As ever these days, the voice of God remained silent in his mind, but James was used to that now. God would speak to him when it was time. Until then, it was enough for him to speak to God. 'I know that you will guide me and help me to do what's right,' he said. He finished by making the sign of the cross.

'I heard you praying,' said Sarah when he came downstairs. 'Does it help to talk?'

James nodded. 'Sometimes I talk to God, and sometimes I talk to Samuel.'

'Your friend? I can tell that you miss him terribly.'

'I do. He was so full of life. And now he's gone. I still can't believe it. Sometimes I forget he's dead and I think of something to say to him, and then I remember all over again that he's dead. It doesn't seem possible. I feel like he must still be here with me. I really do. Do you think that sounds crazy?'

Sarah rested her hand on his. 'No, not at all. When Melanie and I were young our parents died, and I felt exactly like that. For a long time I couldn't accept it. I thought they must be hiding from us somewhere and would return one day.'

'But it's not like that,' said James. 'I know Samuel is dead. I held his body in my arms and watched the life leave him. And yet it still feels like he's here with me. I see his face sometimes, and I talk to him. Is it madness to speak out loud to the dead?'

'No. It's not madness. It's grief. It's the sanest response to a cruel world.'

'I talk to Samuel because I'm so confused about everything,' continued James. 'I used to think that life was simple. Be good. Don't sin. Do what God wants us to do. But now I can't be certain what God truly wants. I'm not even certain what being good means. I need God more than ever, yet God is silent. I can't hear his voice anymore, so I don't know what I'm supposed to do.'

'After all that's happened, can you still be certain that God really exists?' asked Sarah gently.

'He has to,' said James fiercely. 'Otherwise what purpose do we have? There's no meaning to anything.

We're all just surviving, like animals.'

'It doesn't have to be like that,' said Sarah. 'We can find our own meaning.'

'Like what?'

'Well, what would Samuel have wanted you to do?'

James didn't need to think before answering. 'He'd have wanted me to be brave and always do the right thing. But how can I know what the right thing is?'

'Just follow your heart, James. Always listen to your heart.'

He shook his head. 'I was following my heart when I killed Father Mulcahy in the church. And when I killed all those people at the railway station, I didn't even think about my actions, I just did what seemed natural. But that was wrong. I can't trust my heart. I have the heart of a wolf now.'

'No, you still have a good heart, a human heart. I know you do.'

James cocked his head to one side to think about it. 'Samuel had a good heart, even after he'd become a werewolf. He wanted everyone to live together in peace – black and white, gay and straight, old and young, rich and poor. Becoming a werewolf didn't ever change that desire in him, it made it stronger. I want to make his dream come true. And more than that, I want humans and werewolves to live together peacefully too.'

'Make it happen, James. If anyone can do it, you can.'

'I'll try my best. And there's one thing I know for certain.'

'What?'

'I've killed so many people. I'm never going to kill again.'

He left the house then, stepping foot outdoors for the first time in many days. It felt strange to be out again in the fresh air, all alone. He had grown used to having Samuel with him whenever he went out, and he felt the empty space at his side keenly.

The space had a shape, almost as if his friend walked with him still. Tentatively, he reached out a hand to hold Samuel's. It closed on thin air but the feeling that Samuel was there didn't leave him.

Perhaps Sarah had been right. Perhaps he could find meaning in an empty world. As long as it wasn't entirely empty. As long as he could still cherish the memory of Samuel.

'Stay with me,' he whispered to his dead friend. 'I can't go on without you.'

The ghost of Samuel remained silent and invisible, but it gave James the comfort and strength that he needed to continue.

Sarah had given him a wad of money and a list of things they needed. She had told him where to go to find food shops and he headed in that direction now, walking casually, trying not to draw attention to himself. The streets were strangely empty, even though it was the middle of the day. He passed a few people, but they hardly looked at him. There was no reason to, he was just a boy. They didn't know the beast that lived within him.

The house where Sarah and Melanie lived was on the edge of Richmond Park, and he had to walk a good way before he arrived at a more built-up commercial area. The first shop he reached was a burned-out shell. Virtually nothing remained of the building's interior, and cold ash blew across the street, collecting in doorways like drifting snow. The fire must have taken place several days ago and there was nothing to be found here.

The second shop was boarded up with wooden panels across its windows and entrance. Yellow-and-black police crime tape sealed the building and a sign on the door read, *Closed until further notice.*

James trudged on, following the road that led away from Richmond and toward Clapham Common. He was only about a mile from his old home in Mayfield Avenue and he soon began to recognize buildings and landmarks along his route. A curiosity suddenly gripped him. He had not allowed himself to dwell on what had happened to his parents since he had left home. He had been too ashamed to imagine how his mother and father must have worried when he disappeared without trace. But now it was all too apparent. The grief he felt for Samuel must be exactly what his parents felt for him. And at least he had the advantage of knowing exactly what had happened to Samuel. His parents must be ravaged by the uncertainty of not knowing if he was still even alive.

He quickened his pace, following the road, knowing that it would lead him past the place where Samuel had died, but unable to stop. If he could just see the house he had lived in and know that his parents were still safe. If he could perhaps send them a sign that he was still alive …

'Hey, you!'

He had been so caught up with his thoughts that he had forgotten to pay attention to his surroundings. A gang of four strangers blocked his way along the roadside. They were teenagers, about his own age, two white, two black, wearing baggy jeans and a mix of hoodies and leather jackets.

'I'm talking to you, blud,' said their leader, a black youth with his hair in braids. He shoved James roughly on the shoulder.

Samuel, thought James. The boy's black face and hair reminded him keenly of his dead friend, but Samuel would never have behaved that way.

James stepped back and the gang closed in around him, blocking his escape.

'Give us your phone,' said the youth. 'Come on, hand it over.'

'I don't have a phone,' said James.

'Everyone got a phone, innit?' said one of the other kids, a heavily-built guy with a thick metal chain looped around his neck. A flick-knife appeared in his hand and he held it up so James could see. 'Give it to us now, or I'll cut yer face.'

'I don't have a phone,' repeated James, trying to stay calm. 'Please leave me alone.'

'Please?' goaded the kid with the knife. 'Please leave you alone? We'll leave yer bleeding in the gutter if yer don't give us yer phone right now.'

'Please,' begged James. 'I don't have a phone, but I have money. I'll give you half of my money if you leave me alone.' He had promised Sarah he would do the right thing, that he would never harm anyone. But these people were making it so hard for him. The right thing was to use the money to buy food for his friends. The right thing was not to hurt these kids.

The leader laughed out loud. 'Half your money?' he said incredulously. 'You having a laugh?' He looked around at his friends to see if they believed what they'd just heard. 'You'll give us half your money?' He turned back to James and this time his voice was filled with menace. 'Give it all to us, now.'

The kid with the knife raised the weapon and one of the others grabbed hold of James' arms, pulling them tightly behind his back. The knife waved in his face. 'Gimme yer fucking phone too!' screamed the knife-wielder.

'I already told you. I don't have one,' snapped James angrily. The wolf blood was pumping in his veins and his heart hammered loudly in his chest, but he didn't struggle as his arms were pinned back. He wouldn't kill these kids, whatever they did to him. He refused to kill again.

The leader of the gang reached inside James' back pocket and pulled out the wad of cash that Sarah had given him.

'Please don't take it,' he begged. He felt a tear roll down his cheek. 'I need that money to buy food.'

'Yeah?' said the gang leader. 'Too bad. Looks like you gonna go hungry tonight.' He took the money and stuffed it into his pocket.

'Please,' begged James desperately. 'Don't make me hurt you.' Hot tears were streaming from his eyes now. They were giving him no choice. He didn't want to hurt them, but he couldn't return home empty-handed. He wouldn't.

The gang leader laughed again. 'You hurt us? That ain't never gonna happen. You ain't the one holding a knife, innit, blud?'

'Hey,' said the kid with the knife. 'He still ain't handed over his phone.'

Blood boiled in James' veins. He longed to rip at their throats, to sink his teeth into their soft flesh. He had not eaten for days, and the hunger rose inside him, almost uncontrollably. But he had made a promise to Sarah, and to Samuel. He would not kill again.

'I told you I don't have a phone,' he snarled. 'Now give me back my money. This is your last chance.'

Cruel laughter was his only reply.

James screwed up his eyes, struggling to control the rage inside.

These boys were no older than himself. They might have grown up just a few streets away from him. Perhaps if he hadn't come from a good home he would be out on the streets just like them. That boy with the flick knife and the metal chain around his neck might be James. The black-skinned leader with the braided hair might be Samuel, the two of them together out on the streets. James knew how it felt to wield a knife. He had used one on Halloween night to protect himself and the children in his care.

But that had been in self-defence. He had acted to save the innocent. He had not used a knife like these boys, to steal. And Samuel had not ended up in a street gang despite growing up in a poor black neighbourhood. He had made choices. Good choices. At some point everyone had to take responsibility for their own actions.

James twisted in the grip of the boy who held him, moving quickly, wrenching his arms free and hurling his assailant back against the wall. The kid folded up, clutching his body where he had collided against the rough brickwork. James swung round and lashed out at the knife wielder, chopping at his elbow and knocking the knife from his grip. The kid cried out in pain and James brought his knee up into the boy's stomach. He sprawled backward onto the pavement, moaning in agony.

The other two gang members regarded him warily. The leader grabbed hold of the fourth boy and pushed him forward. 'Take him down,' he ordered.

The boy approached hesitantly, his eyes never leaving James' face. He reached inside his jacket and pulled out another knife, a larger one with a fierce blade, hugging it close to his chest. 'Get away!' he called. 'Run!'

'Not without my money,' said James.

The boy came closer, the knife held firmly, ready to strike.

'I don't want to fight you,' said James. 'Just give me my money back.'

The boy lunged suddenly, the knife in his outstretched hand, but James was too quick. He grabbed the boy's arm and twisted it hard. Bones crunched and the arm became loose. The boy screamed and the knife dropped from his grasp. He stumbled and fell, then crawled away, his arm dangling, squeals coming from his mouth.

The gang leader turned and ran.

James ran after him.

The boy was tall and wiry with long limbs and he sprinted fast, but James outpaced him and caught him up. He grabbed the boy by the arm and spun him around. The boy staggered and fell to the ground. He lay there panting, his eyes wide with fear. 'Don't hurt me,' he pleaded.

'I don't want to,' said James. 'Just give me my money back.'

'Yeah, sure, blud,' said the boy. He reached inside his jacket, but instead of pulling out the money, his hand emerged clutching a knife. The knife was the largest James had seen, an evil-bladed weapon with a serrated edge and a bright green plastic handle. The boy rolled to the side and jumped to his feet. He lifted the knife toward James.

James dodged aside, but he was too slow. The knife sliced into his left arm, catching him near the wrist and drawing out a fine spray of blood. The wound stung, bringing James' fury bubbling over. He slashed at the teenager with his good arm, catching him across the face and drawing dark droplets of blood from his cheek. The boy cried out, but James didn't slow. He grasped the boy's knife arm in an iron grip and sank his teeth into the leather jacket.

The thick leather shielded the boy from the worst of James' savagery, but he dropped the knife and screamed as James bit down hard.

James pulled away, a hunk of leather between his teeth, blood dripping from his mouth.

The boy gasped at the sight of his bleeding arm and staggered backward. His fingers began to tremble and shake. He made to run, but dropped to his knees instead, unable to stand. His eyes rolled back in his head and he fell to the ground, shaking all over. An anaphylactic shock reaction had already set in and there was nothing James could do to stop it. He spat the mouthful of leather from his bloody mouth. 'You could have made it easy,' he shouted at the boy. 'Why did you have to make it so difficult?'

But the boy couldn't hear him. He rolled back and forth on the pavement, just the whites of his eyes showing. Blood flowed from his arm and his tongue lolled out helplessly. There was nothing James could do to help him. He bent down and retrieved the wad of stolen money from the boy's pocket.

'Call an ambulance!' he shouted to the other gang members, who were watching from a distance. 'If you want to save your friend, call an ambulance right away.'

But he knew that no one could save the boy now. The

infection was likely to kill him in minutes. Even if he lived, he would become a monster. A monster just like James.

Chapter Fifty-One

King's College Hospital, Lambeth, South London, new moon

'Chris Crohn? Is that really you? Come closer! Let me see you.'

That voice. It was so familiar to Chris. But impossible. The owner of that voice couldn't be here. He couldn't.

'Come closer, I said. I want to look at you.'

Chris felt his flesh creep. He wanted to sneak away. But the voice wouldn't let him.

'It is you, isn't it? Come over here, now!'

Chris crept closer to the hospital bed, eyeing its occupant with fear. It couldn't be him. The man who spoke like that was surely dead. But no, there could be no doubt. The nightmare that had engulfed him had somehow taken a turn for the worse.

Since they'd been brought to the hospital, he had hoped that things might get better, but that familiar voice

Lycanthropic

embodied his very worst fears. He stood in front of the man in the hospital bed, hardly believing what he saw.

'I thought it was you,' said Mr Canning, the headmaster. 'What a nice surprise, meeting you again. And in such pleasant surroundings.' He waved an arm to indicate the hospital quarantine ward. Nurses and doctors attended to the wounded and the sick, but armed soldiers guarded every door, and the windows were securely barred.

The headmaster sat up in his bed, a large cotton pad covering one eye. He looked different to how Chris remembered him. At school, Mr Canning had always dressed immaculately in a suit and tie, his silver hair combed neatly in a side parting. Now he wore pyjamas and his hair was matted and straggly. A thick growth of grey hair covered his chin and neck, and his eyes glittered yellow.

'But you're dead,' blurted Chris. 'That girl stabbed you in the eye with a ballpoint pen.'

'Ah yes, Rose Hallibury, Year 10,' said Mr Canning. 'Such a pretty little thing, and surprisingly resourceful under pressure. My eye is gone, as you can see, but apart from that everything seems to be in full working order.'

Chris stared at the dressing that covered one half of Mr Canning's face. The girl had stuck a pen right through the man's eye. How could he still be alive? 'You tried to eat her,' he accused. 'You ate that other girl.'

'I ate five children in total,' said Mr Canning with satisfaction. 'Four boys and one girl.' He licked his lips. 'I would have eaten Rose too, if it hadn't been for that interfering busybody, Ben Harvey.' He smiled, showing Chris his teeth. 'But what are you doing here?'

'I don't know,' said Chris. 'The soldiers took us prisoner. Me and my friend. It was all a big mistake. We're not werewolves.'

'Are you not?' said the headmaster, his smile turning more wolfish. 'Never mind. I'm sure you can still be of use to me. Oh yes, I'm absolutely confident of it.'

Chapter Fifty-Two

Upper Terrace, Richmond upon Thames, West London, new moon

When James returned to the house in Richmond, he was loaded up with bags of shopping. The knife wound on his arm had stopped bleeding, but it still throbbed with pain. The pain would be his penance, a reminder of the violence he had sworn to avoid, but had committed nonetheless. 'I bought the food and drinks,' he told Sarah. 'But I had to give all my money to the shopkeeper.'

'All of it?' she asked, sounding surprised. She had given him plenty of cash, far more than he ought to have needed.

'Most of the food shops are empty or closed,' he explained. 'I had to walk miles to find one that was still open. They asked how much money I had and demanded all of it. I suppose I could have haggled, but I don't really know how. Shops are supposed to have fixed prices, aren't they?'

'I guess the world has changed,' said Sarah. 'You did well to find food at all, by the sound of it. In any case, we're not short of money.'

She noticed the wound on his arm then. 'What happened? Your arm is bleeding.'

James didn't want to talk about it. 'It's not serious,' he said. 'The bleeding has already stopped.' He didn't want to tell Sarah what he'd done to that street gang. He didn't even want to think about it. 'Don't worry,' he said to her. 'The wound will heal at the next full moon.'

'Let me put a bandage on it,' she said. 'Or a plaster at least, and some antiseptic.'

'I'm okay,' said James, but he allowed her to dress the wound. Tending to his arm seemed to make her happy.

'This is all I do now,' she joked. 'I nurse the sick and tend the wounded.'

'You're good at it,' he said. 'Thanks.' He could tell she wanted to ask him something. 'What is it?' he said.

'You said that the wound would heal at the next full moon,' she said curiously. 'Is that when you change into a wolf?'

'Yeah,' said James. There was no point trying to deny it. The monthly change had become a regular part of his life now, but it must sound very strange to Sarah. 'If I go out and the moonlight from the full moon falls on my skin, then I will change, and any injuries I have will heal.'

'*If* you go out?'

'Yeah, *if*.' He hadn't previously considered the possibility of not going out. He needed to feed after all. But that meant killing. He didn't want to kill again. He wouldn't. If he stayed indoors he would avoid the change.

'What happens if you don't go out?' asked Sarah.

'I don't know,' he said. But the answer was obvious. If he didn't go out, he wouldn't feed. And if he didn't feed, he would die. Perhaps that was the answer. Perhaps that was what God wanted.

'The next full moon is the wolf moon,' said Sarah. 'It's all they're talking about on the news right now. The name seems, well, ... ominous.'

'Yeah,' agreed James. 'It does.'

She finished dressing the wound and went to the kitchen to store the food and groceries away.

Wolf moon. He had asked God to send him a sign. Perhaps this was it. But what did it mean exactly? There was no clear answer, but there was a clear choice. Become a wolf, or don't become a wolf. The choice was his, and his alone.

He paced the house silently, lost in thought. If he never killed again, he would die and join Samuel in Heaven. He had promised not to kill, and the thought of spending eternity with Samuel, never having to make another difficult decision again, held a lot of appeal. But the wolf moon sounded like an invitation. If it really was a sign from God, then it seemed to suggest that God wasn't done with him yet. But what his purpose might be, he had no idea.

Thinking about the next full moon and whether he would go out hunting was just too difficult. It took all his effort to concentrate on the immediate future. He would need to go out again soon, that much was clear. The groceries he had bought wouldn't last long. But there was another reason to go back outside. His parents' house was just a couple of miles away. He could walk that distance easily, provided he avoided street gangs and muggers.

He wouldn't show himself to his parents, not after all he had done. It would be too upsetting for them. How could they cope, knowing that their son was a werewolf? The idea horrified him. It was better if they gave him up for dead. But he would watch over them and see that they were safe. Perhaps he could help them in some way. Perhaps he could take them food.

He would go the following day, back to the shop where he had bought groceries today. He would buy food and leave it on his parents' doorstep. And he would take more care this time, so that he didn't run into trouble.

He was sure that Sarah would give him money again. She was generous. She probably wouldn't even ask why he needed it. But if she did, he would tell her. He needed to atone for his sins.

Chapter Fifty-Three

Battersea, South London, new moon

Liz gazed out of the side window of the patrol car as she and Dean cruised the evening streets of South London. They were on the lookout for trouble and she didn't think it would be long before they found some. Grim faces stared back at her: hostile, fearful, and resentful.

Everywhere they went, from Brixton to Clapham and on to Battersea, the story was the same. These once familiar streets of South London were now hostile territory. Ordinary life had come to a standstill, and antipathy toward the police had reached an all-time high. Since the army had been mobilized and the midnight curfew had begun, many people now regarded the authorities as part of the problem. Maybe entirely the problem. Someone had sprayed *Police and Troops Out Now* in white paint on a wall.

'They hate us,' Liz said sadly to Dean. 'These people

we're here to serve, they just resent us now.'

She could understand it to some extent. The Trafalgar Square massacre was inexcusable, and the curfew and army checkpoints had massively disrupted people's lives. Shops were selling out of goods, and people's freedoms were curtailed. People were angry, and the fact that no wolves had been spotted since the full moon had shifted the focus away from them and onto the actions of the army and the police. She'd tried to explain it to Dean in those terms, but he didn't want to listen. Instead he seemed to relish the opportunity to crack down hard on troublemakers.

'Someone has to deal with the looting, the rioting, and the arson attacks,' he protested. 'Not to mention hunting down the werewolves, wherever they're hiding.'

'I know that,' she said patiently. 'But when people are frightened, they look for easy answers, for someone to blame. Some people even think that the Beast attacks, the Ripper murders and the New Year's Eve rioting were all some kind of government-orchestrated conspiracy. I heard an opposition politician on the news saying that the violence on the streets is the start of a popular uprising in response to an authoritarian crackdown.'

'Idiots,' said Dean angrily. 'What's wrong with people? The police are responding to a surge in opportunistic crime and organized violence. We're here to protect law-abiding citizens.'

'You don't need to lecture me,' she said. 'We're on the same team, remember?'

'Yeah, sorry,' said Dean. 'It's just that this job is hard enough without people criticizing.' He turned the car onto the wide thoroughfare of St John's Road, Battersea. 'Let's keep a sharp eye out around here,' he said. 'This is my local patch. I want to make sure Samantha and Lily stay safe. And that means keeping the thugs off the streets. With any luck we'll catch a few tonight.'

Liz kept her counsel. She hoped for the sake of Dean's wife Samantha and their two-year-old daughter Lily that they stayed well away from any violence. The last thing Samantha needed was Dean back in the hospital, or worse.

But he was right. Returning to St John's Road, the site of the New Year riots, was a grim reminder of exactly why they had a job to do. And Liz's role now seemed to be less like a modern-day police officer and more like a wild west sheriff, patrolling a frontier town and waiting for the outlaws to appear. The fact that she and Dean now carried a Glock and an assault rifle did nothing to assure her that a peaceful shift lay ahead of them tonight.

'Road block coming up,' said Dean.

A military checkpoint closed the road up ahead, and he slowed the patrol car to a halt at the barrier, winding his window down to speak to the two soldiers who approached the car. 'All right, boys?' he said cheerfully. He flashed them his badge and Liz showed hers too.

One of the soldiers nodded. 'Everything seems pretty quiet so far. Probably too good to last.'

'I expect so,' said Dean. 'We're hoping for some action soon.'

'Good luck with that,' laughed the soldier. 'We're just hoping for a mug of hot tea and no one spitting at us.'

The barrier rose and Dean drove through. The patrol car seemed to be just about the only car on the street this evening. When the checkpoints had first appeared, huge traffic jams had formed as people tried to get to work. Soldiers had searched cars and even buses, and the streets of the capital had been jammed into gridlock. But after a few days, people seemed to have given up on driving. Now they stayed home, or went about on foot. It was surprising how quickly people adjusted.

'How are Samantha and Lily doing?' Liz asked. 'Is Lily sleeping better now?'

'Lily's sleeping just fine. It's Sam who lies awake all night worrying. I wish I could be there more for her, but I'm glad I can be out keeping criminals off the streets. That's the best way to make sure they're safe.'

'I'm sure they're safe enough at home,' said Liz. She hoped that Mihai and Kevin were home safe and sound tonight too. She knew that Kevin dragged Mihai everywhere with him. That would have been good, if she could have trusted her father to keep well away from trouble. But Kevin and trouble were old friends and they never stayed apart for long. She wished she could be at home more to spend time with the ten-year-old Romanian boy. She hadn't rescued him from the fire in the community centre just to dump him on her father. But work was demanding all her time right now and she has glad that Kevin had turned up just when he did, even if it was because he was running from the law.

The sound of Dean's phone ringing brought her back to the here and now quickly enough.

'Get that for me, would you?' he said. 'It might be Sam.'

'Sure,' said Liz. She picked up the phone and checked the screen. 'Yeah, it's Samantha calling. Shall I answer it?'

'She's probably just checking up on me, making sure I'm not in any trouble,' he joked.

Liz answered the phone.

The voice at the other end was frightened and panicky. 'Liz? Liz, is that you? Oh, thank God. Thank God. Is Dean there?'

'Samantha, what's wrong?' asked Liz. 'Dean's with me, but he's driving. Can you tell me what's the matter?' She saw the look of alarm on Dean's face and signalled for him to stay quiet.

Samantha's voice was almost inaudible. 'There's someone downstairs,' she whispered. 'Two men, I think. They smashed a window at the back of the house and climbed in. I grabbed Lily and ran upstairs. I'm locked in the bathroom. You have to come quickly.'

'We'll be there in five minutes,' said Liz. 'We're already in Battersea. Did you dial 999?'

'I tried, but the line was busy. A recorded message said

that all the emergency services were fully occupied.' A gasp came over the line followed by a thump.

'Samantha? Samantha? What's happening?'

Sam's voice came back, louder this time. 'Oh my God. They're banging on the bathroom door. They're trying to get in. You have to come now!'

'We're on our way,' said Liz. 'Keep talking to me. Don't hang up.' But the line went dead. 'Shit,' she said.

She didn't need to tell Dean what to do. The car's siren and blue lights were already on and the car was speeding up the road toward his house. 'What's going on?' he asked. 'Tell me what's happening.'

'Two men entered the house. Sam and Lily are safe in the bathroom upstairs.'

'What else? Tell me.'

'The men are trying to get into the bathroom,' said Liz.

She felt the car lurch forward as Dean floored the accelerator. 'If those bastards lay a finger on her …' He didn't need to say what was on his mind.

Chapter Fifty-Four

Leay Street, Battersea, South London, new moon

Dean pulled the patrol car to a stop immediately outside his house and jumped out. Liz followed him. Lights were on upstairs and downstairs but there was no obvious sign of trouble from the outside. Liz had tried to get through to Samantha on the phone again, but she hadn't picked up.

'Samantha said that the men climbed in through a rear window,' she said to Dean. 'She thought there were two men, but there might be more. It sounded like they were burglars.'

Dean had gone to the back of the car and he appeared now with the assault rifle in his hands.

Liz stared at the weapon. 'Is that necessary?'

'Oh, yes,' said Dean. 'I think it is.' He ran to the house and opened the front door with his key. 'Sam!' he bellowed through the open door. 'Sam, we're here!' He entered the house, the rifle raised in front of him. Liz followed.

Dean headed straight upstairs, his feet pounding heavily as he took the steps two at a time. Liz checked the downstairs rooms, but they were empty. She heard a shout from above and ran quickly up the stairs.

Dean was on the landing at the top of the staircase, the rifle aimed and ready to fire. Two rough-looking men stood at the end of the landing ten yards from him, looking scared but undaunted. They were young, perhaps late twenties or early thirties, one of mixed race with long dreadlocks, the other white with a shaven head and tattoos on his neck. Both held knives: one a broad-bladed machete; the other a brutal-looking meat cleaver.

Dreadlock Guy had one arm wrapped around Samantha's neck. His other arm held the machete. The tattooed man held Lily, the meat cleaver at the little girl's throat.

Samantha's clothes were torn away, her underwear on display, the soft mound of her belly clearly visible. Her face was rigid with terror.

'What have you done to her?' shouted Dean, pointing the rifle at the first man's head, his finger resting on the trigger. 'What have you done to my wife? If you've hurt her …'

'They didn't do anything to me, Dean,' said Samantha, tearfully. 'You got here just in time.'

'Yeah,' sneered Dreadlock Guy. 'Like your wife says. We didn't have time to do nothing.'

'You were going to rape her,' accused Dean, his voice rising. 'You were going to rape my pregnant wife.'

Dreadlock Guy shrugged. 'You heard what the chick said. No milk got spilled. No need to cry.'

Dean stared at the man down the barrel of the rifle, his eyes blazing with fire, seemingly too angry to speak. His finger twitched on the trigger of the gun.

'Dean!' cautioned Liz. 'Hold your fire.'

'Yeah, like the lady says,' continued the man calmly.

'No harm done, nothing stolen, nobody hurt. So we all know how this plays out. You let us go. You put the gun down, we walk out of here and nothing nasty happens.'

Samantha's eyes seemed to beseech Dean to do what the man said.

But Dean's finger didn't move from the trigger. 'I'll tell you what we do,' he said. 'You release my wife and daughter. Drop the knives and get down on the floor. I'll decide what happens then.'

Liz knew what Dean was likely to do to anyone who threatened Samantha or Lily. She stepped up beside him and spoke to the man with the machete. 'More armed police officers are on their way now.' It was a barefaced lie, but she was getting good at those. She ought to have radioed for backup, but there just hadn't been time. 'You have no hope of escape,' she continued in what she hoped was a calming, measured tone. 'Drop your weapons and release your prisoners.'

The tattooed man was sweating like a pig. He held the meat cleaver at Lily's throat with knuckles turned white. His eyes darted from Dean to Liz and back. 'Let's do it like she says,' he suggested to his accomplice. 'I don't want to go home with a bullet in my head, man.'

But Dreadlock Guy wrapped his arm more tightly around Samantha's neck. 'No one's getting a bullet,' he said. 'Not while we have his wife and daughter. They're our ticket out of here and he knows it.' He jerked Samantha's head back and she gasped. 'Now drop the fucking gun, big guy.'

Lily began to wail, her lower lip trembling, the quiver spreading to her arms and legs. 'Daddy, help me,' she cried. 'He's hurting me. I'm frightened.'

The tattooed man gave her a shake. 'Stop it,' he muttered. 'I don't want to hurt you.' The handle of the meat cleaver was slick with sweat in his hand and his own arms were trembling just like Lily's. His shaven head shone with perspiration. 'Keep quiet!' he said to Lily. 'I just can't think through that noise.'

The girl cried louder as he shook her, her arms and legs spasming uncontrollably. She began to twist from side to side in his grip.

The man held on to her tighter. 'Make her shut up, man!' he shouted. 'Make her shut the fuck up!'

Dean swung the barrel of the rifle and pointed it at the tattooed man's bald head.

He squirmed, lifting Lily before him as a human shield. 'Don't point the gun at me.' The blade of the meat cleaver sliced through the air by Lily's neck. 'I can't think straight if you point that thing at me.'

Dean didn't move.

The man with the tattoos turned to Liz in desperation. 'Tell him to drop the gun,' he wailed. 'And make the girl shut up. Make her be quiet. She's gotta stay still or I'm gonna cut her.' He gripped the meat cleaver tightly.

'Let her go,' insisted Liz urgently. 'Release the girl and I promise that you'll come to no harm.'

'No!' shouted Dreadlock Guy. 'Don't listen to her!' His hair braids flew as he jerked Samantha in his arms. 'Don't let go of the fucking girl, or else we're both dead.'

The tattooed man ignored him, flicking his eyes wildly from Liz to Dean and back again. 'I'll do it,' he said to Liz. 'I'll let her go. But tell the big guy he's gotta put the gun down.'

In reply, Dean advanced a step toward him.

'Come on,' begged the man desperately. 'Don't do that. You gotta make it easy for me. Don't make me do the wrong thing.'

'Shut up!' the other intruder shouted at him angrily. 'Just shut your mouth!' He tugged at Samantha's hair and she cried out.

Dean's gun swung back in his direction. He took another step closer.

The tattooed man holding Lily was babbling now. 'I don't want to be here no more,' he said to Liz. 'I wish I was at home. Take the girl from me. I don't want her. Just take her.' He lifted Lily in his arms and held the girl out to Liz.

Was it a trick? The man was in too much of a panic to be thinking of a trick. He just wanted to be rid of the girl, to have someone else make a decision for him. She edged along the wooden banister toward him, not once taking her eyes from his. 'Okay, stay calm now. Pass the girl to me. Nobody's going to get hurt here. Just stay calm and pass her to me.'

She moved toward him in small, steady steps, her arms held out to take Lily.

The man's eyes flicked from her to the barrel of Dean's gun and back. Sweat was running from his forehead like a river. He seemed to have forgotten the weapon he held loosely in his hand. 'Take her,' he said desperately, his arms outstretched, as if the girl were a ticking time bomb. 'Quickly. I don't want her no more.'

Lily's tiny form was almost in Liz's reach now. The girl struggled in the man's grip, crying hysterically. 'Lily,' said Liz. 'Can you hear me? I need you to stay still now. Stay very still. I'm going to take you to safety.'

The man's arms were shaking violently. 'Take her!' he screamed. 'Take her from me now!' The blade of the cleaver twitched at his side, the handle dripping with sweat. He held her out for Liz to grasp.

Liz reached out to the girl, but too slowly. Dreadlock Guy lurched suddenly and she saw a silver glint as the machete blade swung toward her.

'No!' cried the other man, shoving Lily forward and letting his own weapon slip from his grasp. He threw his hands in the air.

Liz ducked and the blade of the machete swung over her head. Lily had fallen to the floor, crying. She grabbed at the little girl and yanked her backward, tumbling away from the attackers and back toward Dean.

An ear-splitting crack filled the enclosed space of the

landing and echoed off the walls. The assault rifle jerked in Dean's grip and an empty cartridge spun from its side. Samantha screamed.

Liz tumbled to the carpet, covering Lily with her own body as protection.

A man's voice roared with anger and the gun cracked again. A second spent cartridge landed on the carpet next to Liz.

She pushed herself to her knees and looked to see what had happened. Dean stood like a statue, the rifle still in his hands. Samantha had collapsed to the floor and was wailing hysterically. The two intruders lay dead, each man with a single hole in the middle of his forehead.

Chapter Fifty-Five

Holland Gardens, Kensington, London, crescent moon

The subject of the next War Council was due to be the attack on the hospital. Adam was reluctant to get involved, knowing that he would be unable to be of much use. How could he be a part of the operation now that he could no longer go out of the house? But Snakebite reassured him that he could still be included in the planning.

'How can I help?' asked Adam bitterly. 'I'm stuck indoors, kicking my feet.'

'Don't worry,' said Snakebite. 'I've got a solution to that. The boys have gone to the hospital to record a video of the layout. Come to the meeting and watch the video. You'll be able to see what the army's up to, and how they've secured the access points. You can help with the planning even if you can't go out.'

'Nice one,' said Adam, cheering up at once. 'I can

search for plans of the building and other info online.'

'Sweet,' said Snakebite, punching him on the shoulder. 'We're a team.'

The War Council took place in the basement conference room that afternoon. Adam arrived on time and took up his usual place sitting opposite Warg Daddy and Snakebite. Leanna sat at the far end of the table, brooding silently. Blonde hair covered the burned side of her face, and Adam was glad not to have to look at it.

Warg Daddy seemed to be in charge of the overall planning, with Snakebite as his deputy. The two men acted like military commanders, despite having no weapons and an army numbering just seven foot soldiers. Adam might have laughed, if he'd dared. But even he had to admit that the Wolf Brothers had done a thorough reconnaissance of the exterior of the building.

Snakebite had connected a laptop to the huge wall-mounted TV and was explaining how they'd gathered their intel. 'It's not so easy to travel around the city with all the roadblocks and checkpoints in place. But we managed to send some scouts to survey the target. Meathook and Slasher went out this morning and recorded some footage of the area immediately around the hospital.' He pressed a button and a video began to play on the big screen. It had obviously been filmed from a moving motorbike and was jerky and unclear in places, but it gave a good impression of the geography.

'The main entrance to the hospital is on the northern side,' said Warg Daddy, taking charge. 'Stop the video here, will you, Snakebite?'

The video froze, showing a cluster of buildings. Some were modern; others were older red-brick structures. They crowded together around a cramped parking space filled with military vehicles.

'Tell them about it, Snake,' said Warg Daddy, leaning back in his chair and allowing his second-in-command to give a detailed report.

Snakebite pointed at the image on the screen with a laser pointer. 'The army has set up a roadblock with a checkpoint at the main entrance. They're searching all vehicles and pedestrians who approach the building. The troops are from 16 Air Assault Brigade, which is the British Army's rapid response airborne formation. You can see that they're wearing the red berets of the Parachute Regiment.'

The screen showed a group of soldiers standing at the checkpoint, guns in hand, all wearing the distinctive red berets. Several military vehicles were parked behind them, one of which looked to Adam like a tank. The tracked vehicle was stationed right outside the entrance, its long gun barrel pointing directly at the camera.

'This is a Scimitar armoured truck,' said Snakebite. 'It's designed to offer protection against bullets, mines and improvised explosive devices, or IEDs. The Scimitar packs a 30mm armour-piercing cannon capable of taking out enemy tanks.'

He indicated a second vehicle parked next to the checkpoint. 'This is a modified military Land Rover,' he said. 'It's equipped with a 12.7mm heavy machine gun. It's a belt-fed weapon that'll lay down 750 rounds per minute of sustained fire with a range of up to two kilometres. You don't want to get in its way.'

He pressed another button and the image zoomed in on the soldiers manning the checkpoint. '16 Air Assault Brigade was deployed in Sierra Leone, Macedonia, Afghanistan and Iraq,' he continued. 'The troops you see here are carrying standard-issue SA80 assault rifles. These can fire up to 775 rounds per minute with a range of three hundred metres. The soldiers patrolling the perimeter of the hospital are armed with combat shotguns. They're 18.4mm semi-automatic weapons designed for close quarter use.'

Warg Daddy leaned forward. 'Short range motherfuckers,' he said. 'They'll basically blow the holy shit out of anyone standing at the wrong end.'

'Any questions so far?' asked Snakebite.

Adam had none. The army checkpoint looked to be pretty-well unassailable, at least without heavy weaponry to match, and he was beginning to doubt whether they had any chance of taking the hospital. The Wolf Brothers didn't even have guns, as far as he knew.

Snakebite pressed a button and the video resumed playing. 'This is the main road that runs along the eastern edge of the hospital. The entrance to the Emergency Department is located here, and this is where ambulances enter and leave. You can see that the main hospital building where the patients are being held is on eight floors. The southern boundary of the hospital runs along the edge of railway tracks, with Ruskin Park further to the south. Access from the west is sealed. The site is located right in the middle of a residential area, with housing all around, and lines of sight are very restricted. Soldiers patrol the perimeter of the site on foot, and all access points are controlled by the army. There's a strict quarantine in place, and no one enters or leaves the hospital itself, except to admit new patients.'

He pressed a button and a still image appeared, showing an aerial view of the main hospital building. 'A helicopter landing pad is located on the roof of the main block. This has been turned over to military use, and currently a Lynx attack helicopter is stationed here 24/7. The Lynx is armed with an M3M machine gun capable of firing over 850 rounds a minute, and runs regular patrols, day and night.'

He concluded with a video taken from a distance showing the helicopter swooping low over nearby buildings, completing a wide circle before returning to its rooftop base. The barrel of the machine gun was clearly visible through the chopper's side door.

'Adam,' concluded Snakebite, 'over to you.'

Adam stood up and ran through the intel he had

managed to gather online. He showed a map of the hospital grounds and plans of the interior. But what little he'd managed to find seemed irrelevant compared with the video showing the military presence. He felt like he was wasting his breath. 'It hardly seems to matter,' he said finally. 'They've turned the hospital into a fortress. It looks virtually impregnable.'

Leanna spoke then for the first time since the briefing had begun. 'Looks can be deceptive,' she said. 'As evidenced by Snakebite here.'

'Yeah,' grumbled Warg Daddy. 'We always thought he was a dumbass. Turns out he's a fucking military genius.'

'Explain the plan, Snakebite,' said Leanna.

Snakebite got to his feet again, towering over her. 'What Adam says is partly true. The army have assembled a lot of military hardware here, for sure. They probably think the place is very well protected. But that's their problem, you see. Complacency.'

Adam didn't see. 'But all the entrances are sealed or guarded. How can we possibly get inside? We don't even have weapons, unless you count flick knives and baseball bats. Even in wolf form we're vulnerable to bullets. It doesn't take a silver bullet to kill a werewolf – lead does the job perfectly well. We saw that clearly enough when Samuel was killed.'

Snakebite nodded patiently, scratching at his red beard, giving the impression that he knew Adam would say exactly that. 'The army's used to taking on conventional military opponents. Even unconventional ones. In Iraq and Afghanistan they dealt with terrorists trained in guerrilla tactics. They're trained to handle a wide variety of enemies. But they don't know how to deal with werewolves.'

'Sure,' said Adam. 'But werewolves can't take out tanks.'

Snakebite nodded. He brought up a still image of the tank on the screen. 'The Scimitar armoured vehicle certainly looks dangerous enough. It was designed to punch holes in Soviet-era battle tanks. But if the army boys try to use its primary weapon in such an enclosed space, they'll probably blow themselves sky high.'

'Fair enough,' admitted Adam, 'but what about the soldiers? And the helicopter?'

'The helicopter patrols the air, but only at regular intervals. We can easily avoid it. The main entrance is secured, and the perimeter is patrolled on foot, but the hospital consists of dozens of separate buildings, each with multiple points of entry. The southern boundary lies along the railway track, and the western perimeter is bounded by low walls with several gates. The hospital grounds are almost impossible to defend from a stealth attack. The primary function of the soldiers is to stop people getting out, not in. Besides, most of the soldiers are based inside.'

'That makes it even worse,' said Adam. 'Even if we manage to get inside, how are we going to fight our way to the upper floors of the building to break the patients out?'

Snakebite grinned. 'It's obvious really. There's no need to get anyone out. We'll let them come to us instead. If the plan works we won't even need to step foot inside.'

'Snakebite's plan is so simple it's genius,' said Leanna. 'We simply have to do the one thing they're least expecting.'

'And what's that?' asked Adam.

'It involves you, actually Adam,' said Snakebite, a smile forming on his lips. 'You see, to make the plan work, we need two critical skills. First we need someone with exceptional athletic ability.'

Adam nodded. 'That's me, certainly.' It was good that his talent had been recognized at last. 'What's the other skill you think I have?'

'Bomb-making,' rumbled Warg Daddy. 'Leanna says that if we bring you all the stuff you need, you can build us a bomb.'

Chapter Fifty-Six

King's College Hospital, Lambeth, South London, crescent moon

'Thank you my dear,' said the patient to Chanita.

Mr Canning. He'd been one of the first patients to be brought into the hospital, some weeks before the quarantine had begun. As well as the syndrome, he also had a severe head injury from being stabbed in the eye. His condition had stabilized now and he had been discharged from Intensive Care some days ago. The threat to his life had passed, but it had been impossible to save his eye.

'You are most attentive, my dear,' he said to her, as she changed the dressing on his empty eye socket. 'Most attentive. Indeed, my stay here has been most pleasant, apart from one small detail.'

Chanita continued to dress the wound. She wished that all her patients could be as polite and well-mannered as Mr Canning. He was always so cooperative, and charming too.

He'd been the headmaster of a local school apparently. 'And what is that, Mr Canning?' she asked.

'Do you ever plan to feed us?'

She stopped what she was doing in surprise. Most of the patients with the syndrome never ate hospital food. It was one of the most obvious symptoms of the syndrome, in addition to the yellow eyes. In the early days she had tried to make some of them eat a little fruit and it had literally made them throw up. Doctor Kapoor had believed it was something to do with enzymes in the stomach or microbes in the gut. Some of the patients had agreed to eat cooked meat, but very quickly even that became too unpalatable for them to stomach. How they managed to survive with no food intake was just another of the mysteries that shrouded the syndrome. The only two patients who seemed to eat anything were the new arrivals, Chris Crohn and Seth Salaway. She was beginning to suspect that they may have been telling the truth about not being infected. Perhaps the headmaster was the same.

'Would you like me to bring you some food?' she asked brightly. 'Today I think we have spaghetti carbonara and cheese and mushroom quiche.'

Mr Canning wrinkled his nose at the mention of it. 'That's not really what I was hoping for.'

'It's the only food we have.' It was a miracle that they still had cooked meals in the hospital at all. When Colonel Griffin had announced the quarantine, she had fully expected most of the staff to leave. But well over half had volunteered to stay on, and more had transferred from nearby hospitals. She and the other nurses had made up camp beds in the cafeteria, and the hospital's admin staff were working around the clock providing hot food and drinks. Even senior managers could be found serving up bowls of soup and loading dirty plates and bowls into the dishwashers. Everyone was pulling together and the usual grumblings about under-funding and bureaucratic red-tape had been pushed aside. It was funny in a grim way. All you needed to make the system work was a national disaster.

'I think you know what I'm talking about, my dear,' said the headmaster.

Chanita did. She remembered the first time a patient had asked her for raw meat. James Beaumont. Another very polite patient. She wondered what had happened to him. Since then the demand had been made over and over again. It was usually raw beef they asked for, but sometimes raw pork or even chicken. As if a hospital would ever feed uncooked chicken to its patients.

'I'm sorry,' she said. 'If you mean raw meat, we don't have any.' Mr Canning would have to go without. She finished changing the dressing and turned to leave.

The headmaster's arm shot out to grab her. His fingers held her in a vice-like grip. 'Sooner or later, you'll have to give us something more palatable than cheese and mushroom quiche,' he growled. All traces of his earlier charm had left his voice. 'Every day we get a little hungrier, a little more desperate. Who knows what we might do? A ward full of desperately hungry patients is the last thing you'd want, believe me. Especially patients like us.'

Chanita spoke to him coldly. 'Let go of my arm immediately or I'll call one of the soldiers over.'

Mr Canning looked at the two soldiers on guard in the ward. Both were fully armed with deadly-looking assault rifles. He released his grip on her. 'I'm very sorry about that, my dear,' he said, recovering his composure. 'I don't know what came over me. I'm only trying to help.' The violence that had animated him briefly seemed to have left him entirely and he was his usual polite self again.

He was no doubt desperately hungry. Like many of the bite victims he had gone without food for many days. Chanita wondered if the hospital might find a way to accommodate the patients' needs. Raw chicken was out of the question, but perhaps a rare steak might satisfy them? 'What exactly would you like?' she asked.

'You know what I really fancy?' he said. 'A dog. Or

even a cat. I'd accept a rabbit or a guinea pig if you offered me one. You wouldn't even need to kill them.' He leered at her, showing her his teeth.

Nausea hit her in a wave of disgust. She saw the yellow glint in his remaining eye and realized that this had been his intention all along. He had never expected to be offered any food. He simply wanted to torment her. 'I wouldn't even give you a rat,' she told him.

Mr Canning seemed to brighten at the thought. 'A rat. I wouldn't say no to a rat. Funny you should mention them. Did you know that starving rats will eat each other if they have nothing else to eat? Let's hope that doesn't happen here. That really would be horrible, don't you agree?'

Chapter Fifty-Seven

Upper Terrace, Richmond upon Thames, West London, crescent moon

James had planned to set off early in the morning before anyone got up, but when he came downstairs he was surprised to find Melanie already eating breakfast in the kitchen. It was the first time he'd seen her up and dressed since arriving at the house. She looked much stronger than in previous days.

'Going somewhere?' she enquired, her mouth full of toast and jam.

'Out,' he said. He had intended to sneak away unnoticed and had no desire to tell Melanie what he planned to do. He wasn't sure why. He wasn't doing anything wrong. But going back to his parents' house felt too personal. He hadn't even mentioned his parents to Melanie or Sarah. He guessed he wanted to keep his old life separate from the life he lived now.

The reason was shame, he realized with a start. Shame

of what he had become. He felt his face flush red.

Melanie didn't seem to notice his discomfort, or else chose to ignore it. 'Good,' she said. 'You can take me with you.' She tossed her long dark hair away from her face. 'I've been cooped up indoors for weeks now. It's starting to drive me mad. I need to see the world again.'

James hesitated. 'I wanted to go by myself, actually. Alone. There's something I need to do.'

But Melanie wasn't an easy person to say no to. 'Well, that does sound intriguing,' she said. 'Now I'm definitely going to have to come with you. Who knows what you might get up to if I don't. Besides, if I have to spend one more day in this house with just Sarah and Grandpa for company, I'm going to murder one of them. Maybe even both.' When he said nothing in reply, she gave him a wink. 'I wasn't even joking about that,' she said.

She shovelled the rest of the toast into her mouth greedily, wiping away a smear of butter with the back of her hand. 'So where are we going?'

'Shopping,' said James grudgingly.

'My favourite. You can tell me what we're shopping for on the way. But have you got any money?'

'Sarah gave me some.'

'Good,' said Melanie. 'Sarah looks after all our money. Give it to me and I spend it quicker than you can say Dolce & Gabbana. Mind you, give it to Sarah and she saves it for a rainy day. But I guess it's raining today, isn't it?' she said, glancing out of the window. 'I'll just grab a coat and hat.'

He waited while she pulled on a cashmere coat and adjusted her hat in the hall mirror.

'Come on, then,' she said, slipping her arm through his. 'Let's shop till we drop, baby.'

James led her along the route he'd followed the previous day. This time they were fortunate to avoid any street gangs. The four teenagers he'd encountered wouldn't be hassling anyone else in a hurry, he reflected mournfully.

'Where are we going then?' asked Melanie.

'Clapham Common,' he said. 'That's where I used to live. But first we're going back to the food shop I found yesterday.'

'But we already have loads of food,' said Melanie. 'I didn't eat that much for breakfast, honest.' She paused. 'Ah, I see. Clapham Common. We're going to visit your family, aren't we?'

'It's not much of a family,' said James. 'I don't have any brothers or sisters or grandparents like you. Just my parents. And I don't want them to see me. I just want to make sure that they're all right.'

'Of course,' said Melanie. 'I understand. Why didn't you say sooner?'

He shrugged. 'I kind of tried to forget about them, I suppose. I was ashamed of running away from home, of becoming a werewolf, of killing a priest.' He hesitated, then added, 'I was ashamed of Samuel, or rather, I was afraid of what my parents would say about him. They're devout Catholics, you see. They had no idea I was gay.'

Melanie squeezed his hand. 'Who knows what they thought? Maybe they knew you better than you realized. Why not give them a chance? Tell them, and see what they say. I bet they'd give anything just to know you're still alive.'

James shook his head. 'No. I just want to make sure they're safe, and to take them some food. Then we'll go back home.'

'Isn't your real home with your family?' asked Melanie. 'You're welcome to stay with us for as long as you like, of course, but perhaps you should think about going back to live with your parents.'

'No,' said James resolutely. 'I can't go back there. My old life is over. My home is in Richmond now, with you and Sarah and Grandpa. You're my family now. I just want to do this one last thing. And then I'll never go back.'

Chapter Fifty-Eight

Cabinet Office Briefing Room A, Whitehall, Central London, quarter moon

The Prime Minister peered at the General over her half-moon glasses. 'General, please could you outline for us your preparations for the night of the full moon.'

The Chief of the Defence Staff rose to his feet, straight-backed as always, his uniform immaculately pressed, his medals gleaming, his iron grey hair cut along a ruler's edge. The General always made Helen Eastgate feel like a slob. What did he secretly think every time he looked upon her appalling dress sense, her slapdash approach to grooming, her annoying habit of stumbling when wearing heels? Under the table she had already kicked off her heeled shoes in favour of the comfort of bare feet, and she had a feeling that the General somehow knew it. She tried to sit up straighter in her chair as he began to speak in his precise military way.

'Prime Minister, we are fully prepared for the coming full moon – the so-called wolf moon. Obviously this will be a critical test of our ability to contain the lycanthropes and those who seek to take advantage of the situation.'

The word *lycanthrope* had been Helen's suggestion, based on Professor Wiseman's name for the condition. The General in particular seemed to prefer this word to the term *werewolf*. Perhaps it made him feel more in control of the situation; that he was dealing with a disease outbreak, not a supernatural phenomenon. Nobody outside government seemed to want to use the word however. News networks could gain a larger audience by spreading panic than calming people down. One of the more downmarket newspapers had recently run a front-page headline that read, simply, *WEREWOLVES!*

The General continued his briefing. 'The army will be deployed in strength on the streets of London and in other major cities. These will include Birmingham, Manchester, Leeds and Edinburgh. In London, the Parachute Regiment will lead this task, and I have every confidence that the midnight curfew will be rigorously enforced. The weather forecast for the night is for thick cloud cover, with possible snowfall throughout the day. We do not believe that this will hamper our operations. In fact, the cloud may mean that the moon remains hidden, and it is possible that this will prevent the lycanthropes from changing into wolf form.'

Helen couldn't help herself from interjecting. 'We can't make that assumption,' she said, and immediately felt her neck turn pink as she realized what she'd done. 'I didn't mean to interrupt the meeting,' she added apologetically.

The General didn't seem at all put out by her comment. 'No such assumption has been made, Doctor Eastgate,' he assured her. 'I mention the possibility of inclement weather merely for completeness. We are fully prepared for the worst case scenario.'

'And what might that be?' queried the PM.

'That the lycanthropes mount a fully coordinated attack, that lawless elements come out in force to take advantage of the situation, and that significant numbers of vigilantes and protesters decide to take the law into their own hands in response.'

That sounded like a nightmare scenario to Helen, not merely a worst case.

'And you are confident that you have the resources in place to deal with that?' enquired the Home Secretary.

The General nodded. 'With the combined strength of the army and the police, yes, I believe that we do.'

'What about the quarantine hospital?' asked Helen. 'What happens if the patients try to escape?'

The General waved his hand dismissively. 'Colonel Griffin has briefed me fully on the hospital situation. The patients are weak and under armed guard. He has not expressed any concerns to me.'

Helen persisted. 'But don't you think there's a risk in keeping all the patients in a single location? What if the other lycanthropes try to free them?'

'Doctor Eastgate,' said the General, 'may I remind you that this is a military operation. Colonel Griffin has extensive operational experience under combat conditions. He is more than equal to the task of securing a civilian hospital. The lycanthropes may have caused the police some trouble on New Year's Eve, but I can assure you that they are no match for the British Army. In any case, it is far more likely that their attacks will not be coordinated in any significant way. If you remember, at the last full moon, they appeared singly, or in small groups, at locations across the city. They appeared to have no organized objective, and simply ran amok, killing civilians at random. This time the public has been given advance warning, and few potential victims are likely to be out on the streets. In all likelihood, the night will pass largely without event.'

The Prime Minister seemed satisfied with his report. 'Very good, General,' she said. 'Let us hope that you are right. Keep me briefed if anything changes.'

Chapter Fifty-Nine

Electric Avenue, Brixton, South London, quarter moon

Vijay found Mr Harvey organizing a team of men unloading boxes outside a food shop on Electric Avenue. It seemed weird to see his old biology teacher doing a job like that and it brought home to him just how much life had changed since the school had closed. Vijay needed to change too. It was time for him to step up and show his true mettle. Summoning up all his courage, he went up to his teacher and offered his services to the neighbourhood patrol.

Mr Harvey shook his head. 'It's very good of you to volunteer, Vijay' he said, 'But I need men, not boys.'

Vijay lifted his chin and drew himself up to his full height, but he still only reached the teacher's shoulder. 'I'm fifteen years old,' he protested. That was very nearly true; it would be his birthday in just over a month.

'Sorry,' said Mr Harvey kindly. 'I can't allow you to join

the night watch. It's far too dangerous. But if you want to help, I can assign you to one of the groups going door to door, checking on the older residents, helping them collect their groceries, making sure they're keeping warm, and so on. Often all they need is a friend, someone willing to share a cup of tea and spend a little time chatting. The normal community services have completely broken down, and it's hard for the old people to get out. If you could spare an hour or two a day it would really make a huge difference.'

'Collecting groceries?' said Vijay. It was hardly the heroic role he had hoped for, but if that was what Mr Harvey wanted, he would give it a go. At least it would get him out of the house. His mum had been furious when he'd sneaked out to go and see Rose, but she'd relented when he'd explained about her brother and how desperately he needed medicine. She would certainly approve of him helping out with those less fortunate than himself.

'Okay,' he said. 'But can I ask you about something else?'

'Sure,' said Mr Harvey.

'It's about Rose's brother, Oscar. He's sick. He has cystic fibrosis.'

'Yes, I know,' said Mr Harvey. 'I visited the Hallibury's house yesterday. The family seems to be coping reasonably well, although Oscar has a nasty chest infection.'

'That's the thing,' said Vijay. 'They need special medicines for Oscar, and they just can't get hold of them.'

Mr Harvey frowned. 'I understood from Mrs Hallibury that they have stocks of everything they need for the next few days at least.'

'But that's not enough,' protested Vijay. 'They need more.'

'We're all living one day to the next at the moment, Vijay. My hands are full just keeping supplies of food and other essentials on the move. It's getting harder to find reliable sources at prices people can afford to pay. Oscar seems to be doing all right at the moment. His family know how to care for him.'

'But can you try? Please?'

'I'll ask around. I have various contacts who might be able to source medicines. But I can't make any promises.'

'Maybe I could help,' suggested Vijay. 'I could come with you when you go out to collect stuff from your contacts.'

'No,' said Mr Harvey firmly. 'Dealing with my suppliers is just as dangerous as going out on night patrol. Half of the people I'm buying from probably belong to criminal gangs. I don't dare ask where they manage to get their supplies. To be honest, some of them scare the hell out of me. So just leave it with me, okay?'

'Okay,' agreed Vijay reluctantly. It seemed like helping old ladies was the best his former teacher could offer him.

The news that Mr Harvey was struggling to source essentials like food worried him. He remembered the words Rose had said to him the last time he'd seen her. *It's only going to get worse.* The way she'd said it, about seeing things in a dream, had made it sound prophetic, as if she really knew the future somehow. And prophesy or no prophesy, she might well be right, judging from what Mr Harvey said. Vijay didn't really want to think about the worst, but if he wanted to be of real use to people, he needed to be prepared. It was yet another example of him not wanting to face up to the truth.

Becoming a hero was a lot harder than he'd expected, but perhaps this was an opportunity to do something practical, something that would help to ensure the welfare of his friends and family, however bad things became. He walked home, thinking about the kinds of stuff that they would need to survive if society fell apart completely. Camping gear would be a good start. Some warm sleeping bags, a tent, something to cook with. If he could stock up with useful items, he would be able to demonstrate his street smarts and forward thinking.

He called in at a camping shop close to his house, but it was half sold out already and all the best gear was gone. Other people had beaten him to it.

'Sorry,' said the shopkeeper. 'All our tents and sleeping bags have gone.'

Vijay considered buying a gas cooking stove or a pop-up camping chair, but it seemed like a lame effort. In the end he left empty-handed.

When he reached his house, Drake was arriving at the same time, carrying a large shopping bag under his arm. 'Hey, Vijay, how's it going?'

His friend seemed to be in a good mood. He always was these days. In fact, the worse that things became, the happier Drake seemed to be. Vijay guessed that Aasha had something to do with it. Having a girlfriend made all the difference, and Vijay found his thoughts turning longingly to Rose again.

'What've you been up to?' asked Drake cheerfully.

'I've just been to the camping shop. I was looking for survival gear.'

Drake laughed. 'Aasha's more interested in designer gear. Take a look at this.' He opened up the bag he was carrying and showed Vijay its contents. The bag was stuffed with dresses, jeans and handbags.

'Where did you get all that?' asked Vijay.

Drake cast a furtive glance over his shoulder and lowered his voice. 'I nicked it. It's dead easy to steal stuff at the moment. The world is falling to pieces out there.'

Vijay could hardly believe what he was hearing. 'You stole these things? For Aasha?'

'Yeah. She asked me to get some cool stuff for her. I brought her jewellery yesterday, a nice gold necklace. She liked it, asked me if it matched her complexion, like I know the answer to a question like that. So I said yeah, obviously.' He pulled the jeans out of the shopping bag and held them up for Vijay to see. 'I hope these are the right size. What do you reckon? If they're too big she's gonna kill me.'

Vijay was fuming. 'I can't believe that Aasha asked you to steal for her,' he said. But actually, he could. It was just the kind of thing Aasha would do. Anything that was forbidden, Aasha wanted. She was a rebel through and through.

'Ssh!' hissed Drake. 'Keep your voice down. Don't tell everyone, yeah?'

'You should be ashamed,' said Vijay angrily. 'Sikhs don't steal.'

'I'm not a Sikh.'

Vijay had no reply to that. What was the point anyway? He unlocked the front door and went inside. Drake followed him in and disappeared upstairs to Aasha's room, leaving Vijay standing in the hallway, not knowing what to do.

He knew he ought to tell his parents about Drake stealing for Aasha. Sikhs always told the truth. But something held him back. It was a feeling of hopelessness.

What was happening to him? He wanted to demonstrate his courage, but he couldn't even do this simple thing. After all, what good would it do?

Chapter Sixty

King's College Hospital, Lambeth, South London, waxing moon

Chris stared at the headmaster in disbelief. 'No way,' he said, shaking his head. 'I'm not going to do that.'

'Oh,' said Mr Canning. 'It's not so much to ask, really. Just a small request.'

'No,' said Chris conclusively. He had tried to avoid the headmaster as much as possible since arriving, but Mr Canning always seemed to find him. The ward was small and there was nowhere to hide.

'That's such a shame,' said Mr Canning. 'In that case, you leave me with no alternative. I'm going to have to eat you.'

'What?' said Chris, his eyes widening in horror.

'Yes,' continued Mr Canning. 'It's a kindness really. You see, if I don't eat you, one of these others surely will.' He waved his arm to indicate the other patients in the ward. 'We're all getting very hungry, you know. Hungry folk will do desperate things. If we don't escape from this place by the next full moon, all hell's going to break loose. You're a clever boy. I'm sure you realize that.'

Chris did realize it. It was exactly what he'd been saying to Seth ever since they'd arrived in the hospital. The two of them were the only patients on the ward who ate any meals. Chris had tried his best to persuade the doctors that the fact they were eating normal food must mean they weren't werewolves. But the doctor in charge had insisted that it proved nothing. 'Loss of appetite is just one of the syndrome's symptoms,' he'd told Chris dismissively. 'We don't yet have a definitive test, and in any case, the hospital is on lockdown, so even if you don't have the condition, we have to keep you here anyway.'

Chris didn't really understand how the bite patients could survive without food, but they didn't seem to be growing weaker. If anything they were becoming stronger, and more restless. Violent outbreaks among the patients had become commonplace, and the soldiers had moved some of them to a separate ward in order to keep the doctors and nurses safe. Chris himself would have been attacked by one of the patients just the previous day if Mr Canning hadn't intervened to protect him.

The headmaster reminded him of that now. 'I saved your life, you remember? You owe me a favour in return.'

Chris felt the fight go out of him. Much as he hated to admit it, he needed Mr Canning on his side if he were to survive in this hellhole. 'Tell me again what you want me to do.'

Mr Canning smiled broadly. 'That's more like it. I knew you'd agree in the end. When the next full moon comes, I plan to make my escape. You and your friend can come too, if you like. That's up to you. All you need to do is create a distraction, something that will draw the soldiers to you. Setting off the fire alarm would do the trick. I can do the rest.'

'What exactly do you plan to do?' asked Chris.

'You don't need to know the details,' said the headmaster. 'Just draw their attention and I'll take care of them. Just be sure to wait until the full moon.'

Chris shuddered at the prospect of Mr Canning turning into a fully-changed werewolf. He remembered his encounter with one of the creatures the night of the previous full moon. He and Seth had almost died. But this time, the werewolf would be on their side, at least, if Mr Canning could be trusted. It wasn't as if he had a lot of choice in the matter. 'I'll have to talk to Seth about it,' he said.

'You do that,' said Mr Canning.

'If he says no, then I won't be able to help you.'

'I understand,' said the headmaster. 'But in that case, I really will have no alternative but to eat you.'

Chapter Sixty-One

Electric Avenue, Brixton, South London, waxing moon

The food shop was a long way from Richmond and it took Melanie and James over an hour to walk there. Melanie was glad she'd worn sensible shoes for once.

She was helping James stock up on food when a face from her past appeared in front of the fruit and vegetable counter. 'Ben Harvey,' she muttered, stunned. He was busy stocking the shelves with potatoes and carrots. She stared at him in amazement. It had been six months since she'd last seen him and she'd thought she'd never see him again. Not that she'd ever stopped thinking about him. She'd thought of him a lot recently.

But the last words she'd spoken to him had been cruel. Unforgivably cruel. *You're just a teacher*, she'd told him in a fit of petulant rage. *And you'll never be any more than that.* How could she have said such a thing? She'd been so stupid, she could have slapped herself. Somebody should have slapped her, and slapped her hard. But Ben had been too much of a gentleman to do anything like that. Instead he'd hung his head mournfully and walked away from her in silence. She'd wished a hundred times that she could unsay those words, but words were like arrows. They could never be recalled.

Her neck and face burned red with shame.

'Mel,' he said, equally surprised. 'What on earth are you doing here?'

'Shopping,' she said quickly, trying to hide her embarrassment. 'You know me. What else am I good at?'

He stared at her for a moment, then grinned. Then he laughed. 'I can think of a few things,' he said, and her neck turned redder.

She felt a surge of relief. Relief and gratitude. 'You look …,' she stopped abruptly, unsure of what to say. He looked tired. Older. No, that was being kind. His bloodshot eyes, dishevelled hair and unshaven face and neck gave him a ghastly appearance. Ben had always cared for himself so well. 'You look rugged,' she managed at last. She held her palm to his bearded cheek. It felt soft, rather than coarse. With a decent trim, it might even suit him. 'You could use a proper haircut though,' she added.

He laughed again. 'I've been too busy to worry about my appearance,' he said. 'Or even to sleep much.' He gestured around the shop. 'You were right. Teaching wasn't much of a career after all, so I moved into retail instead. Who knows what I might be doing next week?'

He was mocking her, but his tone was friendly. She could sense no malice in his words. 'I'm sorry about what I said,' she told him. 'It was stupid. I didn't mean it.'

'No problem,' he said. 'I forgave you months ago. How about you? What have you been up to recently?'

'Oh,' said Melanie. She decided not to mention the fact that she'd spent the past two weeks convalescing in bed, and the fortnight before that tied to someone else's bed.

She gave him a smile. 'You know, I'm just a non-stop party girl. The good times don't stop just because civilization is coming to an end.'

He looked her up and down. 'Well, I see that you're still the best-dressed woman this side of the apocalypse.' A frown knitted his brow then and he touched her forehead gently with his fingers. 'What happened here?' he asked, brushing her hair aside to reveal the scar where the maniac with the cricket bat had struck her.

'Oh nothing,' she said. 'An accident with a party game. It's almost healed. I'd forgotten it was still there.'

Ben still looked concerned, but he turned his attention to James. 'Who's this?'

What should she say to that? Meet James, he's a friendly werewolf. We keep him at home. He killed a man, you know, but don't worry, he's perfectly well house-trained now.

'This is James,' she said aloud. 'James Beaumont. His parents live close by. We're just buying some food for them.'

Ben held out a hand to James. 'Beaumont,' he said thoughtfully, shaking the boy's hand. 'Where exactly do your parents live?'

James looked startled by the question. 'Do you know them? They have a house overlooking Clapham Common.'

'Overlooking the Common. Mr and Mrs Beaumont. Yes, I think I do know them.'

'Oh,' said James. 'You do?'

'Yes,' said Ben. He stopped, as if he was trying to remember something. 'They ...'

'They'll be wondering where on earth James has got to,' intervened Melanie hurriedly. 'Come on, James, we need to go and pay for this food. Let's hope you've got enough money or Mr Harvey here might have to throw us out.'

Ben was looking at James in puzzlement, but he said nothing in response.

Melanie steered James toward the checkout, then turned to say goodbye to Ben. 'Take care, Ben. Maybe I'll see you again soon?'

He nodded. 'I hope so, Melanie. I'd like that. It would be nice.'

Chapter Sixty-Two

Electric Avenue, Brixton, South London, waxing moon

A cold sense of dread gripped James, and he couldn't get out of the food shop quickly enough. Fortunately there was no problem with paying for his purchases. He handed over all the cash Sarah had given him, and the Polish shopkeeper took it from him greedily, grunting in satisfaction.

'He knows,' whispered James to Melanie as soon as they were outside. 'That man, Ben Harvey, he knows my parents. He must know about me. What are we going to do?'

'Nothing,' said Melanie. 'Don't worry about it.'

'How can we not?' he insisted. 'He's probably already guessed that I'm a werewolf. Or if he hasn't he soon will.'

'Maybe,' she admitted. 'But I don't think he'll say anything to anyone.'

'Why do you think that?'

'Because I know Ben Harvey. I trust him.'

'You love him, don't you?' said James. 'He loves you too. I can tell.'

Melanie laughed. 'Don't be silly,' she said. 'We're just old friends.'

But James knew that wasn't true. He knew Melanie well enough by now.

'All right,' she admitted. 'We were more than friends once. But that's all over. I hadn't seen him for months. I'd practically forgotten about him.'

James still wasn't convinced.

'Listen,' she said, 'since you're so interested in my love life, it's like this. We dated for a while last summer. We had some fun together. But we were wrong for each other. Or at least, I was wrong for him. It was never going to last. He deserves better.'

They walked along together, heading for Clapham Common. James' nervousness about Ben Harvey had subsided a little after Melanie's assurances, but he still didn't believe her story about Ben. It was typical of Melanie to put herself down. 'Love can never be wrong, you know,' he said at last. 'Samuel taught me that. If two people love each other, it can't ever be wrong.'

Melanie sighed in exasperation. 'Sometimes people can love each other and still be wrong. They can be wrong for each other. Or maybe one person doesn't deserve to be loved. Anyway, Ben doesn't love me, he was just being polite.'

'You do deserve to be loved,' insisted James. 'Everyone does. God loves us all, so even if you think you don't deserve it, you're wrong. Anyway, it's obvious that Ben still loves you. Even I can see that.'

The discussion came to an end when they turned the next corner. The Common stretched out before them, its park-like expanse still perfect, despite everything that had happened. Close-cropped grass gave way to distant trees, and he could even see the duck pond that his mum had taken him to so often as a small child. He felt a tear well up and had to choke it back.

And overlooking the park stood the grand Victorian house that he had once called home. Five stories tall it stood, an end of terrace property with a basement, and attic rooms that had once housed servants. One of those rooms had been his bedroom. He wondered what was there now. Would it be exactly as he had left it, that day he had gone to school and never returned? A memorial, frozen in time? Or would his parents have thrown all his old things away and stripped it bare, ashamed of what their son had done? Of who, or what, he had become.

He turned to Melanie. 'I can't go to the house,' he said. 'They mustn't see me.' He glanced around nervously. 'No one must see me.' What had he been thinking of coming back here? Neighbours, school friends, anyone might see him. What would he say to anyone who recognized him?

'Don't worry,' she said, 'I'll take the food to the door. I'll just ring the bell, hand it over and leave. Okay?'

He nodded gratefully.

'Do you want me to say anything to them? Anything about you? Or shall I ask them anything?'

He shook his head fearfully. 'No, you mustn't tell them anything. Just give them the food, please. I'm going to hide behind this tree.' He gave her the bags of food and went to stand behind one of the bare sycamores that stood at the edge of the Common. He felt vaguely ridiculous hiding there, but it was the only way he could watch and remain out of view.

Melanie crossed over the road and opened the gate that led to the house.

James watched intently as she rang the doorbell and waited. For a while he thought that the house was empty and that no one would come, but then an old woman came to the door, huddled over and wrapped in an old cardigan.

He stared at the woman in surprise. Had Melanie gone to the wrong house? Had he been away for so long that he'd forgotten where he'd once lived? Or had strangers moved into the house in his absence? But then he looked closer and saw that the old woman was his mother. Her hair was almost white in the weak winter light. It had been blonde before. It had always been blonde. She said nothing, just stood on the doorstep looking at Melanie in a state of puzzlement.

An old man came to the door to join her, gaunt and stooped. 'Who are you?' he asked Melanie suspiciously. 'What do you want?' The voice was his father's, but it was cracked and broken. Both his mother and father were broken.

James turned away, unable to look. He had done that to them. He had broken them by his thoughtless and careless actions. He forced himself to look again.

'These are from a well-wisher,' said Melanie, holding out the bags of food.

His father took the bags, his eyes full of confusion.

His mother shot out an arm to grab hold of Melanie's. 'Have you seen him?' she croaked. 'Have you seen my son?'

Tears flooded James' face. He hid his face in his hands, unwilling to look or listen any more.

After a minute Melanie returned empty-handed. 'They took the food,' she said gently. 'They said to thank the person who had sent it, to thank them for being so kind.'

'No!' wailed James. It was too much. He turned from her and began to stride away down the street.

He stopped. A man was watching him from a little farther down the street. A man with a thick beard, wearing a black leather jacket. A motorbike stood behind him. The man stared at him a while longer. Then, as James watched, he turned and mounted his motorbike. A white wolf was emblazoned on the back of his jacket.

James shuddered. *A Wolf Brother.* The jacket was identical to the one Warg Daddy wore. He had hoped never to see that white wolf again.

The man fastened a crash helmet onto his head and started his bike with a roar. He revved the engine hard, making black smoke belch from the exhaust pipe, and rode away down the road, not giving James another glance.

'Who was that?' asked Melanie. 'A friend?'

'No,' said James grimly. 'Not a friend, an enemy.' He turned to face her. 'We can never return here, you understand? We can never come back.'

Chapter Sixty-Three

Brookfield Road, Brixton Hill, South London, waxing moon

'Is no room in here,' complained Mihai. 'And Grandpa Kevin snores like a horse.'

It was pitch dark, but Liz could feel the boy's hot breath against her face. His dark eyes glinted like coals in the blackness.

The boy had a point. The three of them now all slept in Liz's bedroom. Mihai shared her bed and Kevin had squeezed his mattress into the tiny floor space at the foot of the bed.

'You know why we have to share a room,' she told the boy.

'Yes, I know,' he said in frustration. 'Is because Dean and Samantha and Lily can sleep in spare room. Mihai knows that.'

Since Dean had shot and killed the two intruders at their house, Samantha had been too terrified to stay there alone with Lily. Liz had offered to put them up in her spare room temporarily, although quite how long that might be she had no idea. Mihai and Kevin had reluctantly agreed to make space for them.

'But still, is no room in here,' insisted Mihai obstinately. 'And I cannot sleep when Grandpa Kevin makes big honking noise.'

Her father was the only one getting any sleep tonight. He lay on his back, sleeping soundly, the air snorting loudly in and out through his wide-open mouth.

Kevin had helped her move the bodies of the two intruders from Dean's house. They had debated whether or not to report the killings, but technically Dean should never have opened fire on a man with a knife, and certainly not on one who had already dropped his weapon and surrendered. They could have lied about the sequence of events, but Liz hadn't been able to think clearly, so they had panicked and buried the bodies in shallow graves out at the abandoned factory where Dean had taught her to shoot.

It had been a mistake, but there was no going back.

So now she was sheltering two murderers, Kevin and Dean. It seemed to be something of a habit. The second time had been much easier to accept than the first, she reflected grimly. The more deceptions she engaged in the easier they became. Soon she would be telling lies quicker than truths.

It was enough to keep anyone awake long into the small hours, regardless of Kevin's snoring and Mihai's complaints. But it wasn't just the lies and the cover-ups that were bothering her. The next full moon was approaching and she was scared about what would happen.

They were calling it the wolf moon. She had no plans to find out what effect another full moon, wolf or otherwise, might have on her. She would be sure to stay indoors this time, and keep her loved ones safely inside too.

That was the one bright part of this whole situation. She'd always dreamed of having a family to look after. Now she had one in abundance. First Mihai, then Kevin, now Dean, Samantha and Lily too. And when Samantha's baby was born? They couldn't possibly fit a new-born baby in the apartment as well. The newcomers would surely have to move out before then. But while they were still here, Liz was enjoying their company immensely.

'Why you no sleep too?' demanded Mihai from the other half of the bed.

'Because you keep talking to me.'

'Is no one else to talk to.'

There was clearly going to be no sleep for her tonight. 'Tell me what you get up to with Grandpa Kevin all day when I'm on duty,' she said.

Mihai rolled in the bed. 'Is not doing anything wrong.'

'I didn't say you were,' said Liz, although she'd have been surprised if her father wasn't up to something dodgy now and again.

'Is mostly helping Gary the butcher.'

'Is that where you get all the food from?' she asked.

Samantha had expressed amazement that they had so much food in the house. 'I've really struggled to buy groceries,' Samantha had told her the day she'd moved in. 'The shops are all sold out most days.'

Liz hadn't even thought about it before. The food just appeared in her kitchen cupboards and fridge-freezer, and she hadn't ever asked Kevin where he got it from.

'Is no problem finding food,' Mihai told her now. 'Not if you know where to look.'

'And the food Grandpa Kevin finds, is it all legal and above board?' asked Liz.

'Of course,' said Mihai crossly. 'Grandpa Kevin is good man.'

From the foot of the bed came a huge reverberating snore, sounding something like a cross between a warthog and a foghorn. Liz smiled to herself. Despite everything, she was glad her father was back in her life. In fact she had a lot to be grateful for. It seemed that there was nothing better than a crisis to make you appreciate what truly mattered.

'He is a good man,' she agreed. 'Even if he does make a great honking noise all night long.'

In the darkness beside her, Mihai giggled happily.

Chapter Sixty-Four

West Field Terrace, South London, wolf moon

The first fingers of day began to push weakly through the curtains of Rose's bedroom. She lay in bed staring at the ceiling, her arms bathed in sweat that had now turned icy cold. She had barely slept all night, fearing what the wolf moon would bring, fearing even to dream. When she had finally drifted off, an hour before dawn, the nightmare had come again.

Fire swept through her ravaged dreamscape, swallowing all who stood in its path. Burning people staggered through the flames, their cries as terrible to hear as their faces were to see. Wolves ran in packs under the firelight, blood and drool slipping from their open snouts. Soldiers fired at the wolves with their rifles, but the wolves ran on under the full moon, cutting the soldiers down like rag dolls.

Rose screamed in her dream, but the nightmare did not

let up.

A succession of horrors came to greet her.

The headmaster, Mr Canning, the blood gushing from his empty eye socket like a fountain, his mouth twisted in a rictus smile. 'You'll be sorry, Rose,' he whispered. 'So very sorry.'

The dead dogs from the kennels limped past her in a line. 'We trusted you, Rose. But you let them kill us.' She raised her hands protectively in front of her face, but the dogs didn't savage her this time. They stood in a circle, watching, their dead eyes accusing.

Her mother appeared, then her father, then Oscar. She knew what would happen. The wolves rushed forward eagerly and cut them down, tearing at their throats. She stood helplessly as flames advanced, swallowing their bodies.

And something new. Vijay. She had not seen him in her nightmares before. He crept forward uncertainly out of the hellish gloom, not knowing what to do or where to go. Then, when he saw her, he came toward her, smiling with relief.

But Rose felt no relief, only a new dread. 'Why are you here?' she asked him, but she already knew the answer. Everyone she cared for was doomed to die. The wolves came for him, leaping, tearing, biting. They tore him to pieces under the moonlit sky. She woke with the sound of his scream still in her ears.

For a while she lay still, wondering if it had already happened, or if she might somehow still be able to stop it.

Then she remembered. The wolf moon was coming. It would rise tonight.

Chapter Sixty-Five

Brixton Village, South London, wolf moon

Ben Harvey couldn't remember ever feeling quite so angry. He stared at Vijay in disbelief. 'The man said what?' he demanded.

Vijay cowered in alarm as if he feared Ben might hit him.

'Look, I'm sorry,' said Ben quickly. 'I'm not angry with you. You did the right thing coming to tell me. I just can't believe what that man said.'

Vijay had taken up Ben's offer to help out with the Neighbourhood Watch. He'd been going door to door, taking food to the older residents and anyone who had trouble getting out. The old ladies in the neighbourhood had quickly taken a shine to him. 'Such a nice, polite boy,' one of them had told him that morning. 'Always so patient and happy to help.' Ben had smiled. Everyone had a hidden talent, and it seemed that Vijay had found his. But this latest news had come as a shock.

'Tell me again what happened,' said Ben.

'I went to the Polish shop to fetch food as usual,' said Vijay. 'One of Mr Kowalski's sons always puts some baskets aside for me to take to the old people. But today he wasn't there. I spoke to Mr Kowalski instead, and he told me there was no food left. But I could see that he'd just taken a delivery. Mr Stewart was bringing in boxes from the truck outside. There was tinned soup, fresh fruit and vegetables, all kinds of food.'

Ben nodded. He'd helped arrange the delivery himself, with the help of Kevin and his friend, Gary the butcher. They'd managed to secure a big supply of food and groceries, enough to last a good few days.

'So I pointed to the boxes and said that I needed food for the old people,' said Vijay. 'Mr Kowalski said that he was sorry, but he couldn't help. He wouldn't explain why. Then Mr Stewart came in with another box. That's when he said it.'

'What did he say exactly?'

Vijay looked nervous. He couldn't meet Ben's gaze. 'Mr Stewart said that it wouldn't hurt the old people to go without food for a day, especially since they never do anything to help. I said that they had nothing else to eat, and he said that they are old, so they don't need as much. Then when I said that they needed to eat to keep warm in the cold weather, he just laughed. He said that if they got cold enough they'd never need to eat anything again, and there'd be more food for the rest of us. Mr Kowalski didn't say anything. He just looked embarrassed.'

'I can't believe it,' said Ben. 'I mean, I don't doubt what you said about Mr Stewart. I just can't believe the man would be so cruel. And I'm surprised that Mr Kowalski didn't do anything to help. I'll go and speak to him immediately.'

'Wait,' said Vijay. 'There's one other thing I need to tell you.'

'It can't be worse, surely,' said Ben.

'It's about Oscar,' said Vijay, 'Rose's brother.'

'I already spoke to Salma Ali about getting medical supplies delivered to the sick,' said Ben. 'She assured me that she'd make arrangements. Kevin's managed to get hold of a big pharmaceutical delivery, or so I'm told. So that shouldn't be a problem.'

Vijay nodded. 'Yes, I know. But when Mr Hallibury went to ask about it, Kevin told him that he was under strict instructions not to release any of the medicine until further notice.'

Ben shook his head. 'I don't understand what's happening here,' he said. 'I'll speak to Mr Kowalski first, then Ms Ali. I'll let you know what happens.'

The Polish shopkeeper was behind his counter when Ben arrived at the shop. Mr Stewart was there too, stacking the shelves with fresh vegetables.

Ben pushed the door open violently and strode up to the counter. 'What the bloody hell is going on? Vijay Singh just told me you refused to let him have food to distribute to the community. Is that correct?'

Mr Kowalski looked awkwardly around but said nothing. He shuffled some paperwork about and pretended to read it. Mr Stewart stopped what he was doing and came over to join him, a sneer of triumph on his face.

'So it's true,' said Ben. 'I left strict instructions about the fair distribution of food. Why would you disobey me?'

'I just do what Ms Ali says,' said Mr Kowalski sheepishly. 'You must speak to her. Is not my problem.'

'Really?' said Ben. He turned to leave.

'They're going to die anyway, sooner or later,' said Mr Stewart. 'Probably sooner, the way things are heading.'

Ben turned back to face him. 'What did you say?'

The man stared insolently back at him. 'Just thinking out loud. Everyone's entitled to their own opinion. Why don't you run off to Ms Ali and tell her all about it? Be a good little mummy's boy.'

Lycanthropic

Ben fought down his rage. He felt like flooring the man, but what good would that do? Something was very wrong here, and he needed to go to the top, where he could fix it once and for all.

Salma Ali was in her home, and seemed almost to be expecting him. She ushered him into her front room and sat on an elegant chaise-longue, her legs crossed neatly. 'Please take a seat, Ben. May I offer you a coffee?'

He remained standing. 'No. Thank you. I've just been speaking to Mr Kowalski.'

She smiled politely at him. 'Where would we be without men like him? He works tirelessly helping the community, doesn't he? As you do yourself, of course.'

Ben was in no mood for games. 'He told me that you ordered him to stop giving out food packages to the older residents.'

She made no reply, but continued to offer him her smile.

Ben pressed on, determined to say everything that needed saying. 'I also heard that Kevin is refusing to allow medical supplies to be distributed. Is that true? And did you order it?'

'I did order it,' she admitted calmly. 'And I instructed Mr Kowalski to ration food to the elderly.'

'But why?' asked Ben.

'Because we need to plan ahead. I mean to ensure that this community survives this crisis. The food shortage will get worse before it gets better. You know that. There will come a time when there won't be enough to go around. Perhaps that time has already come. What then? Must we all go hungry? Hard workers like you and Mr Kowalski? Brave men like Mr Stewart on the night watch? If that happens, the whole community will crumble. Who will care for the sick and the elderly then? We need to prioritize resources if we are going to survive, Ben. It's a hard fact to swallow, but if you think it over, I'm sure you'll realize the truth of it.'

Her words sickened Ben. 'You've planned this all along haven't you? Those questionnaires you circulated asking how old people were, whether they had any special needs, and so on, that wasn't so you could help people, was it? It was so you could decide who to help and who to abandon.'

'Without my organization and planning, we might all be starving already,' said Salma Ali. 'How would that have helped?'

'So you get to decide who lives and who dies, is that it?' asked Ben, raising his voice. 'You get to play God?'

'Not God, no,' said Ms Ali. 'But someone has to make these decisions. And the people have put their trust in me. You can agree with my decisions or not, but you don't get to decide.' The smile had gone now and her voice was edged with steel. She had one final thing to say before she dismissed him. 'I hope you won't decide to oppose me, Ben. But if you do, I'll take you down, I promise. Don't doubt me for a second.'

Chapter Sixty-Six

West Field Gardens, South London, wolf moon

Vijay was waiting to intercept Drake the next time he came to the house to visit Aasha. He opened the front door even before Drake had a chance to ring the doorbell.

His friend seemed surprised to see him. 'Hey mate,' he said. 'How's it going?'

Vijay regarded him coolly. 'Come inside,' he said. 'We need to talk.'

'Later, yeah?' said Drake. 'I was just going to give this stuff to Aasha.' He indicated a bag he was carrying. Vijay didn't need to ask what was in there. Whatever it was, it was obviously stolen.

'No, now,' said Vijay firmly. 'Come upstairs to my room. You can go and see Aasha afterwards.'

They went up to his room together. 'Sit down,' said Vijay, indicating a chair by his desk.

Drake looked at it, but remained standing obstinately. He dumped the bag on the floor and thrust his hands into his jeans pockets. 'What's all the big mystery?' he asked. 'Why are you acting so weird? Have I done something wrong?'

'You know what you've done wrong,' said Vijay. 'Stealing.'

Drake glanced at his latest bag of ill-gotten gains. 'We talked about this before,' he said. 'You can't stop me.'

'Actually, I can,' said Vijay. 'In fact I can do better than that. I can tell my parents that you've been stealing clothes and jewellery for Aasha. How do you think they would react to that?'

Drake scowled angrily. 'You wouldn't dare,' he said. 'Why would you do that?'

'I would do it because stealing is wrong, and Sikhs don't lie, especially not to their parents.'

'That's wack,' said Drake. 'Aasha would murder you if you pulled a stunt like that.'

'You think I wouldn't?' challenged Vijay. 'You think I'm too much of a coward?'

Drake looked uncertain. He said nothing.

'But perhaps I don't need to tell them,' said Vijay. 'Not if you do something to make up for it.'

'Like what?'

Vijay swallowed. He knew that what he was about to suggest was wrong. Stealing was always wrong. But even Sikh scriptures taught that a poor man stealing bread to feed his family was different from a greedy man stealing money to make himself rich. Perhaps under some circumstances, stealing could be right, or at least justifiable. He had to take the risk if he was ever going to get anywhere with Rose. To Drake, he said, 'Could you steal some medication? Some pills?'

A frown came over Drake's face. 'What? Drugs? I don't know about that, mate. I ain't never done nothing like that. I could get into massive trouble, yeah? Why do you want pills anyway? You don't even drink beer.'

'Not illegal drugs,' explained Vijay. 'Prescription medicine. It's for Oscar.'

'Who?'

'You know. Rose's little brother. He has cystic fibrosis.'

'Oh yeah,' said Drake. 'The little guy in the wheelchair.'

'If he doesn't get the medication he needs, he's going to get really sick. He might even die.'

Drake scratched at the pale wispy hairs that had appeared on his chin these past few weeks. 'It ain't my fault he's sick,' he said.

'No, but this is your chance to do something about it. It's no big deal. You're out stealing stuff anyway, so why not do some good for a change?'

'I dunno,' said Drake. 'I suppose I could have a poke around, see what I can find. Can you tell me exactly what he needs?'

'I've got a list here that Rose gave me. Let me copy it out for you.' Vijay wrote out the names of the medicines in his neatest handwriting and passed it to Drake.

Drake studied the list and screwed up his face at the names of the drugs. 'Flu ... flutic ... I can't read this.'

'Fluticasone,' said Vijay. 'It's a steroidal spray that reduces inflammation in the nasal passage.'

Drake looked at the other items on the list dubiously before flinging it down in disgust. 'I can't get these,' he said. 'How can I steal something if I can't even say it? I've no idea what to look for.'

'Then I'll have to tell mum what you and Aasha did.'

Drake looked at him with something like hate in his eyes. 'You're gonna tell your mum I stole some stuff for Aasha, unless I agree to steal some stuff for you?'

'Yes. Exactly.'

'That's twisted.'

'That's the deal,' said Vijay adamantly. He handed the list back to Drake.

'Why do I need to steal it anyway?' asked Drake. 'Why

can't you just get it over the counter like normal people?'

'Because they're rationing it,' said Vijay. 'It's almost impossible to get hold of some of these drugs. Whenever Rose manages to find a pharmacist with some in stock, they always tell her they can only give her a day or two's supply. But Oscar desperately needs more. If he doesn't get it he might die. And I think I know a place you can get it from.'

Drake seemed to be thinking it over. 'Okay, I'll do it,' he said at last. 'But only if you agree to one condition.'

'What's that?' asked Vijay suspiciously.

'Come with me,' said Drake. 'It's the only way I'll know if I'm grabbing the right stuff.'

Chapter Sixty-Seven

Holland Gardens, Kensington, London, wolf moon

Leanna stared into the bedroom mirror. Like every fitting in the new house in Kensington, the mirror was luxuriously finished, with an elaborately sculptured bronze frame. The artist had stamped the handmade work with their signature. It was a unique work of art, for sure. But no matter the beauty of the mirror, the face that stared back at her was hideously disfigured. She brushed her long tresses away, better to study the blistered and scabrous skin that covered half of her face.

The red sores had healed as much as they ever would. The pain that had sucked her into a vortex of agony had subsided now. But the ravaged skin still itched viciously, and no cream or medicine could ease it. That would pass eventually, she hoped.

But the pits and furrows where the acid had reached deep into her flesh with its burning fingers would never diminish. Neither would her hatred of the woman who had done this to her.

Only the promise of vengeance eased her pain now. She would wear this mask of ruin as a constant reminder of the evil she had suffered.

And she would begin to repay that debt of suffering tonight.

The sound of the bedroom door opening and closing told her that she had company. Warg Daddy's face appeared in the mirror behind her. She let him see her hideous scars for a brief second before hiding them again behind her long hair.

His eyes revealed nothing. He had asked her only once about her disfigurement. She had made certain that he would never mention it again.

'It's time,' he said.

She turned to face him. 'Everything is ready?'

'Everything,' he confirmed. 'The Brothers are waiting for me. Adam too.'

'Good,' she told him. 'And the test subjects?' The people they had injected with infected blood had all reached Stage Two of the condition now – at least those who had survived. They were hungry for blood and ready to be released. The moon would change them to full wolf form, and then they could make their own way in the world, spreading the condition further. Each one was a seed carrying almost unlimited potential to turn humans lycanthropic. A domino effect, cascading onward, inevitably, uncontrollably.

'They've all gone,' confirmed Warg Daddy. 'Just as you ordered.' He paused, as if he expected something more from her.

She kissed him on the mouth, trying to inject some passion into her caress. 'Good luck,' she wished him.

Still he lingered.

'What?'

Warg Daddy seemed nervous in her presence. He often

was. She liked to keep him that way. 'What are your plans for tonight?' he asked eventually.

'Private,' she told him. 'Personal.'

Vengeance.

Her debts would be repaid. And she would begin tonight.

He glanced again at the burned half of her face, now hidden from view beneath a curtain of golden hair.

'Go now,' she commanded. 'I'll see you again in the morning.'

He turned away without another word, and she heard him leave the house with the Brothers.

Once she was certain they had all gone, she slipped out of the house alone, leaving it for the first time since her photo had appeared on the news channels as Britain's most wanted. She smiled grimly. Fame had not been part of her plan, but it seemed that everyone in Britain now knew her face. She pulled her hood over her hair, drawing it tight. Her jeans and hooded jacket gave her anonymity, no matter how hard the police might search for her.

Snow had begun to fall after noon, just a few flakes at first, then heavier as the day dragged on. Now the snowflakes were tumbling down as if they intended to smother the world. The army had gritted the major routes, but the snow covered smaller residential streets in a white blanket. The sky stretched above, white as the snow on the ground.

She moved quickly through the strangely quiet streets, indistinguishable from the few strangers who hurried past. Her footprints were already disappearing under a sprinkling of white.

Chapter Sixty-Eight

Brixton Village, South London, wolf moon

After his confrontation with Salma Ali, Ben went directly to the Hallibury's house to see how Oscar was getting on. The boy had developed a nasty chest infection in the past few days and desperately needed antibiotics.

'It's a bacterial infection,' explained Rose's mother, Jane. 'He often picks them up at this time of year. It's because of the build-up of mucus in his lungs. He needs special antibiotics to treat the infection, and we just haven't been able to get hold of any. When we heard there'd been a medical delivery at the butcher's shop on Brixton Hill, my husband went around to see what they had, but the butcher refused to let him in.'

'I kicked up a bit of a fuss, actually,' said Richard Hallibury. 'The thought that there were drugs that could make Oscar better just out of reach made me furious.'

'I understand,' Ben told him. Salma Ali's words had

made him feel equally angry. Angry and impotent, but he didn't plan to take this lying down. With men like Richard Hallibury to back him up, he had a chance of taking control of this neighbourhood and bringing Ms Ali's budding dictatorship to a quick end.

But a loud rapping at the front door indicated that he might have underestimated her willingness to act.

'Who on earth can that be?' asked Richard Hallibury.

The knocking came again, even louder than the first time. A heavy pounding at the door, from a wooden stick or some other blunt object.

Ben didn't like the sound of it. He glanced out of the front window and saw a group of men gathered outside the house.

Jane Hallibury laid a hand on her husband's arm. 'Don't answer,' she said. 'Ignore them.'

'I'm not a prisoner in my own home,' insisted Richard. He went into the hallway to open the door.

Ben heard shouting. 'Wait here,' he said to Jane and Oscar. He went to see what was happening.

A gang of men had seized Richard Hallibury and dragged him outside. Two of the men held him by his arms. Ben wasn't the least surprised to see that one of them was Mr Stewart. Around ten others were in the mob, some of them carrying heavy tools and other makeshift weapons. Salma Ali stood among them.

Ben strode up to her. 'What the hell do you think you're doing?'

She raised her eyebrows. 'Please calm yourself, Mr Harvey, or I will have to ask for you to be restrained.'

Two of the men came forward and Ben backed a step away from her. It was clear that these thugs would do whatever she asked. 'Explain yourself,' he said.

'Certainly.' Her usual smile was missing. Instead she had what Ben thought of as her *lawyer's face*, stern, serious, simultaneously vulnerable and unassailable. He had seen her use that face many times to persuade people to do what she wanted. She had even used it on him. With that face and that voice, and her carefully chosen words, she had an almost magical ability to connect to people at an emotional level, tapping into their raw fears and dreams, exploiting feelings they didn't even know they'd felt before her speech roused their passion and turned them into a mob.

'We are removing this man into safe custody for the protection of the community,' she said, indicating Richard Hallibury. 'We have eye witness statements that he is in fact a werewolf.'

'That's ridiculous,' said Richard. He struggled to free himself, but his arms were too tightly held.

'Horrifying and almost unbelievable,' agreed Salma Ali, 'But nevertheless true. We also have evidence that his wife is a werewolf too. Take her!' she shouted.

Two more men pushed into the house and emerged dragging Jane into the street. 'I can't leave my children,' she wailed. 'I can't leave Oscar.' She struggled feebly in their strong grip.

Rose appeared on the doorstep. 'No!' she cried tearfully. 'You can't take them away. You mustn't!'

Ben could see Oscar inside the front room, peering anxiously through the window. 'This is outrageous,' he said. He turned to the men who held Jane Hallibury. 'Look at yourselves. What do you think you're doing?'

Salma Ali spoke for them. 'They're protecting their families and their loved ones from these monsters. We've all seen what these beasts are capable of. And we know what will happen to them when the wolf moon comes tonight. At least these two will be locked safely behind bars.'

'That's absurd,' shouted Ben. 'You can't lock these people up!'

At last Salma's smile appeared. 'Actually we can. This is a perfectly legal citizen's arrest. We are acting on evidence to remove a threat to the community. Trust me.'

'I don't trust you,' said Ben. 'And there is no actual evidence against these people, just trumped-up and malicious accusations.'

She remained resolute. 'We have to act in the interests of the group now. The common good takes precedence over individual needs. I'd hoped you would have seen the truth of that, Ben, an intelligent man like you.'

He shook his head. 'I won't allow you to imprison these people.'

'No,' said Salma sadly. 'I know you won't. And that's why I can't allow you to walk away from here. Seize him!'

Chapter Sixty-Nine

Upper Terrace, Richmond upon Thames, West London, wolf moon

Sarah was busy cooking dinner when James returned home from his latest food expedition. She heard him burst in through the front door and come running down the hallway into the kitchen. A dusting of snow rested on the shoulders of his jacket, but his face was flushed with exertion.

'Hey, steady on,' she said. She had never seen him in such an agitated state before. 'Calm down, whatever's happened?'

'Where's Melanie?' he asked breathlessly. 'I need to speak to her immediately.'

'She's with Grandpa,' said Sarah. 'I think she's reading to him.'

James leaned against the door panting.

'Stop and get your breath back,' she told him. 'You look like you ran all the way back from Brixton.'

'I did,' he said. 'That's exactly what I did. I had to get back as soon as I saw what they did.'

'What *who* did, James?' Melanie stuck her head around the door. 'What on earth is the matter? I could hear you from upstairs.'

'It's Ben,' he blurted. 'They've taken Ben Harvey.'

Melanie's face paled. 'What do you mean, *taken*?' Who's taken him?'

'I don't know who they were exactly,' said James. 'But I saw them. A group of men, with a woman in charge. They arrested him and dragged him into her house. They were talking about locking him in the cellar. We have to go and rescue him. We have to get him out!'

Melanie stared at him, uncomprehendingly. 'They arrested him? Are you talking about the police?'

'No,' said James. 'They were like a mob, a crowd of people. The woman in charge said it was a citizen's arrest. They took Ben and two others, a man and a woman. They said they were werewolves.'

'That's ridiculous,' said Melanie. 'Are you sure you understood?'

'Yes!' wailed James.

Sarah calmed him down and got him to go through it all again, filling in the details he'd forgotten to tell them the first time around.

By the time he'd finished, it was obvious that Melanie's mind was made up. 'Okay, let's go and get him out of there,' she said.

Sarah had been listening carefully to James' story. She couldn't allow him and Melanie to rush off on some mad rescue mission. 'But how are you going to get him out?' she asked. 'You don't even have a plan.'

'I'll think of something,' said Melanie. 'I always do.'

Sarah wrung her hands together anxiously. This was so typical of her sister. She was always rushing into trouble, it was like a magnet for her. But it was equally true that she always managed to wriggle out of it somehow. She'd had a few close calls though. It would be better if Sarah went too, to stop her doing anything stupid. But how could she? She hadn't been out for months. How could she do this now?

'I want to come too,' she said. 'I want to help.'

'No,' said Melanie. 'Stay here with Grandpa. If we don't come back, you'll be all he has left.'

Chapter Seventy

West Field Gardens, South London, wolf moon

It was time to go out stealing and Vijay was terrified. His nerves had been growing all day until he'd eventually vomited. Since then he'd felt a little better, but it was still more frightening than anything he'd ever done before, even worse than when he'd been summoned to the headmaster's office for fighting with Drake and Ash.

'Come on,' said Drake. 'It's not so hard. And anyway, this was all your idea.'

Vijay nodded. They needed to get medicines to help Oscar. And Vijay had to prove himself to Rose. More than that, he needed to prove his courage to himself. If he failed at this, he would spend the rest of his life knowing he was a failure. 'Okay,' he said. 'You're sure it's not too dangerous tonight?' The night of the wolf moon had come at last. 'The werewolves will turn when the moon comes out.'

'Not till much later,' said Drake. 'When the cloud clears. And they won't be stealing medicine from the back of the butcher's shop.'

'Yeah, but the police and the army will be out on patrol too. Not to mention the Neighbourhood Watch.'

'They'll all be looking for werewolves, not us. That's why this is the best night to do it.'

'Maybe,' said Vijay.

'Are you just too much of a wimp?'

'No. No, I'm not. Let's do this.'

They went out under cover of darkness, wearing black clothing from head to toe. Drake had given him a black hoodie to wear. 'This is what the pros use,' he told Vijay. 'It'll turn us into ninjas.'

Vijay doubted that, but Drake was right when he said that the hoodies would hide their identities if someone saw them. As long as they didn't actually get caught.

He'd had a tip-off from his contacts in the Neighbourhood Watch that the local butcher, Gary, had taken a delivery of pharmaceutical products the previous day. Gary and that guy Kevin were a shady pair. Vijay wondered how a butcher had managed to get hold of drugs and medicines. He'd asked Kevin about giving some to Oscar, but the man had said he was a businessman and that the supplies would go to the highest bidder. Vijay doubted whether Kevin even knew what kinds of drugs he had got his hands on. He was just hoping they'd be able to find some of what Oscar needed. It was a desperate chance, but the situation was desperate.

'You got that list of stuff we need?' asked Drake as they strode along the back streets to the butcher's shop, trying to look casual.

'Of course,' said Vijay, annoyed. 'How stupid do you think I am?'

'I'll get us inside the storeroom at the back, but then it's up to you,' said Drake. 'I can't even read that list.'

'All right,' said Vijay. 'Look, can you just stop talking? Someone might hear us.'

'Don't matter,' said Drake. 'We ain't done nothing wrong yet.' He pulled his hood tight around his face and took a sudden left turn into a narrow alleyway.

Vijay followed him.

The alley ran parallel to the High Street and they made their way along it to the back of the butcher's shop. The alleyway was unlit and littered with junk and Vijay tripped over an old bicycle wheel that had been dumped there. He cried out as he fell to the muddy ground.

Drake pulled him back to his feet. 'Now who's the one making all the noise?' he said.

A wooden gate led the way up a darkened path to the back of the building. Drake stood nonchalantly with his hands in his pockets, looking up and down the alley a few times. Then he grabbed the top of the gate and quickly hauled himself over. 'Come on,' he whispered to Vijay from the other side.

Vijay tried to copy what Drake had done, but his muddy shoes slipped on the painted wood of the gate and he struggled to gain any traction. He tried again, but it was no use.

'Hurry up,' hissed Drake.

'I can't do it,' moaned Vijay. 'I just can't climb it.' The plan was over even before they had started. He kicked angrily at the bottom of the gate. The gate swung open and he gaped open-mouthed at Drake standing on the other side. 'It wasn't even locked,' he said.

Drake grabbed his collar and hauled him into the shadows. 'Of course it was locked. I just unlocked it from the inside.' He closed the gate and locked it again. 'Now, you'd better be more use when we get inside the storeroom, or else I'm gonna run and leave you there. Got it?'

'Yes,' said Vijay. He would do better next time. It was just nerves that had made him so useless. He had to do better, for Oscar's sake, for everyone's sake. 'I'm sorry,' he said.

'Don't be sorry, be useful,' hissed Drake. 'Now follow me and don't make a noise.' He turned away, slipping silently along the garden path like a black cat.

Vijay followed him, keeping as quiet as he could. When they reached a part of the building that projected out from the main part of the butcher's shop, Drake drew a flathead screwdriver from his pocket. He raised a finger to his mouth to warn Vijay not to speak.

Vijay watched as Drake crept stealthily around the building, poking at the window frames with the tool. Eventually he returned to the first window he'd tried and set to work.

The window looked old and slightly battered. Paint peeled from the rotting wooden frame and Drake forced the shaft of the screwdriver under one corner. He prised the wooden beading away slowly, working methodically from one corner to the next. The lower lip came away in his hands. He placed it carefully on the ground, then set to work on the vertical strips of wood to either side. Soon they were all off and Drake used the screwdriver to lever the pane of glass neatly out of the frame. He propped it against the wall and slipped the screwdriver back into his jeans. 'Easy work,' he said. 'They don't even have a burglar alarm.'

'How are we going to climb in?' asked Vijay. The window was narrow and about five feet above ground. Easy enough for Drake to reach, but Vijay was shorter and had already demonstrated his lack of climbing skill.

'I'll lift you up, then pull myself in afterwards,' said Drake. 'Do you think you can manage?' He knelt down and interlaced his fingers to make a step for Vijay to stand on.

'Yeah,' said Vijay. There was no question about it. He *had* to manage. He stepped onto Drake's hands and reached for the window. Drake powered him upward without warning and he plunged through the gap and into the dark space of the storeroom beyond. He landed head first on the other side but a pile of cardboard boxes broke his fall. Seconds later Drake landed on top of him.

Vijay was furious. 'What did you do that for?' he whispered. 'I might have knocked myself out.'

Drake jumped to his feet and dusted himself down. 'Some things are best done quick,' he said in a low voice. He pulled out a flashlight and shone its beam around the room. The storeroom was about ten feet wide and twenty long, stuffed full of boxes, crates and other containers, like a rather shabby version of Aladdin's cave. 'What does this medicine look like?' he asked.

Vijay shrugged. 'I don't really know.'

'We'd better get looking then.'

Chapter Seventy-One

High Street, Brixton Hill, South London, wolf moon

'Grandpa Kevin, what we buy this time?' asked Mihai. 'Is cigarettes? Is whisky?'

'Never you mind,' growled Kevin. 'Just keep your mouth shut when the Serbians arrive, and everything will be just fine.'

'Me no like Serbians,' complained Mihai. 'Is very bad men.'

The boy obviously sensed that a big deal was about to happen, even though Kevin had been careful not to say anything to him. It was probably Gary's fault. That idiot was puffing through smokes faster than the Orient Express. His hands trembled with nerves every time he lit up, and he kept looking at his watch every thirty seconds.

Kevin gave the butcher a hearty slap on the back. 'Not long to go now, Gary. Zoran said he'd be here anytime soon, and he's not usually late.'

'Yeah,' said Gary miserably. 'That's what I'm worried about.'

'Well stop worrying,' said Kevin crossly. 'You're giving the boy the heebie-jeebies. And when the Serbians arrive, leave the talking to me, right?' The last thing he needed was Gary rabbiting on and messing things up. When guns were on the table and big money was at stake, everyone needed to stay nice and calm. The deal was all arranged. The Serbians would deliver a dozen handguns and half a dozen shotguns, plus assorted ammo, and Kevin had the agreed payment ready and waiting in his shoe box. Zoran was a cool customer to deal with, and everything would be fine at this end too, provided Kevin did all the talking.

The phone in his pocket rang and everyone in the room jumped. He picked it up. Liz. His daughter always seemed to choose the worst times to phone him, but it would be safer to take her call. If he didn't, she'd probably come looking for him, and that would spell disaster. 'Hey, love,' he said. 'How's things?'

As usual, she sounded annoyed with him. 'Where are you? I was expecting you home this evening.'

'No problem,' said Kevin. 'We'll be back soon. Just wrapping things up at the butcher's.'

'Is Mihai with you?'

'Course he is. I'll make sure he's back safe and sound.'

'Well don't be late,' she said. 'You know it's the wolf moon tonight? I want you back in an hour, or else there'll be trouble.'

'Sure,' said Kevin, ringing off. One hour ought to be enough to seal the deal. One hour from now, and he'd be in possession of enough ironmongery to equip a medium-sized gang. With that kind of kit, he'd have more than just money. He'd have power, perhaps for the very first time in his life. It was the next big opportunity, and his hands were ready and eager to seize it.

'Hey,' said Gary. 'Did you hear a noise just then?'

Kevin shook his head. He'd heard nothing, although

his hearing wasn't as good as it used to be. It was probably just Gary's nerves. 'You hear anything, kid?' he asked Mihai.

Mihai glanced toward the storeroom at the back of the building. 'Some noise in back,' he said. 'Perhaps is mice.'

'There ain't no mice in my shop,' protested Gary. 'The only animals you'll find here are dead ones.'

'Well it's probably nothing then,' said Kevin irritably. There was no way into the storeroom except through the shop itself, so no one could be back there. He'd been in there himself not half an hour ago. 'Mihai, why don't you go and take a look?' It might be a good idea to get the kid out of the scene. The less he saw, the better. 'Take your time and have a good look around. We don't want no mice causing trouble, do we, eh?'

'Okay,' said Mihai sullenly, heading toward the back of the shop. 'Is already looking.'

Chapter Seventy-Two

Brixton Village, South London, wolf moon

'I don't want to hurt anyone,' said James. 'I've already killed enough people. I can't do it anymore.'

'Let's hope it doesn't come to that, then,' said Melanie. 'But if it does, I need to know I can rely on you.' The truth was that she'd like nothing more than to hurt someone right now. Whoever had taken Ben was in for a whole lot of hurting if Melanie had anything to do with it. She couldn't afford for James to go all vegan on her now. 'You killed a man to rescue me,' she said. 'Would you rather I was still tied up at the mercy of that psycho?'

James wouldn't meet her gaze. 'I wish there could have been another way.'

'Well, let me know when you think what that might be,' she snapped.

He said nothing but she could see from the way he hunched his shoulders that her words had hurt him. It seemed like she'd learned nothing about the power of her words to inflict harm on those she loved.

'Sorry,' she said gently. 'You know how grateful I am to you. You saved my life. But now we need to save Ben's. And this is no time to be half-hearted. It's all or nothing.'

'I know,' said James. 'But let's try to find a peaceful solution if we can.' They had walked nearly two miles from Richmond, back to the area where they'd met Ben in the shop. 'This is the street where they arrested him.'

'Kidnapped,' you mean, said Melanie. Having been imprisoned for several weeks herself, she had zero sympathy for whoever had done this. 'Take me to the house where they locked him up.'

He led her down several streets. 'This is it,' he whispered. 'The woman in charge lives here. I overheard her giving orders to lock Ben in the cellar.'

'This is the street where Ben lives,' said Melanie. The idea that his own neighbours had imprisoned him struck her as particularly cruel. 'Let's see if we can see anything through the windows.'

James led her to the house. It was a fine property, nicely restored, and larger than Ben's house, which stood opposite. A handsome Victorian house in a suburban London street. The area had been gentrified in recent years and was something of a hotspot with young affluent professionals. It was hard to imagine that a schoolteacher was imprisoned inside, although of course, she had been held captive herself in equally salubrious surroundings.

The houses on this side of the street all had cellars. There were tiny windows below ground level, but it would be impossible to climb through.

'How are we going to get him out?' wondered Melanie aloud.

'There are three people, remember?' said James. 'Ben and two others.'

'Sure,' she said. But in truth she had forgotten about them, she was so fixated on rescuing Ben. She glanced up and down the street, but there was no one in sight. 'Let's take a closer look.'

They crept through the iron gate and up to the front of the house. The building had three floors above ground, and just in front of the house the garden dropped away to reveal another floor below ground level. A light was on in the cellar, but the two basement windows were green and murky, and they could see little through the glass. An iron grille covered the cellar windows and prevented access. James tugged at the iron bars, but they were fixed into the brickwork and wouldn't budge.

'We can't get them out that way,' said Melanie. 'We'll need to go in through the front door instead.'

'But how on earth are we going to do that?' asked James.

'Leave it to me,' she said, giving him a wink. 'You stay here out of sight.' She unbuttoned her long coat and went up to the front door of the house. A brass knocker in the shape of a lion glared back at her. She checked her lipstick quickly in the compact mirror she kept in her handbag and rang the doorbell.

Heavy footsteps approached down the hallway and the door snapped opened a few inches on a chain. A man peered suspiciously through the gap. When he saw Melanie he unchained the door and opened it wide.

'Hi there,' she said, smiling sweetly.

'Well, hello,' said the man.

Chapter Seventy-Three

King's College Hospital, Lambeth, South London, wolf moon

Adam ducked low as the helicopter flew overhead, training its searchlight on the railway line that bounded the hospital's southern perimeter. The Wolf Brothers crouched behind tree cover in the adjacent Ruskin Park, dressed in black, their dark balaclavas making their faces vanish in the night. But the glaring searchlight turned night into day. Their black forms against the white of the snow would betray them if it happened to shine their way.

'It's okay,' said Snakebite reassuringly. 'They don't know we're here. This is just a routine patrol.'

Adam nodded. He knew the plan inside-out, but planning the operation in the safe surroundings of the conference room was different to the deep instinctive reaction he felt to the deafening roar of the Lynx helicopter sweeping overhead. He needed to calm his nerves if he was going to play his part in this mission without messing up. He touched the hunting knife in its sheath at his waist for reassurance.

'The chopper follows the same pattern every time,' continued Snakebite. It will circle once then land on the roof.'

Sure enough, the Lynx swept once more around the hospital's boundary and then slowed to hover directly above the main hospital block. Within a minute it had landed on the pad that in normal times was used for air ambulances.

Now that the searchlight was gone, the sky had turned black again. The moon and stars remained hidden behind the clouds.

Warg Daddy's deep voice rumbled in the darkness. 'Ready? Then go.'

Adam took a deep breath. As the most agile of the werewolves, it was natural that he had been picked for this role. Snakebite had recognized his athletic ability, and had encouraged him to volunteer. Even Warg Daddy hadn't raised any objections. They all knew that Adam was streets ahead of the others when it came to running, climbing and jumping.

He stepped out of the tree cover and darted across the railway tracks. No trains were running tonight. The tracks cut black lines through the virgin snow. He led the Brothers across the cutting and paused at the bottom of the embankment that led up to the hospital.

A low fence at the top of the embankment marked the hospital's southern boundary. Beyond it, two soldiers stood talking. With his keen hearing, Adam could make out their voices even over the high-pitched whine of the helicopter powering down its rotor blades.

He crept up the embankment, cloaked in darkness, and slid soundlessly over the fence, Snakebite at his heels. Slasher and Meathook vanished silently into the shadows to station themselves on the other side. Even if they had made a sound, the noise from the helicopter would have masked it, but they moved without the slightest snapping of twig or rustling of leaves. They edged their way toward the soldiers, waiting for a chance to spring.

Adam crept as close as he dared and waited. After thirty seconds he heard a muted bird call from where Slasher and Meathook had stationed themselves. The soldiers heard it too and turned to investigate.

Adam and Snakebite sprang at them unawares. Two quick flashes of steel and the soldiers' bodies slid to the ground, making dark stains on the white snow. Slasher and Meathook emerged from the shadows to join them.

Snakebite beckoned to the others waiting beneath the trees, and six dark shapes flitted across the railway tracks like bats. Warg Daddy and Snakebite lifted the combat shotguns from the soldiers' bodies. Then the group moved forward again as one, slipping through the narrow gap between two tall buildings.

The rear of the main hospital block lay shrouded in darkness. Lights from upstairs windows shone brightly, but here at the base of the eight-floor tower, they were as good as invisible.

'Good job,' said Snakebite. 'Ready for the next part?'

Adam nodded. 'Sure.' This was his moment. A chance to prove himself at last. This mission depended on him, and he was proud that Leanna and Warg Daddy had trusted him with this responsibility. He owed Snakebite for that. The red-haired giant had backed him all the way, and Adam had felt real comradeship for the first time since becoming a werewolf. He wouldn't let them down. No way.

'You positive you can do this?' asked Warg Daddy.

'Yeah,' said Adam. He looked up at the wall of the main hospital building. Eight floors in total. That was a long way down if he slipped. He'd just have to make damn certain that he didn't.

'Good luck then,' said Warg Daddy.

Adam checked the straps on his rucksack, pulling them tight and shifting the weight to make it more comfortable.

'You don't want to drop what's in there,' whispered Snakebite. 'Or we'll all go up in smoke.'

Adam swallowed. The bomb weighed heavy on his back, but his wolf strength was a match.

He'd had little difficulty making the explosives. All those hours spent attending chemistry lectures and working in the lab as a student had come to fruition, and the Wolf Brothers seemed to have no difficulty acquiring the list of ingredients he had given them.

'The rooftop should be clear by the time you reach it,' continued Snakebite. 'Just plant the bomb, set the detonator and climb back down.'

'No problem,' said Adam.

The moon was still hidden from view. The noise from the helicopter on the rooftop had dropped to a deep throb now and would soon stop completely. It was time to begin the climb.

His eyes traced a path up the wall of the hospital, seeking out any pipes, window frames or other protrusions he could use for the climb. There were none that he could see. The walls of the building were made from concrete and there were no handholds on its smooth surface. But at each floor a narrow concrete lip jutted out, a gap of ten or twelve feet separating each level. A normal human would never be able to scale the building unaided. But Adam was no normal human.

He positioned himself at the base of the building and bent his knees, preparing to spring. With a superhuman effort he launched himself upward and grasped the concrete lip that marked the top of the first level. The upper surface of the lip was dusted with snow, and he felt the cold bite his fingers. Muscles flexing, he hauled himself up onto the narrow ledge, scrabbling with his feet until he was standing flat against the smooth wall, one floor up.

Next to him, light from a window shone into the night,

and he could see people moving inside. Doctors, nurses, patients and soldiers. He waited a moment, but they went about their business, unaware of him clinging to the wall outside the hospital ward. The interior lights made it hard for anyone looking out to see his dark shape as he scaled the wall of the hospital. He let out a breath and readied himself for the next level.

It was harder jumping up from the narrow ledge than it had been from the ground level, but he grasped the lip above on the first attempt. Once again he hauled his bodyweight up until he was standing, this time two floors above the ground. Still no one inside had noticed his presence.

He looked down and saw the Wolf Brothers gathered below, watching his progress intently. Even dressed in black with balaclavas covering their hair and beards, it wasn't hard to tell them apart now that he had got to know them better. There was no mistaking Snakebite's gigantic form, nor Warg Daddy's muscular bulk. The short guy at the edge of the group was Meathook.

Snakebite gave a thumbs-up sign and Adam signed back to show that he was okay.

He leapt up to the third floor, then the fourth and the fifth. He threw a cautious glance up at the sky. The pale moon was just beginning to peek through the thinning clouds. If the change came upon him now, he might well fall to his death. He needed to be quick.

He jumped again, and again, scrabbling breathlessly up the sheer face of the building. At last he reached the top level and stopped to regain his breath. The concrete lip that jutted out above him and ran around the rooftop was thicker and taller than the narrow ledges that marked each floor. To reach it he would have to jump higher than ever. His arms were already aching from the climb, and his hands were chaffed from grasping and hauling himself up the concrete ledges. But he had no choice. He must go up once more.

Lycanthropic

He pictured himself on the starting block of the 100 metre sprint, back in the university athletics ground, poised to win yet another race. The familiar surge of adrenaline flooded his veins, as he prepared himself to spring. No bright floodlights blinded his eyes tonight, but the orb of the moon was quickly lightening in the sky. Every second he waited, the greater the risk of failure.

He closed his eyes and sprang, powering upward with his strong legs, feeling his toes leave the safety of the ledge and into thin air, almost a hundred feet above ground level. He reached out with his long fingers, grasping for the rooftop above. Every nerve fibre in his long body sang as he soared, but the weight of the bomb sought to drag him back down to earth.

It's too far. I'm not going to make it.

He pictured his body tumbling down the side of the building to land in a crumpled heap, the bomb exploding and bringing all their plans to an end.

I must make it.

His flight seemed to last an age, but a fraction of a second later, his hands closed tight around the concrete sill that marked the top of the building, and he was scrabbling with his toes, hauling his feet, then his knees, and finally the whole length of his body up onto the high roof of the building.

I did it.

He lay on his side for a minute, panting breathlessly from the exertion of the climb and the thrill of the final leap. He had made it to the roof of the hospital. In the distance, to the north, he could see the sheer triangular shape of the Shard, London's tallest building, and beyond it a cluster of other towers – the Gherkin, Tower 42, Sky Garden, and the soaring new skyscrapers of Leadenhall Street and Bishopsgate in the City of London.

Thirty feet above his head stood the helipad, a huge metal and concrete superstructure mounted on the roof of the building. Lights from the pad lit up the sky, and he could hear the shouts of soldiers and the tread of men walking up and down the steel staircase that led up to it, but the helicopter's twin engines were silent now.

He crept across the rooftop and readied himself for his final climb.

Chapter Seventy-Four

Brixton Village, South London, wolf moon

The man who had opened the door to Melanie was aged around thirty, with a heavy muscular build. He wasn't unattractive, but the corners of his mouth turned down in a faint sneer, and his eyes glittered greedily. He looked her up and down.

Melanie knew what his eyes saw. All men saw the same. She shifted her hips to one side and watched as his eyes devoured the flowing contours of her body. 'Can I come in?' she asked. 'It's cold out here.' She shook out her long hair to free the snowflakes that had collected there.

'Sure, but, …' The man nodded but seemed puzzled, as if his brain was playing catch-up with his libido. 'Who are you? Did Ms Ali send you?'

'No,' said Melanie. 'I came alone. I heard you had' – she turned her head to look up and down the street behind her, then lowered her voice – 'werewolves.'

The man didn't look too happy about that. 'Might be,'

he said cautiously.

She stepped lightly up to the threshold and laid a hand on his. Even in her heels he was a good few inches taller than her. She lifted her eyes coquettishly. 'I was just curious,' she said. 'But I wouldn't want you to get in trouble with Ms Ali. Just say if you want me to leave.' She kept hold of his hand, rubbing one finger gently along his thumb.

'No need to go,' he said. 'I'm not Ms Ali's poodle.'

Melanie smiled. 'I didn't think you were.' She flitted past him and into the hallway. The house felt warm after coming in from outside. She slid the coat from her shoulders and slipped it onto a coat stand. Then she turned to face him, letting him get a better look at her. 'I'm Melanie,' she said, holding out her hand once more.

He took the hand and shook it carefully, as if it might break in his strong grip. 'I'm Jack. Jack Stewart.'

'Pleased to meet you, Jack.' She glanced around the hallway. A wide staircase led up and a narrower one descended. The lower stairs were unlit and she couldn't see exactly where they led. She forced her eyes back to his face and readjusted her smile.

'So do you live around here, Melanie?' he asked. 'I don't remember seeing you before. And I'm sure that I would remember if I had.'

Melanie laughed. 'Not far away. Not far at all. And I'm certain I've seen you before. What do you do for a living, Jack?'

'I'm a chef,' he said. 'I work at a restaurant in the West End. Or at least I used to, before all the trouble started. I haven't been to the restaurant for the past few weeks. I work for the Neighbourhood Watch now,' he added proudly.

'The Neighbourhood Watch,' said Melanie in admiration. 'That does sound impressive, Jack. And I love restaurants too. I'm such a greedy pig.' She giggled.

'Really?' he said. She could see him eyeing her slender

waistline.

'Oh yes, Jack,' she assured him. 'I have a very healthy appetite.'

His eyes slid slowly up from her waist and came to rest on the curve of her bosom. 'And what is it that you do, Melanie?'

'Oh,' she purred. 'I do whatever men want me to do.'

Her words startled him and his gaze returned to her face. 'Really?' he said. 'You do?'

'Oh yes,' she said. 'I give them exactly what they want. I like to give them some surprises too. And in return they give me what I want.'

He swallowed, his Adam's apple falling, then rising again. 'And what is it you want from me, Melanie?' he asked, his voice growing hoarse.

She sidled slowly up the hallway toward him, and placed both hands against his chest. His heart thumped loudly under her touch and she rubbed him with the palms of her hands. She looked up. 'I want to see … werewolves,' she said. 'Show them to me now, Jack.'

Chapter Seventy-Five

High Street, Brixton Hill, South London, wolf moon

'Over here,' whispered Vijay. 'I think I've found what we're looking for.' A container of medical supplies stood open on the floor in front of him. It was packed with cardboard boxes of all sizes, each one individually labelled.

Drake kicked at the box. 'You're on your own now then, mate,' he said. 'I can't help you no more.'

'Well just hold the flashlight for me,' said Vijay. 'And hold the list where I can see it. I'll see if I can find what we need. And keep a lookout in case anyone comes.'

'Yeah, yeah,' said Drake. 'Don't worry. I ain't gonna forget to do that in a hurry. You do your searching quietly, yeah?'

Vijay started lifting packets carefully out of the container, scanning the label on each one and comparing them with the items on his list. The box was a treasure trove, but he had no idea what half of these drugs were for.

'Why don't we just take the lot?' suggested Drake. 'Or at least as many as we can carry?'

'No,' said Vijay as he read the labels. 'We must only take what we need to help Oscar. Stealing for personal gain is wrong.'

'Yeah, whatever,' said Drake. 'Just do it quickly.'

'This is one of the items we need," said Vijay triumphantly. 'Fluticasone. It's one of the rare ones.' He carried on searching through the box. He managed to find three more of the items on his list. Only one was missing.

'How do you even know how to say these words?' asked Drake, squinting at the list. 'You ain't no doctor or nothing.'

'They're just words,' said Vijay, continuing to rummage through the box. 'I don't need to know what they mean.'

'Yeah, well, as long as you know what you're doing.'

'I do,' said Vijay with a grin. He held a white oblong box up for Drake to see. 'Dornase alfa. This is the one Rose has been trying hardest to get hold of. We've got everything we need now.'

Drake held up the palm of his hand. 'Yo! Teamwork!'

Vijay slapped his own palm against Drake's. 'Teamwork!'

They were gathering the cardboard boxes together when the storeroom door opened.

'Shit,' said Drake. 'Let's get out of here.' He grabbed two of the boxes and ran back to the window where they'd entered. 'Vijay, come on!'

Vijay scrabbled around for the other boxes. He struggled to pick up all three in his hands. One slipped from his grasp and fell to the floor.

'Leave it!' said Drake.

'No,' said Vijay. He hadn't gone through all this just to leave one behind. It might be the crucial one that could save Oscar.

The storeroom light flicked on with a click. The white light was blinding after the darkness and Vijay threw his hands across his face, dropping the boxes again.

'Stop!' said a voice. 'Is caught!'

The voice sounded like a kid's. Vijay took his hands away from his face and saw a boy standing in the doorway. The kid was even smaller than him and had a shock of brown hair sprouting from his head. He looked like he didn't own a comb. The boy's eyes were a deep nut brown and stared at Vijay with determination. Despite the kid's small stature he stood tall, like he owned the place. He was the boy who always hung around with Kevin and Gary, Vijay realized. He had never heard him speak before.

'Stay here,' commanded the boy. 'I go fetch Grandpa Kevin and Uncle Gary. Then you in big big trouble. Is bad thing to steal,' he said contemptuously. He turned to go.

'No,' said Vijay. 'Wait. We weren't stealing, really.'

The boy turned back to face him and looked pointedly at the boxes that Vijay had dropped. 'Is stealing,' he insisted. 'Is very bad.'

'We weren't taking anything for ourselves,' said Vijay. 'A friend of ours is very ill and needs medicine to make him better. We were just trying to help.'

The boy regarded him with suspicion. 'You steal medicine?'

'Yes,' said Vijay. 'We only took what we needed. We couldn't find it anywhere else.' He picked up the dropped boxes to show to the boy.

'Who your friend?' demanded the boy.

'His name is Oscar. Do you know him? His sister is called Rose. They live not far from here.'

The boy seemed to recognize the names. 'Oscar is boy who rides in wheelchair?'

'That's right,' said Vijay, nodding vigorously. 'He has cystic fibrosis. He needs these drugs to keep him alive.'

The boy seemed puzzled by the strange medical term. 'And you only take medicine for Oscar?' he asked.

'Yes.'

'No other stuff?'

Vijay shook his head.

The boy frowned, his smooth skin furrowing as he decided what to do. At last his mouth widened into a grin that revealed several missing teeth. 'Okay,' he said in a hushed voice. 'You steal drugs for Oscar and I no tell.'

'Thank you,' said Vijay gratefully.

'But help tidy up first,' said the boy, pointing at the boxes scattered over the floor of the storeroom. 'Is very messy thieves.'

Chapter Seventy-Six

Brixton Village, South London, wolf moon

The man called Jack looked at Melanie uncertainly. 'Werewolves?' he said. 'I'm not supposed to let anyone near the prisoners. Ms Ali said not to let anyone in. I shouldn't really have let you come inside.'

'I understand,' she said. 'They must be very dangerous. And there's only you to guard them.'

He nodded. 'I'm not scared of them, though.'

'No,' said Melanie. 'Not a strong man like you.' She continued to rub his chest with her fingertips. 'It's just that I'm really curious. I've never seen a werewolf before. Perhaps I could just have a quick peek? Then we could carry on our conversation upstairs.'

'Yeah, okay, let's do that,' he said. He didn't move though.

Melanie drew away from him and walked to the top of the cellar stairs. 'Are they down here?' she asked. 'In the basement?'

He nodded.

'Come on then,' she said, pulling him by the hand.

They descended the narrow stairs together, Melanie leading the way. A short passageway at the base of the staircase led to a wooden door. The man flicked a switch and a light flickered on overhead. The door was reinforced with roughly-sawn two-by-two struts, and an external bolt had been freshly added. The floor in front of the door was still flecked with sawdust. A brass padlock and chain kept the bolt secure.

Melanie clutched the man's arm tightly. 'Are they in here?' she asked breathlessly, her eyes as wide as she could make them.

'Yeah,' he said. 'But don't worry, they can't escape.'

'Could I just see them for a few seconds?' she asked. 'If you're with me, I'm sure I won't be frightened.'

He looked nervous. 'Are you sure you want to?'

Melanie nodded her head solemnly.

'And then we can go upstairs together?'

'Yes,' she said. 'I'd like that very much.'

'Okay, stand back.' He pulled a key from his back pocket and twisted it in the padlock. The lock clicked open. He slid the lock from the bolt.

She could see a leather belt strapped around his waist holding a sheathed knife, but he didn't take the knife out. Instead he grabbed hold of a metal rod that was propped against the wall and held it in his right fist. Then he slid the bolt aside and cautiously pushed the door open.

Melanie had expected to find a dreary space with rough-hewn walls, but instead the basement was a comfortably furnished spare room containing a double bed with floral patterns on the duvet. A man and a woman sat together on the bed holding hands and another man was seated on a wicker chair. Melanie's heart leapt in her chest when she saw that the seated man was Ben.

He jumped to his feet. 'Melanie?' he asked incredulously.

'You know her?' said the man called Jack. He raised the metal rod and swivelled to face her. 'Is this a trick?'

'Don't you catch on quickly, Jack?' said Melanie. She jerked her knee up into his groin and he doubled over in agony.

Within seconds Ben and the other man had grabbed him and wrestled him face down to the floor.

'You bitch!' he screamed, twisting his head and spitting at her. 'You filthy fucking bitch!'

'Talk dirty to me, why don't you?' said Melanie. She bent over and slid his knife from its leather pouch. 'Or actually, you could just shut up.' She ground the tip of her heel into the small of his back. The man screeched.

Chapter Seventy-Seven

High Street, Brixton Hill, South London, wolf moon

A large white van pulled up outside the butcher's shop, and three men jumped out, slamming the doors behind them and looking around at the empty street.

'It's the Serbians,' said Gary unnecessarily, stubbing out the cigarette he'd lit just a few seconds earlier. 'They're here.'

'Yeah, yeah, I can see that for myself,' said Kevin. 'Now stay calm and just remember what I told you. Keep your lips zipped and leave the talking to me.' It was good that Mihai was still checking the storeroom out the back. With any luck, they'd get the business done and dusted before he returned. 'Now go and open the door to them,' he said to Gary.

The butcher tugged at the door with his meaty arms and the three men came into the shop without a word.

Zoran entered first, a large rucksack slung over his shoulder. The Serbian boss resembled a slab of raw meat himself – a mountainous man with broad shoulders, heavy arms and fleshy jowls. His eyebrows were bushy and his hair luxuriant, even though it had long since turned the colour of steel. Only his lips were thin, and his eyes were small and beady like a pig's. His gaze swept around the room, missing nothing.

Behind him came his two henchmen, one of them even more heavily-built than Zoran, the other whip-thin, with a sharp face and enormous oversized ears. Kevin had never been introduced to either of them, nor heard them utter a word. It was always Zoran who did the talking. The two thugs stood behind their boss, their hands in their pockets and scowls on their faces.

'Right, Zoran?' said Kevin, striking a friendly tone. 'You're bang on time.' He saw Gary cringe at his choice of words. Perhaps that hadn't been the best welcome for an arms dealer. He sought to ease things over quickly. 'You're a busy man, Zoran, just like me, so let's get this transaction done and we can all go home, right? We've got everything you asked for just here.' He pointed at the wooden crates stacked neatly in front of the counter. 'Everything packed up just as you asked. Check it if you like, it's all there.' Damn it, he was starting to babble like an idiot. It was all Gary's fault. The fool had put him on edge with his worrying. He looked to the Serbian man for confirmation that all was in order.

Zoran nodded toward the crates and spoke a few words in Serbian. The two henchmen started opening up the crates and checking their contents.

'You'll find everything's as agreed,' said Kevin. 'Nothing missing.'

Zoran made no reply, but waited for his men to do their work.

Kevin began to wonder what had happened to Mihai. The boy had only gone to look for some non-existent mice in the storeroom. What could be keeping him? He'd probably seen the Serbians and decided to stay at the back of the shop. That was fine with Kevin. It was bad enough having to worry about Gary blurting out something stupid. He didn't need the boy here too. In fact it would have been smarter to have left him at home with Liz. But the best ideas always seemed to come too late.

The Serbians took their time, working methodically through the contents of the crates, leaving nothing to chance. But eventually they finished their work. They nodded at Zoran and moved back into position behind him, one either side of their boss.

Kevin's nerves were at breaking point, but he was good at keeping his emotions under a blanket. 'All good?' he said chirpily. 'Right then, let's see what you've brought us.'

The Serbian boss smiled at him with his thin lips. 'Yeah, all is good,' he agreed. 'Apart from just one small thing.'

'Uh,' said Kevin. 'What's that?' He glanced nervously at the two henchmen standing with their hands in their pockets. He didn't like those men at all, neither the thin one nor the fat one. He didn't like anything about them. He especially didn't like the way their pockets bulged.

'Unfortunately the deal is off,' said Zoran. 'We didn't bring any guns to give you.'

'Oh,' said Kevin, a horrible sense of dread creeping over him. 'Why's that?'

'Because we brought guns to kill you instead.'

The two henchmen brought their hands out of their pockets and there were pistols in them. One gun pointed at Gary, the other at Kevin.

'It's very much easier this way,' explained Zoran, his piggy eyes shining with greed. 'Now we can take what you agreed to give us, plus everything else you have in your store, and we don't need to give you anything in return. It's an elegant solution, don't you agree? I'm surprised you didn't think of it yourself, Kevin. I thought you were smarter than that.'

Kevin had thought he was smarter than that, too. 'Come on, Zoran, this isn't the way to do business. We're trading partners, right? We have a lot more deals to make, a great future ahead of us.'

Zoran shook his head sadly. 'I don't think so, Kevin. In fact I think our trading partnership is now over. But you should be happy. I am teaching you a valuable lesson for the future, you know?' He pulled out his own gun and raised it level with Kevin's head. 'But unless you and Gary start loading the entire contents of your shop into the back of our van right now, I don't think you'll have any future at all.'

Chapter Seventy-Eight

King's College Hospital, Lambeth, South London, wolf moon

'When are we going to do it?' hissed Seth.

Chris had reluctantly agreed to help the headmaster escape. After all, what choice did he have? Set off the fire alarm or be eaten. That was no choice at all.

He shrugged. 'The headmaster said not to do anything until we can see the light from the full moon.'

Seth peered through the hospital window. 'When will that be? I can't see anything out there.'

Chris nodded miserably. The sky was overcast and dark. Light from streetlamps and from the hospital itself cast a faint glow over everything, making it impossible to tell if the moon was out or not. 'Maybe it will never happen,' he said hopefully.

The other patients were all on edge, pacing around the ward, growling whenever they approached Chris and Seth.

One of them had already been removed kicking and screaming from the ward by the soldiers after he'd grabbed at a doctor. It was like being locked in a Victorian lunatic asylum. Chris half expected the other inmates to suddenly begin howling at the moon.

Only Mr Canning seemed calm, sitting silently in his bed, not moving, just watching everything that happened with his one good eye. When he caught sight of Chris looking his way he winked.

Chris shuddered. 'We'll just have to watch and wait,' he whispered to Seth. 'Maybe Mr Canning will give us a sign when he's ready, or perhaps the other patients will all go mad when the moon comes out.'

Seth looked startled by the prospect. 'Do you think they will? What then? What if they all go berserk and start attacking the soldiers?'

'Then I guess Mr Canning won't need us to create a distraction after all.'

'What if they start attacking us?' asked Seth. 'What if they try to eat us?'

'I don't know,' snapped Chris. He wished Seth would pull himself together. 'Stop trying to think of all the bad things that might happen. Let's just hope everything goes according to plan and Mr Canning keeps his part of the bargain. Then we can escape with him and get out of this madhouse.'

'Good thinking,' moaned Seth. 'Trust the werewolf. Sounds like a plan. What could possibly go wrong?'

'It's the only plan we have,' said Chris angrily. 'If we don't do what he says, he's promised to kill us.' That wasn't strictly true. The headmaster had promised to kill Chris. He hadn't specifically mentioned killing Seth too. But Chris wasn't going to say anything about that now. He needed to keep his friend as motivated as possible. Instead he tried to reason. 'If we help Mr Canning, he's promised to help us too. And just to remind you, the headmaster is the only person who's offered us any help since this whole apocalypse thing started.'

'Okay,' agreed Seth. 'So when are we going to do it?'

Chris sighed in frustration. 'If you ask me that again I'm going to turn loopy myself,' he said. He glanced out of the window one more time. There was a pale light in the sky that might just have been the moon. 'Come on,' he said. 'Let's do it now.'

Chapter Seventy-Nine

Brookfield Road, Brixton Hill, South London, wolf moon

There was a fierce knocking on the front door of Liz's apartment, and the sound of a key turning in the lock. The door opened and Mihai tumbled through, his eyes wide and staring.

Liz rushed to him and gathered him in her arms, but he struggled free of her embrace and began shouting, his arms waving expansively as he sought to grasp the English words he needed. 'Is big problem. Grandpa Kevin needs help.'

'What kind of problem?' she asked. 'What kind of help?'

He gave her a look of exasperation. 'Is no time to tell. Help now, please. Is emergency.'

She tried to calm him down, but the boy waved his hands in agitation. 'Come to butcher's shop,' he said. 'Come now. You and Dean, come already.'

'Tell me what happened,' insisted Liz.

'Bad men with guns come,' said Mihai. He mimed the pistols with his fingers. 'They say shoot Grandpa Kevin and Uncle Gary.'

Liz pulled a face. 'Oh God,' she muttered. 'What has that fool gone and done now?'

Dean appeared in the hallway, the Glock in his holster, the carbine in his hands, his boots already on his feet. 'Never mind what he did. Let's go and sort this,' he said.

She hesitated. The night of the wolf moon had come and she had promised herself not to set foot outdoors. But the situation gave her no choice. 'All right,' she agreed.

Mihai seemed relieved. He dragged her by the arm toward the door, 'Okay, no time to talk. Must come now.'

Liz stopped him before he could drag her any further. 'Dean and I will go immediately,' she said. 'But you must stay here with Samantha.'

Dean's wife had already appeared from the kitchen, and she took hold of Mihai's hand. 'Don't worry,' she said. 'We'll stay here together and keep safe.'

'No!' protested Mihai.

'Yes,' insisted Liz.

Samantha gave Dean a quick hug. 'Take care!'

He kissed her on the cheek. 'I will, love. You stay here with Lily and Mihai. Keep the door locked and call me if anything happens.'

They ran to the butcher's shop, Liz struggling to imagine how her father had got tangled up with armed men. She remembered the food that kept mysteriously appearing in her kitchen cupboards, the meat that filled her freezer. She'd guessed he was up to no good – Kevin always was – but she'd never imagined him getting in this deep.

'What do you think's happened exactly?' asked Dean.

'I don't know,' said Liz. 'It sounds like an armed raid on the butcher's shop. Either that, or else they've got mixed up with bad company.'

'Very bad, if these men have guns,' said Dean. 'Here, have this.' He held out the Glock for her to take. 'Go on, it's yours,' he said when she hesitated. 'I taught you to shoot for a reason. I've got the rifle, and if we're going up against an armed gang, then we both need firearms.'

'Okay,' agreed Liz. 'But don't shoot unless there's no other choice. Dad mustn't get hurt.'

'Should we call for backup?' asked Dean.

Calling for armed backup was standard procedure in any firearms incident. In normal circumstances, Dean wouldn't even have asked her before making the call. But Liz had almost forgotten what normal circumstances were. 'I don't want Dad to get into trouble,' she said. 'Let's check out the situation before we involve anyone else.'

The butcher's shop was only a couple of minutes away. They approached it from a side street, keeping low behind a brick wall along the side of a terraced house. Dean went in front.

'What can you see?' asked Liz. She pushed up behind him so she could see too. A thin layer of snow covered the ground, making her trousers turn wet and cold. But at least the snow clouds had covered the sky, making the dim circle of the wolf moon barely visible behind them.

The area was well lit with streetlamps. No cars moved along the road, but a tall delivery van was parked right outside the butcher's shop, the rear of the van open and facing them. Wooden crates and cardboard packages were stacked inside. 'That doesn't look like a meat delivery,' said Dean.

A group of men emerged from the butcher's shop. 'It's Kevin,' whispered Liz. 'And his friend, Gary the butcher.' The two men were carrying more crates in their arms. Three strangers followed them, holding guns. 'Shit,' she breathed. She'd hoped that Mihai had somehow been mistaken, or that something had got lost in translation. But it was just as he'd described. *Bad men with guns.*

The armed men glanced warily around them, but the

street was empty of pedestrians. The spectre of tonight's wolf moon was keeping law-abiding citizens safe in their houses. Kevin and Gary placed the wooden crates carefully inside the van and went back into the shop. The armed men followed.

'How do you want to play it?' asked Dean.

'There are three of them at least,' said Liz. 'Maybe more inside the shop or in the front of the van.'

'Right,' said Dean. 'We're outnumbered, but at this distance I could probably take one or two down before they even know we're here.'

'No way,' said Liz. 'If you do that, they'll just kill Dad and the butcher. We need to play it safe. I say we wait and watch. It looks like they're clearing out the stock. They might just drive away when they've got everything they came for.'

'Maybe,' said Dean. 'Or they might decide to leave no witnesses alive.'

'I won't kick off a firestorm without a good reason,' she said. 'It's my father who'll get killed if we screw up. We do it my way.'

Chapter Eighty

High Street, Brixton Hill, South London, wolf moon

Kevin wondered how Mihai had managed to vanish out of the storeroom. Probably scarpered out of the window when he heard the trouble unfolding in the front of the shop. He glanced up and saw that one of the window panes was missing. That was a smart trick. He'd always known the kid was bright. If he'd been a bit slimmer and a few years younger he might have tried hoisting himself up and out himself. But the thin Serbian had followed him into the storeroom, gun in hand, so there was no chance of that.

He lifted another of the crates and carried it out of the storeroom to the waiting van. Every step was an agony, and not because the crate was so heavy. What hurt him most wasn't even the betrayal. He'd known that Zoran's loyalty extended only as far as he could see a profit, and he had no problem with that. Business was business after all.

Kevin might have done the same if the roles had been reversed. What caused him almost physical pain was having to load his entire stock into the back of the bastard's van.

Kevin had built his growing business empire through hard graft and determination. He'd poured his life savings into this venture. Chances like this came once in a lifetime, and then only if you got lucky. He would never get a chance like this again. It wasn't just boxes and crates he was carrying into the Serbian's van. It was his hopes, his dreams, his future. 'Bastards,' he whispered to Gary. 'Dirty treacherous bastards.'

Gary was virtually in tears himself. 'My old man passed this shop down to me,' he muttered. 'The last thing he said when he was lying on his deathbed was, *Take good care of the butcher's shop, Gary. I'll be looking out for you when I'm up in Heaven. I'll be sure to put in a good word for you.* Those were his last words. Now look at the place. There's nothing left. I let him down, Kevin. I failed the old bugger.'

The thin Serb with the cruel face prodded Gary in the back with the barrel of the gun. 'No talking. Keep working.' It was the first thing Kevin had ever heard him say.

'Bastard,' he muttered under his breath. *You can never trust a foreigner*, his dad had told him more than once. Quite a few times in fact. And he'd been right. Apart from Mihai, of course. That boy was all right. Kevin was glad he'd got out safely. He wondered if he'd ever see the kid again. He wondered if he'd see his daughter, Liz. She'd be mad with him after this, but he could live with that. If he could just see her face one more time, he wouldn't even regret the collapse of all his hopes and dreams.

In front of him, Gary stumbled in the road and dropped the wooden crate he'd been lugging. It crashed to the ground, splintering open. Bottles of whisky spilled onto the hard pavement, some breaking open, some rolling into the gutter. The sharp smell of the amber liquid quickly reached Kevin's nostrils.

He'd thought Gary had tripped, but quickly realized it had been deliberate. The butcher spun round and threw his fist at the nearest Serbian, the fat one. It smashed into his big round face like a joint of ham.

The man reeled back and Gary went for him again, his thick arms pumping like pistons as he pummelled him in the face, the neck, the chest. The man fell back and raised his arm.

'No!' shouted Kevin, but his voice was drowned out by the firing of the gun. A single shot to the head and Gary collapsed in a heap among the broken whisky bottles.

Damn, that had been bloody stupid. Gary had never been the sharpest knife in the block. But desperate men do desperate things. He hoped no one else would do anything desperate.

He stood motionless, wanting to raise his hands in the air, but too afraid to let go of the crate he was carrying. One wrong move now and it would be curtains for him too. 'Don't shoot,' he begged. 'Don't shoot, or there'll be no one to carry the rest of the crates.' It sounded like a pretty lame reason once he'd said it out loud, but he couldn't think of a better one right now. He held his breath.

Zoran barked out some command in Serbian, and Kevin shut his eyes and held his breath, waiting for the shot to come. It didn't. He opened his eyes again and breathed out. The man who had fired the shot kicked Gary's lifeless body with the toe of his boot. 'He's dead,' he said to Kevin, his face hard. 'Carry on loading.'

Chapter Eighty-One

King's College Hospital, Lambeth, South London, wolf moon

The clouds were thinning rapidly as Adam began his final ascent to the helipad on the hospital's rooftop. This last part of the climb was easier, as he was able to grab hold of the metal pipework that snaked up the side of the structure. The greatest risk was that he might be spotted before he could position the explosives and set the detonator.

According to Snakebite's intel the pad should have been clear of soldiers by now, but instead he could hear men shouting to each other overhead. That didn't matter. He had to complete the mission regardless. In fact, if they were preparing the helicopter for another patrol, it was even more vital to detonate the bomb before it took off.

He hauled himself quickly up the rickety pipework and reached the top of the landing pad. Peering over the edge he was greeted by a bustle of activity. The soldiers seemed to be readying the Lynx for flight. The attack helicopter stood in the middle of the pad, measuring perhaps fifty feet in length. Soldiers were completing the refuelling, and others were conducting last-minute checks. The two-man crew were already in position in the cockpit, and as he watched, the third crew member, the gunner, climbed up behind the pilot and co-pilot and positioned himself by the door-mounted heavy machine gun. The twin turboshafts of the helicopter spluttered into life and its rotor blades began to slowly turn.

Holding on tightly to the metal frame of the helipad with one hand, Adam swung the heavy rucksack from his shoulders and attached his home-made bomb to the main supporting structure of the pad. This was the first bomb he had ever made, and it was as-yet untested, but he was pretty confident it would work.

It has to.

Too much was at stake for it to fail.

He carefully connected the detonator wires to the device, checking they were secure, and began the downward climb, spooling out the wire from its coil as he went. It was a long way down, but climbing down was easier than ascending, and he no longer had the weight of the bomb on his back to worry about.

The milky form of the moon peeked through the clouds, growing brighter with every passing minute.

It mustn't come out from behind the clouds. Not yet.

He dropped from the helipad and moved to the concrete ledge that overhung the rooftop. The sight of the ground a hundred feet below him gave him a moment of vertigo, but he closed his eyes to block out the view and backed himself carefully to the edge of the roof so he couldn't see the drop.

Don't look up. Don't look down. Just focus.

It was the same when he raced at the athletics track. Worrying about times and performance and personal bests was a certain way to lose a race. You had to clear all conscious thought from your mind. He could do that. He knew how.

He gingerly lowered himself down from the rooftop until he was hanging by his fingertips from the concrete lip. He let go.

No past. No future. Just the drop.

A moment later his feet hit the ledge below and he landed like a cat.

One floor down. Seven more to go.

The wire uncoiled down the building as he jumped from floor to floor. He was halfway down when his foot missed the ledge.

His left leg shot out into space and he crashed onto the concrete lip, landing painfully on his right knee. He scrabbled for purchase, scraping his palm against the rough concrete. He almost dropped the detonator coil, but his quick reactions kept disaster at bay. He crouched on the narrow ledge, breathing heavily.

He wiped his forehead with his free hand. The air temperature was below freezing, but his hand came away damp with sweat.

Clear the mind. Breathe. Think of nothing.

His old coach, Brian Wooley, had taught him that trick. Poor old Brian. The coach hadn't been entirely useless. It was a shame that Adam had killed him. But Brian should have known better than to rouse his anger.

Clear the mind. Breathe. Think of nothing.

Down the side of the building he came, dropping from ledge to ledge, until at last he reached the ground.

When he landed, Warg Daddy reached out a meaty palm and gave him a hearty slap on the back. 'You did it,' he said, and Adam could have sworn that the Leader of the Pack had admiration in his voice.

'Well done, Adam,' said Snakebite, taking the coil of detonator wire from him.

While Adam had been putting his gymnastic skills to good use, the Wolf Brothers had been busy, priming the other bombs around the base of the building. Now they were all ready to detonate.

They had to be quick. The next foot patrol would be along shortly, and high above, the sound of the helicopter had grown to an intensity that indicated it was just about ready to take off. They had only seconds to spare.

Snakebite pushed the button on the detonator box. For a second there was silence. Then a huge explosion ripped through the night. A red fireball ignited in the sky, followed quickly by a second thunderous explosion as the freshly-refuelled Lynx went up in a ball of yellow flames. Even at ground level they felt the wave of heat from the rooftop inferno.

The sound of tearing metal followed as the helipad tipped sideways, its support struts twisting and buckling under their own weight. Broken girders and pipes began to fall from on high, and then the twisted wreck of the helicopter itself toppled over the edge of the building and plummeted to the ground on the far side of the hospital.

Simultaneously, Snakebite detonated the incendiary bombs that the Brothers had placed around the edges of the hospital, and a great curtain of flame roared up the sides of the building, engulfing it in fire, shattering glass windows and sending tongues of orange flames deep inside.

The plan had worked, just as Snakebite had promised. They had done the very last thing the soldiers were expecting. Instead of entering the building to free the prisoners, they had set the hospital itself ablaze. Now all they had to do was wait.

Above them the moon emerged at last from behind its silvery veil and Adam felt its cold light caressing his face. After the tension of the climb, the moonlight brought a soothing calm. Hair began to sprout from his skin as the change came once more. It had been a month and he had almost forgotten the delicious agony of becoming a wolf.

Chapter Eighty-Two

High Street, Brixton Hill, South London, wolf moon

The sound of the single gunshot echoed loudly around the High Street. The body of the butcher lay dead in the middle of the street, a bullet wound to his head. Curtains twitched in the windows of nearby houses but no one dared step outside.

'Shit,' said Dean, raising his rifle to fire.

Liz grabbed at the barrel of his gun. 'No!' she hissed. 'My dad's right in the firing line.' The man who'd killed the butcher had lowered his gun. The men exchanged words and her father began moving forward again, the wooden crate in his arms. The immediate danger had passed, but if Dean started shooting, her father's chances of getting out alive were minimal.

'How are we going to do it then?' asked Dean. 'They're likely to kill him when they're done, just like they killed his friend.'

He had a point, but opening fire now wasn't the answer. 'We can't just go in all guns blazing,' she said.

'What then?'

'We'll negotiate.' She stood up, making herself visible over the top of the wall. She wished now she'd had the foresight to put on a bullet-proof vest. 'Drop your guns!' she shouted, trying to sound a lot more confident than she felt. 'You are surrounded by armed police officers.' She held the Glock out in front of her.

The three armed men looked in her direction and dropped back cautiously, taking cover around the side of the delivery van.

'It's working,' said Liz. 'Show them the assault rifle.'

Dean got to his feet too and pointed the G36 in the men's direction.

'Drop your weapons!' he shouted.

The men stood still, watching and waiting. They didn't seem frightened, just wary. One of them, a tall broad-chested man with thick grey hair walked calmly over to Kevin and held a gun to his temple. 'All right,' he called back in a heavy Eastern European accent. 'Show yourselves.'

Dean cursed. 'They're calling our bluff. They've guessed it's just the two of us.'

'They can't know for certain,' said Liz. 'They're just trying their luck.' She shouted again to the armed men. 'Drop your weapons and release your prisoner! You are surrounded by firearms officers.'

The tall man dragged Kevin into the middle of the street and stood behind him, the gun at his head. 'It's difficult to surround someone when there are just two of you,' he called. 'Now drop your weapons and put your hands in the air, unless you want this one to die too.' He shook Kevin by the arm.

'What now?' whispered Dean.

'We have no choice. Do as he says.' Liz bent down and carefully placed the Glock on the ground in front of her.

She stood again, raising her hands above her head. 'Do it!' she said to Dean.

She could tell he hated it, but he obeyed her command, putting the rifle down and holding his hands high.

'That's good,' called the man who held the gun to Kevin's head. 'Now stand back away from your weapons.'

The other two men came over and grabbed the guns. The barrel of a handgun jabbed Liz in the small of her back. 'Move it,' said the man who had taken her Glock. She started walking over to the van. Dean and the other man followed close behind.

'Sit down there,' said the tall man, pointing to a spot on the pavement near the van. 'Don't move and don't talk. You can watch while we finish loading.' He released her father from his grasp. 'That means you, Kevin,' he said. 'Load the last of the crates. And don't try any funny business. You saw what happened to Gary.'

'Okay, Zoran,' said Kevin. 'Just one more crate to go. Then you'll have cleaned me out completely.' He shot Liz an exasperated look.

'That's how I like things,' said Zoran. 'No loose ends to trip me up.' He reached out an arm to stop Kevin, grabbing hold of him and turning him to face Liz. 'Talking of loose ends, do you know this woman?' He pointed at Liz with the gun.

'No,' said Kevin. 'Never seen her before.'

Liz turned away, but Zoran had seen the way Kevin had looked at her. The man scanned Kevin's face closely. 'I think you two do know each other,' he said eventually. 'In fact, I think I can see a family resemblance. Who is she? Your daughter?'

'What?' said Kevin, doing his best to look surprised. 'Come on, my daughter, a copper? How likely is that?'

Zoran smiled. 'That would be funny,' he agreed. 'So if she's not your daughter, you won't mind if I shoot her?' He trained his gun on Liz.

'No! Don't shoot her!' said Kevin. 'All right, all right, I

admit it. She's my daughter. But what difference does that make?'

'Oh, it makes a big difference,' said Zoran. 'Like I told you, I hate loose ends. And there's no end looser than an armed copper with a personal grudge against me. I don't think I'll be able to sleep very easily knowing she might be coming after me. What do you think?'

'No,' begged Kevin. 'You mustn't harm her. Please, I swear on my life she won't come after you. You mustn't do anything to hurt her.'

Zoran turned to his two compatriots. 'What do you think, boys? Shall we let the nice police officers go home? Or would you sleep easier knowing they were safely out of harm's way?'

The two men said nothing in reply. They knew a rhetorical question when they heard one. The thin man raised his gun and pointed it at Liz.

'Kill her,' ordered Zoran. 'Kill them both.'

Chapter Eighty-Three

Brixton Village, South London, wolf moon

James had hidden himself in the shrubbery at the front of the house to wait. He'd watched the front door open, spilling warm light into the darkness. Melanie had stood in the light, talking to a man inside the house. James couldn't see the man, but Melanie had spoken to him like a long-lost friend or a lover. A few seconds later she was inside and the door had closed behind her, swallowing the light.

James waited patiently outside.

A thin layer of snow dusted the garden. It had stopped falling now, but dark snow clouds still drifted heavily overhead. It was already past moonrise. He wondered if the wolf moon would put in an appearance tonight. He could feel its gentle pull even behind the curtain of clouds. It tugged insistently at every nerve ending, drawing him with a power he could not resist.

He hadn't made a decision to come out tonight. The

decision had been taken for him, as if forces larger than himself were at work. Whether it was the moon, or God, or fate, he couldn't say. But if the clouds cleared before he returned home, he would change. He had no choice in the matter.

But he still had one choice. Whether to kill, or not.

'I won't,' he whispered. For a moment it seemed as if Samuel's ghost crouched beside him, a swirling translucent form in the darkness. Or it might have been his breath in the freezing night air. 'I won't kill,' he said. 'I promise not to. Whatever happens, I will shed no blood tonight.'

He didn't want to think about the consequences of not hunting. How long could he survive without feeding, without the sweet taste of meat and the trickle of hot blood between his lips? Already he had grown weak and tired. A whole month had passed since he had last tasted flesh. Could he endure a second month? A third? There was no way of knowing. He needed to take things one step at a time. And for now that meant helping Melanie to rescue Ben.

A shout came from the basement room of the house. A man bellowed in anger, followed by a scream. James jumped to his feet and rushed to the front door. 'Melanie?' he called, banging his fist against the wood. 'Melanie, are you there?'

'No,' said a cold voice from behind him. 'But I am. Don't say you've forgotten me already, James. I haven't forgotten you. I never will.'

He froze and turned. At the iron gate stood a young woman dressed in jeans, her face shadowed by a hooded jacket. From within the shadows her eyes shone blue and cold.

'Leanna.' He had hoped never to hear her icy voice again, had fooled himself that he was free of her. 'What are you doing here?'

She opened the gate and stepped onto the short path that led up to the house. The wrought metal gate slammed shut behind her. 'Believe it or not, I'm here for you, James,' she said. 'One of my watchers spotted you nearby, so I waited for you to return, and followed you and your pretty friend right here. Are you really so surprised to see me? I thought you might have guessed.'

The Wolf Brother. James had been right to fear him when he'd seen him watching outside his parents' house. But he hadn't thought Leanna would follow him tonight. He'd been stupid. He should have known that she would never let him go that easily. 'What do you want from me?' he asked her.

'Oh, just one thing,' she said. 'Vengeance.' She threw back her hood, and thick blonde hair tumbled over her crystal eyes. She brushed the hair aside. One side of her face was hideously burned and blistered. She turned it toward him so he could see.

James recoiled at the sight of her.

Leanna turned her cold gaze on him, blue eyes flashing angrily. The skin around her right eye was red and cracked, like a lava flow from a volcano. 'Horrifies you, does it?' she snarled. 'Think how I must feel, seeing this every day in the mirror. The only thing that makes it tolerable is knowing that one day the person who did this to me will suffer far worse than she could possibly imagine.' She smiled. 'But first I'll take my revenge on you. You're a traitor, James. A traitor to me, and to your species. And it's time for you to pay the price.'

'I'm no traitor,' he said defiantly.

Leanna's eyes narrowed and seemed to become even chillier, if that was possible. 'You took the side of humans against wolves,' she accused.

'They were just kids, like me,' said James. 'They didn't deserve to die. I did the right thing. I would do it again.'

'They were prey,' she said flatly. 'Nothing more.' She began to walk up the path toward him.

She meant to kill him, that was plain enough.

He could fight her, but he was so tired of fighting, tired

of praying to a silent God and groping in the dark for guidance. He could offer himself to her instead. It would be easier than struggling on, pointlessly, day after day, growing ever weaker. It would be easier than battling against the wolf blood that surged inside him even now, lusting for blood, always lusting after human blood. And he could be with Samuel again, now and forever.

'I visited your parents earlier this evening,' said Leanna. 'I took them a food basket, just like you did. They were very grateful. They welcomed me into their home. But they didn't get to eat any of the food I took them. I ate them instead.'

'No!' he shouted. 'You're lying.' But a cold dread had seized his heart.

'I thought you might say that,' said Leanna. 'So I brought you some proof.' She slid a hand inside her jacket and drew out a photograph. 'Recognize this?'

The photo brought back instant and vivid memories. It had been taken at his first day at the Catholic Boys School on Mayfield Avenue. An impossibly young version of himself stood awkwardly outside the gate to the school, dressed in his brand new uniform, his shoes polished to a bright shine, the sleeves of his blazer too long. 'You'll grow into it soon enough,' his mother had promised him. He choked back the tears as he remembered.

'This photograph took pride of place on the mantelpiece in their front room,' said Leanna. 'It seems they still loved you, even after everything you'd done.'

'No,' said James, but what was he denying? She spoke the truth. His parents were dead. Everyone he held most dear was dead. His mother and father; Samuel too. Every hope, every desire, every dream was dashed. Nothing remained in this world for him now.

Leanna licked her lips greedily. 'You defied me once,' she accused. 'But you will never defy me again.'

'No,' he said, willing for it to end quickly. He bowed his head before her. 'Take me, then.'

'What?' Her voice cut the air like a knife.

'You can have me,' he told her. 'Take your vengeance. Kill me now.' He stepped toward her, head dipped, arms clasped behind his back.

She backed away from him. 'No,' she cried, 'Not like this!'

He looked up. 'How then?'

'Run!' Her anger blossomed into red hot fire. 'Fight!'

He shook his head sadly. 'No,' he said. What was the point? He had no fight left in him. 'Do it quickly.'

Already the pale form of the moon was peeping through the clouds above. He felt the moonlight brush his skin. The hairs on his neck began to tingle.

He would change in seconds. And then what? He didn't want to find out. 'Do it!' he commanded.

But Leanna held back. She would not touch him. She bared her teeth in frustration and rage.

'Do it now!' he insisted, but she stood her ground.

The change began, slowly at first. His fingertips throbbed, his clothing tightened, his breaths came faster. There was nothing he could do to stop it. Fire flowed from his heart as the wolf blood quickened in his veins.

Leanna was changing too. The pale skin of her face rippled as fine golden hairs pushed through, concealing her disfigurement. The nails of her thin fingers began to twist, turning longer, sharper, iron-hard. Her mouth contorted into a sickening grin as sharp canine teeth emerged, glinting white as the snowy ground around her. She let out a triumphant howl as the change flooded through her.

The change was reviving James, restoring vigour, just as Samuel had once given him the gift of a new life through love. The transformation accelerated as skin and bone reshaped themselves under the pull of the wolf moon. Muscles thickened as his limbs grew strong, and he dropped to all fours. Energy coursed through him again. And hunger too, more hunger than he could have imagined. He growled at Leanna and raked the ground with long claws.

Already Leanna was in full wolf form. She opened her snout in triumph, exposing long teeth like icicles, snorting white breath toward him. 'Yes,' she hissed with satisfaction. 'Like this. Wolf to wolf.' She padded slowly up the path.

Voices came from within the house behind him. A man's voice: Ben's. Then Melanie's. The front door of the house began to open.

Leanna laughed cruelly. 'You can be my main course, James. Your parents were my hors d'oeuvres, and your friends will be my dessert.'

'No,' he cried. He roared at her with anger. 'I won't let you.'

She paced toward him, eyes shining yellow, mouth a cage of white teeth. 'You have no power over me,' she snarled. She scratched at the ground in anger, getting ready to pounce. 'I am your queen now. Queen of all werewolves. And you shall do as I command.'

James stood his ground between her and the others. He would never let her pass. 'You are no queen,' he told her. 'Look around you. Everything you touch you destroy. You are queen of nothing.'

He threw back his head and howled.

Chapter Eighty-Four

King's College Hospital, Lambeth, South London, wolf moon

Chanita woke with a start. She grabbed rest whenever she could these days, slipping into oblivion in minutes, the warm relief of sleep taking her into its welcoming arms like a lover snatching a quick kiss. She never knew how long she might sleep, or how long it would be before she could rest again.

The sound that had shattered the silence of the night was loud enough to wake the dead. A fire alarm, ringing frantically. She had heard another sound too. An explosion. More than one. The hospital must be under attack.

She sat bolt upright and leapt from her makeshift bed in a single movement.

A fire here, in the hospital?

They had to evacuate immediately, or it would be a catastrophe. She thought of all the patients sealed into quarantine. How could they get everyone out safely?

But if someone was attacking the hospital, was it even safe to leave? And what about the quarantine? The risk that the patients might escape was unthinkable.

But there was no time to think. Events were unfolding too quickly. She dashed onto the ward and saw chaos. Patients were up and about, rushing to and fro, and the doctors and nurses seemed unable to control them. The two soldiers on guard in the ward shouted for order, but no one took any notice. They raised their rifles, but stopped short of firing. There was too much movement, and the patients seemed scared, not violent.

'Everyone stay calm and return to your beds!' she shouted, but the noise was too loud and no one seemed in a mood to listen. Instead she turned to the soldiers. 'Help me unlock the doors. We have to get everyone out of here.'

The two soldiers regarded her uncertainly. 'We have orders to keep them here unless authorized.'

'Move!' she screeched at them. '*I'm* authorizing you! We'll burn to a crisp if we stay in here!'

That got them moving. One of them brought out a bunch of keys and went to the main exit door to open it.

'What are you planning to do?' asked the other soldier. 'We were told to keep the patients quarantined even in the event of a fire. Our instructions are to wait for help to arrive.'

'You heard the explosions,' Chanita told him. 'This is no ordinary fire. The hospital is under attack.'

'Okay,' agreed the man. 'Come on, we'll escort the prisoners down to the main entrance hall and wait for further instructions.'

Chapter Eighty-Five

Brixton Village, South London, wolf moon

Ben left Mr Stewart lying on the cellar floor and closed the door tightly shut, slamming the bolt home and locking the padlock. He slipped the key into his pocket. 'He won't be going anywhere in a hurry,' he said. He still had no idea how Melanie had found out that he'd been taken prisoner, but there would be time to ask questions later. 'Come on,' he said. 'Someone might come back at any time. We have to get out of here.'

She wrapped her arms around him and gave him a kiss on the mouth. 'I'm just so relieved that they didn't hurt you.'

'I'm okay apart from a few bruises,' he said. 'But I might not be if we don't make a run for it.'

Richard Hallibury led the way back up the stairs, holding the steel rod in front of him. His wife, Jane, went next, then Melanie. Ben checked the locked door once more, then followed, clutching the hunting knife that

Melanie had taken from Mr Stewart.

He reached the top of the staircase when he heard the sound of a wolf howling outside.

Richard stopped abruptly in the hallway.

The sound was unmistakable. A wolf, right outside the front door of the house. It continued to rise and fall for several seconds before dying away.

'Let's go out the back way,' said Ben. 'We can't go out into the street with a werewolf on the loose.'

He started to back away, but Melanie grabbed his arm. 'Stop. It's just James. I left him out there. He must have changed in the moonlight.'

'Your friend is a werewolf?' said Ben. When he'd first heard that James was the Beaumont's son, he'd guessed as much, but still, he'd been reluctant to accept it. Now hearing it from Melanie's own lips brought the truth crashing home. James Beaumont was the boy that the police had suspected of killing that Catholic priest in his confessional. 'Will he attack us if we go out?' Every werewolf that had been captured on video had killed or attacked someone.

'James would never hurt me,' said Melanie fiercely. 'He saved my life.'

But Richard Hallibury seemed sceptical. 'We're not going out there with a werewolf, whoever he happens to be.'

'Let me go first,' said Melanie. 'I'll talk to him. Then you'll see.' She opened the front door and looked outside. She was greeted by the howling of a second wolf.

Chapter Eighty-Six

High Street, Brixton Hill, South London, wolf moon

The thin man aimed the handgun at Liz's chest. She sat immobile on the hard pavement, the blood pounding noisily in her temples. He stood too close to her to miss. If she tried to move she was dead. And Zoran still held his gun to Kevin's head. She could do nothing. Dean crouched next to her, breathing hard, looking for a way out, a straw to grasp. But they were both out of options.

'Kill her,' ordered Zoran. 'Kill them both.'

Was this the end? After all she had been through, was she now to be gunned down cold-bloodedly in the street just minutes from her own home by armed robbers? She'd known the risks when she'd signed up to become a police officer. She'd seen fellow officers shot, stabbed, and even bitten to death. Her colleague Dave Morgan had been killed by the *Beast of Clapham Common* only a month previously. It looked like she'd be joining him. She wasn't sure if she believed in God or in an afterlife, but she was about to find out.

The thin man's finger closed around the trigger.

Above her the sky was lightening as the moon pushed through the wispy remnants of the snow clouds. She'd done her best to stay indoors tonight, refusing to risk exposure to the moonlight. But fate had brought her here anyway, only to bring her life to a brutal and untimely end. A few more seconds and she'd be lying dead in the road outside the butcher's shop.

'No!' A figure darted out from behind the delivery van. A small, skinny waif, his brown hair like a thatched roof, dashing out of the shadows. Mihai.

No. He couldn't be here. She had left him safe at home with Samantha. She had forbidden him to come. She opened her mouth to shout, but it was already too late. The boy leapt at the thin man, jumping onto his back, grabbing at his arms and pulling with all his strength. 'No shoot Liz!' he screamed.

The gun went off. The noise from the gun and the pain from the bullet struck her at the same time. Mihai's frantic efforts had shifted the man's aim. Not enough to miss completely, but to hit her arm, not her chest. Blood from the wound splashed her face, turning her vision red, as her ears rang with the noise of the shot and the sound of her own scream. She clutched at her arm to stem the flow of blood, but the crimson liquid coursed freely between her fingers. At point blank range the bullet had gone clean through and she was bleeding out. She fell to the ground as the pain swallowed her up.

The thin man spun like a windmill as Mihai clung to his neck, arms flailing wildly. 'No shoot!' he shouted again. 'No kill!'

Another shot went off, this one high as Mihai struggled with his opponent.

Her father used the moment to make his move. He

struck out at Zoran, ducking down and barrelling forward into his broad chest, using the wooden crate he held as a battering ram. Zoran fired at him, but the shot went wide. He staggered back as Kevin powered forward.

Dean seized the moment too, kicking out at the big man who stood over him. The man's legs buckled under him and he went down hard. Dean threw himself onto him and grappled his opponent, rolling over in the street. The gun skittered out of the man's hand, but he fought back with powerful blows to Dean's face and chest.

It was all Liz could do to stop herself slipping into unconsciousness. The pain from the bullet wound was overpowering. She gripped her left arm with her right hand, trying to staunch the bleeding, but her sleeve was quickly turning red. If the bullet had severed an artery she would probably bleed to death before medical help arrived. Her breaths were shallow and quick, more like gasps, and she could feel the pressure of panic bubbling up in her chest like a thick liquid. Her head felt cold as ice, then hot as fire. She rolled over and vomited.

Mihai still clung to the thin man, his hands over the man's eyes. The man swung wildly trying to throw him off, but the boy clung on, his dark eyes burning with fury. The man raised his gun and fired off another shot, seeming not to care where it went.

Zoran had fallen to the ground as Kevin's crate crashed open, but he rolled quickly and was back to his feet in seconds. He aimed his gun at Kevin. Kevin grabbed it as it went off, shooting high. The two men struggled to wrest control of the weapon. Zoran kicked out viciously. Kevin twisted and stamped his foot against his opponent's knee. They tumbled to the ground in a knot of limbs and grunts. The tussle for the handgun went on.

The silver moon looked down on Liz with kindness. She felt its rays like feathers caressing her face. She had tried to avoid it, done her best to free herself from its relentless pull, but fate, destiny, or just cruel chance had aligned with the moon against her. She gave herself up to it.

The soft moonlight soothed away her pain, bringing clarity to her thoughts. It raised the hairs on the back of her neck and sent smooth ripples of calmness to block the panic that had threatened to take her. She lay still and let it do its work.

Dean and his opponent were trading blows. Grunts and slaps rang out in the night as they rolled and fought, like dancers moving to some grim rhythm.

A fire surged through Liz's wounded arm, from her shoulder to the tips of her fingers. Her flesh was remaking itself from within. She cried out in a mixture of pain and ecstasy as the wound closed and knitted together as if it had never been. The bleeding stopped. Still the moon smiled down, sending its strange power, making her its creature.

Mihai cried out as the man finally threw him off. The boy crashed to the ground and lay on his back, winded. The man stood over him, aiming his gun. 'Stop!' he called out. 'Stop fighting or the boy dies!'

As soon as Kevin heard, he gave himself up to Zoran immediately. 'Please, don't harm the boy,' he begged. He kneeled on the ground and raised his hands, allowing Zoran to take control of the gun.

Dean also rolled away from his opponent. The thin man kept his gun pointing at Mihai.

'Don't you dare,' said Kevin. 'If you harm one hair on his head, I'll kill you with my bare hands.'

Zoran stood over Kevin and dusted himself down. The gun was in his hand again. He turned it toward Kevin. When he spoke, his voice cut like a razor. 'No one tells me what to do.'

The healing fire in Liz's arm receded. The damage was undone, the flow of blood quenched, the flesh made whole again. She flexed the arm and all pain was gone. New strength came to her, rising like a flood, filling her with power. Time was slowing, just as it had under the last full moon. Her mind grew sharp, her senses clear. The moonlight bathed her, changing her still. Her fingers ached as her nails twisted outward, hardening into blades. They hungered for flesh. They whispered to her, begging for violence.

Zoran placed his boot against Kevin's neck and pushed him roughly to the ground. 'Enough,' he said. 'This ends now.' His finger caressed the trigger of the gun.

Liz rose to her knees, and then her feet, almost weightless. Her limbs pulsed with pure energy. Her long fingernails were like claws, thirsting for blood. Her teeth ached for the taste of flesh.

'Kill the boy,' ordered Zoran. 'Kill him now.'

The thin man's face remained expressionless. His finger pulled the trigger.

A sound fell from Liz's lips unbidden. She felt faces turning toward her. Eyes widened slowly in surprise. The sound that came from her mouth was a roar.

She had already crossed the distance to Mihai. She didn't know how. The bullet made a grey blur through the air. She snatched at it with her fingers, and dashed the shot from its path. It dropped to the ground like a tamed beast.

The thin man stood still as a statue, his arm outstretched.

She spun in the air, striking him with her foot. He opened his mouth to cry out, but no sound came. His eyes rolled slowly toward her. She spun again and opened his throat with hands like blades, drawing thin red trails across the whiteness of his neck. The man looked surprised. She spun a third time as he began to fall sideways, and landed lightly as his body hit the ground. Droplets of blood beaded his neck like a grisly necklace.

Still the moonlight powered her on. Her lungs drew air and she felt a new release of energy flooding her body, threatening to break her if she refused to let it flow.

Blood, whispered her fingers. *Flesh*, begged her teeth.

The thin man lay still now and Mihai was safe. She turned to face the others.

Zoran's face had blanched white. The gun trembled in his fingers like a petal in the wind. She flew at him, another roar issuing from her throat, and grabbed at him. She spun once again, ripping his arm from its socket, twisting it loose so that his weapon fell harmlessly. The sound of his scream fuelled her hunger for more violence. On she sped to the third man.

The big man was already turning to flee. She landed on his back, sinking fingers like claws into his shoulders, tearing at the meat that covered his bones. He toppled forward and she clung to him as he fell.

When she rose again her lips were blooded and the man lay dead. She didn't remember how it had happened. The sweet taste of his flesh overwhelmed her senses.

More, demanded her teeth. *Give us more*, said her claws.

A dark cloud swallowed the moon and Liz's strength drained away like an electrical plug being pulled from its socket. She crashed to her knees, gasping for breath. Time speeded up again.

Zoran was running. Kevin crawled across the ground, reaching for the gun. His fingers found it and he rose up, his arm reaching out. He fired a shot, and another. The third shot found its target. Zoran lurched and staggered, then fell, sprawling in the road. He rolled once and lay still. Kevin calmly lowered the gun.

Chapter Eighty-Seven

Brixton Village, South London, wolf moon

Melanie stared out through the open doorway, unable to accept the evidence of her own eyes. She had thought to see just one wolf, James. Instead, two golden-haired beasts faced each other, panting, snarling and clawing the ground. The wolves snorted hot breath like dragons, the nearest with its back turned to her, the other gazing straight at her. Its yellow eyes radiated hate like a wave of cold piercing her skin. Something in its gait or expression told Melanie that this was a she-wolf.

She had thought she could never feel fear again, and she did not feel it now so much as taste it on her tongue. She opened her mouth to scream, but the scream wouldn't come. Ben clutched at her arm, pulling her back toward the safety of the house, but she shook him off and stood on the threshold staring back at the yellow-eyed wolf.

The wolf nearest the house twisted its huge head to

look at her. Its eyes glowed yellow too. 'Run,' it growled. 'Flee!'

This beast was no stranger to her. She had seen it before, and she knew its voice. James. He looked nothing like the other wolf now she looked more closely. His shoulders were broader, his hair thick and sandy-coloured, his body lean but muscular, whereas the she-wolf was slender and its coat was of the finest silvery gold.

James had rescued her once already in wolf form, saved her from certain death at the hands of a madman. Now he was preparing to fight for her again. He was ready to risk his life for her a second time. She would not allow it. 'Come on,' she said to Ben. 'James needs our help.'

Jane Hallibury cowered back along the hallway, her face full of terror. Her husband stood before her, seeking to shield her with his own body. But Melanie knew that hiding would do no good. If that other wolf killed James, it would come for them next. It would tear down the solid wooden door as if it were cardboard. It would track their scent wherever they ran, and those hate-filled eyes would follow them relentlessly until hungry jaws closed tight on soft flesh.

'Give me the metal rod,' she said to Richard Hallibury, holding out her hand for the weapon he had taken off Jack Stewart. When he hesitated, she shouted at him in fury. 'Give it to me!' Reluctantly he handed it over.

She turned to face Ben. 'Will you stay and fight?'

He gripped her shoulders and gazed into her eyes, searching for something. She opened herself to him, holding back no secrets, and he must have found whatever it was he sought, because at last he nodded firmly. 'Yes,' he said, raising the hunting knife in his right hand. The edge of the steel blade glinted under the bright light of the moon.

Outside, the she-wolf snarled angrily. James turned back to face it, but too late. It sprang at him, spittle flying from its open muzzle as it locked its jaws around his throat and raked his neck with sharp talons.

James rose up to meet it, wrenching his head free of the creature's jaws, and gouging at his opponent with his own long claws.

The she-wolf hissed and clung on tightly, but James jerked free of her grasp. Her claws left bloody ruts in his cheeks, but he pulled away and dropped to all fours again.

He stood sentinel in front of the door of the house, blocking the way to her. 'Run!' he hissed again at Melanie. 'I will hold her here.'

'We're not leaving you,' Melanie called back. 'We'll help you fight.'

'No!' bellowed James. 'You mustn't! She'll kill you.' He sprang at the other wolf, his claws outstretched, seeking to drag the she-wolf to the ground.

His opponent was ready for him and dodged aside, biting his back as he flew past. Then the creature turned its cold gaze to Melanie and started to run.

It came at her like a whirlwind, and it was all Melanie could do to strike at it with the metal bar as it rushed into the house. Ben slashed at the beast with his knife, but the wolf powered past him and flew at the others.

Melanie spun round to see the wolf's jaws locked around Richard's throat. He had put himself directly in its path to protect his wife. Jane screamed, but Richard had no breath to scream or shout. His body shook limply from side to side as the wolf's teeth cut into him, and slumped to the floor, lying still in a pool of blood.

His wife screamed again.

'No!' shouted Ben. He stabbed at the wolf with the long blade of the hunting knife, but the beast twisted and turned in the narrow space, dodging his thrusts.

Jane Hallibury stood stock still, unable to lift her eyes from the bloody mess of her husband. The wolf turned to face her, its tongue dripping red on the hallway rug. It seemed to smile.

Melanie ran at the monster, the steel rod held high. She

opened her mouth as she ran, a long battle scream pouring out before her. When she reached the wolf she finally found the word she had been looking for. 'Bitch!' she screamed, and brought the rod down along the creature's back with all her strength.

The wolf buckled under the blow, screeching in pain. It rolled over, jaws snapping in fury, deadly claws flying in all directions. One claw caught Jane's leg and she toppled over, falling next to the still body of her husband. The wolf sprang back to its feet in a second. It sank its teeth into Jane's soft flesh and ripped her open, from her pale throat to her breastbone. She gulped for air, but her lungs filled instead with her own blood. The monster roared with fury, thrashing its victim from side to side as it took its kill.

Ben rushed at it again, blade slashing and thrusting. He nicked its side, but the beast was filled with a wild rage and seemed to feel no pain. Instead it charged at Melanie, yellow eyes burning for vengeance.

Melanie clutched the metal rod tightly. She had no time to swing it, but brought it up to meet the headlong dash of the wolf. It met the wolf full-on in the chest, but the beast was too strong for her. She felt her legs go from under her as the full force of the creature knocked her backward, sweeping the rod from her hand as if it were a straw. The wolf landed on top of her, jaws snapping, talons reaching to tear at her limbs. Helpless, she lay pinned to the floor, the wolf's face just inches from her own, its teeth like bloody daggers. 'Now you die, pretty one,' snarled the wolf.

Suddenly James was on her, biting at the she-wolf with all his strength. His jaws closed on her neck but came away with just fur. He butted her face with his head, forcing her back. The she-wolf rose up to meet him and their muzzles locked together as the two wolves spun in a vicious pirouette.

The she-wolf fought savagely but James was stronger.

Slowly he forced her backward, away from Melanie. He grappled her with front and rear legs, scratching skin and fur with sharp talons. The two wolves snarled and roared as their teeth clashed together once, twice, three times.

Then, in a flash of pale fur, it was over. The she-wolf bolted for the door, running like the wind. It rushed from the house, leaping the iron gate easily and vanishing down the street. Melanie collapsed with relief, lying breathlessly on the floor of the hall. The smooth wood felt reassuringly real and solid against her back.

Ben came to her and held his palm tenderly to her face. 'Melanie, are you all right?'

She nodded. Miraculously she had survived. She rubbed her back. 'A little bruised, that's all. And you?'

'Not a scratch,' he said. He wrapped his arms around her then and lifted her up. A second later his lips were on hers.

She kissed him passionately but briefly, then pulled back. 'What about James?'

The sandy-haired wolf stood on the doorstep, looking out into the dark street. Up above, the clouds were already regathering, blocking the light of moon and stars. James began to change once more, from wolf to human. His cloak of fur shrank away as his muscles writhed beneath his skin. Melanie had seen it happen before, but she watched in fascination as creature became boy again. He was no longer a boy though, but a man, bearded, with eyes aged beyond his years. He stood naked and hunched in the doorway, leaning against the door frame for support, panting breathlessly. He looked back mournfully at Melanie.

She pushed away from Ben and ran to him. 'You're hurt,' she cried. 'How badly?'

Leanna had carved bloody furrows in the boy's cheek, and his neck was scratched with red lines. His fingernails dripped blood, and when he turned she saw a raw bite mark on his shoulder. He lifted his wet fingernails to the light. 'That's Leanna's blood,' he said in a weak voice. 'I think she came off worse than me.' Then his gaze came to rest on the two corpses lying in a tangle of limbs. 'Who are they?' he asked with tears in his eyes.

Ben answered him. 'Richard and Jane,' he said. 'They were friends of mine.'

'I'm sorry,' said James. 'I tried to stop Leanna.'

'You did your best,' said Melanie. 'You protected me and Ben.'

Ben seemed unable to look away from the bodies of the husband and wife. 'I know their children,' he said. 'I have to go to them. They don't live far from here. I need to make sure they're safe, and tell them …' He stared down at the twisted remains and tears ran down his cheeks.

Melanie gripped his hand hard. 'We'll go together,' she said. 'And then you'll come back to Richmond with us.'

Ben looked dazed, as if he barely understood the horror of the night's events. 'Richmond? But my house is just across the road.'

'You can't stay there, not after everything these people have done to you. You'd be lynched for sure.' She drew him to her and kissed him once more, holding him tight against her breast. 'Your home is with me now, Ben. I should never have let you go.'

Chapter Eighty-Eight

King's College Hospital, Lambeth, South London, wolf moon

Chris Crohn was rushing for the exit of the hospital ward when he felt a hand grab him from behind. An all-too familiar voice rasped in his ear.

'Well, that was very clever of you,' said Mr Canning. 'I didn't even see you set off the fire alarm.'

'I didn't,' said Chris. 'I was getting ready to, but it just went off by itself.'

'I know,' sneered Mr Canning sarcastically. 'So I'm really under no obligation to keep my part of the bargain, am I?'

'You can't eat us,' spluttered Seth. 'You mustn't.'

'Really?' said Mr Canning in a puzzled voice. 'Can't I? Why ever not?'

'Because ... because ...,' burbled Seth. 'Because I don't want you to.'

'Quite,' said the headmaster. 'But you'll have to come

up with a more compelling reason than that.'

'Because we can still help you,' said Chris desperately. 'We're not out of the building yet. Anything could happen.'

'Wise words,' agreed Mr Canning. 'Come on, then. Let's go. But stay where I can see you and don't try anything funny.'

They followed the rushing crowd out of the ward and down the main hospital staircase. The exits from wards on other floors were opening and hundreds of people were forcing their way into the crowded stairwell, all hurrying to escape the fire.

'Where do you think the fire is exactly?' enquired Mr Canning. 'I heard two explosions from above and more from below. They sounded like bombs. Who do you think can be attacking the hospital?'

'I've no idea,' said Chris. 'And I don't really care. Let's just get downstairs as quickly as we can.'

When they arrived in the ground floor entrance hall, soldiers were organizing an evacuation. The main doors had been opened wide and patients and staff were being ushered through into the parking area immediately in front of the hospital.

A broad smile spread over Mr Canning's face. 'I smell freedom,' he said. 'But stay close. I might still need you yet.'

Chris and Seth followed him out through the doorway and into the open air beyond. The night was freezing cold, but it was the first time Chris had stepped outdoors in weeks. Mr Canning was right. Freedom wasn't far away.

The army had sealed off the area and were lining the patients up in a zone a short distance from the main hospital building. Bright floodlighting bathed the whole area with white light. The burning wreck of a helicopter had crashed onto the ground nearby, and fires raged at each corner of the main hospital block, quickly filling the night air with choking smoke. Chris covered his face with his hand to keep out the stench of burning. The area immediately around the exit was clear of fire however. It was as if the attackers had deliberately left a safe route so that the hospital could be easily evacuated.

A clipped military voice was booming over a loudspeaker. Chris recognized Colonel Griffin, the man in charge of the hospital. 'Please remain calm,' said the Colonel. 'An orderly evacuation is underway. Patients will be taken away from the hospital in batches of a dozen. Please form into lines and await your turn. No harm will come to any of you as long as you remain calm. There is no immediate danger from the fire.'

A convoy of military vehicles was waiting at a checkpoint beyond the sealed-off area. Soldiers ushered the first batch of patients through the checkpoint and into the vehicle, which then drove off. A second vehicle immediately took its place.

Mr Canning groaned. 'They're going to take us to another hospital. I haven't come this close to freedom just to let some self-appointed autocrat whisk me away to a different prison. Come with me,' he snapped at Chris. 'I need you to create another diversion. And try to do it properly this time.'

He grabbed hold of Chris and marched him over to where the head nurse, Chanita, was helping to organize patients into lines ready for evacuation. Two soldiers were standing next to her, making sure the patients did what they were told.

'I need you to distract those soldiers,' said Mr Canning.

'How do you want me to do it?' asked Chris. He eyed the tall burly men with their assault rifles with trepidation.

'Like this,' said Mr Canning. He grabbed Chris with both hands and shoved him toward the soldiers.

Chris crashed into the back of them, knocking one of the men to the ground and landing on top of him. 'I'm sorry,' wailed Chris. 'Someone pushed me. Please don't shoot.'

The soldier struggled to get back to his feet, but before he could, Mr Canning flew at him, jerking the assault rifle out of the man's hands and pushing him back down. The headmaster stomped down hard on the soldier's face and swung the butt of the rifle at the second soldier, knocking him flying. Before Chris knew what had happened, the headmaster had the soldier's assault rifle in his hands and was pointing it at Chanita's head.

'Everyone stop what they're doing right now,' bellowed Mr Canning over the noise of the crowd. 'Nobody move, or the nurse dies.'

All evacuation activity ceased abruptly. The other patients backed slowly away from the headmaster and his hostage. Soldiers advanced cautiously, their rifles trained on Mr Canning.

The headmaster didn't flinch. He pushed the rifle barrel against Chanita's neck. 'Lower your weapons, or I'll kill her,' he said calmly. 'Don't doubt for an instant that I will do what I say. I have nothing to lose.'

'Do as he says,' ordered Colonel Griffin over his loudspeaker. 'Let him leave through the checkpoint.'

'No!' shouted Chanita. 'You can't allow him to go free. Not after everything we've done to try to contain the infection.'

But the soldiers fell back as instructed, lowering their weapons.

Chris watched horrified as Mr Canning forced Chanita forward with the barrel of the gun and followed her toward the exit. He gave Chris a broad smile as he walked past. 'Thank you, Mr Crohn,' he said. 'Your assistance is much appreciated.'

Chris felt his neck turn red and hot. 'No,' he said. 'I'm not your assistant.' The idea that he had somehow helped this monster to escape was too much. Without thinking he rushed at the headmaster and grabbed at the rifle. There was a series of deafening roars as the gun went off, firing rounds into the air. Chris pushed at the rifle with all his strength, hoping to knock the headmaster off balance. For a second or two he thought he might wrestle it free, but his opponent was far too strong. Mr Canning wrenched the weapon from his grasp and shoved him aside.

The butt of the rifle struck Chris in the jaw and he toppled backward into Seth's arms. The two of them collapsed in a heap on the ground.

His eardrums were ringing from the gunshots, but he could hear voices screaming and shouting all around. He looked up and saw that Chanita had managed to break free from the headmaster. But Mr Canning still had his gun and was making a dash for it. More gunshots followed, but whether it was Mr Canning or the soldiers firing he couldn't tell amidst the chaos.

But now something else was happening. The night sky had cleared at last and the moon made a bright circle above the burning hospital building. All around him the patients were changing.

Hair sprouted from skin. Muscles rippled beneath tight clothing. Jaws parted to reveal sharp white teeth and fangs. The night was suddenly filled with bestial grunts, growls and wails. Chris stood dumbfounded, watching in amazement.

An arm grabbed his and pulled him out of his daze. 'Come on,' yelled Seth. 'Quick, before they eat us!'

Chapter Eighty-Nine

High Street, Brixton Hill, South London, wolf moon

Liz stared at her bloody fingernails and hands. Her clothes were red too from the men she had killed. More blood left a tangy taste in her mouth. She spat it out in disgust. She had slaughtered two men, one with her bare hands, one with her teeth. Her gut twisted in horror at the realization. If she hadn't already been sick she might have emptied her stomach a second time.

It had happened again, the moonlight change, just as she'd feared, but worse this time. She'd been out of control. The moon had become her mistress, making her do its dark work. She had done it willingly, lusting after violence and death.

But at least her loved ones were safe.

'Liz!' Mihai ran to her and she swept him up in her arms, hugging the boy tight against her chest. 'You killed bad men!' he said in awe. 'How you do that?'

'I don't know,' she said. 'I don't understand what happened.' She had not become a wolf. What had she become? Some kind of whirling dervish. Some kind of killing machine.

Dean gave her a quick hug too. 'You all right?' he asked.

'I think so. I don't really know.'

'Well, you're better off than this lot,' he said, pointing to the three bodies sprawled in the road. 'That would have been us,' he added, 'if it hadn't been for you.'

Liz nodded, unsure of how she felt. They were all killers now. Her, Kevin and Dean. But she would do the same again to protect the ones she loved. At least the street was still deserted. None of the residents dared unlock their front door. But they must all have seen what happened. She would have to worry about that later.

'That was incredible,' said Dean. 'I'm glad you were on our side there.'

'Yeah.' She wondered how close she'd come to harming him, or Kevin, or Mihai. She would surely never have done that, even when the bloodlust took her. She had acted to protect them. But if the moon hadn't gone when it had, what else might she have done? She had no way of knowing.

She turned to Mihai, remembering that she was supposed to be cross with him. 'Why on earth did you come?' she demanded. 'I told you to stay at home with Samantha.'

The boy glared at her indignantly. 'I save you from bad man with gun. You should say thanks.'

'What about Samantha?'

Mihai looked shamefaced. 'I give her slip. I run out when she busy with Lily.'

'I'd better call her,' said Dean. He pulled his phone from his jacket.

Her father loped over, limping on one leg. 'All right,' he said. 'Good job done. Now let's get these boxes back inside the shop.'

Liz gaped at him. 'Are you joking? You almost died just now. I nearly lost you. I nearly lost all of you. And you're thinking about your boxes.'

'Don't get me wrong,' said Kevin. 'I'm very grateful for being rescued.' He eyed the body of Gary, still lying in the road where he'd been shot. 'Shame about Gary. But there's no reason to lose the stock.' He hefted a crate from the back of the van. 'Come on. This stuff's worth a fortune. I ain't leaving it out here for anyone to make off with.'

In the end she agreed to help.

Dean rang off, confirming that Samantha and Lily were safe in the apartment. 'She was relieved to hear that you're safe too,' he said to Mihai.

Between the four of them it didn't take long to carry everything back inside the shop. Kevin took the keys from the van's ignition and locked the van. 'Handy vehicle that,' he said. He'd already gathered up the weapons that the men had dropped. 'I reckon we did all right in the end,' he said cheerfully. 'Apart from poor old Gary. You just never know which way things are going to turn. Funny old world, eh?'

Chapter Ninety

King's College Hospital, Lambeth, South London, wolf moon

Colonel Griffin watched in horror as the carnage unfolded. His men backed away from the army of wolves that had suddenly appeared in the hospital grounds beneath the light of the moon. The creatures padded forward, cautiously at first. But their eyes were filled with hunger and fury, and they began to run at the soldiers, leaping at them and snapping with huge jaws.

'Fire at will!' ordered the Colonel.

The soldiers didn't need to be told. Automatic gunfire drowned the sounds of wolf howls. But the screams of dying soldiers still rang in his ears.

Wolves tore at flesh with teeth and talons, ripping throats and limbs. The huge beasts surged forward like a tsunami, overpowering the soldiers before they had a chance to reload their weapons or turn and flee.

He looked for Chanita but the crowd was too large and

moving too fast. Men, women and beasts, all rushing in different directions. Doctors and nurses fleeing for safety, soldiers firing in desperation. And seemingly from every direction came wolves, ravenous after a month in captivity, hungry for blood, hungry for freedom, and hungry for vengeance on their captors.

Then he saw her, sheltering near the checkpoint. 'Chanita!' he shouted. A soldier shielded her from attack by a brown-haired wolf with slavering jaws. The wolf leapt and the soldier opened fire at point blank range, blasting the wolf between the eyes. The beast fell to the ground, dead.

More bodies of wolves littered the ground, but the casualties were mainly on the human side. Doctors and nurses were cut down and savaged by the dozen. Soldiers fell too as the sheer number of wolves overwhelmed them. The remaining few pulled back toward the military vehicles. And still the wolves surged forward, jaws snapping, claws tearing. Their victory howls filled the air, drowning out all other sounds.

'Withdraw!' ordered the Colonel over his loudspeaker. 'Fall back!'

He ran to where Chanita stood, blood spattered over her face, but apparently uninjured. 'Are you all right?' he asked. 'Are you hurt?'

She shook her head.

'Let's get out of here. Now.'

The battle was lost. The only imperative now was to evacuate the surviving troops safely. 'Fall back!' he ordered again.

It had hardly been a battle, more a massacre. The handful of soldiers still on their feet followed his order, retreating to relative safety behind the Scimitar armoured vehicle, dragging wounded colleagues with them. More bite victims, reflected Colonel Griffin. More wolves to join the pack at the next full moon.

The machine gun in the Land Rover opened up once it

was safe to fire, clearing a circle around the survivors and keeping the attacking beasts at bay.

Already the creatures were starting to disperse. Bodies of dead wolves lay heaped on the ground where they had fallen, but dozens or even hundreds more had escaped into the night. Their howls echoed from the nearby streets.

The sound of approaching fire engines joined the howls of the wolves, and he could hear the thud-thud-thudding of helicopters in the distance. Reinforcements were arriving, but it was all too late. The army would never find the escaped wolves now. They would have to be hunted down, one by one. But each wolf had the capacity to infect countless more victims before they were caught. He had not just lost a battle tonight, but perhaps a war.

Chanita squeezed his hand. 'It wasn't your fault,' she said. 'You couldn't have known this would happen.'

He said nothing in reply. He *had* known that something like this might happen. It was his job to anticipate. His combat experience had prepared him for unconventional warfare, and this was the most unconventional situation he had ever encountered. But he had allowed events to run out of control, and the blame for that lay with him. He looked up and the silver moon shone down on him, a stark symbol of everything that had gone wrong tonight.

And towering over him, a reminder of how desperately he had failed, the blazing inferno of the hospital sent jets of orange flame high into the sky overhead, filling the air with choking smoke as ash rained down across the surrounding city blocks.

Chapter Ninety-One

West Field Terrace, South London, wolf moon

Vijay felt like a conquering General returning with victory before him. He was light-headed with excitement. The medicines he clutched in his hands would prove his bravery beyond all doubt and deliver him his just reward. Rose's heart.

And they would cure Oscar too. He mustn't ever forget that. He mustn't allow himself to become selfish in his moment of triumph. He must remain humble at all times, or else what good would Rose see in him?

He ran to her house and knocked quickly on the door. What would he say to her? He didn't know. The words would surely come when he needed them. He would be brave, he would tell her that he loved her. And when she saw what he had brought, and how brave and resourceful he had been, she would say she loved him too. He knocked again, louder this time, unable to wait.

The door opened and Rose stood there, silent. What had happened to her? She looked terrible. Dried tear tracks stained her pale cheeks. Her skin was flushed pink and her red hair dishevelled. She regarded him through blackened and bloodshot eyes.

'Rose?' he ventured timidly. 'What's wrong?'

She didn't respond, but stood in the doorway, her thin arms dangling limply at her sides.

A wave of dread came to Vijay. Was he already too late? No! That was unthinkable. 'Is it Oscar?' he asked. 'Is he …' He couldn't finish the sentence, but let it hang in the air between them.

A tiny shake of her head reassured him. 'But what, then?' he asked. But he could hardly wait to show her what he'd brought. He held the boxes of meds up for her to see. 'Look what I've got. I found everything on the list you gave me. Fluticasone, dornase alfa, the whole lot.'

She brightened a little at that, but still seemed very subdued.

'Can I come in?' he asked. As his excitement turned to disappointment he suddenly became aware how cold it was outside.

Rose let him in, saying nothing.

'Here,' he said, passing her the packets of pharmaceuticals. 'You must give these to Oscar. But first tell me what's wrong.'

'They took Mum and Dad,' she said. 'And Ben Harvey too.'

Vijay gaped at her. 'What? Who took them? Why?'

'Ms Ali and the Neighbourhood Watch. They accused them of being werewolves.'

Vijay blinked. He could hardly understand her words. 'Werewolves?' How could anyone have thought that? 'Mr Harvey was one of the leaders of the Watch. How could that happen?'

'Ms Ali did it. The men grabbed them and took them away. I'll never see them again.'

'No!' cried Vijay. 'Of course you will. We'll go and find them. We can break them out, or … or … they'll realize they made a mistake and let them go.'

Rose shook her head despondently. 'No,' she said. 'They're as good as dead.'

Vijay stared at her uncomprehendingly. He had arrived so full of confidence. Now everything looked hopeless. But he wouldn't turn back now. He couldn't. 'Sit down,' he said. 'There's something else I have to tell you.'

Her eyes gazed back unseeing, but she did as he told her, and sat on a chair.

He sat opposite her, then changed his mind and dropped to one knee. 'Rose, I tried to tell you before, at the hospital, but we were interrupted.' She stared at him for an instant, then looked past him, her eyes unfocused. He pressed on. 'There's only one way to say this, Rose. I love you. I've loved you since the first time we spoke, outside the school. Do you remember? You stopped me and you knew my name, and I wondered how someone so pretty could have noticed me. I wanted to say it ever since, but I wasn't brave enough. Well now I am. And I'll say it again. I love you, Rose. I'll love you forever.'

He could hardly think for the thudding of his heart in his chest. He stopped breathlessly and waited for her reply. His declaration had been a silly gush of words. Far too many. He should have slowed down and thought more about what he wanted to say. But it was too late now. The words were out. He had said them at last, and that was all that mattered.

She looked down at him and held his gaze with her green eyes. His heart soared and he took hold of one freckled hand in his. Her skin, so smooth and delicate, looked even paler against his own chocolate complexion. He gripped her hand tightly, not caring that his palm was sweaty, not wanting to ever let her go.

'I'm sorry,' she said in a quiet voice.

His heart came to a shuddering halt. Suddenly he could

no longer hear it beating, he could only hear a ringing in his ears. Time seemed to stop and he felt a wave of bile rising in his throat. His flesh turned to ice and her hand suddenly felt hot as fire in his.

'I can't love you,' she said, and each word was like a spear piercing his chest. 'I'm so sorry. You have to go.'

'No,' he cried. He must have forgotten to tell her something important. Didn't she know what he'd done for her? For Oscar? 'I stole those medicines. I'm just as strong as Drake. Stronger. I stole to help Oscar. I just wanted to help.'

'I know,' said Rose. Her face had hardened like steel, as if the words were painful for her to say, and she needed to force them through her lips. 'You are stronger than Drake. Much stronger, and braver too. And I appreciate what for did for Oscar. But I can't love you. It's impossible.'

He knelt silently for a moment, still holding her fingers, not wanting to let go. She didn't pull away from him, but sat there, looking sad. And then he realized how foolish he must look, kneeling on the floor, pouring out senseless words, clutching desperately at the hand of a girl who did not love him, who had never loved him, and who never would. He got to his feet and stumbled away from her. 'I'm sorry,' he said. 'I should never have come.'

Chapter Ninety-Two

King's College Hospital, Lambeth, South London, wolf moon

Warg Daddy sniffed at the cold night air. A rush of smells assaulted him. Billowing smoke, falling ash, the burnt flesh of those trapped in the hospital inferno. He smelled diesel fumes as military vehicles, fire engines and ambulances arrived at the scene, far too late to save the building or its occupants. The acrid smoke from the fire sharpened the pain in his forehead and he tried to shut it out.

He smelled wolves too. Hundreds had escaped into the night, making their own way to freedom. They were the seeds of a new generation of werewolves, spreading the condition far and wide in unpredictable patterns. The rise of the werewolves was unstoppable now, just as Leanna had promised.

The plan had gone well. But his work here was not yet finished.

He had changed into wolf form all too briefly this night. For a while he had tasted freedom, felt the wolf blood surge through his body, run on all fours, and feasted on the dead. The pain in his head had eased a little. But already the clouds had swallowed the moon, and he and the Wolf Brothers had returned to human form. They had recovered their scattered and tattered clothes and taken clothing from the fallen soldiers. They had gathered the soldier's weapons and amassed a good supply of SA80 assault rifles and combat shotguns. The Brothers would make good use of those in the days and weeks ahead.

He had one more task to do.

He sent the Brothers home with the cache of weapons, keeping just Snakebite and Adam by his side. He waited until the three of them stood alone by the burning hospital.

'Good work, Adam,' he said. 'We couldn't have done this without you.'

'Thanks,' said Adam. 'But it was all down to Snakebite's plan.'

'Yeah,' agreed Warg Daddy. 'It was a good plan. A clever plan. An excellent plan.' He rubbed the spot on his forehead where the pain was greatest. It ached all the time now, unrelentingly, and no amount of painkillers seemed to help. But the pain in his head wasn't his biggest problem.

He could see the pride in Adam's face, the way his eyes shone in the light of the flames. Adam had never once lost his pride. Even when Warg Daddy had gone out of his way to belittle him in the War Councils. Even when the Brothers had taunted and goaded him. Adam Knight had remained a proud man throughout.

Warg Daddy had never permitted a rival to his leadership and he wasn't about to start now. He'd seen the hunger for power in Adam's eyes the very first time they met. He knew that desire to always be first, to win at all costs. He had only to look in the mirror if he wanted to see it. And Adam was one of the first werewolves, a close confidant of Leanna. A doctor too, using medical words with Leanna that Warg Daddy would never understand. A man like that would never be subservient to another.

Snakebite had seen it too. Snakebite saw everything these days. And he had a solution to every problem as well.

'Snakebite's plan isn't quite finished yet,' Warg Daddy told Adam. 'There's still one final job to do.'

'What?' asked Adam, a suspicious look replacing the pride of the previous moment.

'Tidying up loose ends,' said Warg Daddy.

Snakebite raised his assault rifle and held it to Adam's chest. 'Don't worry, Adam. We'll tell Leanna you died bravely in battle. We'll say you died a hero. She'll never find out the truth.'

Adam gasped. He clearly hadn't seen this coming. He wasn't as clever as he thought. 'No,' he said. 'Please, I'm begging you. Don't kill me.'

'We have no choice,' said Warg Daddy. 'There can only be one leader. And I'm already Leader of the Pack.'

Adam's eyes darted wildly back and forth between him and Snakebite. 'Let me go then,' he begged. 'I'll run from here. I'll go far away. You'll never see me again, I promise.'

Warg Daddy weighed his words. 'Maybe you'd do as you say. Or maybe not. It's not a chance I care to take.'

Adam's face contorted with fury. He spat at Snakebite. 'I thought you were my friend,' he said. 'I trusted you.'

'You were a fool to trust me,' said Snakebite. 'And a fool shouldn't expect to live very long in this world. In fact, your time's already run out.'

For a moment nobody moved. Then Adam's body seemed to blur. He moved so fast even Warg Daddy didn't see how he did it. He had already turned and run several paces before Warg Daddy became aware that he had gone. Incredible. He'd had no idea Adam's reaction times could be so fast.

But Snakebite already had the rifle aimed. He pulled the

trigger and Adam's dash for freedom came to a halt as abruptly as it had begun. He stumbled and fell, his life spilling on the ground before them.

The rich smell of blood rushed up to meet Warg Daddy and he twitched his nose in response. But he would not eat the body. Even Adam deserved better than that. 'Good job,' he said to Snakebite. 'Well done.'

Snakebite lowered the gun. 'It was a pity, really. He could have been useful to us. But the risk was too great.'

'It was,' agreed Warg Daddy. 'Will you miss him? You two became quite good friends in the end.'

Snakebite shrugged. 'I did what I had to do. Perhaps I'll miss him a little. But no regrets, that's always been my motto. What about you? Any regrets?'

Regrets? It was something Warg Daddy had been mulling over a lot lately, and there was no harm now in letting Snakebite know what was on his mind. 'I miss the old days. Before we became werewolves. Before my head began to hurt so much. Before the world began falling apart.'

'Really?' asked Snakebite in astonishment. 'But you always dreamed of being a werewolf. It's why you brought the Wolf Brothers together. It's why you named yourself Warg Daddy.'

'Yeah,' admitted Warg Daddy. 'That's true. But life was simpler back in the old days, before we met Leanna.' His problems had been easier then, the solutions less painful. He rubbed his head once more. The headaches had only begun after she had turned him lycanthropic.

Snakebite nodded. 'I think I understand.'

'No,' said Warg Daddy. 'I don't think you do. You can't really know what it's like to be a leader unless you've been one.'

'Yeah,' said Snakebite. 'There's only one Leader of the Pack, isn't there?'

'That's right.'

They stood together for a moment, looking at Adam's

body lying on the frozen ground, watching the fire that still raged in the hospital. Snakebite's red beard glowed bright in the firelight as if it were afire itself.

Warg Daddy broke the silence. 'Adam was right about your plan, you know. It was smart. Very smart.'

'Thanks.'

'But perhaps a little too smart,' concluded Warg Daddy sadly. 'You've become clever, Snake, these past weeks. Cunning, devious. Much too clever all round.' He raised the shotgun and pointed it at Snakebite's head.

The big man started to move, but his reaction speed was nowhere near as fast as Adam's had been. Warg Daddy fired the gun.

The recoil from the blast was much more powerful than he'd expected. It blew him back several feet before he regained his footing on the icy ground.

Snakebite's body jerked backward before crumpling and falling. His arms swung out to each side and he toppled heavily like the giant he was. He didn't move again.

Warg Daddy stooped to examine the remains. The shotgun had blasted a large hole in Snakebite's head, and his entire torso was peppered with shot. Blood oozed from dozens of entry points and trickled out onto the snowy ground. His face was almost entirely unrecognizable, save for his red beard.

Warg Daddy slung the combat shotgun over his shoulder. It was a good weapon. He could grow to like it.

He picked up the rifle that Snakebite had dropped and turned away with regret. Snakebite had been a good companion, the nearest he'd ever had to a friend. But when you were leader, you couldn't really afford to have friends. It was lonely at the top, but someone had to do it. He had started to depend too much on Snakebite to do his thinking for him, and that would never do. A leader had to think for himself and not rely on others. And a man as clever as Snakebite had become could never be trusted. He was better off with grunts like Slasher and Meathook, simple men who did exactly what he told them, even if they had no particular talents other than their love of violence.

The moon had vanished completely behind the clouds now and Warg Daddy didn't think he'd get a chance to be a wolf again tonight. He began the long walk home, alone.

It had been a good night, all things considered. A job well done. And two of his biggest problems had gone away too. He quickened his pace at the thought of it. The walk back to the house in Kensington was long, but sometimes it was good to spend time on your own. He wasn't sure if it was his imagination, but his headache was starting to hurt less than it had done for a long time.

Chapter Ninety-Three

West Field Terrace, South London, wolf moon

Rose sat in the chair after Vijay had gone, sobbing uncontrollably. Her shoulders quaked and she wailed as the grief took her and threatened to burst her heart wide open. She had known that Vijay would come. She had known for a long time what he would say. She had seen it on his face often enough, and in his eyes too, and had waited patiently for him to say the words, and now he had. If only she could have told him that she loved him back. But she couldn't. Her words would have killed him.

Everyone she loved was doomed to die.

The dreams had shown her that. First the dogs at the kennels had died. But that had been just the beginning. The dreams had grown darker, showing worse to come. Her parents' bodies, twisted and bloody, cast aside like piles of rags. Oscar too, torn to shreds by some unknown horror.

The dreams were coming true. The dogs lay dead and buried. Wolves stalked the streets. Soldiers shot and killed. She had seen it and it had happened. Now her parents had been taken. She would not see them alive again. Only Oscar remained, and the dreams had shown her his fate. Even with the medicine Vijay had brought, he would not live. She had seen it. She knew it.

To save Vijay she had turned him away.

If she had told him the truth, that she loved him too, he would have become like the others. He would have been cursed. And he would die.

She sobbed again, the knowledge of her dreadful choice battering at her heart afresh. He had proved his bravery to demonstrate his love for her, but she had been braver still, to deny her love and send him away. And he would never know the sacrifice she had made.

She would never see him again, but at least he would live.

'Rose?' Oscar's voice cut through her grief. 'What's happened? Why are you crying?' Her brother spoke to her from his wheelchair in the hallway. 'I heard Vijay's voice. And then I heard you crying.'

'Come here,' she said, beckoning to him, still sniffling, trying to stem the tears.

He pushed the wheelchair toward her and she leaned forward to hug him. He hugged her back as tightly as he could, but his arms were limp with weakness. He coughed violently, and his whole body shook.

'Look what Vijay brought for you.' She showed him the medicines.

Oscar's eyes lit up. 'Wow. Awesome. I should take them right away, shouldn't I?'

'Yes,' she said. She dried her eyes and stood up. She must be brave still, for Oscar's sake. 'I'll fetch you a glass of water. Wait here.'

She walked steadily to the kitchen and filled a glass. She

needed to calm herself down and focus on Oscar, on the medicines. There was still a slender chance that the dreams had lied, that Oscar could be saved. Vijay had braved danger to bring him this chance. The least she could do was take it with both hands. If there was any chance at all, there was still hope.

And if the dreams proved to be false, she could go to Vijay and explain. She could still do that. All was not lost, yet.

A loud crash shook the house as a heavy weight smashed against the front door. The timber of the doorframe began to split. Another crash broke the lock, and the door flew open.

Rose screamed. A figure from her worst nightmare stood in the doorway.

She dropped the glass of water and flew to Oscar in the front room. 'We have to get out of here,' she cried. She turned the wheelchair and shoved it toward the door, but it was already too late.

Mr Canning blocked their way.

The dreams had not lied. The man she had thought was dead had returned, just as her nightmares had warned her.

The headmaster had changed. His hair, always neatly combed and parted, now stood like a forest. A thick and unruly beard covered his chin and neck, right up to his ears. But he still wore a dark suit with a waistcoat and tie. And incongruously, a black patch over one eye, like a pirate.

Mr Canning stroked his bushy beard. 'I do apologize for my appearance,' he said. 'I haven't been allowed to shave for a long while. They seemed not to trust me with a blade for some reason. But then, look what you did to me, armed only with a ballpoint pen.' He lifted the patch and showed her the place where his eye had once been. He laughed hollowly before covering the empty socket again. 'Do you like my eye patch? I took it from a costume shop on the way here. My suit's new too. I liberated it from a gentlemen's outfitters that was being looted. Just because the world is ending, there's no reason not to keep up appearances. Quite the contrary, in fact.'

Rose backed away from him, drawing Oscar with her.

The headmaster advanced into the room.

'You didn't expect to meet me again, I suppose,' he said. 'But I have thought of little else these past weeks. I knew I would escape one day, and I knew exactly where to find you. You didn't think of leaving? No, why would you? You imagined you were safe. The adults around you reassured you of that. Too bad they lied.'

He took another step toward her.

Oscar coughed and the headmaster regarded him sympathetically. 'That's a very nasty cough you have there, young man. It's the time of year for sickness, isn't it? It was always the same at school.'

'You're a werewolf,' accused Oscar when he had finished his coughing fit. 'Rose told me.'

'Yes, indeed,' said Mr Canning in a conversational tone. 'But you know what — and this might surprise you — becoming a werewolf was the best thing that ever happened to me. I've always hated kids, you see. Now I get to eat them.'

Rose backed toward the window. If she could just keep the headmaster talking, perhaps there was a chance. She had escaped from him once before, and this time the stakes were even higher.

He certainly seemed happy to talk. 'It's hard to believe I ever became a headmaster, isn't it? Do you know why I first went into teaching?' He gave Oscar a lopsided smile that showed his long teeth. 'I thought I could make a difference.' He turned his attention back to Rose, watching her with interest as she searched the room for a weapon, an escape route, a chance to live. 'I know,' he said. 'It's pathetic, isn't it? The beauty is that now I really can make a difference. The difference between life and death. Extraordinary. So everything worked out all right in the end. For me, at least. Not for you. Definitely not for you though, little Rose. You should have killed me when you had the chance. I'm sure you realize that now. You're such a bright girl.'

She grasped at a vase on the mantelpiece and gripped it tightly. It might buy her a second if she smashed it over his head.

'But you didn't kill me, so I won't kill you. I can't be fairer than that. But you took something valuable from me.' He lifted the eye patch again so that she could see the empty eye socket beneath. 'So I'll take something from you in return.'

He lowered his eyes to Oscar.

'No,' pleaded Rose. 'Not Oscar. Take me instead.'

Mr Canning shook his head. 'That wouldn't be fair. And you know me. I'm a stickler for fairness. You stole my sight, so I'll take your brother in return. I'd say that's more than fair.'

He moved quickly, shooting out his arm and grasping Oscar's neck in a choking grip.

Rose lifted the vase and brought it down over his head, but it was as if she'd brushed him with a feather. Oscar's face turned purple as the headmaster began to throttle him.

She dashed herself against him, screaming like a banshee, struggling to dislodge his grip, but Mr Canning stood like an oak tree with unyielding arms. She battered him with her fists, but his fingers dug in to her brother's throat like iron roots. Oscar struggled for breath, and his eyes bulged as Rose grappled with Mr Canning. The headmaster stood unflinching as Oscar's life slowly ebbed away.

When her energy was finally spent and her voice was too hoarse to scream, he finally unlocked his fingers and allowed Oscar's body to slide to the floor. 'There,' he pronounced. 'It's done.'

Her brother had spent the entirety of his short life

fighting to breathe. Now his battle was over. Rose fell to the floor, prostrate over him, unable to see him through her tears.

'You won't ever see me again,' said Mr Canning as he left. But Rose knew with a cold certainty that she would see him every time she closed her eyes to sleep.

Chapter Ninety-Four

Brixton Village, South London, wolf moon

James' energy was all spent. The moon change that had fed him so much power and enabled him to fight off Leanna had drained him of every last drop of his strength. It was all he could do to hold himself upright against the hallway wall. He tried to take a step unaided but stumbled and fell, unable even to support his own weight. He sprawled helplessly on the floor.

Melanie crouched at his side. 'James!'

'I'm all right,' he assured her. 'Just weak.' It wasn't his injuries from the battle that had weakened him. They were superficial, just bites and scratches. It was the hunger that left him so drained. A whole month had passed without feeding. He hadn't eaten since he'd killed that young woman at the firework display on New Year's Eve. He had vowed not to touch human flesh again, and had kept his promise. Now he would pay the price.

He hadn't realized before how much energy the change

demanded. To transform from human into wolf and back again was exhausting. When he had changed previously, blood and flesh had powered him. This time he was running on empty. He wanted simply to lie down and sleep.

Melanie shook him gently. 'Come on. We have to get away from here. The people who imprisoned Ben might be back any moment. We have to flee.'

'No,' he said. 'You go. Leave me here. I'll be all right.'

She shook him harder. 'No,' she said, more insistently this time. 'If you think I'm going to leave you behind after everything we've been through, you must be out of your mind.'

He allowed her to pull him upright so he was sitting on the floor. He realized he was stark naked. He shivered, noticing the cold for the first time since becoming lycanthropic. He had thought that werewolves couldn't feel the cold. 'My clothes,' he said. The clothes he had worn were nothing more than rags strewn over the floor now.

'I think I have a solution to that problem,' said Ben. 'Wait a moment.' He ran off down the stairs to the basement room. Angry shouts came from below but after a minute Ben reappeared with a bundle of clothing in his arms. He grinned. 'Mr Stewart very kindly offered to give you his own clothes.'

James allowed Melanie and Ben to dress him. They hauled him to his feet and put their shoulders under his arms to half-drag, half-carry him.

'Can you walk if we support you?' asked Melanie.

He took a few tentative steps with the others taking most of the weight. 'I feel like a slab of meat,' he complained.

'Just one step at a time,' said Melanie.

He let them lead him out of the house and across the street. He was too weak to resist.

'This way,' said Ben. 'Richard and Jane's house isn't far.

But I don't know how I'm going to break the news to the children. The boy is ill. How are they going to manage without their parents?'

'I don't know,' said Melanie. 'Maybe we can help.'

It wasn't far but they made slow going of it. James wondered how long it would take to get all the way back to Richmond. Hours, at this rate. As they entered West Field Terrace, he smelled burning.

Before long the others smelled it too. 'Oh God, what's that?' asked Ben. A red glow lit up the far end of the street. Black smoke poured from one of the terraced houses. 'Come on,' said Ben urgently. 'I have a dreadful feeling about this.'

They trudged grimly along the pavement toward the fire. By the time they reached it, there was no longer any room for doubt. 'This is the Hallibury's home,' said Ben, aghast.

Fire had already consumed the building. Bright flames danced from windows upstairs and down. Black smoke billowed into the night sky, and high above, bright sparks dashed from the chimney stack. The front door was still in place, but inside the house was a sea of flames. A crowd of neighbours watched as the building burned.

Ben set James down against a wall and hurried forward. 'What are you doing?' he shouted at the people gathered in the street. 'There are two children in that house!' He rushed to the front door, but already flames were licking through the letterbox. The heat of the fire was intense. 'Have you called for a fire engine? Why aren't you doing anything?'

One of the neighbours appeared with a garden hosepipe and started spraying water onto the base of the fire. Another emerged clutching a bucket of water, but their efforts were futile. Other people were carrying valuables from the neighbouring houses, hauling items to safety in case the fire spread.

'We called for a fire engine,' a woman said. 'They are

coming, but it's too late to save the children.'

A man gave Ben a shove. 'I recognize you. You're one of the werewolves. What are you doing here? What do you care about the children?'

'I'm not a werewolf,' protested Ben. 'Don't be so stupid. And why is it too late to save the children?'

The woman shrugged her shoulders. 'Look for yourself.' She gestured to the raging flames. The front door of the house was on fire now too, and more flames emerged from the top of the house as the roof began to collapse. The crowd retreated to a safer distance. 'It was the girl who started the fire in the first place,' explained the woman. 'She ran into the road screaming that her brother was dead and there was nothing worth living for. The next thing we knew the house was burning.'

'Oscar dead?' said Ben, appalled. 'And Rose? The girl?'

The woman shrugged again. She turned her gaze back to the burning building. Little more than a shell remained already. No one could still be alive inside that inferno.

The man who had challenged Ben returned with two other men. 'How dare you show your face around here,' he said. 'This is all your fault. You and your kind. You did this.'

Melanie pulled Ben by the arm. 'Come on. We have to get out of here. It's not safe.'

Ben was in tears, but he helped her lift James back to his feet. James placed his arms around their shoulders and let them lead him away. The men watched them leave.

Ben cried as they set off slowly on the long walk back to Richmond. James wanted to cry too. He hadn't known these children, Oscar and Rose. He had done his best to save their parents from Leanna, but his best hadn't been good enough.

He thought of his own parents lying dead in their home. They had died because of him too. A sense of futility overwhelmed him. His feet dragged along the pavement as he stumbled along. 'I need to rest,' he said to

Melanie. 'Just for a minute.' They sat him down on the cold pavement against the post of a streetlamp. He inhaled deeply, trying to get his breath back after the exertion of walking. He was broken and wasted, no use to anyone like this.

And if he didn't feed, he would grow weaker and become even more of a burden. But what choice did he have? 'I promised,' he muttered. 'I promised not to kill.'

Melanie and Ben exchanged glances. 'Come on, James,' said Melanie. 'Let's get you home.'

He had a choice. There was always a choice.

'I'm going to make a new promise,' he said as they lifted him back to his feet. 'I'm going to change.' The memory of Leanna's fury was enough to seal his decision. He had fought her off this time, but she would never give up. He knew that her hunger for vengeance had only been fuelled by her defeat tonight. And the sight of the burning building with the children inside, and the savaged corpses of Richard and Jane reinforced his determination.

He had made a promise to Samuel. He had promised never to kill again. But Samuel had already lain dead when he had made that vow. Samuel was gone and he must finally accept it. *I will never forget you, my friend.* But he was ready to walk his path alone now. It was time for a new promise.

He turned his head to look at Melanie. 'I swear to protect you, whatever happens,' he told her solemnly. 'I vow to make myself strong again so that I won't fail you next time you need me. I will never allow anyone to hurt you, or Sarah, or Ben again.'

He was still weak, but his wolf hunger rose up inside, raging stronger than ever. This time he would use it. He would feed it.

He would never deny his true nature again. If Samuel had taught him anything, it was surely that. For better or worse, he was a lycanthrope, a werewolf. And werewolves hunted for prey.

His tears were all gone now, and though he still needed his friends' help, he walked easier, he walked quicker. He was eager to begin again.

Chapter Ninety-Five

Herne Hill, South London, wolf moon

Chris and Seth staggered away from the burning hospital, seeking safety. Machine gun fire still crackled behind them, and they hurried from it as quickly as they could. They passed the wreckage of the helicopter lying by the roadside, not wanting to peer too closely in case dead eyes stared back at them from inside the cockpit. A few last wolves streaked past them under the silver moonlight. One snapped its jaws at them as it went, but seemed too intoxicated by its unexpected freedom to put much effort into it.

Somehow they had survived.

Grey ash rained down on them as they stumbled along the roadside. Chris's jaw throbbed viciously where Mr Canning had struck him with the rifle butt, but he was still alive. Starved, frozen and terrified witless, but nevertheless alive. He could hardly believe it.

'I'm cold,' moaned Seth. The red glow of the fire lent a

devilish touch to his friend's pointed beard. Seth's unruly hair had grown even longer during his spell at the hospital and it now nearly covered his eyes completely. He tried to flick it away, but it was useless. It fell back over his face almost immediately.

'Cold?' shouted Chris angrily at his friend. 'We were almost burned, shot and eaten, not to mention robbed, beaten and humiliated, and after all that, you're complaining about the cold?'

'Yeah,' said Seth miserably. 'It's freezing out here.'

Chris shivered, despite his anger. Seth had a valid point. They wore nothing other than flimsy hospital pyjamas, gowns and slippers. Chris had carefully stockpiled all-weather survival gear, and now here they were wandering around in the snow dressed in their nightwear.

The body of a doctor lay on the ground up ahead. Blood pooled all around, but his white coat looked warm enough despite the red stains. Chris carefully removed it. 'Take this,' he said to Seth.

Seth accepted it with trepidation but slipped it on over his gown. 'It fits.'

'Good.' Chris pulled his own dressing gown tight around his middle. If they kept moving, he would probably stay warm enough. Perhaps Seth would agree to a time-share option on his coat.

'What now?' asked Seth. 'Everything's gone wrong. We've lost all our stuff. We don't even have a map. We might as well go back home.'

'No,' said Chris. 'We can't go back. We have to keep going. On foot if necessary.' He plodded on determinedly into the night, one foot after another. After all, it was how a journey of a thousand miles was supposed to begin. And what other options did they have?

'But where?' asked Seth.

'We follow our original plan. We head west.'

Seth hurried to keep up with him. 'Why west? We could go anywhere. Like north, east, south. Somewhere not so far away. What's so good about west?'

'I already explained,' said Chris. 'We need to go where there are fewer people. We need to get out of London as quickly as we can, then steer clear of the major population centres. West is best, Seth.'

'I don't know,' said Seth, but he didn't make any other suggestions.

After a while Chris stopped feeling quite so cold. He wasn't sure if it was because he was warming up, or if he was getting frostbite. It was probably best not to think about it.

Up ahead a girl appeared, walking slowly down the middle of the road.

'Who's that?' asked Seth.

Chris glared at him. 'Will you stop asking dumb questions? How am I supposed to know?'

The girl came closer. A teenager with red hair, wearing just a thin top with bare arms. She looked vaguely familiar. She might be one of the girls from Manor Hall School. Chris had never paid much attention to the kids. He wondered what she was doing wandering around in the middle of the night all on her own. Then again, why was he here wearing a dressing gown and slippers? Perhaps there was no good reason.

The girl walked past, appearing not to notice them. Her pale freckly skin was visibly shaking from the cold.

Seth stopped. 'Hey,' he called to the girl. 'Are you okay?'

She stopped and turned back, seeming to see them for the first time. But she said nothing.

'Are you cold?' asked Seth.

Still the girl said nothing.

'Obviously she's cold,' said Chris. 'Everyone's cold apart from you. Why don't you give her your coat?'

'My coat?' said Seth. 'Then I'll be cold too.'

Chris took it from him and draped it over the girl's shoulders.

She looked at him. 'I've seen you before,' she said. 'Was it in a dream?'

Chris frowned. 'Maybe it was at school,' he suggested. 'I used to work at Manor Road.'

Seth came over to join them. 'You dreamed of Chris?' he asked the girl. 'Like, freaky.'

The girl's eyes seemed to gaze into the distance. Chris wondered if she was on drugs.

'Where are you heading?' asked Seth.

The girl shook her head. 'Nowhere.'

'Why don't you come with us, then?' suggested Seth.

'What?' said Chris. 'She can't come with us. Why did you say that?'

'Because she looks like she needs our help.'

'We're the ones who need help,' insisted Chris. 'Where is your brain?'

The girl gave no sign she'd heard them.

'Come with us,' said Seth again, ignoring Chris's protests.

'Where are you going?' she asked.

'West,' said Seth. 'West is best.'

'I'll come with you then,' said the girl. And she did.

Chapter Ninety-Six

Houses of Parliament, Westminster, London, waning moon

Once, she had hoped to be remembered as the Prime Minister who brought the nation together, delivering a dynamic economy, improving the hopes of the many, and fashioning a Britain ready to face the challenges of the twenty-first century.

Instead she would go down in history as the PM who presided over her country's descent into anarchy.

She had come straight from the latest all-night COBRA meeting to the Houses of Parliament without a chance to rest. Exhaustion tugged at every fibre of her being, but the House had been recalled for an emergency sitting, and her announcement would not wait. Sleep would come later, if it came at all.

Earlier that morning she had taken a call from the US President, who had accused her of being personally responsible for the global spread of the werewolf due to her government's failure to contain the threat. The facts hadn't seemed to interest him a great deal, and she had concluded that his main purpose in calling her had been to vent his anger at someone for an extended period of time. It had left her feeling isolated at a moment when she most needed solidarity from her peers. But that was proving to be elusive. The President of France had been equally belligerent when she'd spoken to him. Werewolves at the port of Calais had run amok under the wolf moon, slaughtering freely among the refugee camps. He'd left her in no doubt that in his opinion her policies were to blame. In response to the attacks, vigilantes and protesters in French ports had set cars, coaches and goods vehicles alight, resulting in many more fatalities. He seemed to think that was her fault too.

The options now were limited, and all her choices seemed to be made for her. The latest news from Colonel Griffin had taken away her last hopes of containing the disease.

Her aides ushered her into a packed House of Commons and she took her seat on the front bench, flanked by the Home Secretary, the Foreign Secretary and other members of her Cabinet. Members of Parliament filled the green leather benches of the chamber on both sides of the house, and more stood before the oak doors at its entrance. The Chamber buzzed with the sound of speculation and rumour, the atmosphere tense and expectant.

The Leader of the Opposition sat on the bench opposite, no more than a few feet away from her. His eyes were wary and gave away nothing. She wondered whether he would lend her his support, or if the way ahead would be even lonelier than she feared.

It is too late now. My decision is made.

'Order! Order!' The words of the Speaker of the House of Commons cut through the hubbub of the Chamber, and the hum of voices dropped quickly to a hush. 'The

Prime Minister will now make an announcement to the House.'

She rose to her feet and lifted her tired eyes to take in the historic Chamber, seeing its oak-panelled walls and galleries through a veil of sleep deprivation and a feeling close to despair. The architect Sir Giles Gilbert Scott had rebuilt the Commons Chamber in 1945 in an austere style reflecting the post-war mood. Her mood today was similarly downbeat, and yet to her eyes the Gothic architecture of the building seemed outdated and irrelevant. It felt totally out of place for the announcement she had to make today.

Am I also outdated and outwitted by this strange, new enemy?

Despite having heard nothing but bad news for the past twenty-four hours, she was determined that she would not be beaten. If necessary she would hold the country together against its foes by sheer force of will.

Some of her foes sat on the benches opposite, looking mutinous. A few of the Opposition politicians jeered and heckled as she stood, but there were also murmurs of support and a few cheers. 'Order! Order!' bellowed the Speaker insistently, and despite the huge turnout the House fell eerily silent as she took her place at the despatch box in the middle of the Chamber.

She had debated many times and on many subjects in this place. But the time for debate was over.

'Thank you, Mr Speaker,' she began. 'As you are aware, for the past month this Government has done its utmost to contain the outbreak of the disease known as lycanthropy, together with the other threats to the nation's safety.'

Fresh heckles greeted this announcement, but she ignored them and pressed on. 'A cornerstone of our policy has been to contain carriers of the disease in a secure hospital controlled by the army. I regret to inform you that this policy has failed. As you may have already heard on news reports, the quarantine has been breached, and the suspected lycanthropes have escaped.'

Shouts of 'Shame!' and 'Resign!' erupted from the Opposition benches. The Speaker intervened once more to silence them.

Once order had been restored, she continued. 'We are left with few choices, none of them good. The breakout from the hospital marks an end to our opportunity to extinguish the werewolf threat quickly. Instead we must now prepare ourselves for a long and difficult struggle. Our allies in other countries are turned inward, dealing with their own security matters, and so we face this challenge alone.

'It is not the first time that Britain has stood alone against a seemingly unstoppable enemy. None of you will need reminding that Mr Winston Churchill stood in this very Chamber and contemplated similar threats. He did not shirk from his duty, nor give in to the enemy, and neither shall we. Mr Churchill had nothing better to offer his citizens than blood, sweat and tears. I fear that I can offer no more.'

She wondered what her illustrious predecessor had really been thinking as he spoke those words. Had he known the true gravity of the threat the country had faced at that time? She was certain that he had. Britain had been confronted by a militarily superior enemy, ruthless in its ambitions. She feared the same was true now. The best she could hope for was that she would somehow blunder through this crisis and come out the other side. How many would be dead by then she dreaded to think. The cause seemed almost futile. Perhaps Churchill's feelings had been the same. She gazed around the room at the faces turned expectantly in her direction. Did it really make any difference what she said or did now? But yes, the fate of millions of ordinary people depended critically on the decisions she must make. She must not flinch from her duty.

'I have today instructed the Home Secretary to take

measures to halt all international flights, blockade all ports and barricade the Channel Tunnel with immediate effect. I have asked the Foreign Secretary to contact our embassies abroad and notify them that they must now act alone, and that the safety of their own staff must be their primary concern henceforth.'

A great outcry greeted this announcement. She waited patiently for it to subside.

'I have authorized the Secretary of State for Defence to take all necessary measures to control and if possible prevent the further spread of lycanthropy. The full capacity of the British Army, Royal Navy and Air Force will be at the disposal of General Sir Roland Ney, Chief of the Defence Staff, and the police force and other emergency services too, should he deem it necessary. From today, all reserve forces have been called up, and the fleet has been recalled, including the aircraft carriers, HMS Queen Elizabeth and HMS Prince of Wales.

'Finally, in order to be ready for any eventuality, the General has requested that all four of our *Vanguard* class nuclear submarines be deployed and fully operational, and I have granted him permission for that to happen.'

A few more calls of protest greeted this last statement, but the House was largely shocked into silence.

She felt utterly drained as she made her final pronouncement before leaving the Chamber. The arcane tradition of addressing her comments to the Speaker of the House did little to dampen the magnitude of her words. 'Mr Speaker,' she declared, knowing that her statement would be heard by every man and woman in Britain and beyond, 'this country is now in a state of war.'

To be continued in Wolf War, Book 3 of the Lycanthropic series …

If you enjoyed this book, please leave a short review at

Amazon. Thanks!

About the Author

Steve Morris has been a nuclear physicist, a dot com entrepreneur and a real estate investor, and is now the author of the Lycanthropic werewolf apocalypse series. He's a transhumanist and a practitioner of ashtanga yoga. He lives in Oxford, England.

Find out more at: stevemorrisbooks.com

Printed in Great Britain
by Amazon